"A BRILLIANTLY UNSETTLING STORY BY A SERIOUS AND GIFTED WRITER!"
—*Cosmopolitan*

"You know, we could get this over with right now, Miss Longden."

"What do you mean, 'right now?' "

"Well, I was just thinking. If you wanted to just . . . *resign,* then you wouldn't have to go through all the trouble of going to Los Alamos and getting examined by those nuclear doctors."

She stood up. "You don't understand, Deckman. I *want* to go to that examination. This thing here is just a charade."

"A what?"

"A lot of bullshit."

A SHORT LIFE

A novel about a woman's special kind of courage

A SHORT LIFE

THOMAS B. ALLEN

A BERKLEY BOOK
published by
BERKLEY PUBLISHING CORPORATION

Published by arrangement with G. P. Putnam's Sons

G. P. Putnam's Sons
200 Madison Avenue
New York, New York 10016

Acknowledgment: *A Book of Americans*,
by Rosemary and Stephen Vincent Benét
Holt, Rhinehart and Winston, Inc.

SBN 425-03946-3

BERKLEY MEDALLION BOOKS are published by
Berkley Publishing Corporation
200 Madison Avenue
New York, N. Y. 10016

BERKLEY MEDALLION BOOK ® TM 757,375

Printed in the United States of America

Berkley Edition, FEBRUARY, 1979

THIRD PRINTING

To Scottie, more than ever

1.

I BEGAN WRITING about Judith Longden on the night she died. I did not know much about her then. I had only enough information for a short newspaper story. And my paper was not much interested in the death of a young factory worker on a highway in Oklahoma. "You went a helluva long way to cover a car crash," somebody on the desk said to me that night. He was right. There was not much to Judith Longden as a dead woman.

All I knew that night was that Judith Longden worked in a plutonium plant, that she had some information about the plant, that she was on her way to meet me and give me the information, and that before she could reach me she died.

From that night I wanted to know her. From that beginning, standing in a motel room in a strange place, I felt involved, somehow involved. I even felt a personal loss and, if not sorrow, then bitterness. She was only twenty-six years old. And she had died, alone, on a highway, in her smashed-up car, the victim of bad luck and perhaps homicide.

At first I did not know what I was going to do about her memory, if you can have a memory about someone you have never met. I started by writing a memo for the files of my paper, the *Washington Post.* A reporter writes a memo like that not for publication but on the chance that the information may be of interest to the newspaper in the future. The memo is filed away, sometimes for years, until that day when the truth (or what passes for the truth) finally can be printed.

But my memo for the files soon became something beyond a memo. And I had to ask myself, Whose files are you writing for? At the age of forty-six, I had reached a point in life and in newspapering where I wanted to try to follow a story beyond the last line in a column of type. I wanted to write a story thoroughly, at least once in my life.

And there was something else, too, something I have trouble setting down. I was becoming obsessed with the need to know more about Judith Longden. I saw myself dealing with her leftover life, that part of her which she never was to live, that part of her which she might have known if she had not set out to meet me.

She had wanted to tell me about what was wrong in the place she worked. I began to feel I owed it to her to find out what it was she had wanted to tell me.

Owed it to her. Thoughts like that made it inevitable that she would become a part of my life. I owed a debt for the first time in a long while. I found myself taking an indefinite leave of absence from the *Post* and asking a friend to keep an eye on my apartment. I live alone, not exactly because I want to. But there's no need to go into that here.

I learned newspapering at a time when a reporter was not supposed to get involved. Nor was a reporter allowed to waste a reader's time by recounting all the troubles involved in getting a story. A reporter was supposed to write objectively and not reveal his sources.

I can't do that with Judith. She is my principal source. Nor can I write objectively about her. I think too much of her. I know too much about her. So much. And yet so little. But that often happens with people, even with people who are able to know each other.

I have fragments of her. There is her journal, with such entries as this:

> JULY 9: Gasket in Glove Box No. 9 leaking again. Room on respirators for two shifts. Three workers exposed to airborne plutonium particles. Concentration beyond MPC [maximum permissible concentration].

She began the journal when her life and her job merged, about a year before her death. The journal ended on the day I was to have met her.

Other fragments came from people who knew her in life. One of them was her mother. I talked to Judith's mother in the city where Judith was born and buried.

She was born in the base hospital of the Naval Air Station at Corpus Christi, Texas, and she was baptized Judith Anne Longden in the Catholic chapel by a chaplain, a Jesuit, whose Boston accent reminded Judith's mother of home. Judith's father, Paul Longden, was a chief aviation gunner's mate. Judith had been conceived in the Golden Wings Motel, about two miles from the main gate of the air station. Her mother, Janice Macauley Fogarty, was thirty-one years old and had a Navy widow's job as a clerk in the commissary. Janice Macauley had married Lieutenant (j.g.) Michael Fogarty late in World War II. They had tried to have a child, but they had not been able to. Lieutenant Fogarty, a pilot, was killed in an automobile accident on Okinawa a few weeks after the war ended. In the Golden Wings Motel, seeing Paul Longden's tattoos for the first time (bluebirds, one over each nipple, and a U.S.N. with eagle on the upper left arm), Janice Fogarty had known he would make her pregnant and that they would, as a result, get married. Mrs. Longden, who is now divorced from Paul Longden, told me all of this within twenty minutes after meeting me.

Another fragment, from Judith's friend, Barbara O'Neill. One of Judith's earliest memories was the sound of her parents arguing about her. The arguments had something to do with her name. Her father always called her Judy, and her mother always called her Judith. And sometimes one would tell the other, "She's *your* child."

Judith also told Barbara O'Neill about what Judith called her first life, the life before the one that began—and ended—in a place named Caslon Wells, Oklahoma. In her first life, Judith was a daughter and then a student. She was about to graduate fourth in a high school class of 236 when she learned she was pregnant. She told her mother—and it was then that her mother told her about the tattoos looming over her in the motel and the feeling of inevitable pregnancy. "It just goes on, from one of us to the next one," Judith's mother said. "You're being me all over again." And that first life kept going on: pregnant woman, married woman, wife, mother. Then it ended, and she started a new one, a short, fatal life.

I have found other fragments. They are Judith's tapes. When I first started writing about her, I did not want to use the tapes directly. I drew back from putting her words on my paper. Instead, I would listen to the tapes for hours, letting them spin in my mind, absorbing her voice, wondering about her, picturing where she was and how she looked when she was talking into her recorder. And then I would set down what she said, reconstructing from her words but shielding her words as much as possible. I told myself that by withholding her words I would be writing objectively, and I would be protecting my source. But my source was dead. I was kidding myself.

Now, starting again, trying to write again (perhaps trying to straighten out my own feelings about Judith), I know I have to do more than use the tapes. I will have to share them. They are hers, not mine. I know that. They form the memory she would have had of herself, the memory she wanted to preserve.

Now her memory has passed on to me. I entered her life through her death. It is a strange way to make a friend, but that is what happened. She has come to mean a lot to me. Even if I had not begun to want to know about her, though, I would have wanted to know what it was she was going to tell me and why she died on her way to meet me.

I think I did find out.

Judith Longden and I were to meet on Monday, October 19. The meeting was set up by Harry Skirvin, a vice president of the Nuclear Workers Union. I agreed to the meeting when I talked to Harry in his office at the union's headquarters in Washington on Thursday, October 15. About all he told me was that a female worker believed she had been contaminated by plutonium in a place called the Caslon Nuclear Facility somewhere in Oklahoma. Harry said the worker had been active in the union local at the facility and had information about poor safety practices there. And Harry said she had other information about "something else, something big."

I believe now that it was my conversation with Harry which reduced the number of remaining days in Judith Longden's life to four. Events moved swiftly after that conversation, for at about 3 A.M. on Friday, October 16, Judith's apartment was raided.

Curiously, I found no taped description of what happened that morning. Perhaps it was too much of a violation of herself, a kind of rape that she could not describe in the cool, confident voice of the tape. She did talk about the raid—to Harry, to Barbara, to her friend Art Reeves—but she did not tell it to her recorder, to herself. The only reference to the raid on a tape was something she said on one made later that day. She was talking about a meeting with the boss of the Facility. Then she interrupts herself:

"They came in about 3 A.M. That's when this goddamn awful day started. At 3 A.M. That's when I knew it wasn't a game anymore. [There is a rare pause. Usually, her tapes are filled with her fast delivery of sparsely worded remarks.] But I don't want to talk about that now. Or maybe ever."

2.

THE ACHE ABOVE her eyes had become a throbbing that seemed to move about inside her skull. She lay back on the bed, staring at the white ceiling instead of the flickering gray screen. She thought about turning the thing off, but then she decided that its hum might help her go to sleep, that the rolling chords of *Rock of Ages* might help her wake when the station signed on with the country preacher show. She and her headache and her sleeplessness had gone to the dark end: Late . . . then Late, Late . . . and now blank. But the Tylenol was wafting through her mind, the throbs were fading, and the night at last was going away.

The throbs came back suddenly, urgently, and loud, so loud that they seemed to be outside her head. It was a pounding and her name was part of it: *Ju-dith Long-den, pounding, pounding, Ju-dith Long-den, pounding* . . . And now she was awake, and now she knew that someone was pounding on the door of her apartment. She heard herself say, "Who is it, please?" and she knew she was awake because she realized she was saying something that sounded absurd.

She was moving slowly, clicking on the bedlamp, getting out of bed, wrapping a blanket around herself—*judith longden, pounding, judith longden, pounding*—into the living room, flicking the light switch by the door, checking the chain latch, pulling back the bolt, turning the brass latch above the knob, turning the knob—and through the black slit came a laminated identification card bearing a man's face, name, and in red block letters RADIATION SECURITY. She did not recognize the face or name.

"Emergency," a muffled voice said. "Open up. Emergency."

She tried to push the door closed, but something was pressing against it; the door would not move. The jaws of a tool appeared, closed over the lock chain, and snapped. The door pushed against her, and she stumbled back. She ran back to the bedroom, slammed the door, jammed a chair against it, and hurling herself across the bed, grabbed the phone. She dialed O and when after six rings the operator responded, she said, "Get me the police."

"The sheriff?"

"The police, the sheriff, the police," she shouted into the phone. "The police."

"They know about this," said the muffled voice from behind the bedroom door.

Almost simultaneously, the voice on the phone said, "Sheriff's office. Deputy Burke speaking."

"My name is Judith Longden. Somebody just broke into my apartment."

"Where is the apartment, m'am?"

"Forty-two hundred North Arroyo Drive in CW West, apartment 1-C."

"You Judith Longden? You work for Caslon?"

"Yes, but what . . ."

"We know about this, m'am." There was a click, but she gripped the phone more tightly and listened to its hissing.

The chair was moving slowly, and the bedroom door was opening. She kept her eyes on the door and dialed another number. The chair's back legs snapped and it fell as the door was flung open all the way. In the doorway stood a man in white boots, long white gloves, and bright orange coveralls that seemed to glow. An orange hood covered his head and draped his shoulders. Where there should have been a face there were fragments of a mask: a dark, oblong window for eyes, a white, doughnut-like bulge for a nose; in the doughnut hole small metal petals fluttered to the sounds of breathing.

"We're just here to do a job, honey. Not a damn thing is going to happen to you." The fluttering blurred the voice. It was hard to talk through a respirator. She knew that.

The ringing went on. *Art's not home.* She wanted to call someone else—who?—but she was afraid that if she hung up the phone she would not be allowed to pick it up again. Still staring at the man in the doorway, she started talking to the ringing. "Art. Art. Please come over right away. They're here. They broke in. Plant Security. The sheriff won't come. Art . . ."

"Art's not home, honey."

She hung up the phone. She could see two other men entering the apartment. They were dressed the same as the first man. One was carrying a long metal toolbox. The other had what she realized was an alpha-ray counter for large-scale scanning. The man who had forced open the bedroom door seemed to be in charge. The other men lumbered up to him and were given orders that Judith could not hear. He turned back to her. "Stay here," he said. "We'll do this room and the bathroom last. Do what this tells you to do." He tossed her two packages wrapped in thick plastic. She broke the seal on the smaller package, spilled the contents onto the bed, and picked up a stiff card labeled *Instructions.* She recognized the objects from the emergency decontamination kits at the plant, but something had been added: a douche.

She looked up at the doorway. The man already was in the kitchenette; she could see him squatting in front of the stove. The other two men were taking the paintings and posters off the living room walls and piling them onto her new brown sofa. She heard a tinkle of glass. That would be the watercolor, the splash of blues and green. *"You need some bright colors in here," Art had said. "Happy twenty-sixth."*

The men lifted the sofa, and one of them called to the third man, the leader. He grunted and walked over to the apartment door, which he propped open with an armful of books he scooped off a shelf. He was taller—larger, it seemed, rather than taller—than the others.

"What are you doing?" Judith shouted. "What the hell are you doing?"

As the sofa disappeared, the large man, in surprisingly fast strides, entered the bedroom and stood over her. She was still holding the douche package in her right hand. His faceplate was opaque. She would never be able to identify him.

"Look, honey. You go into that goddamn john and you do

what you're supposed to do, including dosing your cunt. And then you put on the decon garment and come out of that goddamn john and sit here on this bed. Now move your ass."

She tried to gather up the articles on the bed with one hand while clutching the blanket with the other. It was no use. The blanket started to fall away, and she dropped things on the floor. The man grabbed the blanket and said, "You don't need this. Move it!"

In one motion she pulled the sheet in her left hand and rolled off the bed. Shrouded, she picked up the objects and crawled through the open bathroom door. She locked it. She was safely alone, at least for the moment, but that was all. There was no window, no way out. She tried to make sense of what was happening. They were checking the apartment for radioactivity. No. For plutonium. Maybe planting it, and saying they had found it. She had been getting paranoid about plutonium. That was Art's word, really. Paranoid. He had said she was thinking like a paranoiac. And the day after he said that, he had handed her a printed card that said, "Just because you are not paranoid doesn't mean they are not out to get you." The card was under a small, pineapple-shaped magnet clinging to the refrigerator door.

She decided that she had nothing to lose by doing what she had been told. She went through the procedure. Shower and shampoo. Spray the decontaminant from the aerosol can. Wherever the chemical touched her, the skin hurt as if it had been severely sunburned; the rash, she knew, would last for at least twenty-four hours. She rubbed a washcloth, impregnated with a lesser dose, around her face, the back of her neck, under her arms, and around her ankles—wherever skin may have been accidentally exposed through the protective clothing she had to wear in the plant. She pulled through her hair a rubbery brush whose bristles squirted decontaminant. She cut her fingernails and toenails to the quick, then sprayed the raw skin.

So far it was a standard exercise in emergency decontamination. She had done all this before. She did not even need to read the instructions. But the douche was something new. She looked at the *Instructions* card. *(OVER)* was written in felt-tip pen at the bottom of the card. On the other side, also in felt-tip pen, was lettered: "Warning: Female employees must douche. They may use their own personal method, providing this special decontaminant is used. It is mild and does not sting."

The plastic squeeze-bottle did not have the look of a mass-produced product. Unlike the other articles in the decontamination kit, the bottle did not bear any trademark or warning. It was special, unique. Too special.

Following procedure, she had dumped everything she had used into a big orange bag. She knew Security would check the contents of the bag. She also knew that she did not want to use the douche. She squirted most of the douche liquid, a clear fluid vaguely smelling of lemon, into the toilet. Then she took a small plastic bottle of Tylenol from the medicine cabinet, dumped the tablets into the toilet bowl, rinsed the bottle, filled it with the douche liquid, and flushed the toilet. She opened the bag containing the decon suit, a blue polyester jumpsuit with feet, and shook it out. It looked like standard issue. Before stepping into it, she taped the Tylenol bottle to the inside of her upper right thigh. She tossed the empty douche bottle into the orange bag. Then she zipped up the jumper, opened the door, and walked through the bedroom to the living room.

There was nothing in the living room. Only the outlines of paintings and posters on the walls, the outline of a rug on the floor. The chairs, the lamps, the end tables, the sofa, the bookshelves, the books—all were gone. The two windows were like black holes in the bare walls: the curtains and the plants were gone. Everything was gone.

In front of her, across the space where there had been a bookshelf-divider, she looked at the little square of space she had called her kitchen. The cabinets over the sink gaped open. They were empty. She could see that even the scallop-edged shelf paper was gone. Two men were carrying the stove out the door. The third, the big man, was crouched in front of the open refrigerator. He was slowly moving a black tube over the food on the shelves. It seemed strange to see some things the way they should have been: the milk carton next to the mayonnaise jar, the eggs in their niches on the door, the butter in its little hinged-door chamber. But then he swept everything into an orange bag like the one in the bathroom. He wiped the black tube on a dish towel that still hung over the sink and dropped that into the bag. He put the tube into the long side pocket of his coveralls.

She wanted to hurl herself at him, rip off his hood, smash his face with the wrench that lay on the floor next to him. She started to move toward him—not walking, but shuffling, as in a dream. He turned, facing her, and picked up the wrench. They stared at each other for a long moment. She heard the other men coming in the front door. By the time she could reach the door they would be up the five steps from the street entrance and standing in the hall, blocking her way to the outside.

She sat in the middle of the living room, legs crossed at the ankles, hands resting on her knees. She closed her eyes to what was happening, but she could hear it, and she could feel it: the sound of their thumping walk, and the resonance at the base of her spine. The squeak of wood—that was the bed being taken apart. The scraping of furniture across the floor. The grunting and heaving to get the refrigerator through the door. The echoing of an empty apartment. The labored, fluttering breathing of those who emptied it.

"OK, honey. On your feet."

She stood and opened her eyes. There was nothing, nothing at all, except the black telephone on the bedroom floor. The phone looked like an exhibit of a phone—unreal, but a clever imitation.

"You left the phone," she said.

"It's against telephone company regulations for us to touch a telephone," he said.

She began to laugh, and she felt herself going out of control.

He grabbed her shoulders and shook her hard.

"Quiet down, goddamn it. Keep your goddamn mouth shut. Now assume the position."

She knew at that moment who he was. *Assume the position.* P. J. Feeney, the guard on duty at the main gate. *Assume the position.* That was what he always said. P.J. Feeney. The women—some of the women—called him Pussy Feeley.

She turned stiffly toward him and put her hands to her side. He removed the black tube from the pocket and ran it swiftly along the outside of her left leg, then the right. He swept the tube across the top of her feet. He paused, and, wagging the tube, tapped her inner ankles. "OK. Open up."

She moved her left foot slightly to the left. "More." He tapped her ankles again. The other men sat on the floor, their backs against the wall. She knew he would put on a show for them.

"Come on, honey. Open up." She placed her feet about eighteen inches apart. Pressing the tip against the inside of her right leg, he moved the tube slowly upward. Her leg quivered as the tube neared the bottle taped to her thigh. But the tube did not touch the bottle.

She heard the detector click as he passed the bottle, and she was sure he had also heard the click and had seen the red flash on the dial near the tip of the tube. He did not react, and neither did she.

He held the tube at her crotch for a few seconds, made a sawing motion for the benefit of the spectators, and said his well-worn line: "Nuthin' hot here."

He moved the detector down the other leg. Then, starting from her right hip and going up her side, down the inner right arm, up the outside of the arm to the neck, he outlined her with the tube. "Turn around." She felt the tube cross her head, touch the nape of her neck, and follow her spine to the cleft of her buttocks. What moved down the cleft and down first one leg, then the other, was, she knew, not the tube but Feeney's lightly laid hand.

"Turn around. Now the tonsils." She opened her mouth and he inserted the tube. She tried to keep her tongue away from it. "No biting," he said. "I don't like girls to bite it." He withdrew the tube, and holding it like a rolling pin with both his hands, he ran it down her chest to her stomach, his fingers dragging across her breasts.

He motioned for the other men to leave and then went through the bedroom to the bathroom. From where Judith stood, she could not see what he was doing. But she heard the crash of bottles as he emptied the medicine cabinet, and she assumed that he had made sure that the empty douche bottle was among the objects in the orange bag. He came out of the bathroom with the bag slung over his shoulder. His right arm was crooked through the opening of a toilet seat, whose cover flapped against his leg.

The sight of the toilet seat jarred her. Up to now what happened could have been a parody of moving-day. But this was a ripping out, a violating, a show of obscenely brutal power.

He walked past her, opened the hall door, and put down his burden. He took off his right glove, reached into his pocket, and pulled out a packet of papers. He held them out to her, and she walked across the room to take them at arm's length. He donned the glove and went out.

She closed the door behind him and, leaning against it, looked at the papers. On top was what appeared to be a routine letter from the Atomic Energy Commission, which apologized for "the emergency radiation detection incident" and reminded her that she had been told of the possibility of such an incident "as a condition of employment in the nuclear industry." She skimmed the rest of the papers, for she knew the gist of what they would say. A radiation-security "survey"—the official term for such a raid—could yield items showing no trace of radioactivity, highly contaminated items, or material only lightly contaminated. A raid that turned up no indication of radioactivity could look very much like a mistake, and Judith had never heard of that kind of a raid. More often, some items were labeled "lightly contaminated" and were taken away for a quarantine of indefinite length "in protective facilities."

The seized items—which usually included family photographs, private papers, and personal documents—were routinely photographed by Caslon, ostensibly as a service to the owner in the event they had to be destroyed. Material deemed highly contaminated was placed in 55-gallon drums, which were sealed and buried in a dump for dangerous radioactive waste.

One of the papers she had been handed was an inventory of every "disposable" object in her apartment, from pieces of furniture to each book by title; the thoroughness of the inventory did not surprise her, though she did feel intimidated by the realization that someone knew so much about her and her possessions. After each item was a "replacement cost" figure, which would be paid if the item had to be destroyed or buried. There was a Caslon check for $300 for "restoration expenses (to be accounted for)," authorization for transportation at company expense to a motel "for two (2) nights, single occupancy," and, finally, a Federal travel voucher.

• • •

The voucher was for a prepaid, roundtrip ticket between Tulsa and Albuquerque, to be picked up at Tulsa airport on the day after next—Sunday, October 18. A notation on the voucher said that from Albuquerque "available Atomic Energy Commission ground transportation will convey subject employee of Caslon Nuclear Facility to the Atomic Energy Commission Medical Center in Los Alamos, New Mexico, for a full-body count physical examination to determine possible reaction to possible effects of plutonium toxicity."

She went to the window and saw the big blue disposal truck pulling away from the curb. A white car with *Sheriff* and a gold star on its door appeared from around the corner of the apartment building, passed the truck, and led it down the empty highway toward the first thin light of a chill fall day.

3.

I WAS FIRST told about the raid by Harry Skirvin on the night of Monday, October 19. Harry gave me some of the vivid details—the snapping of the lock chain, the methodical moving out of the furniture—but he did not tell me much more. He said he wanted the story of the raid to come from Judith Longden's own lips. That is the way he put it. He also said that he wanted to whet my curiosity. It was late when he said that, and he knew I was getting tired of waiting for Judith Longden.

We began waiting a little after seven o'clock in the Boomer Room of the Cherokee Motel on Oklahoma Route 85, about halfway between Tulsa and a cluster of streets called Caslon Wells, where the Caslon Nuclear Facility is located. Judith Longden worked in the plutonium processing plant at the Facility.

Harry and I had met only once before, about two months earlier. I was covering an energy hearing on Capitol Hill, and I asked Harry a few questions about his testimony. I am what is called a general assignment reporter. I go where the desk tells me to go. That day it was to the Hill because the regular energy man was in California or some place. Talking to Harry on the Hill that day, I got the feeling that he was an overseller. He was pushing a story—something about a union campaign to make nuclear-fuel processing safer—and he was pushing too hard.

I had a similar feeling soon after I walked into the Boomer Room. We were sizing each other up and talking small talk. I took out my notebook and spread it open on the table. That usually stops small talk.

I wrote Harry's name at the top of the page and said, "OK, Harry. Let's go over this again. Her name is Judith Longden, right?"

"Can't we just talk, Phelan?" He pointed to the notebook. "Without that?"

"Some background stuff, Harry?"

"Yeah. You know, off the record."

I closed the notebook. "No good, Harry," I said. "I mean, none of that off-the-record bullshit. I came all the way out here for a story, not a goddamn union briefing. If I thought you were going to PR me, I wouldn't be here. It's a long trip, Harry."

"OK. OK. What you want, you can have. Just ask me."

"Fine, Harry. What I'd like first is that we just have our beer in peace and then go up to my room. Leave word for her at the desk. I have a recorder up there, and I would feel a lot better if what we talk about is on that tape. OK?"

"OK. I guess the recorder is OK with me." He sighed. He was a man used to paying dues for what he wanted. And my dues were not that much.

"And you'll tell her it's OK? I want her to talk that way, too, Harry."

"Sure. Christ, she's used to it. She's got a little tape recorder in her car. Talks to it all the time. I had to tell her—" He hesitated for a moment. "I had to tell her to put the union stuff in a log, a journal she called it. 'Not on tape,' I said. 'People can fool around with tape.' And she said 'Fine. That's fine with me. The tape's mine, not the goddamn union's.' "

He took a small sip of his beer, trying to keep the level in his glass the same as the level in mine. To speed up the process, I drained my beer, and, of course, Harry did, too. He was an adaptable man. I had looked him up in the *Post* library. There was not much: the standard handout biography from the union, a couple of small clips, a cross-reference to another file on a union official who had been killed in Caslon Wells during a Facility strike. I would want to ask Harry about that dead man, a man named Scinto.

Harry realized I was staring at him, and he looked away. His oval face was saved from roundness by a chin dimple as deep and sharp as a notch. His eyes were black. He never squinted. His thick, gray-flecked eyebrows matched the mustache flaring beneath his broad, flattened nose. His hair, grayer than black, swept back to the edge of the collar of his shirt.

He stood and picked up a silver-gray Stetson that had occupied the chair next to him. He laughed, embarrassed. "My western costume," he said. The hat had a three-inch brim, a high crown, and what Harry called a mule-kick crease.

Harry had grown up in Texas and Oklahoma and had been an oil rigger before becoming a union professional. He had acquired his sharp, crisp speech pattern in Washington, I guessed, because he was not talking that way now. He was sounding like a westerner. I wondered if he was conscious of this. Lyndon Johnson could do that, I've been told. But it bothered people back home. They thought that a man with two voices might have two faces.

My room was on the upper deck, overlooking the highway. I always forget to ask for a back room. There was not much traffic outside, but there was enough to produce a faint background vibration to our conversation. Harry was giving me a little that was specific and much that was general. And he had a way of coming around to saying things instead of saying them directly. It turned out, for instance, that he had not told Judith Longden to keep a book on what was going on in the Facility. That had been the idea of Dick Scinto, the local union official killed in a strike about a year ago.

There seemed to be no connection between Scinto's death and whatever it was that was going on now. The basic union complaint seemed to be that Caslon was a company that ran a sloppy plutonium plant. As a result of that sloppiness, some of the plutonium got on, or into, I didn't know which, one of the employees. It just happened that the employee with the contamination was also carrying around a notebook and jotting down safety violations.

I was wondering if there was a story here for me at all. And I was wondering about Judith Longden. I looked at my watch. I remember that. It was 8:35. She was supposed to be here at eight. I was getting edgy. What was I going to tell the desk? Maybe I could do a feature on sagebrush.

I heard a siren, and I remember that, too. But I cannot honestly say that I gave it much thought at the time. If I thought anything about the siren, it would have been a thought about its sound. It did not sound like a siren in Washington, a yodeling, modern, urban siren. It sounded old-fashioned. A western siren.

At nine o'clock, Harry dialed 9 for an outside local call. He got no dial tone. He dialed zero for the motel operator and was told that there was trouble; she could not make outside connections. She would call him back when the trouble was cleared.

"The phones are funny around here sometimes," Harry said. "Funnier than they are in Washington."

"Washington's phones usually work, at least, no matter who's tapping them," I said. I showed my irritation. "Are you telling me that this is part of some plot against the union?"

"You think we're paranoid, don't you? Me. Judy. The union."

"I didn't say that. But to make any odd thing that happens part of some plot against you . . ." I stretched and went to the window. I opened the drapes. There was little traffic. Maybe, I thought, maybe I'll be able to get some sleep. Harry was still on the side of the bed, staring at the phone. "I'd just as soon lie down, Harry," I told him. "It's been a long day. I won't turn in yet. Why don't you just go back to your room? When the operator calls back, I'll ring you right away. Better still, I'll knock on your door. OK?"

Harry went to the door. "OK," Harry said. "Look. She'll be here. This isn't like her . . . OK. I'm going."

As soon as the door closed, I took a large manila envelope from the shelf in the open closet between the bathroom and the door. I opened and closed the thin brass wings of the fastener on the flap until they broke off. I did not lift the flap.

I had found the envelope when I had entered my room for the first time. For a moment I thought it was some kind of welcome package. It was stuck in my Gideon Bible, between the pages of chapters 6 and 7 in Paul's Second Corinthians. My anonymous mailman had circled two verses. I don't like people who mark up books, and so my mailman was off to a bad start with me. And I don't think much of Paul, either.

The circled verses were: "Be ye not unequally yoked together with unbelievers: for what fellowship hath righteousness with unrighteousness? and what communion hath light with darkness?

"And what concord hath Christ with Belial? or what part hath he that believeth with an infidel?"

I have since looked up *Belial,* which is another name for Satan. I guess what I was being told was to watch out for evil doers. I peeked into the envelope. I saw 8 × 10 glossy photographs, a looseleaf notebook, and some papers bound in a file. From that glance, I got the impression that I was supposed to look through this envelope before my meeting with Judith Longden. Presumably, the contents of the envelope would give me information about her before I actually talked to her. I decided that I did not want that kind of prejudgment, and so I did not examine the contents just then. Paul wasn't the only man who could resist a temptation.

The phone woke me up at 10:15. I had fallen asleep watching something on television that I could not remember. I clicked it off in the middle of a local furniture store commercial, put on my shoes, and went to Harry's room. I only had to knock once.

Harry flung open the door. As I closed it behind me, he was dialing the phone. He motioned for me to come in and pour a drink from a bottle of I. W. Harper on the bureau. Harry hunched over the phone. I could not understand the words. It was a short conversation.

Harry hung up and spoke rapidly.

"He says she left. He says he's worried. But he didn't say why."

"Who is 'he,' Harry?" I asked. He nodded when I held up the bottle. I poured a couple of inches into his glass, a little less into mine.

He took a sip of the drink before he answered me. "I called Art Reeves. He works at Caslon's. He's . . . he was . . . I don't know. I guess he still *is* her boyfriend."

"Why did you call him? Does she live with him?"

"Not any more. She used to. They both worked there. They . . . they sort of broke up, I guess. He just quit. The day of the raid, he quit. I called him because he had called me, just before you came into the lounge. It was about seven.

"I was just sitting here, thinking about the meeting, not worrying. I was paged to the phone. I thought it might be Judy, and I thought, 'Oh, shit, she's not coming.' I knew, you see, that she had had a tough day—well, a tough couple of days. But I had got a message from her. She had left a message here this afternoon, when I was out. All it said was, 'See you at eight.' That's all. I shouldn't have been worrying. But I was.

"I grabbed the phone out in the lobby, and I said, 'Judy, Judy, baby. You all right?' Well, it was Art, and, I guess, he didn't like that. He's still in love with her, I guess. Anyway, what he was calling about was to tell me that cars were following her. Well, that's happened lots of times, and . . ."

"Wait a minute, Harry," I broke in. He had hinted at some intimidation, some harassment, but he had not acted worried about her. I caught his feeling of unease, a feeling I could not understand. I don't believe in premonitions, but I do believe that feelings are contagious, that worry can spread in a room like smoke. "Wait a minute," I repeated. "Why didn't you tell me this before? Has she been threatened? Is she in danger?" I was not really worried about her. I was thinking about the story and how *threatened* and *danger* could improve it.

"I didn't want you to think I was hyping, Phelan. Things like this had happened before. Scinto. That's still unsolved. Not that . . . I mean, I'm not *that* worried about Judy. She can take care of herself. She really can.

"Anyway, Art said he wanted to tell me she was being followed—by a car and a pickup—and she wanted Art to draw off one so she could slip away and get to her own car."

"Go slower, Harry. She was at her place, calling Art . . ."

"No. Not her place. I told you—the raid? Her place was cleaned out, Phelan. Really empty."

"OK. So where was she calling Art from?"

"She was at a friend's house."

"Another boyfriend?"

"No. Barbara O'Neill. Another worker. Anyway, she was working out a way for Art to draw off one of the cars. And he called me to tell me he had done that. And I also think he called to see if . . . if she had got here early."

"So what if she had?"

"Well, it would make him think that she and me . . . Well,

we used to know each other pretty well."

"OK. I get it. But she was all right? She wasn't chickening out?"

"No. Art said she was really looking forward to it, to meeting you. She had stuff with her, too."

"What kind of stuff?"

"I don't know exactly. Art said it was in an envelope."

I thought of the envelope in my closet. "A manila envelope?"

"No. He said it was a company envelope. One of those inter-office ones, with the holes in it."

"Do you know what she was going to give me, Harry?"

"Not exactly. But she'll be here in a minute." He looked at his watch. "Ten thirty. She'll be here."

"What does Art think happened?"

Harry had finished his drink. He was sitting on the bed, staring at the glass. "Art says he's going to call the sheriff. He says he wants to find out if there's been an accident or anything."

I sat on the chair next to the bureau, facing Harry. He poured us each another drink, then went back to the bed. I wondered what he was thinking about. The story was getting complicated. I was sorting a new set of questions in my head. There was not much use in asking Harry any questions, though. It was clear now that whatever Judith Longden was going to give me would be something only she could give.

The phone rang.

Harry grabbed the receiver and pressed it to his ear. "Jesus," he said. "Oh, Jesus." He looked across to me, his eyes wide and glazed. "She's dead, Phelan," he said. "She's dead."

4.

HARRY TALKED NONSTOP about Judith Longden on the drive out Route 85. My tape recorder was on the seat between us, and he knew he was talking to it as well as to me. The drive, at frighteningly high speed, lasted only a few minutes. But it was time enough for me to learn quite a bit about Judith.

" . . . Scinto and she, well I don't know exactly what they were. He was a married guy. She had just come here when she met him. I didn't meet her until after he was killed. I came out here to keep the strike going. He was killed early in a strike, a stupid strike.

"She saw him go down when he was shot. And the night before, they'd been in bed. 'Just that once,' she said. 'Just that once.'

"One thing I do is I judge people fast. I thought, the first time I saw her, I thought, she was OK. I guess I do it on how people sound. Like you, you sound all right to me, Phelan. You don't have a first name Phelan, do you?"

"It's Francis, Harry, if you must know. My mother called me Franny. I made kids call me Phelan." He was looking toward me, and to keep his eyes on the road as much as to hear more about Judith, I said, "You were saying she sounded all right."

"Honest. No bullshit. Swore like a trooper. I still can't get used to the young broads doing that. So anyhow, because my name is Skirvin and his was Scinto, I guess, she got me mixed up—at least my name mixed up—with his. I said something about how good she sounded to me. I felt funny saying that, just meeting her like that and sitting there in Jack's, a joint in Caslon Wells."

Harry said there were machines—voice-stress analyzers—that were supposed to be able to do what he did, and he thought that someday he would like to test out his judgment against the machine's. His system was simple. If someone spoke too fast, it could mean the speaker was lying; too slow, with too many gaps, could mean the speaker was lying and not doing it very well. There was a perfect frequency that Harry's ear could detect, and that was the frequency of an honest person.

"Right away. I mean, she hadn't spoken ten sentences, right away, I felt I was talking to one of the most honest people I had ever met. I told her about the system, about thinking that the way people *sound* is a way to make a judgment about them."

" 'I know what you mean,' she said. 'It's funny, but you sound a lot like Dick. I trusted his voice. And him. I trusted him.' That's what she said."

Harry seemed to be searching the highway, looking for her, for where she died. He began speaking softly, and I began listening more closely, trying to hear the honesty, not in his voice but in *her* voice, in the words of hers that he was repeating to me.

"She said she trusted me, and then she started talking a little about how Scinto and I were similar. 'Maybe I'm not saying your name right,' she said. 'But your name, it sounds like Dick's. And even a little how you look, it's as if there's a *sameness* about you and him.'

" 'Judy,' I said, 'Judy, I'm no shrink. But I think you should lay off that stuff about me being like him, like Scinto. It's loading too much on yourself. You've got a lot to carry already.' "

Harry told how she paused and how tears came to her eyes. I could picture her, though in my mind then she had no face; just the presence of a face I did not know. I could picture her wiping her eyes with the tips of her index fingers, raising her hands to her forehead, and in one swift movement pulling the long strands of her hair aside, as if to better look at Skirvin. But she was still far away, seeing Dick Scinto, seeing him die.

"I didn't get any response from her, and I tried again. I said I knew she had been through a lot and I didn't want to make things worse for her. 'But if you want to do something about Dick Scinto,' I said, 'if you really . . . cared . . . for him—'

"And she said, just like lightning, 'You mean did he fuck me?' I almost fell out of the booth. 'Is that what you mean?' she said. 'Yes. It happened one time. One night. The night before they killed him. So what? What the hell is it to you?'

"Jesus!" Harry said then, and he said it again now, to me, to the recorder. The words, coming back for her and from time, hit me the way they must have hit him. "Jesus. Just like that, she said it, 'You mean did he fuck me?'

"I was trying to get her reaction to a report I had on Scinto. I thought it might help in handling the strike. There was no use trying to clear up the murder. We both knew that."

"What was the report?" I asked.

"A lot of accusations about Scinto. I just wanted her to see the report, to tell me about it. I was here cold. I knew practically nothing about what was going on out here.

"I wanted to tell her about the report so that one person around here would know what was in it. I told her to hold off on any judgments until she heard me out. 'Honest to Christ,' I said, 'I don't believe what is in it. But I want to know why somebody decided I should see it.' "

I interrupted him to ask how he had got the report. I was not surprised by his answer: in the pages of a Gideon Bible when he checked into the Cherokee Motel. I told him my story and asked him what verse was circled. He said the folder had been between Psalms 9 and 10. No verse was circled, but the title of the ninth psalm was underlined.

"It was, 'Praise of God for executing judgment.' I remember telling that to Judy. I told her it was like somebody was trying to tell me that Dick Scinto was killed because it was God's judgment."

I had lost my image of Judy sitting in that place, listening to Harry. I was thinking of the two reports—one on Scinto, now dead; one on Judith Longden, now dead. I had questions to ask, and I could not afford the luxury of hearing Harry reminisce. But as I started to ask him about the report on Scinto, headlights flashed on our side of the road, just ahead.

Art Reeves' car was pulled off the highway facing us as we

approached. Harry drove up on the shoulder. The beams of the headlights of the two cars merged over a concrete slab. The slab covered a culvert, linking a ranch driveway with the highway. Art said it was here that Judith Longden's car smashed up. That's what he said, "Smashed up."

After Harry introduced me to Art, the three of us stood there in that glare. Art talked rapidly. He had got his information from the deputy and from the rancher who had heard the crash and phoned in the report.

"The sheriff says she went off the road heading east, cut across the road into the westbound lane, hit the culvert, and spun up it. The deputy who found the car said it hit the edge of the slab . . ." He pointed, and his hand vanished in the darkness beyond the glare. "The windshield, actually, that's what hit, and the edge just kept going and it hit her, hit her right on the forehead. The deputy said she couldn't have felt a thing."

His voice was perfectly under control. I had seen them like this, the people who tell about accidents involving people they know. They seem so calm before the shock hits.

"I think we better take a look at that car, Art," Harry said. He was trembling, and his voice was thick. "Did they tell you where they took it?"

"Highway Garage—in Wells. Guy I know runs it."

Art got a flashlight from his car, and we went down into the shoulder-deep culvert, backtracking along it for about fifty yards. On the grassy shoulder were two parallel tracks that cut in at a diagonal from the highway and ended at the lip of the culvert. Art flashed the light along the tracks, and crouching we could see them heading toward the highway.

Art lined up the flashlight with the tracks, aiming it toward the opposite wall of the culvert. The concrete was gouged there. As we slowly tracked back to the slab, we found other fresh gouges, a couple with faint smears of red paint.

A six- or seven-inch piece of the edge of the slab had been broken off, but the missing piece was not in the logical place—directly below. We began looking for it, for no apparent reason. It had not occurred to any of us why it was important to look for that piece of concrete. And yet here we were, looking under the slab, poking the light through the darkness. Art, hunkering low, shone the light on the underside of the slab, where one of its edges bit into a patch of earth along the lip of the culvert. He wondered, he said later, whether the piece of concrete had somehow been jammed up there. What his light picked up, though, was a sliver of red glass that had sliced into the dirt like the blade of a knife.

He showed it to us. "Tail light, I think," he said. We climbed up the side of the culvert, crossed the slab, and walked a short distance along the culvert. None of us had spoken much through this, but we were all coming to the same conclusion: we were looking for something that was not there. Harry said it first. "This side's full of crap." He pointed toward the slab. "The other side, where the car hit, it's been cleaned out. They've swept it clean."

"Who's 'they,' Harry?" I asked.

He glared at me, impaling me in the darkness, an intruder on his rising private grief. "The ones who killed her. I don't really know who they are. It doesn't matter, Phelan. *They* killed her. I know they did."

I wanted to say that to me it still looked very much like an accident. I had picked up enough information about Judith to know she was strung out. And merely by driving the rental car from the airport I had learned that a western highway is a high-speed rodeo.

"OK, Harry. Sorry. Let's go look at the car. But you're in bad shape. Can I drive?"

I followed Art to Caslon Wells, or rather tried to keep up with him. My introduction to the town was blurred. Art screeched to a stop at a dark garage on the far end of the straight-line business section that flanked Route 85.

Art jumped out of his car and ran to a trailer in back of the garage. In a minute he reappeared. With him was a tall young man who said his name was Dave and that he would open the garage.

When he switched on the overhead fluorescent lights, they flickered, and for a moment I could not quite understand what I was seeing. The flickering reflected off a mass of translucent plastic in the middle of the garage.

"There she is," Dave said, and we all had the same horrible thought.

But he meant the car. It was wrapped in thick plastic, which was sealed in many places with shiny gray tape. Coming closer, peering at the package, I could see, as if through turbid water, a mangled, faded-red Volkswagen bug. Its hood was up and twisted. The driver's door gaped open. The seat and backrest were intact but blotched with blood. The steering wheel looked as if it had melted and then had been folded, its two black semicircles hanging against the steering column like the skeletons of wings. The windshield was a maze of cracks surrounding a jagged hole roughly the size and shape of a football. The hole was precisely where the driver's head would have been when the car hit an obstacle and the driver's body was catapulted forward. But on the drive to the garage Harry had told me that Judith always wore a safety belt and was angered when her passengers refused to wear theirs. Maybe this one time—in a hurry to meet me . . . I felt a twinge of guilt, the first feeling of involvement.

Art was trying to talk Dave into removing the plastic sheeting from the car.

"No soap, Art. The deputy says that car stays just that way. I ain't even supposed to be letting you *look* at it, I think."

"Who wrapped it up?" I asked. I doubted that deputy sherrifs carried yards of heavy plastic in their patrol cars.

"The people from Caslon," Dave said.

Harry looked at me, as if to say *They.* Then he turned to Dave. "Who from Caslon? Anybody you know?"

"Yeah. That big shot the guys call B.O. and Cap'n Deckman and two other guys. One guy works up there. Comes in here with his car. But just gas. He won't let anybody touch it. A Jag?"

"Kovacs," Art said. Then to me: "Security. A Security guy." I wondered why Art had singled out that one man, the man from Security. I asked who B.O. was.

"Bailey Orr," Art said. "The super of the Facility."

I had not had a good chance to look at Art before. Now, under the harsh light, he looked to be in his early twenties. He had a long, pale face, the kind that does not see much sun. His light blond hair was close-trimmed. He was a slight, slope-shouldered, narrow-hipped young man, but he acted so tight and tense that he seemed wiry and strong.

I sensed that he wanted to talk a little more, and I tried to draw him out. I asked him, "What do you think happened?" I assumed that he would continue to be calm and would begin to open up to me. But he was so calm that I guess he figured he could ignore me, and that is what he did.

He crouched down with his flashlight at the back of the car. "Look at this," he said. We gathered around, trying to see through the plastic, through the reflection. Art handed the light to Dave. Holding the plastic with his left hand, Art traced a finger of his right hand along the cowling, from a few inches to the left of the tail light to a few inches on the other side. Shards of red glass edged the frame of tail-light housing like teeth in a battered jaw.

"What do you think, Dave?" Art asked.

"Clipped," Dave said. "Looks like somebody clipped her. Sure does. Not what Cap'n French says, though. Not what I *hear* he says. Now I wasn't there all the time, you understand. It was Deputy Bim Beardsley that called me to tow the wreck in. But he told me what the Cap'n said. Bim, well, he says that people sure was actin' like it was a big accident, considerin' it was just a single fatal—sorry, Art, didn't mean no disrespect.

"Bim says he got this message from the dispatcher that there was an accident on 85. He heads to it and he finds it, and sees that the driver is . . . is, well, pretty certain dead. But he calls for an ambulance from the firehouse in Wells. And he calls in the license number and the name of the driver. Well, he says about five minutes later, he gets a message from Tulsa. On the state police band? And they tell him that Cap'n French will be there and will take jurisdiction. Well, technically, the state troopers, they can do that, it bein' a state highway. But it hardly ever happens.

"The ambulance from the firehouse was just about to roll—I get this from Ike Meadows? A volunteer who's a customer? Well, just about to roll, and *they* get a call. From the deputy guard at the Facility? And he says that the Facility will respond. And in a minute that Facility ambulance is roarin' past the firehouse."

"But what was it that this Captain French said?" I asked. I identified myself, but it did not seem to make much of an impression on Dave. "And do you have his first name?"

"Hell, no, mister. I just call him Cap'n French. He rolls through here quite regular. He's in charge of the state police around here, but his headquarters is in Tulsa. He says that what happened was he thinks the driver was on drugs and that she fell asleep. That's what Bim says Cap'n French told him."

"Where can I find this Bim Beardsley?" I looked at my watch and began estimating how much time I could spare before I had to call in and give the desk some kind of story.

It was still a story then. I paid little attention to Art and Harry as they began talking softly to each other. They had withdrawn to a corner, as far as they could get from that shrouded car. But they kept looking at it as they talked.

I gave Dave a five-dollar bill for use of the phone in the garage office for a while. I managed to convince the sheriff's office to give Deputy Beardsley a message to phone me at the garage and I managed to convince the state police dispatcher in Tulsa that it was urgent for me to get in touch with his commanding officer, who was fully identified for me as Captain Gerald P. French. The dispatcher told me I could reach Captain French at the Caslon Nuclear Facility.

French's voice was courteous but hard: "I don't have anything to say to you, Mr. Phelan. This is only an automobile accident."

"But I understand you personally investigated it."

"Not *investigated,* Mr. Phelan. I visited the scene, that's all."

"Why?"

"I don't have time to talk to you, Mr. Phelan. I am sorry. I just have . . ." I thought we were cut off, but in a moment French was back. "Yes," he was saying distantly, as if he had been talking to someone and was turning his face back to the receiver. "OK. Mr. Phelan. I have a suggestion. Why not come out here to the Facility tomorrow morning and the folks out here will answer your questions. You just come here to the main gate at nine o'clock, Mr. Phelan, and tell the guard you want to talk to Cap'n Deckman. He'll be expecting you."

French hung up before I could ask him why his state police duties included being a PR man for Caslon.

A few minutes after I hung up, the phone rang. It was Deputy Bim Beardsley. He said he would be going off duty at midnight and would meet me then at the coffee shop in the motel. He sounded like a friendly cop.

I phoned the paper and dictated a short story. I would lose most editions, but at least I was covered. Essentially all it said was that a woman had been killed in an automobile accident on her way to a meeting with a *Post* reporter. It certainly was not much of a story, as the desk man reminded me. I promised more for tomorrow.

Harry and Art had decided that Art would go to Barbara

O'Neill's and break the news to her. Harry would try to notify Judith's parents, or at least her mother. He believed she lived in Texas somewhere; Corpus Christi, he thought.

Harry would stay at Art's, since they knew they would be up most of the night. They were mourners now, and the weight of a death was drawing them closer, making me more of an outsider. There was not much I could do. Dave said he would be able to find a cab for me. I said I'd wait there in the garage. Harry's hand was trembling when I gave him the car key.

The cab was an old and battered Plymouth that once had been blue but now was faded and flecked with rust. The driver, whom Dave called Jim, was not talkative, at least with me.

"Need gas," he told Dave. Jim got out of the cab and stood next to Dave while he pumped the gas. Jim's mouth worked sideways as he talked. His eyes kept straying to me in the back seat. I could not hear what the two of them were saying, but I certainly could guess the topic.

Jim had not needed gas, since Dave only managed to get three gallons into the tank. They talked for a few moments after Dave hung up the hose.

On Route 85, I noticed as a passenger what I had not noticed as a driver: the road was arrow-straight.

"Is it like this—is the road straight like this—all the way to Tulsa?" I asked. I wanted to get some kind of conversation going, get some local color.

"Mostly."

"So she sure didn't go off at some curve, I guess," I said.

"Who?"

"The woman in the VW. Judith Longden. The accident."

"I don't know about no accident."

On his dash I could see a citizens' band transceiver and a police receiver, the kind that monitors all public-safety frequencies and locks on one when a message is transmitted. Even as he spoke, the receiver had locked on the sheriff's dispatcher reciting a couple of stolen-car license numbers. At that moment, Jim finally figured out that the receiver made him a liar, and he turned it off.

I suddenly realized that Caslon Wells was a small, tight

place, where a stranger—or troublemaker—could be spotted, watched, and perhaps even controlled. I was quite sure that Jim knew where and when I was going to meet Bim Beardsley. Radios must be like an old-fashioned telephone party line out here. French would know where I was, and Caslon would know. But so what?

And then, for an instant—so swiftly that I hardly knew the thought had flashed—I pictured Judith Longden on this road on this night, thinking about being watched, being followed. For that instant, I had felt her paranoia. Nothing mystical, but a feeling of sympathetic vibrations.

Thinking about her, trying to put together what I had learned, I could not see her. I did not know how to even imagine what she looked like. But when I got to the motel and entered my room, I still did not want to look into that envelope. I was postponing the possibility of finding out something about Judith Longden that I did not want to know.

5.

BIM BEARDSLEY TURNED out to be a man about my age. He had a large waist, but was not otherwise fat. Bus drivers get to look like that. I supposed Bim was more a driver than a walker, a walker to the side of the highway. I imagined there was never much need to walk fast because the victims were probably almost always dead when he rolled up to their smashed-up cars and pickups and trucks.

"Yep," he told me, "Head-ons, that's what they mostly is. One boy all full of booze headin' east and somebody else, he's headin' west, mindin' his own business or talkin' to the missus or maybe feelin' up his girl, right? And then—*Bam!*" He struck his fist on the brown Formica counter. We were on our third cup of coffee. It was nearly two o'clock.

We were good friends by now, thanks to my having been, like Bim, in the U.S. Navy. And also because I am a professional listener. "*Bam!* They gets each other right between the eyes. That's the way they always is."

Bim paused and leaned forward, hunching toward the reporter in a gesture I had seen cops and lawyers and other news sources use so many times as a signal: confidential information. "But not this one. Somebody killed in a single-car accident? It just don't happen. They's usually not fatals, you see. The single-car ones. That's what's a little funny. This was a fatal. That's what I told Cap'n French. I said. 'It's a funny one, Cap'n.' And he said, 'Bim. You keep your big goddamn mouth shut about this, you hear?' "

I asked Bim what was funny about this accident. He composed a long memoir about his encounters with accidents involving drunks and what he called sleepy-heads. Finally, he got to tonight.

"Now, like I told you, somebody falls asleep, somebody's drunk, they just sort of gradually let go. There's a crown in the middle of the road, right? So the car just almost naturally goes over to the right. The car just slips off the road, and the feel of *that* happenin', well, it would wake the dead. At the last second, they see what's happenin', and they grab the wheel or they hit the brake. Well, they gets banged up—maybe real bad. But they don't get killed. And drunks? I've seen a drunk hit another car head-on. Guy in the other car: dead. The drunk: alive. He's so rubbery and all. Well, you know. You've heard, I'll bet, even back where you come from, they says that God watches over drunks. Lot of truth to that. Lot of truth."

I nodded, hoping that the tape would last. Bim was fascinated by the tape recorder. On many people the effect is to make them much more talkative than they would be in front of a pencil and an open notebook.

"So, Bim, let me go back over what you say. You figure that the driver didn't fall asleep, probably wasn't drunk. Well, let me ask you two questions, Bim. Why didn't Captain French figure it the way you did? And what do *you* think happened?"

"Hell, Phelan, I *told* Cap'n French what I figured happened. And I don't give a real goddamn. I'm going to tell you. Those goddamn state troopers, they thinks they're the little green apples of God's creation."

I asked Bim to start from the beginning, from the time the sheriff's office was called. I was starting to see the accident scene now, building a picture that I could trust. By translating Bim's words into my own, I think I can put the accident scene on paper. His eyes were sharp, and I think he's honest. I'm relying on him to give me the truth.

Bim was in the sheriff's office when a rancher, Bob Mulhall, called. Deputy Timothy Burke answered.

"Tim? Bob Mulhall. Looks like you got a wreck in front of my place."

"Bad?"

"One car. One of them Volkswagens. Girl in it, and she's dead."

"Sure?"

"Well, I'd bet you ten bucks on it."

"No bet. Well, I'll be sendin' Bim. Bye, Bob."

When Bim Beardsley arrived, the first thought he had was that the car was on the wrong side of the road. Then he realized that it had cut across the highway.

The car looked as if it had been slung in the culvert, its left wheels on the bulge of the curve, its right wheels on the bottom of the curve. The right front fender and the forward portion of the hood were jammed under the concrete slab that crossed the culvert. A piece of the slab had broken off and lay on the right side of the hood, near the windshield.

The driver's head was protruding, face down, through the windshield. Beardsley reached his right hand through the hole in the windshield and pressed his fingers against the driver's throat near the jawline and felt for the pulse of a carotid artery that he knew would pulse no more. But he had to check.

Bim had some trouble maneuvering down the curve of the culvert, but he managed to yank the driver's door and brace it open against his back. He swept the beam of his flashlight around inside. The steering column had penetrated the driver's abdomen. The steering wheel was bent forward, and the driver's hands still clutched it. Bim had never seen this happen when the driver was a woman. She had bent the wheel with the force of her last burst of strength.

When the car slammed into the slab, the driver had shot up and forward. Her moccasins were in the blood on the floor. Her stiff arms had acted as levers as her body catapulted. Had she not been gripping the wheel so fiercely, she probably would have been thrown through the windshield.

A gospel group was singing:

> By cool Siloam's shady rill
> How sweet the lily . . .

He reached around the driver and switched off the radio.

Bim was required to check seat belts for his fatal-accident report. The driver was not using a seat belt. He looked on the seat and then on the floor for the driver's pocketbook. A woman driver usually keeps her pocketbook on the seat next to her. Bim needed the pocketbook because that was where the driver's license would be. No pocketbook.

There was a tape recorder on the floor, and tape cassettes were scattered around, on the floor and on the seat. They had apparently spilled out of the glove compartment. Most of the cassettes had what Bim described as plain labels; a few had the recording artists' photographs on them. He did not recognize any of them. There was a tape deck mounted on brackets under the radio.

On the seat next to the driver was a large envelope. Bim was about to go through it in search for some identification when he saw what he knew as a Caslon employee tag on a chain around the driver's neck. The tag had been flung around and hung down the driver's back.

The tag was a temporary one; Bim particularly remarked about that because he had wondered whether the driver had been a good-looker, and he was disappointed that the tag had no photo on it. The name on the tag was Judith Longden. He went back to his car and called in.

"Timmy? Bim. Got a fatal. You better call them card sharps at the fire station and tell them we're goin' to need an ambulance out here to take the body to Weaver's. Name's Judith Longden. No driver's license. A bitty VW. License TA 6571."

"Hold on, Bim. You say Longden?"

"Yep. Caslon ID tag."

"Bim, you keep away from that car! You hear?"

"Say again."

"You stay there until . . . until you hear otherwise. But keep away from that car! There's some trouble with that girl, Bim. Caslon-type trouble. Out."

Bim, a man of routine, had never heard of such a thing. Keep away from the car? He shrugged and walked along the shoulder, looking for the spot where the car had entered the culvert. He was trying to figure out the accident for his report.

The car had been going east and for some reason had cut across the highway, across the shoulder—he found the tracks now—and into the culvert. Bim eased himself into the culvert and spotted the gouge where the front of the car hit. Bim imagined the driver struggling with the car. If it had hit the wall head-on, the car would have ended up athwart the culvert and probably would have rolled over. But he surmised that the car struck the curving wall at just enough of an angle so that the car would be spun slightly; for an instant the car would have been parallel with the walls of the culvert. But it landed on the right wheels and heeled up the left wall. Bim found another swipe, faintly streaked with red paint.

She would be trying to keep the car upright now and trying to stop it before she hit that slab. He had to hand it to her. She wasn't giving up. He got the idea then of what it was she was planning—if a plan could be made in about one-quarter of a second. Bim figured that she was trying to go *up* the wall. He had seen trick drivers do it.

If she had gone up the wall a bit more, she might have nicked the slab, even flipped over. But she might have made it. She had also given herself another chance. By trying to get the car to veer to the left, she was probably hoping to hit the edge of the slab on the passenger's side. She had almost made it. If she only had had her seat belt on, there would have been a chance. He wished she had been wearing the belt.

Bim could not stay away from the car. He went back to check the seat belt again. She was a good driver, a damn good driver, he decided. Not all good drivers use seat belts. But those who do not use them just lock them on the seat. She had not done that. The left strap of her belt had been hanging by her side.

Bim went around to the passenger's side and got that door open. The end of the other belt strap was lying in the blood on the floor. He did not want to pick up the buckle to examine it, but he did. In the flashlight's beam, the buckle looked all right. When the body was taken out, he would try to lock the belt to see if the buckle was defective. That is what he hoped, though he never had a chance to do it.

He wanted to look at the wheels. He was sure they would be turned slightly to the left. He flashed his light under the slab and crouched down. He was right. The wheel was pointed slightly to the left.

There was still something strange about the accident. Why had she gone off the road? He went to the back of the car. Most of the glass had been broken out of the right tail light, whose housing had been smashed in. To the right of the housing was a crease about two feet long, parallel to the bumper. The left tail light was intact, there was no crease on the left side, and the bumper and the bumper guards were undamaged.

The back of the car could have been hit like that in some previous accident. But Bim doubted that. He decided to retrace the tracks in the shoulder to the other side of the highway, looking for skid marks—and bits of red glass. Just then, he heard his radio crackle. He went back to his car and responded. It was the state police dispatcher.

"Sheriff 301. This is Tulsa SP. Please acknowledge."

"Four-five, Tulsa. Three-zip-one on the air."

"Stand by, 301. Cap'n French is lookin' for you."

In a moment French's voice was on the air. "Bim. You just keep everybody away from that car. We're sending in a decontamination team and a Caslon ambulance. I'm on my way. That car might be hot, Bim. Radiation. Got it? Over."

"Got it, Cap'n. Three-zip-one off the air."

Bim ambled across the highway, following the angle of the tracks on the shoulder. He thought he saw fresh skid marks on his side of the highway, but he could not be sure. In the eastbound lane, however, he found what he was expecting: four pieces of red glass, including the curved top peculiar to the tail light on a VW.

Captain French, driven by a state police corporal named Perry, arrived with siren screaming. Bim, who hardly ever used a siren, was going to say something about scaring the bunny rabbits. But French gave him what Bim calls "that Patton look," and Bim decided to remain silent. French ordered Perry to rig a white nylon rope on a perimeter about fifteen feet all around the VW. Perry used a cottonwood sapling and flare stanchions as stakes. French walked around the shoulder side of the rope barrier, but did not venture into the culvert. French averted his eyes from the car.

"Cap'n. Can I cover her up?"

"What? I told you. No one . . . Goddamn it, Beardsley. Take your light off her."

"I thought the Cap'n wanted to see what happened. Sorry, Cap'n." Bim shone the light on the chips of glass in his hand and told French, "I think she was clipped, Cap'n. Looks to me like some drunk hit her hard as hell, and then he just kept goin'."

"Give me those, Beardsley," French ordered. He was a short, stocky man with white eyebrows and a thin white mustache. His brow had three permanent lines exactly aligned with the brim of his hat. Bim dropped the glass into French's outstretched hand. French hefted them for a moment. His brow lines rippled. Then he flung the bits of glass into the culvert. Bim heard at least one strike the car.

"What happened, Beardsley," French said, "was that this young lady, who drinks *and* takes drugs, fell asleep at the wheel. She didn't have much sleep last night, you see. Shacking up. We know quite a lot about that young tramp, Beardsley. Quite a lot."

The next siren belonged to the Caslon Facility ambulance, which pulled up on the shoulder next to Beardsley's car. Another car, a black Ford LTD, stopped behind the ambulance. Beardsley walked toward the car, waving it back to the highway. But when the driver got out, Bim recognized him. It was Captain Deckman, chief of Security at the Caslon Nuclear Facility.

"Evenin', Cap'n," Bim said. He respected Deckman's past—he was a former Texas Ranger—but, like most lawmen, Bim was never quite comfortable with a man who turned in his badge to work for a company.

Deckman shook hands and chatted with Bim for a moment while three other men got out of the car. Bim knew two of them: Orr, the Facility superintendent, and Kovacs, Deckman's assistant. The third man Bim vaguely recognized as "some Washington doctor or something like that," who frequently visited the Facility.

The four new arrivals withdrew a few yards and began speaking to each other, stomping the cold ground, turning up collars to the wind. In a couple of minutes a Caslon panel truck, coming from the direction of Tulsa, swung off the highway and stopped in front of Beardsley's car. The truck's headlights swept across the shattered windshield. Bim wanted to say again that the Judith girl ought to be covered up, but he did not speak.

Bim recognized the panel truck and the two men who emerged from it. Their names were Fred and Bill. No last names. Bim calls them Mutt and Jeff. He thinks they are not what they seem. "Funny fish," he says of them. "Mighty funny fish." They stood leaning on their truck, talking softly, while waiting to hear what to do. Bim was waiting, too, curious about who was going to take charge. Remembering the Scinto case, he was sure it would be Kovacs.

When Dick Scinto had been shot, about a year before, Bim had noticed that Kovacs seemed to outrank Deckman. "Well, you know," Bim says, "that man Kovacs, he always wears suits, eastern suits, and Cap'n Deckman always wears a Caslon uniform, like a guard's, only a little fancier. Well, it's like that in a lot of places. I mean, the man wearin' the *suit,* that's the lawman in charge."

So Bim was not surprised when he saw Kovacs step away from the other three men and walk to the ambulance. Kovacs jabbed his right index finger in the general direction of the VW and gave some orders Bim could not hear. Kovacs passed French and merely nodded at him. French started after Kovacs, but he waved French away. Kovacs went to the panel truck, shook hands quickly with Bill and Fred and issued more orders.

The two ambulance attendants adjusted the spotlight on the door so that its beam touched Judith's head. They wore yellow coveralls, and now they put on black respirators, which covered the lower half of their faces. They went into the culvert carrying a body bag and a basket.

As if an invisible string jerked the head of each man there, everyone else turned away simultaneously when the ambulance men began wrenching the body out of the wreckage. There were sounds of breaking glass, tearing cloth. They finally climbed up and placed their burden in the ambulance. All others turned back, eyes now on the black hole in the windshield.

Fred and Bill, meanwhile, had put on white coveralls and hoods with elaborate respirators that drew air from backpacks. The men also put on gauntlets and stepped into white shoe-covers they tied tightly around the ankles. All this was done with slow ceremony.

They then took two radiation detectors from the truck. The one Bill carried to the ambulance was about the size of a small toolbox. He toted it by a handle on the top. In his right hand he held an instrument that looked like a pancake turner; this was attached to the box by a cable. Fred's detector was larger; it looked like a floor waxer, but from the way he hefted it, the detector seemed to be about as heavy as a long-handled shovel.

Bill ran the smaller detector over the ambulance men, the

open door of the ambulance, and finally over the dark-green body bag inside the ambulance. Bill wrote something on a small clipboard attached to his belt. He nodded to the attendants. They stripped off their coveralls and respirators, tossed them on the body bag, slammed the door, and got into the ambulance. It started off immediately, in the direction of Tulsa.

"I thought they were takin' her to Weaver's in Wells," Bim said to French.

"The body's going to the nuclear medicine research lab in Caslon Memorial Hospital in Tulsa," French said.

"Where they goin' to take the VW—Texas?"

"This is national security business, Beardsley, and there's no room for foolin' around. Now you get on the radio and you call a good wrecker you can vouch for. I'm impounding the car in Caslon Wells until further notice."

"Would that notice be from Mr. Kovacs, Cap'n?" Bim looked so guileless when he spoke that French started to nod. Then he flushed and said, "Get goin', Beardsley. We want that wrecker pronto."

Holding the detector close to the ground, Bill traced the route of the attendants from the ambulance to the edge of the culvert. He put aside the detector and took up his pencil and clipboard. Fred was already in the culvert, poking the detector in and around the car and calling up a litany of car parts and NC's: "Driver's seat, NC . . . Passenger's seat, NC . . . Steering wheel, NC . . ."

Deckman, Orr, and the unidentified doctor from Washington all got back into the LTD and started the car so they could turn on the heater. After Bim called in for the wrecker, he walked over, hoping Deckman would invite him in. Deckman shook his head. The men in the back were seated as far from each other as they could get. They were looking straight ahead.

Bim went back to the edge of the culvert, where Kovacs was supervising the wrapping of the VW in sheets of plastic that Bill had fetched from the truck.

"What'aya doin' that for, Mr. Kovacs?" Bim asked in his most stupid cop's voice. "Don't NC mean 'no contamination?' "

Kovacs looked Bim up and down as if he could not believe that Bim stood there. "It's so nobody can put any contamination *in* it," Kovacs said. "The car's impounded. Evidence." He did not say what the evidence was for.

Kovacs had a large Caslon inter-office envelope in his right hand. Bim was quite sure that it was the envelope he had seen in the VW because there was blood on it. Bim figured that it contained something stiff because otherwise Kovacs would have folded up the envelope and put it in his topcoat pocket.

At Kovacs' feet was a yellow plastic bag. It was closed by a wire wrapped around its neck. But Bim could see the outline of what he took to be the tape recorder and cassettes he had seen in the VW. Bim lifted the bag, saying, "I guess you want this in the truck." Kovacs grabbed it from his hand. Bim had held it long enough, though, to touch the sides and satisfy himself that the bag did contain what he thought it would.

Kovacs did not put the bag down. He immediately carried it and the envelope to the LTD and put them on the back seat between the two silent men. Each looked briefly at the delivery, but neither touched it.

When Dave's Highway Garage wrecker arrived, Kovacs again supervised, making sure that the plastic sheets were wrapped and taped under the car. One of the hubcaps had come off during the car's carom along the culvert. Bim started down to get it. Kovacs ordered him away.

"I don't want anybody touching anything but my men," he said. "It's . . . it's a matter of liability insurance."

The wrecker was about to leave when the doctor from Washington got out of the LTD and, borrowing a flashlight from Dave, made a quick inspection of the VW. He walked up to Kovacs and spoke to him, pointing the beam of the light toward the rear of the car. Kovacs took the flashlight from the other man and went back to the VW, as if he were going to take a closer look at it. Instead, he handed the flashlight to Dave and told him to leave.

As soon as the wrecker pulled onto the highway, Kovacs had Deckman, French's driver, Bim, and Bill arrange their vehicles so that all their headlights shone along the culvert and shoulders. Then Kovacs, Bill, and Fred, with brooms and brushes taken from the panel truck, began sweeping the culvert and putting the debris in yellow plastic bags.

"Now why in blue-balled blazes are they doin' that?" Bim

asked, leaning on the window of French's car.

The corporal, a young man who had Indian blood in him, smiled at the sight. "They don't do it very good," he said. "But I think what they're doin' is coverin' up tracks."

Bim leaned back, confident that he had told me all there was to tell. I only had one question.

"If she was hit, couldn't it have been the Caslon truck?" I had begun to be suspicious of most of the people Bim had put at the scene.

Bim laughed. "Hell, Phelan, I just *look* like a dumb cop. I really *ain't* one. Don't you think these big blue eyes looked at that panel truck, and at that Ford LTD, and even at Cap'n French's car and the ambulance, too? It's sometimes a funny place, that Facility. I always try to keep a step ahead of 'em. But nope. No marks on any of them vehicles that I could see." He made a sound—*aunh, aunh*—while shaking his head. "Aunh, aunh," he said again, and I knew they were words for *no*. "It wasn't one of them." He paused for just an instant and looked around. "Not that some of 'em wouldn't."

It was 4 A.M., and we were conspicuously alone in the coffee shop. Anyone happening by would see him talking to me, and I sensed that this would do neither of us any good. I mentioned this to Bim, but he waved it off. Talking to people about things that bothered him was obviously more important to him than staying out of trouble by keeping his mouth shut.

"Not that some of 'em wouldn't," he repeated. "I don't know who, Phelan. But somebody did that little girl in. That weren't no accident."

6.

WHEN BIM LEFT, I went up to my room, telling myself that I would get a little sleep before I went off to the Caslon Nuclear Facility. But I knew I was not going to go to sleep right away. The envelope was waiting for me. There was no reason to put off examining the contents. I had to know more about Judith Longden.

The photographs were in an envelope within the envelope. I put them aside for a moment and picked up a blue looseleaf notebook. I flipped through it; the notebook seemed to contain a chronology of her career at the place where she worked, the place that, in one way or another, killed her. I knew that then. At that moment in the motel, I knew that.

I looked back to the first page of the notebook. The page was mostly blank, as if there was more to tell, but no one or no way to tell it. All that was printed on the page, near the top was this:

LONGDEN, JUDITH A. EMPLOYEE NUMBER 807
Height: 5'3" Weight: 97 lbs. Age: 26 Marital Status: Divorced

I put down the notebook and picked up the envelope of photographs. Again I hesitated about looking into the envelope and I wondered why. Looking back on those moments of hesitation, I know that I had begun to imagine a Judith Longden, and I did not want to spoil my image. She had not yet been consciously in my mind as a real person. I had thought about her on the edge of reality. She had become a faint impression, lodged in what seemed to be my memory. It was as if she were a friend from long, long ago—someone only dimly remembered.

And now I could see her just by removing photographs from an envelope. It was open at the top, with a little notch that allowed a crescent of margin and black to show. I pulled the photographs out and fanned them out on the bed.

There were seven glossy, 8 × 10 photographs. To help me identify the participants, someone had typed information on the backs, and the impression of the letters appeared backwards on the participants, branding them in odd places.

I sorted through them.

A woman kneeling in front of a man, performing fellatio. The man is black, broad-shouldered, gleamingly muscular. The slim, dark-haired woman has her naked back to the camera. The photograph is well lit, even well composed. The names on the back are *Judith Longden and Bar Pick-up.*

A man and woman in bed, a sheet over them, both apparently sleeping, on their backs. The photograph could have been taken from the angle of a high window. The names on the back are *Judith Longden and Art Reeves.* The man looked like Reeves, and I assumed the woman was Judith Longden. A beautifully tranquil face. I stared at that face and at the faint outline of a slim body. I knew this was Judith Longden.

A grainy enlargement of a portion of this photograph, showing the table on the woman's side of the bed. Circled with a grease pencil is an ashtray in which are the remains of what the words typed on the back says are *Grass Joints.*

Two women engaged in mutual cunnilingus. One of the women appears to be the same woman who was performing with Bar Pick-up. The other woman is stocky. Their positions and the angle of the photograph are such that their faces cannot be seen distinctly. The names on the back are *Judith Longden and Barbara O'Neill.* I doubted that the woman who was supposed to be Judith Longden was Judith Longden. Barbara O'Neill, her friend? Could she be this other woman? Short hair, full, slightly pendulous breasts; slim, stunning legs.

There was also a photograph marked *Judith Longden and Dick Scinto.* I had never seen a photograph of Scinto. But the woman with him—awake, smiling, her face turned toward the man—looked like the woman I had decided was Judith Longden. She was nude, her face and body in a tense profile. I felt a senseless shame because I was looking at her—looking at a dead woman. But I could not take my eyes from her.

I compared this photo with the woman-and-Art photo. I was sure it was the same woman. An identification photo of the real Judith Longden would be easy to get. And then I would know for certain. But I felt that I knew already. I was seeing this woman in two moods, for even in sleep there was a mood to her: tranquillity, a radiance of tranquillity. And, with Scinto, a woman of intensity.

There were two photographs marked *Harry Skirvin and Judith Longden.* In one they are in a parking lot. She—for now I was certain it was she—is getting out of a car that looks to be a Ford Galaxy. Harry is at the trunk, putting in or taking out a large suitcase. She is wearing a light-colored pair of slacks and a dark, V-necked, long-sleeved jersey. She has a light-colored raincoat over her left arm. Her hair is longer and lighter than it is in the Judith-and-Scinto photograph.

On the back of the photograph it says, *Phoenix Airport, Harry Skirvin and Judith Longden.*

The second photograph, the clearest of all, was apparently taken from a ceiling fixture. There is a motel-room look to the place. The lens apparently is wide-angle, and so there is a slight distortion that somehow intensifies the reality. I assumed that many photos were taken, perhaps by a motor-driven attachment. This is a selected photo, but not a staged one.

I wondered what the motive was in selecting this. It is a beautiful image.

She is lying on her back, a small woman, eyes bright, lips half open. All that can be seen of her is her head and her pale arms and legs enwrapping the man named Harry. He seems to be hovering above her, but they are joined, so joined. He is grasping the white sheet, and the creases are radiating out from his clutching so that it looks as if her head is haloed by faint rays.

I looked at the photographs again and again, telling myself that I had to do this for the story I was working on, but realizing that I was kidding myself; I was straying into an outrageous, senseless infatuation. I put the photographs back in their envelope and tried to get my mind off them by leafing through the blue loose-leaf notebook again. *CP 047-22-807 6 of 12* was written on the bottom of the cover in white ink. At the top, written in block letters, also in white ink, was CONFIDENTIAL.

I turned to the back to see where the notes on her employment ended. The last entry was a reference to the "survey" of her apartment on Friday, October 16. But there was more. Several pages had been clipped to the back cover of the notebook. They looked like a report. I saw a date, October 18—only two days ago—and an address, the Atomic Energy Commission Medical Center in Los Alamos, New Mexico.

All this was too complex for so early in the morning after so long a day. It did occur to me, though, that someone had wanted me to see this report, see those photographs because that someone—Harry's *they,* I suppose—expected that I would be writing about a living person. Or did they want me to think that? Was this planted in my room to make me think that Judith Longden's death had not been anticipated? Thinking was making my head hurt.

I wanted to get a couple of hours of sleep at least, before driving to the Facility for my 9 A.M. appointment. But I could not sleep for what seemed like a long while. I kept thinking of the woman in those photographs, not thinking of her as an image. Thinking of her as a woman named Judith Longden. And, just before I finally fell asleep, thinking of her as someone not quite dead.

I was still half-asleep when I pulled out of the Cherokee and started toward Caslon Wells on the only road that would take me there, Route 85. There was not much traffic, which is a phenomenon I fully appreciate as an inhabitant of a city which is a continual traffic jam. I had expected more morning traffic and had allowed myself too much time to get to the Facility, which was about nine miles west of town.

I looked at my odometer. It would be right around here that she went off the road. The driveway slabs across the culverts all looked the same, but I had no trouble knowing which was the one. I pulled off the road and got out of the car, leaving in the frost a trail that tipped the coarse, ankle-high grass. It seemed so long since I had been here, and it seemed so slight a place compared to the intense one that Bim's memory had reconstructed for me. I knew I could trust Bim's memory. I guess I just wanted to feel the place again. I stood with my back to the highway, my breath streaking the air.

I heard brakes screech, and I turned to see a battered black pickup knife off the highway and stop at an angle in front of my car. I was mugged once in Washington, and just before I was jumped I had the same feeling I had at this moment. Both times, I felt: too late. I tried to get a good look at the truck and the faces of the two men who had hopped out and were running toward me. Too late. I took a step toward my car, but they were already on me.

One spun me around, grabbed my elbows, and drew my arms back. The other brought his left knee into my groin. I pitched forward. He brought his right knee up hard against my chin. I remember thinking it would be a good idea to become unconscious, and that is what I did.

As I fell to the cool grass, I closed my eyes. I heard noises far away, and I decided, as if deep in a dream, that it was a car roaring away.

I don't think I lay there long. I got to my knees and lost some scrambled eggs and an English muffin. I lay back for what seemed like a few seconds. Then I stood up. I was surprised that I felt so intact. In pain, but intact. I got into the car, locked the doors, and looked in the rear-view mirror. I had not lost any teeth. There was a red mark on my chin. My lower lip was bleeding and was already puffing up. My testicles were aching, but closer examination showed I had caught his knee on the groin itself, where I had a blue-and-green bruise about the size of a six-footer's kneecap.

I decided that I had been handled very lightly by two people who had known what they were doing. I assumed that if I had not obliged them by stopping and getting out of the car, they would have forced me to a stop—or forced me off the road. It took an instant for me to realize the significance of what I had just thought: maybe Judith Longden hadn't stopped for them, and so they had slammed into her.

I'm essentially desk-bound. The feelings of fear are very unfamiliar to me. But, suddenly, there they were, so standard: weakness in the knees, sweat on the spine, palpitating heart. For the first time in six years I wanted a cigarette.

As I began to calm down and concentrate on driving, I remembered what a friend in the CIA had once told me. He said that sometimes the nicest thing that can happen to you is to have the opposition let you know they're around. When you don't know they are there, he said, it may be because they are going to kill you. So I had met the opposition. But, of course, I did not know who they were.

I tried to concentrate on the scenery for the next few miles. Bim had told me that Route 85 was laid out in the 1920's to connect Tulsa and Oklahoma City and that once there was nothing along the road but fence posts, barbed wire, and tumbleweeds. But with each new discovery of an oil pool under the dusty soil, a few shacks and a cafe would hook onto Route 85, and a town would be born.

One of those towns, about thirty miles west of Tulsa, was Caslon Wells. It was founded by the late U.S. Senator Frank B. Caslon, who also founded the company that bears his name. The town is about one mile long and a dozen or so blocks wide. The natives call the place Wells, I guess because that's what they can see. The oil wells are marked by donkey engines whose stubby black arms ceaselessly semaphore on ranches and, in the town itself, on a few meticulously maintained lawns of imported turf.

Route 85 splits the town. I drove straight through. I thought about stopping at the sheriff's office to report the assault, but the word sounded eastern, and I pictured the locals, including even Bim, having a laugh over someone who tried to make a crime out of a scuffle so mild that he could walk away from it.

About half a mile outside of town I stopped to pick up a hitchhiker, hoping to pump him for casual local information. He was a young, short-haired man in an army field jacket and jeans. He was carrying a lunch box, the old black kind, humped to carry a thermos. He told me he worked at the Facility and he was late as hell.

"We're on three shifts up there. Well, they change those shifts so *god*damn fast that you're just gettin' used to bein' on the eight-to-four and they put you on the goddamn four-to-midnight. And, well, by shit, there's *no* way you get used to *that* fucker. Jesus. I mean you can't do nothin', nothin' at all. No drinkin'. No fuckin'. Nothin' but you sleep and you get up and go to work and you go to sleep again. So anyways, I'm on the eight-to-four, and I don't set my fuckin' clock and the old lady don't wake me. And then my goddamn pickup won't start. Christ. I'll lose two goddamn hours."

I speeded up, as much to help him as to get myself to the Facility a little ahead of time. I needed some coffee. But as the speedometer passed fifty-five, my passenger said, "Christ, mister. You better slow down. It's fifty here, and the state cops, they really watch this stretch. Couple of Caslon people wrapped up here—not hurt bad. But lost time. How those bastards hate lost time. Anyhow, B.O.—that's the super, we call him that—well, B.O., he just called the state police. And they started stoppin' people. They just stop them when they're leavin', usually, so's it won't slow down production. I mean, if Caslon wanted them to let people *speed* to work and back, I mean, if *that* was good for Caslon, then you can bet your ass that the cops wouldn't mind at all. When they say Caslon *owns* the highway patrol and the sheriff, too, they just aren't blowin' it out their ass. I mean, they own *everything*. So you'd best slow down. It's fifty here."

He sighed and looked out the window. I wanted to ask him about Judith Longden, but I had a hunch that her name would shut even him up. So I just asked him what he did at the Facility.

"I'm in P Plant," he said, looking sideways at me. The tempo of his speech slowed down as he spoke, and I could not decide whether caution or weariness was causing it. "I mostly work in SX. You know, where they extract the plutonium from the fuel rods? I mean, mister, I mean I *really* touch that stuff. I really get a chance to touch it, you know?" His voice lowered. "How interested are you, mister? Where you from? This car, it's got Oklahoma plates, but it ain't from here. This is Mr. Hertz's car, mister. Where you from?"

"My name is Phelan and I'm from Washington."

My passenger sat up straight, put his lunch box primly on his lap, and looked directly out the windshield. He had so obviously clammed up that I knew I could do no harm to our conversation by asking him if he knew Judith Longden.

"She got killed last night," he said. "She stuck her goddamn nose into a lot of things." He turned to me and, barely opening his lips, said, "Let me out."

I told him I was going right to the Facility.

"That's what I figure," he said. "You let me out of this fuckin' car right this fuckin' minute."

I stopped. He jumped out without a word and began walking rapidly. I could see a sign about three hundred yards ahead.

The turnoff to the Facility was a straight, two-lane road that ran for half a mile between Route 85 and a group of buildings on a slight rise. A high wire fence paralleled both sides of the road. Black-lettered words on a large white sign proclaimed: NOTICE. ALL VEHICLES AND PERSONS WILL BE SEARCHED WHEN ENTERING AND LEAVING. Another sign announced that it had been 1,139 days since there had been an accident at the Caslon Nuclear Facility.

I drew up to a guardhouse and a closed gate. A sudden wind stirred the dust from the shallow culverts along the road. The car ahead of me moved forward and stopped at the guardhouse. The driver held up a plastic identification tag worn on a chain around his neck. A guard checked a name on a clipboard. The guard wore a khaki shirt and trousers and, tilted low over his mirroring sunglasses, a visored blue cap with a C-in-a-diamond badge.

I got a closer look at the badge when I pulled up, identified myself, and was directed to a visitor's parking space next to the guardhouse and outside the fence.

I had seen that badge's symbol—Caslon's square blue C-in-a-diamond trademark—throughout the countryside. Alongside each small farm house were tall white natural-gas cylinders bearing the symbol. It was on the warning signs that stood over buried Caslon pipe lines, which sometimes surfaced as long, rusty smudges on the rangeland. Caslon country.

I got out of the car and walked to the pedestrian gate. To the left of the gate was a large parking lot. About half the vehicles in it were late-model American cars; the rest were pickups. I saw one Volkswagen, a micro-bus.

A guard met me at the gate and escorted me toward a building flanked by two flagpoles. On one was the American flag; on the other, Caslon's. The wind was rippling the halyards on the flagpoles. The halyards' snaps clanked in a faint tolling, and the flags whipped, giving sound to the wind. The flags' shadows flapped on the sunny wall of the building. A small sign near the glass doors said, ADMINISTRATION.

All the buildings scattered around were white and two stories high, but some were large and some were small. They were linked by sidewalks. I could see white lines on some of the sidewalks, but none on the one I was walking. I asked my escort about this. He shrugged without speaking. I felt the irritation I always feel on a military base or around people following orders.

There is never any use arguing. I submitted to the finger-printing (thumb of right hand only) and was given a temporary identification tag on a chain. I also had to sign a form saying that I would not hold Caslon responsible for any accidents that might befall me on company property. I wondered just where company property began and ended.

My escort, whose own ID tag was in his shirt pocket, remained silent and nameless as we left the Administration building and headed along a sidewalk—this one with a white line down the middle—toward the largest building on the site. Projecting from it was a long, closed walkway that ended with a double-door. As we approached, I asked my guard—as I now thought of him—if he would please inform me where he was taking me.

"This is the Plutonium Processing Plant," he said. "They said they'd meet you in the conference room. You first." He opened the door marked IN.

A chest-high counter ran the length of the walkway. Behind the counter were two guards. They nodded to us and checked my ID against a paper. My guard hurried to the other end of the walkway and went through a door marked SECURITY PERSONNEL ONLY.

On my side of the counter the walkway ended at a stall hung with a curtain of narrow metal strips. I passed through the strips, which clung to me for a moment. At that moment, I thought of Judith Longden passing here and the strips clinging to her body. I did not want to think about her then, but I did.

A door beyond the curtain opened, and there was my guard. He told me, rather proudly, that the door would have stayed closed if any weapons had been detected on me.

The door opened into a wide central hall. At either end of the hall was a metal stairway, clangorous, I imagined, at the changing of shifts. To the left was a booth made of thick, floor-to-ceiling sheets of glass. A guard sat in the booth. To the right of the booth was a door without a doorknob. As we approached, the guard in the booth nodded and apparently pushed the button that opened the door.

We entered a large room, part of which was partitioned into a labyrinth of half-walled small cubicles. Beyond the cubicles were some fully-walled offices. I found out later that the cubicles were where Personnel conducted interviews and administered tests. The walled offices belonged to Security. The Big Room, as it was called by employees, was shared by Personnel and Security. Both union and nonunion employees accepted as fact that the two departments were actually one—Security.

The conference room was behind a door flanked by the offices of Deckman and Kovacs. I wondered why Security needed conferences, and why its headquarters was in the plutonium plant and not in the Administration building. My guard left me at the door.

The men around the oblong table introduced themselves. They had a narrow range of reactions when I told them what had happened to me on the highway.

Captain Deckman said he was shocked, and he did manage to look shocked. I'm sure he knows the area pretty well and is not surprised by any kind of local violence. Orr, "speaking for management," as if that would somehow help, said he was sorry to hear about this, and I'm sure he was. A man named Rosen, Dr. Samuel Rosen, had been introduced as an AEC official from Washington. I assumed he was the unidentified man Bim had seen at the accident. Rosen mumbled, "Incredible. Incredible." His face assumed what to me was a familiar look: the expression of a Washington bureaucrat who finds himself in a situation or location which has produced still another problem to solve or obfuscate.

Kovacs did not say a word. He looked me in the eye and almost imperceptively shrugged. He had a good head of black, tightly curly hair, but I thought of Kojak, and I wondered how much he had profited by having a name that reminded people of a tough TV detective. I would like to know more about Kovacs, I decided. At that moment I also decided that I had met a member of the opposition.

"And there's something else," I said. "Somebody got into my room before I checked in and left me a set of photographs.

They are supposed to be of Judith Longden engaged in various sexual acts. In case any of you are interested, there are two Judiths in the photographs. One I assume *is* Judith Longden. The other I assume is a Tulsa hooker. Lots of things happen when people have sex, but I've never heard of a case where a woman grew new ear lobes by straying from straight intercourse."

"For the record, Mr. Phelan," Orr said, "I want to say that I have no idea what you are talking about." He looked at the other men for supportive indignation, but they had been up all night and were too tired to give him much.

I told them that I had also received a blue loose-leaf notebook marked confidential and that it was now locked in the motel safe. (It was locked in my glove compartment.) I said I assumed they knew about the notebook, since it appeared to be one of several copies. I said that I intended to use the notebook for background.

No one said anything, so I plunged on. I said that I had to file a story by 3 P.M. and that I hoped there would be no objection if I started interviewing them.

"You can start with me, if you like," Kovacs said. Smiling, he turned to Deckman. "OK, Captain?" Deckman nodded. "Can we use your office?" Deckman nodded again. At that time I did not know for certain that Kovacs surreptitiously outranked Deckman. But by the way Kovacs was acting, I was sure he was in charge. I was satisfied then to talk to anyone who could give me any information. Later, I became more wary.

7.

A GUARD BROUGHT in a pot of coffee and left. Kovacs and I both drank it black. He was seated at Deckman's rolltop desk. I was in a straight-backed chair to the side. He pulled out a sliding shelf. I put my cup on it and then my tape recorder. He did not object.

"First, Mr. Kovacs, I would like to find out what happened to the envelope that Judith Longden had in her car last night. She was bringing that envelope to me. There were also, I understand, some tapes."

"I don't know of any envelope." He paused for a split-second, and I wondered whether I was supposed to read the pause as a threat or a surprise. "And I don't know of any tapes . . . other than some cassettes for the tape deck in her car. Songs, that sort of thing." He had a long yellow legal pad, the kind that Nixon made famous. He wrote down something. "I'll check into your inquiry, though."

"Thanks. I'll be sure to remind you."

I wrote a couple of words in my notebook, looked at the tape recorder, and wrote a number. When he asked, I told him that I keep track of questions and answers by jotting down the numbers in the recorder's tape-inch counter. He seemed to enjoy hearing about what he called a new technique.

"I'd like to go back to where you think all this started."

" 'All this?' I'm afraid you'll have to be more specific, Mr. Phelan."

"OK. Miss Longden reported being contaminated—the most recent time—on last Wednesday. Correct?"

"Correct."

"Well, maybe you can start from there."

Kovacs leaned back in the old swivel chair, intertwined his fingers, and stretched his arms forward until several knuckles cracked. "OK," he said. "We start with Wednesday. She goes to work and somehow gets contaminated. She did not know how. The air-sample filter papers don't show it. I'll explain about them later, if you want. Usually, that would be enough. But we have an employee with a contamination report, and so we put the room she was working in on respirators—meaning that everyone in that room has to wear masks that would filter out any plutonium in the air.

"She is decontaminated in the HP—Health Physics—room. It's a standard procedure. You can look it up. Anyway, she is successfully deconned. She monitors herself—checks herself out. And agrees: no contamination left on her body. She's given what are called bioassay kits, so there will be a three- or four-day record of her urine and feces. And she goes home. Am I going too fast?"

"No. Keep going. I may have some questions about technical terms when you're finished. But this is fine."

"OK. Now comes Thursday. She goes back to work. And after a while she *feels* . . ." He leaned forward and tapped the sliding shelf. "She *feels* she's contaminated. Anyway, she calls an HP technician who runs an alpha scanner over her. And, by God, she *is* contaminated. She's got traces of airborne plutonium on her hands, though she was wearing gloves in a glove box, and on her neck. There's a little in her hair, too, and in her nose. The HP does a nasal smear and gets a count.

"The HP, following strict procedures, declares the room on respirators again and takes Longden—*Miss* Longden—to HP. She's decontaminated. Similar drill to the day before. She's upset, almost hysterical. But she's clean. The monitors say so. She can read the monitors. She knows she's got no contamination on her body.

"After the first incident, I got—that is, Captain Deckman got—a report and asked me to check it. What he had heard was that Longden was trying to create an incident. If you have a copy of the chronology—and I sure as hell don't know how you got it—then you'll see that she was quite the little agitator. Nothing wrong with that, ordinarily. A pain in the ass to management, maybe. But nothing awfully big. Except in a place handling . . . in a place like this, a production plant, people—not just management, but fellow workers—get to not appreciate agitators. There are some other factors giving us concern. But I'm afraid there are aspects of this case that I cannot openly discuss."

I pushed the OFF button on the recorder and asked, "You mean strategic nuclear material? Diversion of plutonium? And, going back. . . ."

He interrupted. "It's *special* nuclear material. It's not called strategic any more."

"Because strategic sounded too much like the stuff for making a bomb?" He did not answer. "Again, getting back to another point you made. You mentioned co-workers who did not appreciate what you call her agitating. Are you suggesting that a co-worker may have tried to kill her?" As I said this, I started the recorder.

"The preliminary finding of the state police, as you may know, is that she died in an automobile accident as a result of falling asleep at the wheel. No foul play. She was taking drugs—maybe prescribed, maybe not. The state police are trying to find legitimate prescriptions. She fell asleep. No foul play."

I had a feeling Kovacs did not often repeat himself. I wondered how the police were going to find anything when all her possessions were gone. But I pursued the plutonium. "You strongly implied," I said, "that she had somehow been involved with the theft of plutonium. Is that an accusation?"

"Let's just say that we did not know what was going on. We took a look at her car and at her locker. No evidence that there had been SNM—special . . ."

"I know. . . . ."

"SNM in the car or locker."

"Did she know you checked them?"

"No."

"Does that mean she was under investigation?"

"No. We have a wide latitude in dealing with employees. It's all legal. They sign waivers, et cetera.

"OK. We began discussing what to do. HP does a reading on the bioassays she had brought in. And HP can't believe what they see. It's off the dial.

"The urine and the feces that she brings in on Thursday

show incredibly high readings. She is *entering* the plant with contamination. She goes through the shift and, as I told you, reported *feeling* she was contaminated. She's been fooling around with plutonium. Whatever happened to her had not happened in the course of work. Something funny was going on.

"While she is being deconned on Thursday, we start drawing people into the discussion of the problem. Rosen was here . . . on another matter. But he's Washington, AEC, and so he's in on this very big. He's worried. We've got a problem. Longden and plutonium are getting together. There's no doubt of that. We just don't know how.

"Phelan, it was *in* her, passed through her. That's what the bioassays told us. Big amounts. It didn't make sense."

I guess I looked puzzled, because Kovacs began speaking more slowly. "What I mean is this. Usually our P Plant contamination incidents—which are rare, by the way—involve airborne plutonium. The worst that can happen is that it gets in the lungs. I'll give you some medical stuff on that later. To get plutonium into your feces and urine in the amounts she was showing—well, it looked to us at first that she had to be *eating* it."

"Jesus, Kovacs, You're trying to tell me. . . ."

"I am telling you that we came to the conclusion, on the basis of the first monitoring of the bioassays, that she had been *consuming* plutonium, either deliberately or accidentally."

"I have a lot of trouble believing that, Kovacs."

"So did we. So did we. But . . . Well, there was another theory that didn't make sense, either. At first."

"What was that?"

Kovacs' hand reached toward the recorder, but stopped. He drummed his fingers on the sliding shelf. I got the impression he was acting. He was too deliberate a man for pausing indecisively like that.

"OK," he said, sighing. "I guess you will appreciate how delicate this is. I hope you won't print anything about it. The woman deserves some regard, being dead."

"You tell me. Then I'll tell you if we'll print it."

"All right. There is a possibility that she was smuggling plutonium out of the plant in her vagina or her rectum."

I tried not to react. For some reason, I didn't want to give him the satisfaction of reacting. Somehow, his play-acting about whether he would tell me this had been worse than if he had told me straight out. I though of him—or someone very much like him—arranging for the photographs. I was infuriated at him, sorry for Judy. (I remember realizing that I thought of her as Judy for the first time at that moment.) But all I said was, "Do you have anything to back up your theory?"

"A couple of things. And I want to warn you, this is going to be a little. . . ."

"Raunchy?"

"Yes. Raunchy, I suppose. First, the urine and feces samples were peculiar. To put it as simply as possible, the amounts and types of plutonium were not consistent with consumption of plutonium. It took some very, very sensitive tests and interpretations to . . ."

"You'll have to run that past me again, Kovacs. I'm having trouble understanding this, let alone believing it."

"Can't blame you. OK. Plutonium, as you know, is radioactive and has a half-life—a long one—of 24,000 years. Only half of a given amount would be left in 24,000 years, but there still would be radioactivity. It would take about 250,000 years for it to be no longer radioactive. I guess you know all this in general."

I nodded, saying, "I still can't see . . ."

"The point? Plutonium also has a half-life in the body. If you get some in you, some of it stays; the overwhelming percentage is excreted. Plutonium particles in the GI tract, for instance, get out of the body faster than particles in, say, the lungs. Eventually, about ninety-nine per cent of the plutonium is excreted in the urine and feces."

"Well, wouldn't a lot of plutonium in her excretion indicate she *had* eaten it?" The professional currents were flowing in me. I guess they are deep enough so that I didn't let myself be bothered by the images of Judith Longden eating plutonium. I forgot about her and concentrated on asking him questions. "I mean, if there were signs of a lot of plutonium, what other explanation would you come up with?"

"That *was* the first explanation. She was poisoning herself or being poisoned. A stupid way to poison people, by the way. Precisely because it does pass through so fast. But not as fast as happened in this case. There was *too* much. And there was something involving an article of food, a salami, that was so incredible that . . ."

"A what? Salami?"

"Found in her refrigerator by the survey party. Covered with plutonium. You'll see . . . Incredible. And another matter . . ." He reached over and punched the recorder's OFF button, very decisively.

"There may be a national security angle to this other clue," he said solemnly. "We can pretty well tell where a sample of plutonium came from by analyzing the isotope ratio in it. Plutonium-239 is what we work with most here, but there's always a presence of plutonium-240, another isotope, or, more technically, a nuclide, and americium-241, another radioactive element. In each work batch . . ."

"Excuse me, Mr. Kovacs. What is your background? Are you a physicist or what?"

"My background? Plant executive. That's enough, isn't it? If I worked in a button factory, I'd just naturally make it my business to know a lot about buttons. I'm that way. Curious. May I go on?"

"Sure. But I can't help wondering why you're telling me this information about isotopes off the record."

Kovacs sighed. "It's a strange world, nuclear energy, Mr. Phelan. There used to be a lot of secrets. Now there are hardly any. I went off the record because information about how we can track down missing plutonium could be of interest to the opposition."

"The what?" Sometimes I believe in a kind of telepathy, not as a way to read minds, but as an unknown sense that somehow, without warning, picks up the presence of a word or a phrase hovering in the air. I was startled by his use of the word I had been thinking. *Opposition.* The CIA man I know uses that word for something or someone the CIA is up against. I had been thinking that I would want to talk to that CIA man, Phil, about what he knew of all this. Now I heard that CIA word in this room. And so, amazed, I had said, "The what?"

"People who would try to . . . divert . . . plutonium. Anyway, the isotope ratio in her excretion was not consistent with the isotope ratio of the plutonium she had been working with on Wednesday or Thursday. In fact, the ratio was the same as that of some MUF—material unaccounted for—we were aware of."

"We?"

"Caslon. The Facility. It was a tiny amount. And that is entirely off the record." He pressed the button again, and the tape began to whir in silence for a moment, while he started ahead.

"OK," he finally resumed. "We suspected she may have been smuggling plutonium, and we made one more check. When she was decontaminated on Thursday, we had a female HP check her vagina. There was an indication of plutonium. And then, through Rosen, we set up an examination of her, a *thorough* examination of her, at Los Alamos."

He did not tell me about the phony douche, of course, and he did not tell me the brutal details of the raid. I had been able to imagine Judith when Harry talked about her. There was an honesty that helped to develop the picture. But Kovacs was lying, smoothly lying, and I could not get a picture of her.

I would have to talk to other people to find out what had happened in her last days. And in the days before that, I knew. In the days before that.

". . . When we did come to the conclusion that she was coming in contact with plutonium in some unauthorized and probably criminal way," Kovacs was saying, "we couldn't wait. We knew that plutonium was being diverted." He stepped up his tempo. "We notified the AEC, again through Rosen, that the incident had gone over from one involving safety to one involving safeguards. Do you know the difference, the significance?"

"No."

"Safety: making sure employees and the general public are not hurt by anything we do in the Facility. Safeguards: making sure the wrong people don't get SNM. Safeguards is a different ball game, Phelan. It's very serious stuff.

"From here on, I have to be careful what I say. But I will say this. We thought someone was getting plutonium out of here and that somehow Longden was involved. We decided we had to inspect her apartment. For all we knew, there was plutonium there. We could not warn her."

"Did you yourself go to the apartment?"

"I was in the party outside. Three people went in."

"All men?"

"Yes."

"HP technicians?"

"No. Security force. Guards."

"Armed?"

"I'd rather not say."

"Well, can you tell me what happened?"

"I can do better than that. I can give you a copy of the survey party's report. It's confidential, but I'm sure you'll be discreet."

"Sure. Just like you."

He smiled and stretched his arms and interlocked fingers in that knuckle-cracking gesture. The interview was over. I shut off the recorder and wrote something in my notebook.

"More numbers?" he asked.

I nodded. But what I had written was a word, *opposition.*

8.

KOVACS WAS THE only one who gave me an interview. Deckman, of course, did not talk; Kovacs did all the thinking for both of them. Rosen signaled that he would prefer to be interviewed on his own turf; I told him I would call him when I returned to Washington. Orr said that a messenger, from company headquarters in Tulsa, would deliver a company statement to the motel by two o'clock.

I did not like the idea of waiting around for a company handout that would say how Caslon regretted this unfortunate accident. So I called Art from a highway phone book. He asked me to come over right away. He had found two pages that Judith had made, apparently just before she had got in her car and driven off to meet me.

Hearing her voice, watching Art and Harry listen to her voice, I began to know her. She began to achieve dimensions in my mind. I not only learned about her but I also got some idea of what it was she had been bringing to me. I had something to check. It was only a number: 43719. But the number had come from her lips.

We listened and we talked and we listened again. I listened mostly for the truth in that voice. I could get the details later; they were flowing from her tape to one in my recorder. What I was getting from her was an understanding of what had happened on the last day of her life. I would find out about the other days later. I would piece together what I heard from her voice and from the living voices of others. But now I was hearing her tell me about yesterday—incredibly, *yesterday*—the day we were to have begun to know each other.

The voice began by telling how she reported for work on the eight-to-four shift.

"That son of a bitch Feeley—Pussy Feeley—was on the gate and he gave me a temporary ID," the voice on the tape said, indignant, but level. "I asked him where my permanent one was, and he told me it was being processed. I said that they had had it since Friday, here it was Monday, and where the hell was it?"

" 'So what?' the bastard said, and he told me to report to outer change room 4. 'Light duty,' he said. 'I guess they're afraid you popped a cherry at Alamos.'

" 'And up yours, Feeley,' I said. And he touched me, just below the belt, Art, with the alpha-scanner tube, and he said, 'Tell me honey, which was better, the wound probe at Alamos or Reeves last night.' He said exactly that, Art. Jesus, I can't take much more of this. Jesus, Art. Why are they doing this? I've just got to get it out, Art. Get it out. I guess I'm talking to the tape because I want to tell you before I tell a stranger, that reporter guy—Flynn or somebody—that Harry's bringing. Art, if you want, you can let him have the tape, OK? The tape's yours, not mine. It's yours. Maybe I'll tell him about it, Art. But I want to say, 'If you want it, Mr. Flynn, then you'll have to get it from my boyfriend. My boyfriend, Art.' How's that sound, Art?"

There was a touch of hysteria in the voice now. When she was talking about what happened, the voice was clear and under control. But when she talked about herself directly, or, now, when she talked about Art, the hysteria speeded up and raised the pitch of that young, vibrant voice.

"Feeley wasn't fooling me about why I was in that goddamn change room. It wasn't light duty. It was because they wanted to hold me somewhere, some place where they could question me. You know that old dodge, Art . . ."

Art told me later that a worker was usually assigned to a change room while Security examined his or her locker or car, or while Security questioned the worker's friends. The change-room complexes had been built to fulfill AEC security requirements. The rooms were hardly ever used. Workers found it easier and faster to change clothes in the locker rooms adjacent to the change rooms and then enter the RMA, the radioactive materials area.

". . . I walked in, and right away I heard the door close behind me. I guess there was a guard there, in the hall. There was another one in the guard station. He had left his door open a little. I didn't recognize him.

"He was the only other person in the room. I moved a couple of benches around and I took out my journal, the one I guess I'll be giving to Harry and the reporter. I started working on it. And I guess I got so carried away I didn't hear the hall door open. But I smelled something. B.O. Well, his goddamn cigarette. I bet he *knows* I can't stand the smell of cigarettes.

"I turned around, and there he was, big as life and twice as ugly. He just walked to the end of the bench I was sitting on, and he stood there and stared down at me. You know how he smokes—cigarette in his right hand, his left hand like a little cup for the ashes.

"He smoked like that for almost a minute, or it seemed that way, and then he flicked the ashes into the cup of his hand, and he lifted up his leg—like he was a dog that was going to piss—and he put the ashes in his cuff. I hear his cuffs are asbestos lined.

"And he was shaking that wing of his, you know how he does? Twitching while he talked, but that's the way he always is all the time. I wasn't feeling nervous or anything until he opened his mouth and spoke to me. I never heard his voice so edgy. 'I'm having some visitors today,' he said. And he looked all spruced up. But that's all he said, for like a whole minute, it seemed. 'I'm having some visitors today . . .!'

"He said it again, I mean, just the words, 'Some visitors.' He was trying to scare me, and I was wondering how far the son of a bitch was going to go. I was glad the guard was there. A witness, I thought. Honest to God, Art, I was that scared . . ."

Bailey Orr can be a menacing man. He is not subtle, and from Judith's words it was not difficult to conjure up his confrontation with her.

"Some visitors," he repeated. He raised his foot to the

bench again, this time to crush out the cigarette. He touched the index finger and thumb of his left hand to the tip of his tongue and pinched the butt. Judith could hear the whisper of the last spark. He dropped the butt into his cuff. Then he shook a Chesterfield out of a pack he carried in his shirt pocket and lit it with a lighter that bore the C-in-a-diamond Caslon trademark.

"They're going to be asking questions," he said. "Like you do."

"FBI?"

"What makes you say that?"

"I know they're in town, and you know I know."

"You think I know a lot more than I really know." His arm stopped flapping for a moment. "But I do know they haven't talked to you—yet."

"That's right."

"OK." The flapping resumed. "But you're going to talk to a certain other party. Tonight."

"That's right, too."

"I have no way of stopping you . . . but . . ."

"Right, again."

"But I want you to know a couple of things. First, there are not just millions of dollars tied up here. There are *hundreds* of millions of dollars. Hundreds. In fact, I heard people say billions, but I can't ever think that high; it don't make sense. But that's the first thing. Big money. And I don't need to tell you, there's no way—no way—anybody with no money can turn around people with big money.

"The next thing is people. Not much more than 200 people working here all together. But that's a lot of Caslon Wells. This place is a place where they have jobs, good jobs. They don't like to hear any talk about the place being so bad it ought to be shut down. I don't need to tell you the folks around here can get riled up about things—or people—they don't like.

"Now I'm not saying that there'd be anything wrong with your health if you kept working here. But I *am* saying if you don't like it here, you go work somewhere else. There ain't no need for you to endure all this suffering here, now is there? So I don't know why you stay. Unless it's just plain to cause trouble."

He suddenly stood straight. His foot hit the floor hard.

"Before I talk to those visitors," he said, glaring down at her, "I want to know what's your game. What's your goddam game? I'm asking you . . ."

Judith's tape told us that she responded by asking him questions about his game. About something called a criticality incident and about the keeping of plutonium records. I would find out about these issues later.

" 'Why are the plutonium records so fucked up?' I asked the son of a bitch, and he said, 'Watch your language, young lady.'

"And I asked him, 'How come you pulled inspectors off the fuel-rod assembly line?''

"And before he could answer, I told him that that's the kind of stuff I was going to tell the reporter.

"And Orr said, 'You silly-ass woman. You go telling things like that, and you figure those damn Feds will be all over this place, sticking their noses in, telling us what to do. Well, you're all wrong. The Feds are on *our* side. You got it all wrong, all wrong. It's you that's in trouble. It's you.'

"The phone rang, and they told him his visitors were there, and he left. And I decided that I was going to leave, too, Art. I decided it was about time I got out of that damn place."

The guard unlocked the door so she could go to the cafeteria at lunchtime. A worker she did not recognize—probably, she said, some Pinkerton in work clothes—fell in behind her and sat at the other end of her table, sipping coffee. She believed that people at nearby tables were looking at her. She heard a woman say, "Oh, it's just what's-her-name. From the union."

She hurried to the side door of the cafeteria and ran down a deserted hall to the main-floor lobby. There was no one in sight in the entrance hall. Getting out was always easier than getting in. She said she had early-exit permission, and the guard did not question her. The door at the outer end of the walkway tunnel clicked open. She began running.

She ran against the cold, dry wind to the parking lot and swiveled through the rows of cars to her Volkswagen. It was parked in her assigned parking space in the row farthest from the Facility buildings. (When she had become recording secretary of Local 1010, she had been moved from the first row to the last. All union officers were put in that row.)

The VW sped through the inner gate, which was not manned between shift changes. She looked, as she always did, at the sign outside the plant. She had a mild obsession about that sign ever since the first day she came to work. The sign said, SAFETY FIRST; 1,138 DAYS WITHOUT LOST-TIME ACCIDENT.

She slowed for the outer gate near Route 85. They may have phoned ahead to stop her . . . But the gate slid open, and the guard in the kiosk waved. She was out.

Not alone, though. Quivering in the shaky side mirror was the image of a dirty white pickup.

She said she had expected a green Impala. "That's what's been following me mostly," she said. "A green Impala. I've been getting used to it."

The tape brought Judith's voice to life: "So I came here, Art. It's a nice place, Art. Such a nice place. I think sometimes, what the hell, I'll come back. It's not just that I don't have any place now. Not even a goddam toilet seat to call my own, Art. It's not that. It's that I think I really want to come back to you. I'll see you tonight, Art, after I talk to that reporter guy. Harry told me his name. Flynn? Something like that. After I talk to him, Art. I'll be back. This was a nice place, Art."

Art, who had been listening to the tape, turned to me and said, "I want to talk to you, Phelan, about her. You've got to write more about her than just that she was killed. Not just that she was killed. She was more than that."

Harry said nothing, and neither did I. My mind was on another thought, a silly thought, but I kept having it: I wish she had known my name.

9.

ART TOOK THE tape out of his machine and replaced it with the second one he had found. Before he played her second tape, we tried to piece together what had happened between her recordings. The picture of her last day was becoming more clear in my mind. I was steadily thinking of her now as Judy, but I feel compelled to write of her as Judith. I don't know why.

Art's apartment was in what had been the loft of a converted barn set back about fifty yards from a side street at the east end of town. The barn was now an antique gift shop and on most weekends an auction site. The big clapboard farmhouse itself had long since disappeared under a grid of plots for small, flat brick houses with dusty front lawns and cluttered car ports.

The apartment was reached by a steep outside stairway that ended at a small landing. Beyond the tiny kitchen was a bathroom, a bedroom, a living room, and what Art called his dope and music room: water pipes, quad speakers, incense burners, tape deck, a few books, including a couple of hollowed-out ones in which, as a joke, he stashed grass.

When Judith reached Art's apartment, she stood on the back of the couch in this room, where Harry, Art, and I now sat, and looked out one of the high, narrow windows that faced the street. The white pickup that had been following her had parked in front of a house a block away. Two men were in it, one wearing a red cap with CAT on the front. She had seen that man before.

Judging the line of sight from the pickup, she decided it was possible to slip away without being seen. The men were watching her car, which she had pulled up along the side of the barn opposite the stairway. As long as her car was parked there, she figured they would just sit and watch it.

"She was getting more and more scared, I think," Art told Harry and me as he hovered over the tape deck in his music room. "She knew I wasn't going to be home until about five. I'd quit Caslon, you know, and I was in Tulsa, looking for a job."

"No. I didn't know," I said sharply. I felt that he had walked out on Judith when she needed him, and I was unreasonably angry at him.

"Yeah. On Friday, the day of the raid. It's a long story . . ."

"I'd like to hear it someday," I said. There was an edge to my voice, and he caught it. Her words were still echoing in my mind. She had sounded so alone.

"OK. OK," Art said. "But right now we're trying to figure out yesterday, right? OK. I had told Judy I'd meet her at Barbara's around five. I guess we'd eat there, and then she'd leave from there to meet you guys . . ."

I interrupted him again. "Why Barbara's? Why not meet you here?"

"A couple of reasons, I guess. We . . . she . . . We used to live here, and she felt funny sometimes about . . . about staying here again. But the main reason, I think, is that she had to pick up something at Barbara's."

"The tapes!" I exclaimed. "There were tapes in the car, and Kovacs grabbed them! She was going to bring them to me. And her journal. She said she was working on it. Kovacs must have grabbed that, too."

"Hold on," Art said. "You haven't heard the rest of what happened." He pointed to the machine, but he still did not play the second tape.

"From what I've heard and from what Harry and I figured out before you got here, she began to get really worried when she stood up there"—we all three glanced at the window—"and looked out again. She must have known then they were really after her.

"I left things the way I found them." He showed me a cable that snaked out of the machine to a yellow sling chair. On the chair was a green sweater. "Mine," Art said. "She gave it to me for my birthday." And under the sweater was a microphone.

"You'll hear her say, at the beginning of the second tape, that she 'rigged the gear for auto.' That means she patched the recorder so that it was sound-actuated. The tape would run only if the mike picked up a certain level of sound. She knew her way around recorders." He pressed a button on the recorder, and her voice again entered the room. She was speaking rapidly. Unlike the voice on the first tape, this one had a timbre of panic.

"Second tape. Rigged the gear for auto. May not have time to hide tape. Just looked out window. The man in the red cap got out of the truck.

"Put in this tape, hid mike. He's heading for the driveway. Can't hide this tape. Hope you find first one. Hope I can talk to you. Got to get out. Anybody comes in, maybe won't find mike. Goodbye, Art . . ."

There was a faint buzzing sound. Art shut off the recorder.

"That's just the first part," he said. "Before we get to the rest, I think I can fill in a little. I talked to Barbara last night. Talked a lot, for me and Barbara.

"What happened, I figure, is that she ran down the stairs and got around the back of the barn without old red cap seeing her. There's no noise on the tape of anybody coming in the door, and I think the mike would pick that up. So I figure that the guy just came into the driveway. Maybe to scare her. Maybe to get her to take off. And that's what she did.

"She must have jumped over the fence in back of the barn and ran up a side street to Route 85. She crossed the highway and headed for Barbara's. She told Barbara she was about halfway down the street when she saw a green Impala parked almost in front of Barbara's. She had seen that car following her, and she didn't want whoever was in it to see her.

"When she saw the Impala, she ran back to the highway and went a block east to the next street. She cut through the backyard that backs up to Barbara's and ran in. Barbara doesn't lock her door much.

"Barbara told her the Impala had been watching the house.

We had seen it before, all of us, since the raid and before we went to Los Alamos, which was on Sunday. You know about Los Alamos?"

I told him I had some kind of report from Kovacs, but I hadn't had time to look at it. I wanted to know about Judith and yesterday more than I wanted to know about anything else.

"OK. Barbara said Judy started strutting around the kitchen, making believe she was B.O., flapping her arm and all, and, Barbara thought, covering up that she was scared.

" 'B.O. has to know what those guys are doing in the Impala,' she said. 'I'm sure they've all got those old-buddy CB's and they're telling each other right now that I'm gone, cleared out of that goddamn place.'

"She didn't like CB radios, you know. She said they reminded her of her . . . her ex-husband, Michael. His handle was Papa Bear and he wanted her to get a CB and be Mamma Bear. Can you imagine? Her being Mamma Bear?"

He laughed, the way people do at Irish funerals. It is not laughing at death or the dead but at a good memory of the dead. Harry smiled, and so did I. Art was right. I couldn't imagine her that way. I could not imagine her at Barbara's, either. I asked Art to describe Barbara's apartment. He glared at me. He had the idea, I suppose, that I was a reporter trying to get some colorful details on the life of the dead woman.

"In the kitchen," Art said. "They were in the kitchen. It was—it is—just an ordinary kitchen. But neat. Barbara's neat as hell."

I've since seen Barbara and her kitchen. It is neat. What Art did not realize was that I did not want colorful details; I wanted an understanding of what was going on. But I was anxious to hear her voice again, and so I just nodded, and he resumed talking.

"They argued—well, Barbara said *discussed,* but she's awfully, well, *mild* most of the time—they argued about the box, the box in Barbara's closet, and . . ." Art looked at me and rapidly filled me in.

Art said that the box in the closet in Barbara's bedroom was a square wooden chest with a worn leather handle. Its lock and hasp were brass, and there were riveted brass plates on its corners. It had belonged to Barbara's grandfather, a traveling jewelry salesman. It had a false bottom.

"So there was something hidden in it?" I asked. I practically lunged at him. I could not contain my sudden fascination with that box. I thought of the journal, of information that might be in that box. Once again, Art looked disgusted. At that moment, I certainly was the reporter on a story, and I couldn't blame him for his reaction.

"I don't know. Barbara didn't tell me, and I didn't ask." It looked as if his eyes strayed toward Harry for an instant as he added, "The less known"—with a slight shrug—"the better."

He took a breath and went on. "She used a lot of gestures—fingers to her lips and all—to convince Barbara that the place might be bugged." Art looked startled, swept his eyes around. "Hell, *this* place might be bugged. I never thought of that . . . Anyhow, Barbara said they took the box upstairs to Barbara's landlady's apartment. It's a two-story house, and Mrs. Jordan, the landlady . . . well, you'll see it. The idea was that Judith would wait up there, on the second floor. . . . In case, just in case . . . Well, she was convinced now that they were really after her."

"You mean to kill her?"

Art and Harry looked at each other. I was convinced of the exchange of glances this time.

"I don't know. Maybe that. Maybe just to get her, to talk to her. Anyway, what happened next is that Barbara had to go to work."

"So all we have for finding out what happened next is what's on the second tape?" I asked.

"Pretty much," Art said. "And what I know, from later, from when she left to . . . to meet you."

He pressed the button. The sound of a door opening. Footsteps. The dialing of a phone. Muffled voice. A phone rings once. Muffled voice. Footsteps. Sound of door opening and slamming. Again, the sound of a door opening. Footsteps, more than one set. Chairs scraping. Then her voice: "Get to Wells much?" And a man's voice, deep, drawling: "Once a month about. Just in and out. Pick up instruments, drop them off . . ."

We were hearing what the microphone picked up in two distinct fragments that seemed like one. It did not make sense. There were more fragments, rolling off the tape that way. By the time the tape ended, though, there were links between the fragments. Judith eventually spoke on the tape and gave us an idea of what had happened.

From her words and from Barbara's and Art's recollections, I was able to follow Judith through those fragments and assemble them into a narrative that covered the rest of that Monday, that last day that was then yesterday. I would be able to understand much of that day. But on that tape I would hear that number, 43719. And it would be a while before I would find out what that number meant. Judith never did find out.

Judith had stationed herself at the windowseat in Mrs. Jordan's living room, which was directly above Barbara's. She looked through the organdy curtain. The pickup was now parked behind the Impala.

Barbara roared out of the driveway on her motorcycle, heading for the four-to-midnight shift. As soon as the motorcycle turned onto the highway and disappeared, a man got out of the Impala and went back to the pickup and talked to the man in the red cap, who was leaning out of the passenger's window. The man from the Impala wore a gray suit and a low-crowned, narrow-brim gray western hat. Judith recognized him as a man who called himself Geiser.

She crawled along the living room floor to the kitchen, where she found a phone and called the Cherokee Motel. She asked for Harry Skirvin's room, but the operator told her that Mr. Skirvin was not in his room and asked if there was any message. "Just say I'll see you at eight," Judith said. "See you at eight."

She stayed in the kitchen by the phone. Her plan was that she would call the sheriff's office and identify herself as Mrs. Jordan if she heard anyone coming up the back stairs. She knew then, as she had known since the raid on her apartment on Friday, that the sheriff's office would not respond to a call for help from Judith Longden.

She heard someone enter Barbara's apartment. She could hear the sound of movement, of search, she assumed. But no voices. She decided only one of the two or three men had entered.

She heard the front door close and she crawled back to the

window. The man called Geiser was walking down the porch stairs. He got into the pickup, on the driver's side. The man in the red cap sat next to him. There was still one man, whom she had never got a good look at, in the Impala, which stayed in front of the house. The pickup started, made a U-turn, and headed for Route 85.

Shortly after 5 o'clock, the phone rang downstairs. It was Art. He had arrived home, seen her car parked outside, and entered his apartment expecting, of course, to find her there. When he discovered she was not there, he called Barbara's. He did not see the microphone, which had picked up his entry, walking around, and telephone dialing.

Judith could hear the phone ringing below her, and she knew it had to be Art. As soon as the phone stopped ringing, she dialed Art. He answered on the first ring.

She told Art to go to Barbara's and walk right in. He thought she sounded strange.

She ran down the back stairs and through Barbara's apartment to the front door. She crouched next to it, hand on the knob.

In five minutes she heard brakes screech in front of the house, a door slam, and the sound of feet hitting the stairs and porch floor. As soon as Art's hand was on the knob, she turned it and pulled the door open. He almost fell on her.

She put a finger to her lips, crawled out of the entrance hall, and at a far corner of the living room, stood. She took him by the hand and led him upstairs to Mrs. Jordan's.

She told him to leave immediately and to act as if he had looked for her inside and had not found her. She said she thought the people following her might be confused; they might still not know she was in the apartment. She told him to roar away in the hope of drawing off the Impala. She said that she would duck out of Barbara's back door and run to his place, where she would get her car. She planned to drive directly to the motel, hoping that she would be on her way before her pursuers figured out what had happened. (Half of her plan succeeded. Art did draw the Impala to a town about thirty miles west. He called Harry from there after seeing the Impala suddenly stop and U-turn back toward Caslon Wells.)

Judith was carrying a large brown Caslon inter-office envelope. Its flap was tied down by a red string that ran between two cardboard buttons. On the other side were lines on which names and office numbers were written, as a record of use; there were two rows of perforations so that a mail clerk could tell whether the envelope was empty. Art recognized a few names and numbers: Orr, Fenwick, Metal. Lab 5. Through the perforations he could see dots of manila and dots of shiny black.

He said he asked her what was in the envelope.

"My . . . my stash, Art," she said. "My very, very good stuff."

He said he asked her if that was what she was taking to the reporter, to me.

"Yes," she said, "I'm showing him this and I'm telling him where there's more. At Barbara's. At your place." She told Art about the tape hidden in the hollowed-out book and about the tape still in the recorder and about the sound-actuated microphone.

She spoke quickly, intensely, he told us, his own voice quick and intense.

" 'Let's *go*,' " she said. And then she pulled me out of Mrs. Jordan's back door and down the stairs to Barbara's."

She shooed him toward Barbara's front door. But he stood in the doorway between the kitchen and the living room, and he was able to see the back door. Judith dashed out of Barbara's bedroom, where she had picked up a jacket. She ran out the back door. The door did not latch. It blew open. Art ran back to close it.

She was at the back fence. She dropped the envelope. Art saw her pick it up, open her jacket, and stick the envelope into the waistband of her jeans. Then she vaulted, one hand, over the fence. Her open jacket flared about her like a bright blue flame. Art watched her for a moment, a blur of blue that whirled around the corner of the house on the next street. She was gone.

10.

"THAT WAS THE last time I ever saw her," Art told Harry and me. He had shut off the tape deck. It was at this point on the tape that the door is heard opening for the second time. Judith is walking into the kitchen, with at least one person, a man who has a drawling voice . . .

Later, as I reconstruct her last day, I play my copy of the tape again and again. By skipping to the end I can get a brief account from her about what happened after she leaped over Barbara's backyard fence and began running to Art's.

I have shuttled often through the time of that day and night, feeling the time, thinking about her, remembering the route I walked from Barbara's to Art, remembering, too, the fear I myself knew in Caslon Wells. I think I now can take her along that route on that night.

The wind was stripping the last warmth from the day. There was no moon. A few cars already had their lights on when she reached Route 85 and crossed to the north side. Concrete platforms spanned the culvert paralleling the highway. On each platform was a silvery mailbox mounted on a pipe. Each concrete platform was a bridge to a driveway and a house set back from the highway. The lights were going on in the houses, and behind each living-room window flickered a blue-edged cluster of color.

When she reached Art's house, she saw a Caslon panel truck in his driveway. Two men in white coveralls were doing something to her car. As she came closer, she could see that they were checking the VW for contamination. Each man had a wiper, a specially treated cloth, sticky on one side for picking up radioactive particles too small for the eye to see.

They had managed to unlock the car. They took smears of the seats, the steering wheel, the switches, door and window handles, the gear-shift knob, the accelerator, brake, and clutch pedals. They worked swiftly, dropping the wipers into a yellow plastic drawstring bag.

She had not seen them before. They said they were from Caslon Technical Services and worked out of the corporation headquarters in Tulsa. One man was tall and looked like a polar bear, paunchy, narrow-headed. The other man was short, slim, and aggressive. She asked them their names. They gave only first ones: the little one, Bill; the big one, Fred.

A few hours later they would be checking the VW again, and under Kovacs' careful direction they would shroud it in plastic sheets.

When they tell her they need to make a phone call, she invites them upstairs. The door opens, and they walk into the kitchen.

"Get to Wells much?" she asks.

Fred's voice, deep and drawling: "Once a month about. Just in and out. Pick up instruments, drop them off. Recalibrate 'em, decon 'em. That sort of stuff."

Chairs scraping. Faint voice of Bill on telephone, apparently calling Tulsa to report in.

New voice [Bill, obviously in charge]: "Well, that's it, buddy. Home time."

"Ever have to decon an employee's car before?" Judith asks.

Fred starts to speak. Bill cuts him off. Fred tries again. "Not exactly," he says.

"What's exactly?" Judith asks.

"Well, he wasn't exactly an employee. I mean, he was dead."

"For Christ sake, Fred," Bill commands. "Let's go."

"Who was dead?" Judith asks, a clipped control to her voice.

"The union guy. You know, the one that was killed."

"Scinto?"

"Yeah. Scinto," Fred says. "We checked out his car, his house, garage. Looking for any of the stuff."

"Plutonium?"

"That's it, Fred," Bill says. "You got a big dumb mouth. Now let's get the fuck . . ."

"You watch out how you talk," Fred says. Sounds of movement: [Is he standing over Bill?] "She's a lady and you ain't supposed . . ."

"Yeah. Yeah. Let's go, Fred. Let's go."

"When you checked that Scinto's car, you find anything?" Judith asks.

"Naw. He was clean as you are."

"What were you looking for in the VW? What did they tell you?"

"Nothin'. They never tell me nothin'."

"Come on, Fred," she insists. "They must have told you something about me."

"She's pumping you, Fred. For God's sake," Bill says. "They told us *that.* They told us she'd pump us."

"What else did they tell you?" she asked. If she now turned to face Bill, they would be standing almost eye to eye.

"They said you were cute—and they just didn't mean your face," Bill says. "They said you ask a lot of questions."

"One more. What would you have done if I hadn't come along? One more again. Or did you know I was coming along? Did a little white pickup tell you?"

Sounds of movement. The door opening. Bill speaks, apparently from near the door: "Go turn the truck around, Fred. I'll be right down." Door closes as footsteps are heard on the outside stairs.

The voices of Bill and Judith are faint. They seem to be standing near the door. Judith has probably maneuvered herself so that in speaking to her Bill is facing in the direction of the open door to the music room and the microphone. They speak quickly and furtively.

"You wouldn't want to tell me what's in that envelope, would you?"

Rustling sound that may be Judith zipping the jacket, perhaps to protect the envelope, which is probably still in the waistband of her jeans.

"No. I wouldn't want to tell you . . . Not unless you can tell me what 43719 means."

"What?"

She repeats the number.

"I don't have the least idea what that number means, honey," Bill says. "And if I did, you can bet your little ass I wouldn't tell you." Sound of door opening. "You're as cool as they said you'd be. Cool little bitch, they said." Sound of door closing.

She stands on the back of the couch and watches the truck go down the driveway and turn toward the highway. She goes out on the landing at the top of the stairs and keeps in her sight the white beams and the red dots of the truck as it angles through the streets and finally vanishes.

She goes into the music room again. She does not disturb the microphone under the green sweater. Someone else might come in after she has left, she explains. The recorder will automatically shut off at the end of the tape. In fact, this will be the last voice on the tape: her voice, quite clear and calm as she quickly tells about the check of her car, her visit with Bill and Fred, and the moments up to this moment. She pauses, and then she says: "Oh, I'm cool, Art. I'm really cool. A real cool little bitch." She laughs.

She finishes her beer, makes a peanut-butter sandwich, showers, and changes her blue turtleneck shirt for a yellow turtleneck shirt, which she had brought from Barbara's.

Sound of a door opening and closing.

It was a little after seven, time to go to meet the reporter.

11.

WHEN THE TAPE ENDED, I had three questions. Who was the man in the red cap? Who was Geiser? And what did the number 43719 mean?

"The guy in the red cap I don't know," Harry said. "But we both saw him, Art. Remember? At Carry's Place? He was with Geiser."

Art nodded.

"I sure as hell know Geiser, if that's his name," Harry said. He stood and began banging his right fist into his cupped left hand. "The first time I saw Judy, that was the time I saw that son of a bitch. Judy and I were in Jack's. I was asking her about"—He glanced at me, somehow making me understand that the missing words were *Dick Scinto*—"about the strike, trying to get a line on the strike. And then I saw Geiser. He was in a booth across from ours.

"I told her to go to the john and look at the guy but don't let on she was looking. She came back and she said it was a guy who worked in Personnel. She was sort of naive then. She didn't really know how they operated in that place. Like that Personnel is really Security. Anyhow, I told her I knew him. He has a couple of names. Geiser's one of them."

Harry sat down again. He seemed suddenly older and tired. "I was called into a strike at a nuclear fuel-processing plant near Houston a couple of years ago. There was trouble. One of our guys, an organizer, was killed. Hit by a car. Hit and run. Geiser was the son of a bitch we thought drove the car. He's a small-town hood. Did time in Texas and in a federal prison somewhere. I'll bet you one thing, Phelan. I'll bet he has a perfect alibi for last night. The son of a bitch."

Art went into the kitchen and asked if we wanted a beer and something to eat. Without realizing it then, we had the same meal Judith had had. We were sitting around the kitchen table. Art was saying something about how she liked peanut-butter sandwiches, and then Harry blurted out: "Why did she make the tapes?"

For a moment I didn't realize why Harry sounded so upset.

"Did she know?" he asked. "Did she figure they were going to get her? Did she think they were going to kill her? Or maybe it was something else."

Then I thought I knew what Harry was thinking. It was occurring to me, too.

"You mean," Art said, "did she do this because she was going to kill herself? These are like suicide notes? Is that what you mean?"

Harry nodded.

"It's been going through my mind," Art said. "Listening to her, that's been going through my mind." He began speaking slowly, summoning a memory. "I remember once she was talking about her husband, Michael. She called that her first life. And coming here, her second life. I said something about, well, you'd have to be dead for there to be that new life. It doesn't sound right now. But when I said it, well, I was sort of kidding but, I guess, sort of probing, too. I never knew much about that first life of hers. Anyway, she said, that the first time, when she saw that her life wasn't working out, well, she didn't kill herself, she just walked off. She said that if she ever felt that way again, felt that life wasn't working out, she wouldn't walk out; she'd do something else. That's what she said."

I asked him if she specifically said she would kill herself. He did not, or would not, remember her exact words.

"She was capable of it," Harry cut in. "She could do it. She had the guts to do it. That's what you need. Guts. You know"—looking toward me as if I'd understand—"Hemingway."

"He was out of his mind," I said. "She wasn't. And what about the smashed tail light? And all the running, and the evading, the worrying? And that envelope. We heard that on the tape. She wasn't going to drive herself off the road. She wasn't thinking about killing herself. I think she was thinking about *getting* killed."

I tried to change the subject. I asked them about the number 43719. Neither had any idea what it could mean. I wondered if Barbara might know. I suggested that we call her. They looked at each other for a moment, as if each hoped the other would speak.

Then Harry said, "She's not here . . . She's taking the body to Corpus Christi. For the funeral."

Harry suddenly stood and walked toward the door. He turned around. "I feel like such a son of a bitch. She's the only one going, you know. We aren't going to the funeral. None of us. Just Barbara."

"She handled everything," Art said, picking up his share of a confession. "Judy didn't have a dress, you know. All her stuff was gone. Barbara bought her a dress. I don't even know what goddamn color it was." His eyes filled up, and he could not speak. He folded his arms on the cold metal-topped table and lowered his head upon them.

I tried again to change the subject. I remembered Harry's telling me that she had said something about *Way Out in Idaho* when he tried to tell her in code about bringing her records to me. He had said, "And you'll bring your records? The country music records? My friend would enjoy hearing them."

"Yeah. I'll bring them," she said. "I'm sure he'll like *Way Out in Idaho.*"

I asked Harry if he had figured out what that had meant. It seemed like a question that would get their minds off Judith's funeral.

"I don't have the least idea," Harry said, sounding annoyed. He probably figured I was just fishing for color for a story. I tried to think of another question.

Suddenly, Art lifted his head. "Jesus," he said. "Jesus. That was a song we kidded about once. Kidded. It must sound to you like that's all I do. It's a working song. On a folk song record I've got." While he continued talking, he led us back into his music room. He found the record, and put it on the turntable. Before he let down the tone arm, he finished talking.

"We were listening to this one night, and this song came on. She said, 'Isn't that where they buried those men?' And I said,

'What men? What the hell are you talking about?' Well, I hadn't heard about that. But she had. She knew all kinds of things, mostly bad things, about nuclear energy."

He paused, looking toward Harry. I could see that Harry knew what Art was talking about. The room had not been as silent all day long. I sensed each thinking about the other, each thinking about where he had fitted into Judy's life and Judy's fate.

"It was in Idaho, in 1960 . . ." Art began.

"It was in 1961," Harry cut in. "January 3, 1961, at the AEC test station in Idaho Falls. Sorry. But *I* know about that one, too.

"A small nuclear reactor went supercritical," Harry continued. "The three guys working in it were killed . . ."

Now I broke in. "By the reactor? I've seen AEC handouts that say no one's ever been killed in a reactor accident."

"No *civilians* maybe," Art said. "These were guys from the armed services. It was an SL-1 reactor, for places like military bases in Greenland. Anyhow, the bodies were so hot, so radioactive, that when they were buried—Jesus, when I think of it—that when the bodies were buried, they had to be put in special caskets. Concrete. Lead. God knows what else. And their heads and hands were cut off. The heads and hands had been so much more exposed, you see, that the heads and hands had to be buried separately, as high-level waste. They were buried with the high-level waste in the dump at the AEC site in Idaho. Just like the crap from P Plant, like the stuff from Judy's apartment. High-level waste. Heads and hands, buried in the ground. In Idaho." He put the tone arm down, and the music started, slow and twangy.

. . . Way out in Idaho, way out in Idaho
A-working on the narrow-gate, way out in Idaho.
. . . When I got to Pocatello, my troubles, my troubles
began to grow . . .

The song went on as Art finished. "When she was telling me about those guys, and we were listening to this, she said that she hoped she wouldn't have to get it that way. She said she hoped that she'd be buried whole. Honest to God, Phelan, she sat here in this room, and that's what she said."

. . . Oh it filled my heart with pity as I walked along the track . . .

• • •

When the record player turned itself off, each of us waited for another to speak first. Finally, Harry said, "So she said that to me, *Way Out in Idaho,* because she saw something? Saw she was going to die? I can't believe it. I can't."

I blurted out: "Neither can I." Perhaps I spoke up a bit too quickly, but we all were ministering to our consciences. "She was scared—and in one day here, I can tell you, who could blame her? She wasn't going to kill herself. She was going to see me. She wanted to talk. She made these tapes to back herself up, to give herself a record."

"She used to do that, you know," Art said. "Make tapes about what she was thinking. A sort of diary, she said."

I thought of that bag of tapes that Kovacs took from the accident scene. "Used to?" I asked. "Why did she stop?" For some reason, I decided not to mention the tapes found in her car.

"I don't really know," Art said. I had noticed that people around Art's age often used *really* as a way of signaling a white lie. I pressed him.

"You must have an idea why."

"Not really. It's just that I *think* she was taping stuff now and then, but it was private. And there was the journal. She said, a couple of weeks ago, I guess, she said that the journal was where she was putting everything now. But she said the journal was about Caslon and plutonium more than it was about her. So maybe—well, it's what I *think*—maybe she stopped the tapes because she was concentrating everything on the journal."

"Where's the journal then?" I asked. But I thought I knew. I pictured it going into that bag that Kovacs had.

"I don't know," Art said. "I guess she was taking it to you. I guess it was in the envelope."

Harry was beginning to act restless. He finally said that he planned to fly back to Washington that night. He said he could do more there than here. I said I thought I could, too. We made a date to meet when I returned to Washington.

Harry followed me back to the motel. I felt safer, seeing his car behind me on that highway that seemed to be filled with pickup trucks. Any one of them could be out to get me, I thought. And the word paranoia glided through my mind.

Harry and I talked for a while in the bar, and he casually gave me a few insights into Judith's character. She was beginning to become more real. I knew I was going to have to bring her to life in mind if I were ever to find out what it was she had wanted to tell me. But the journal, the tapes, so much about her was gone.

I was thinking this at the bar after Harry left to check out. I felt a touch of the maudlin coming over me. So I paid my bill and left.

I went to my room, feeling if not defeated at least dejected. I looked forward to quiet and privacy. No more talking. Maybe no more thinking. Then I opened the door. Coiled on the bed, in the warmth of a patch of fading sunlight, was a rattlesnake.

I backed out of the room and hurried—I did not run—down the corridor to the elevator. There was no one at the counter in the lobby when I walked up to it. I hit the bell a couple of times, and a tall, slim man who looked like a young Gary Cooper emerged from an office behind the counter.

He laughed out loud when I told him about the snake. He said he would send a black porter up with a wire noose. "Niggers know how to take care of these things," he said. "And they're immune, you know."

I said I didn't know.

He asked me if I had any friends in Wells. I said I did. I wanted to add "provisionally." He said, "Well, Mr. Phelan, some friend is just tryin' to scare you. That's all. It's an old trick around here." He leaned forward. "Now you wouldn't be foolin' around with any boy's woman up there, would you? Mind you, I'm not bein' nosy. That's what it's usually about, though. Cheatin'. Now that snake, it wasn't goin' to do nothin'. I mean, you *saw* it, right? Well, that's the point, Mr. Phelan. It was there just to tell you to watch out. That's all."

I wondered how much he knew about what went on in his motel. Paranoia again: a Caslon-controlled motel. I must have been staring into space because the desk clerk tapped me on my arm with a bony finger. "Mr. Phelan?" he said. I looked up at him. "Two messages." He handed me a telephone message slip and a long white envelope whose return address was Caslon headquarters in Tulsa.

When I thanked him and turned away, he asked, "You'll be staying with us for a while?"

"Maybe a long while," I said, and I headed for the bar.

Over a beer, I jotted in my notebook, in a very personal shorthand, the basis for a story. The handout from Caslon did not say anything, of course, but I grudgingly gave the company a couple of quoted paragraphs. Being of the old school, I refrained from writing about the attack on the side of the highway and the rattlesnake on the bed.

I knew I was delaying a return to my room. I also knew I did not want to call in the story from a phone in the bar. I was becoming suspicious about phones, but I reminded myself that I was not going to be dictating any secrets. Whatever I said on the phone would be in the paper the next morning.

I had practically forgotten about the telephone message. I was to return the call of a Mr. Smith who had called me from a number I did not recognize. The area code was for suburban Virginia.

I gingerly entered my room. The bed was clear. For the first time in my life, I put a chair against a door, the back jammed under the knob, just the way they do in the movies. I drew the drapes and pulled the phone as far as possible from the window. I sat on the floor, back propped against the bed. From where I sat I did not think I would be hit by a bullet fired through the window. I was feeling not only frightened but also embarrassed.

When I got the desk, I gave a rewriteman the Virginia telephone number and asked him to have a copy aid (we used to call them copyboys) check it in the criss-cross directory, which lists telephone numbers numerically with subscribers' names. In the office I developed the habit of looking up anonymous call-back numbers. I would get the name from the criss-cross, run the name through the file, and sometimes wind up with the advantage of knowing quite a bit about the anonymous party before I returned the call.

I began dictating the story. I devoted quite a bit to the mystery surrounding Judith's death. ("Mystery surrounding" is about the best I could do, considering the rattlesnake, I told the rewrite man.) I was told once again that I had gone quite a way to cover a car smash-up. I did not say anything.

He told me that the Virginia number did not appear in the

criss-cross. The copy aid was sharp enough to try out the number on a telephone company friend. The friend said the phone number was not only unlisted—a reporter can sometimes pry that out—but also was "sensitive."

"Don't tell me any more," I said, and the rewriteman got the message that I did not trust my phone. I chatted with him innocuously for a couple of minutes, feeling curious and somewhat intrigued by the sensitive number and also by the quest for Judith and the story she was bringing me.

I was about to hang up when one of the assistant national editors came on the phone and in very few words said the story was not very much and I should come home. The paper, he said, was tired of letting everyone try to be an investigative reporter. I said I was trying to be a reporter, period.

We went on and on until a higher-ranking editor broke in to say I was trying to bullshit a two-bit story into a serial. I said I had a lot of leave coming. He did not say anything. I said I wanted an indefinite leave of absence. He said, "Keep in touch and send in your expense account." I said I was going to Judith Longden's funeral. On my own time and at my own expense. I also said something about her being my friend. He did not say anything for a moment. And then, his voice softer, he said, "OK. I guess you have to play it out on your own. But it's only an obit, Phelan. An obit." He hung up.

I gave myself about ten minutes to cool off and then I picked up the phone and dialed 0. But when the operator asked me for the long-distance number, I told her never mind. If the number is sensitive, I could at least take an elementary precaution.

I left the lights on when I slipped out of my room and down a fire exit stairway that opened to the outside. I found my car, and opened a back door. The car was empty. There was no one in the parking lot to notice me as I opened the front passenger's door and the interior light went on. A police bomb expert had once told me about the ways a car bomb can be rigged to go off: opening of the driver's door (since the driver, not the passenger, is the target); under the seat (a cigar box fits nicely) or under the car (detonated electronically from a distance); a pressure switch sewn into the upholstery (very rare because it's so easily spotted); under the dash (feel for something taped there); under the hood (very tricky). I had got that far with my inspection when I remembered that the bomb expert had told me why under the hood was tricky: opening the hood to look for a bomb can be a secondary way to set it off. He told me a way to get around this.

I felt silly, but since I had gone this far, I decided to do it. I took off my belt, hooked the buckle into the hood-release handle, and lay the belt under the driver's seat. I opened all the windows to keep flying glass at a minimum. Then I sprawled on the floor of the car, reached my arm under the seat and grabbed the belt.

Car bombs are highly directional and usually put in place by professionals. One mounted under the hood and placed behind the firewall would be aimed to hurl shrapnel at the driver. If the seat was empty, the shrapnel would be absorbed by the backrest of the seat. The shrapnel pattern would be centered above where I lay, so presumably I would be safe.

I yanked the belt. The hood sounded as if it had sprung open. Nothing else happened.

I sheepishly made the last inspection: under the hood. This is the oldest and crudest kind of car bomb, dating back to the 1920's. Professionals scorn it today. The bomb consists of explosives hooked up to a spark plug. Such a bomb has to be powerful because the explosion is located so relatively far from the driver. It is frowned on by bomb planters because it has a way of killing innocent people and getting authorities riled up. I did not expect to see one. But there it was, connected to a spark plug.

I was seized by a nausea-inducing panic. I leaned forward, letting my head enjoy the cool touch of the hood. Then I looked more closely at the bomb. I recognized it from my childhood. I hadn't realized they still made them. We called them buzz bombs: firecracker pops, sparks, smoke. They were supposed to scare you, not kill you.

Another kind of rattlesnake.

I disconnected it, hands shaking because the initial fright had not yet ebbed and because anger was already surging up. I forced myself to stop and think, to plan. I decided to drive directly to the airport in Tulsa and change cars. I would also make my call from one of the booths there; they would have to be safer than the booths here. I would break the speed limit to the airport, and to anyone who was watching me, it would look as if I had been convinced I should leave town.

• • •

Just to make my trip to the airport plausible, I made inquiries about the next flights east. I also got a new rental car. Then I found a phone booth and called the Virginia number, using my telephone credit card so there would be a record of the call.

I did not immediately recognize the voice of "Mr. Smith," but when he said, "I called you from Langley," I knew who was on the other end of the line. *Knew* might be too strong a word, though. I did not know his real name or much about him. Even here I will only call him Phil. He works for the Central Intelligence Agency.

Phil is a key figure in what is known in Washington as the intelligence community. His job is to help news people—up to a point. He is a trustworthy man; courteously uncooperative sometimes, always intensely cynical, but reliable—up to a point. That point is self-preservation, the most important reason for Phil's dealing with news people. He calls us assets.

"What did you want to talk to me about, Mr. Smith?" I asked. Only a CIA type as sophisticated as Phil would dare use Mr. Smith as a cover name.

"That person you were supposed to meet last night. That person had an accident. A real accident."

"How do you know that way back in Langley, Mr. Smith?"

"We get very good accident reports. We are very smart here." He paused for a moment. "You are calling me from a pay phone across from the TWA reservation desk in Tulsa International Airport. You just turned your Ford Granada into Hertz and very cleverly went to Avis to cover your trail. You got a Nova. You don't know it yet but your license number will be AT 8563."

"I had some trouble with the Granada."

"You could have had more."

"Is that what you're calling about?"

"Something like that. People are watching you, Phelan. We plugged in, through the Bureau, late today. You're in the middle of something. The feds are trying to find out what it is."

"So am I."

"Do yourself a favor, Phelan. Do your finding out in D.C. Caslon Wells is *terra incognita* to the Bureau. They won't tell you that. The Federal Bureau of Investigation doesn't tell people things like that. They could have told that reporter in

Arizona, you know. And those civil rights guys, in Mississippi, way back in the '60's. But they didn't. So we are. Getting reporters killed is bad for the country's image. It's dangerous out there, Phelan. I'm passing the word, as a friend."

"You're holding back, Phil."

"Sure I am. You want to know more, you come to D.C."

"OK. You can tell the Bureau they can have the night off. I'll stay in Tulsa tonight at least. There's—" I started to say there was someone I wanted to talk to, but I stopped short and then started the sentence again: "There's still one thing I want to know, though. I want to know how do you know there was an accident."

"It's hearsay from the Bureau, Phelan. I haven't seen the stuff, but I'm assured there is plenty of very hard evidence that your friend"—I wondered why he used that phrase; the sound of *your friend* stung me—"died an accidental death. No one had her hit. You understand?"

"No. Nothing. I understand nothing. Especially your calling me."

"You call me at this number when you get to D.C., Phelan, and maybe I can do some clarifying for you. See you soon." He hung up.

I picked up a razor, toothbrush, and shirt and checked into a motel at the airport. I thought about calling the Cherokee so they would not worry about me. But I had a better idea. I called Bim Beardsley's home and left a message with his wife for him to call me as soon as possible. I asked her not to tell him this until he got home. I didn't want my message on the Caslon Wells radio party line.

Bim woke me about 1 A.M. I told him about the incident on the highway and the rattlesnake and the buzz bomb. I told him I was holed up in a motel in Tulsa but would be coming back to Caslon Wells. I said I wanted the law to know what was going on just in case I was the victim of any more pranks.

"There sure are some bad sorts on the loose around here," Bim said, sounding worried. His tone surprised me. "That stuff up there, that plutonium, it's like that heroin you got back East, Phelan. Makes a lot of people do things they just naturally wouldn't want to do."

Bim, as usual, was right. What this is about is plutonium. I know no more about plutonium than I do about rattlesnakes. But tomorrow I was going to get educated.

12.

HARRY HAD TOLD me that in the last few months Judith had been learning all she could about plutonium. She told people, including Art and Barbara, that she did her studying in the main public library in Tulsa. Actually, she was visiting a young physicist who was on the faculty of a small college in Tulsa and was a consultant to the Nuclear Workers Union.

Harry had told me about the physicist at the bar. He obviously had not wanted to speak at Art's about Judith's secret visits. I suppose Art might not have believed it if Judith had told him she was going to Tulsa to talk to a physicist, especially if Harry had been the one who had set up the meeting.

The physicist, Dr. Alice Radnor, had been working with Judith to set up a series of meetings on nuclear hazards for Facility employees. Harry was frank about the motive. The union was soon to be challenged by the company in a decertification election. Employees would vote on whether to have the Nuclear Workers Union continue to represent them. Since only a minority of the employees belonged to the union, the chances were strong that the union would be decertified.

"Judy convinced me to make safety an issue," Harry had told me at the bar. "She was getting stuff to show that the place was unsafe. The union was going to bring Alice Radnor into the picture as an expert on the dangers and the need for better protection. And the protection would come from the union. We'd deliver hard bargaining, a strong grievance system, and so forth. It was an issue. *Not* a crusade. Jesus.

Not a crusade. But I guess Judy saw it like that. To her, I guess, it was getting to be a crusade."

I met Alice Radnor in her office, a windowless room in a small stucco building at the edge of the campus. A blackboard filled most of one wall. The other three were lined with bookshelves; there were few books on the shelves, which were stuffed with papers, boxes, pamphlets, and booklets. The boxes had large numbers and letters written on them. I tried in vain somehow to make a 43719 out of them.

Radnor saw my eye straying to the boxes. "I'm writing a book on contamination," she said, waving toward the boxes. "All organized in those."

I politely asked the title.

"The publisher wanted to call it *Radioactive Contamination in Man,*" she said. "I changed the last word to *People.*" She jutted her chin. I nodded vigorously. I certainly did not want to argue with her about anything. She radiated intelligence. I was intimidated by the amount I could feel in the room.

I told her that Harry had been secretive about her meetings with Judith. I wondered why. I also mentioned the 43719 puzzle.

"Puzzle?" she asked. "It's merely a set of numbers. They don't have any significance that I know of."

That seemed to settle it for her. She was a very positive person. She was probably a little older than Judith, I figured. About thirty. Her hair was dark and short, cut in clean angles about her face. She had long fingers, stiff on hands that sawed the air in horizontal sweeps, punctuating her words.

"As for secrecy," she said, "that was Mr. Skirvin's idea. I certainly have nothing to hide. My consultations are my business."

I told her I did not know much about Judith or about plutonium. I said that Harry had told me Judith found out about things by asking questions, and I said that was my way, too. I also said I felt as if I had a debt to pay.

Radnor understood that. Quite suddenly, she said, "Judy's death was a surprise to me but not a shock." Her words did not sound as cold as they look on paper. There was a fatefulness to what she said. Not a eulogy perhaps, but at least a kind of tight-lipped, rarely awarded admiration.

Radnor was not someone who appreciated much small talk. I told her I needed to know something about what it was that Judith was trying to accomplish. I asked her if she considered the Facility a dangerous place.

"I visited there once. I wanted to see the Caslon Facility on my own. I talked myself in as a prospective employee. Some men were in the back of the plant. Between shifts, I assume. A couple of them had peashooters. They were aiming them at a black man off to the side. He slapped his head a couple of times and then ran toward the peashooters. They playfully wrestled for control of the peashooters, and then they went inside. I picked up what they had been shooting. Fuel pellets. Plutonium covered by a thin shell of ceramic. If a pellet had broken on impact and a fair amount of it had entered him through his eye or mouth, say, he would have been mortally wounded. That would be an extreme possibility, but a possibility, nevertheless."

She shook her head, both hands sawing toward her throat. "I couldn't believe it."

She quickly came back. "Now. Safety. A soft word for dealing with something so deadly. Plutonium is usually called the most toxic substance on earth. This depends on how and what you are gauging. I saw a fatuous statement issued by someone in the nuclear industry. He proceeded to prove that cyanide and rattlesnake venom were more deadly."

I could not resist telling her about the rattlesnake.

She shrugged. "Yes. And the obscene phone calls and the threatening letters. And the surveillance. Very crude types in the industry out here."

"All these things have happened to you?"

"Not the rattlesnake. But a certain number of paranoia-inducing incidents. Car being followed. That sort of thing. I was not going to mention them. I suppose, in truth, that is why Mr. Skirvin did suggest a certain amount of secrecy. Now, getting back.

"Plutonium. Very radioactive. But the radiation doesn't penetrate very well. A piece of cardboard can shield you from it. The problem, though, is that its radiation is intense. It can cause fibrosis of the lungs, and lung cancer. It can get into your liver or into your bone and stay there, doing damage, undoubtedly inducing cancer.

"Am I going too fast? Well, you're recording. Very well. In the human being—the plutonium worker—plutonium on the skin is not much to worry about. It washes off. The skin is a barrier, like the piece of cardboard. But getting it on your skin is alarming, because it proves that the stuff is in the air. And if it is in the air, you can breathe it. Then plutonium is very dangerous.

"The particles are in a kind of suspension called an aerosol. If the particles are of a certain size, they may be coughed up, or blown out of the nose with mucus. Those of a more critical size, however, will burrow deep into lung tissue. Plutonium oxide is insoluble. It will stay there, in the lungs.

"Another problem: It is extremely difficult to detect plutonium within a person. Again, the simplest barrier stops the rays. If it has entered the body and has been secreted in various places, then it may be that the monitors will show no significant contamination."

I told Radnor what Kovacs had told me: the widespread radiation detected in Judith's apartment during the raid; the suspicions that her contamination was somehow self-inflicted. I did not mention Kovacs' suspicions about Judith's being a plutonium smuggler.

"What do you think happened?" I asked. "Does any of what Kovacs said make sense to you? Could plutonium get into her apartment, into her food?"

Radnor walked to the blackboard and began doodling: stick figures, stick trees, childlike sketches of houses. She turned around and began throwing the chalk up and catching it, in rhythm to her speech.

"Deliberate or accidental? That's what it comes down to, doesn't it? Did she contaminate herself? Cut a hole in a glove in a glove box, that sort of thing?" She put the chalk in the blackboard's counter.

"No. I think it is more likely that someone was trying to scare her. A version of the rattlesnake. They are fools there, you know, most of them. They have no idea what they are dealing with. It could be sneezing powder the way some of those fools handle it. Wait until everyone was out of the room for a moment—if they would even care about that—and then hold a little plutonium dioxide, a powder, near the intake vent in the hall. Or better, in that alleyway. I think Judy said there's a service alleyway that runs along the inside of the wall. I think they could find an intake vent there, too, or could get the powder into a pipe or blow it through a tiny hole. All sorts of ways. The point is this, yes, there were dozens of people there who would do that, thinking they were scaring her, not killing her, or at least not putting her life into grave danger."

"Do you feel she was going to die?" I asked. I felt shocked at my own voice. I had not intended to sound emotional. I guess the tone surprised Radnor; she looked at me quizzically for a moment.

"The question is too general. Do I think that her life was shortened by what happened to her? Absolutely. Do I think she would die of cancer? Almost certainly. Can I tell you how long she had to live? No. I don't think anyone could do that."

"What about the apartment? Would you care to speculate about that?"

"It's beyond my competence," she said quickly. "That raid involves what they call safeguards. Ask Dr. Rosen about that."

"Rosen? The AEC man. I thought he was a physicist."

She smiled for the first time. "He is. But his specialty is safeguards. I thought you knew. There are many kinds of physicists, you know." She returned to the cluttered table that served as her desk.

"As a physicist, I'm supposed to think certain things," she said. "Such as the most significant fact about plutonium is this. A metric ton of plutonium, about 2,200 pounds, can produce nearly five point five billion kilowatts of electricity. It would take about two million tons of coal or nine million barrels of oil to produce that much electricity.

"People in the industry talk about 'risk acceptance.' They say that we've learned to accept risk in driving automobiles and we'll just have to accept risk using nuclear reactors. I don't know how many times I have heard someone say it's more dangerous to drive a car than to work in a nuclear facility. I am sure that Judy heard that one, too."

I said I knew of at least one accident: the reactor in Idaho that Art and Harry had told me about. In mentioning it, I also said that Judith had feared a similar fate.

"At least she was spared what happened to them," I said.

"But it did happen to her, you know," Radnor said. Her voice lowered. "Like them, the men in Idaho."

I asked her what she meant.

"I heard this from a friend at Caslon Memorial Hospital, here in Tulsa. He said that the nuclear medicine research lab has her lungs, her liver, her kidneys, her stomach, her tongue, and her uterus."

13.

I HAD THOUGHT I would fly directly from Tulsa to the funeral in Corpus Christi. But I did not. I could not go to Judith's funeral because I did not know her well enough then.

Instead, I returned to Caslon Wells. No one seemed to have missed me at the Cherokee. I did the chair-braced-against-the-door-and-drawn-shades number. I holed up with some beer and cheese I had bought in Tulsa. And, as Bim had suggested, I called his house to leave word where I was. He had told me he would be keeping his eye on the Cherokee, and I wondered if that meant the management would be a bit more careful about letting people into my room.

I spent the rest of the day and much of the night reading what I had—the reports, the notes—and listening to what I had taped. What I did know about Judith then was centered on her life as a worker. I knew little about her as a person. Yet, I knew even then that what she did in the Caslon Nuclear Facility was not merely a job. It had begun to become what Harry called it, a crusade. Her job had become her life.

I had got the feeling that Art had not supported her much in her crusade. I wondered about Barbara O'Neill.

On Thursday, I went to see her. Her name and address were in the slim Caslon Wells phone directory. She lived on the first floor of what had been a two-story, one-family house. I found out later that it was in what was considered "the old end" of town, where it had first hooked onto Route 85. The conversion of the first floor into an apartment marked the beginning of the nuclear boom in Caslon Wells. (Judith's was in the west, or "new end," of Wells in a complex built by Caslon as part of the boom.)

I rang the doorbell, but there was no answer. The doorbell button was under a brass nameplate that said B. O'NEILL. Over that was another doorbell button and a brass nameplate that said JORDAN. Its front porch was festooned with scrollwork. There was a wooden swing suspended on chains hooked onto the porch roof. The house had character: solid, self-sufficient, conservative, maybe even smug. I wondered if the inhabitants had similar traits.

I went around back. In the driveway, next to a motorcycle, was a white panel truck with Caslon's diamond symbol on the side. Two men in yellow coveralls were walking from the backyard toward the truck. They were carrying what I assumed were alpha-scanner monitors. One man was tall, the other short. Mutt and Jeff. Bill and Fred.

"Hi, Bill, Hi, Fred," I said, trying unsuccessfully to see who answered to what. The big one scowled, but said, "Hi." The small one just scowled.

There was a woman in the backyard. She was standing between another two men in front of an oddly shaped brick structure that was perched on concrete blocks and shaded by a shedlike corrugated-iron roof. I found out later it was a pottery kiln.

The men were both dressed in dark suits and dark topcoats. At first I thought they were dressed identically, but there were differences in the shades of their dark clothes. And one, the slightly older of the two, wore a snap-brim hat of the 1950's. I assumed they were FBI agents. Bim had told me that Caslon Wells was swarming with them. At breakfast in the motel I had been mistaken for one by a new waitress. Apparently, any man not in a Stetson was assumed to be from the FBI.

As I approached the trio at the far end of the narrow backyard, the man in the fedora turned and walked rapidly toward me. He placed himself in front of me, forcing me to stop. He showed me his identification and asked me my name and my business; I'm sure he knew both.

Agent Trumbull was polite enough, though he did want me to leave, at least while he and his partner were there. But he knew that I knew that he did not want to make a very large matter out of my presence, and so I took a step to the side and continued walking toward O'Neill. Trumbull fell in step on my right, as he had been trained to do. I resisted the temptation to put my right hand in my raincoat as if I were reaching for my heater.

Trumbull introduced me to O'Neill, in tones that seemed to encourage any latent desire she might have to evict me. She did glare at me when she said hello. I assumed that she was blaming me, or imparting some blame toward me, for Judith's death. The idea struck me hard. I had not got that feeling from either Art or Harry.

I concentrated on what seemed to be going on. O'Neill was standing in front of the kiln. She was piling firebricks inside a kind of oven that was about the width of a fireplace and twice as deep. The outer brick wall of the structure was held together with angle irons. A silvery gas tank, with a Caslon symbol on its side, sat on a rack nearby. A pipe ran from the tank to burners rigged under the kiln.

The younger, hatless agent was taking notes as O'Neill methodically placed the firebricks inside the opening. "And again, please, what would be a typical temperature in this kiln, Miss O'Neill?"

"I've tried to tell you," she said. Her voice was tired and soft. "I've honestly tried to tell you. Potters measure in 'cones,' pyrometric cones. The cones tell the working heat, not the temperature." She handed the agent a thin slab of clay to which were attached three tall, gleaming white pyramids, each about an inch and a half high. She stooped over and picked up a similar slab of clay. But on this slab two of the three pyramids were bent over, as if they had melted. "This was a cone-eight firing," she explained. "Each cone had a heat or temperature equivalence. In this case two cones —numbers six and eight—have bent; number nine hasn't. See? It's still standing. So this was a cone-eight firing."

The agent had stopped making notes somewhere around the first cone-eight. She had explained it clearly enough, but it did not make a great deal of sense to an outsider.

"And the temperature? The maximum temperature in this kiln?" The agent valiantly tried again.

"I suppose it could go to cone-ten or eleven. Maybe 2,400 degrees Fahrenheit." She paused for about three seconds. "Call it 1,300 Celsius."

The agent nodded, closed his notebook, and put it in his pocket. He looked to the older agent, who pointed to another slab of fired cones on the ground. The younger man picked up that, along with three firebricks and a small rectangular shelf. The older man gave O'Neill his card and a receipt for the materials. With one last suspicious glance toward me, the agents marched off.

I asked her what that was all about.

"I've been answering a lot of questions for the last few days, Mr. Phelan. I don't know how many more I want to answer. Especially questions I don't *have* to answer. Yours, I mean. I don't have to answer yours, do I?"

I thought I detected a touch of hysteria in her voice. Judith had been buried the day before. From the looks of O'Neill, she had been going steadily since Monday night. And from what Art had begrudgingly said in praise of O'Neill's mental and physical health, she was no pill popper. I assumed she had been doing it all on her own adrenaline. And maybe there was not much left.

I judged she was usually a little overweight but had just lost three or four pounds. Somehow, her face, though round, seemed drained. She had Irish blue eyes, and long, lustrous black hair. While she was talking to me, she looked directly at me, her eyes on mine. Only after a while did I realize that what I had first taken for a glare of resentment was her typical way of looking, peering, at people.

I said that I just wanted to find out what it was that Judith planned to tell me. I said that the only way I could do this was by asking questions.

"She used to say that," O'Neill said. "She used to say that all she wanted were answers. Sorry I snapped at you. . . ."

"You didn't snap at me, Miss O'Neill. I doubt if you're even capable of it."

She shrugged. "Would you like some tea?"

We walked to the neat, bright kitchen in silence. She took my coat, and it seemed I no sooner sat down than she was pouring tea from a sturdy ceramic teapot, brown with a dark orange glaze. We drank from mugs of similar color.

By the second mug of tea we were through with my recital of what I knew and what I did not know. Then she began to tell me about the funeral.

"Her mother and father were there. They're divorced. But they were there. It was a Catholic church. I shouldn't have been surprised. But she wasn't a practicing Catholic. No church at all. I tried to stay in the background. I told them I was her friend, and they thanked me for coming. But they did not want to know anything about . . . about her life here.

"I don't know. Maybe they were in shock about it, but it seemed strange. I got the feeling that to them it was simply an automobile accident. I didn't go into anything beyond that. And . . . And anyway I guess I tried to avoid the family. In the back of the church, and in one of the last cars to the cemetery, was her ex-husband, Michael. A fat young man. I hadn't expected a fat young man. He did not have the child, their son, with him. But a woman was with him, a tall, blond-haired woman, with her hair up. Well, I shouldn't be talking about *that,* should I? A woman's hair."

Somewhere during the recital of the funeral she had begun to cry, not sobbing, but crying: a flowing of tears. She dabbed at them with her napkin. The motion disturbed her cat, which had been sitting on her lap. The cat leaped to the floor, sniffed around my legs, then jumped up on my lap.

O'Neill reached over to push the cat away.

"That's OK, Miss O'Neill. I like cats."

"Very unconvincing, Mr. Phelan. People who like cats don't say that. Just push Grayfur down."

"No, really. It's fine."

Grayfur settled it for us by jumping down. But his interruption had been welcome. I had been about to ask her the color of the dress Judith had been buried in. That would have been a stupid question then—or at any time, I suppose. Thanks to Grayfur, I didn't ask it.

I told her I planned to go to Corpus Christi and see "Miss Longden's—Judy's—relatives." After that remark, I used "Judith." I think Barbara O'Neill understood my problem in referring to Judith, and I even think she understood that I was having a larger problem, trying to deal with a dead woman who had assumed life in my mind.

O'Neill began telling me about the FBI and the backyard kiln, which she disconcertingly pronounced *kil.*

"I've been determined not to be paranoid through all this," she said, seeming to relax even as she spoke. "But I am quite sure that someone very thoroughly went through this house while I was in Corpus Christi. I noticed it when I got home late last night. I came back from the airport on my bike—motorcycle. I noticed a car in front of the house.

Well, *that's* not exactly new, as you have probably heard. Anyway, as soon as I got into the house, the front-door bell rang. And there were the men from the car. They were the men you just saw: Agents Trumbull and Brooks."

She poured me another cup of tea and, frowning slightly, looked toward the back door.

I asked her what was wrong. I wondered about her paranoia.

She laughed. "About the *kil.* I was going to load it. I have some planters, hanging planters? And mugs. I have. . . . I have a little sale the first weekend in December. I'm away behind."

She asked me if I would mind continuing in the basement. I said that sounded fine. I certainly wanted to humor her.

We went into a small room that had been closed off from the furnace and the usual paraphernalia of a basement. She put on a gray, streaked smock. The room was coated with a thin film of gray dust. Gray objects—raw-clay mugs, bowls, planters, vases—stood on the gray shelves. In a corner of the room was what she called her wheel. She sat on a board seat and began kicking a large flywheel connected by a shaft to a smaller wheel. On this she hurled a blob of wet clay. When her kicks got the wheel going fast enough, she stopped kicking and pressed against the blob, centering it by the strength in her hands and arms.

There was something strangely attractive about her. Head down, hair falling forward, arms and shoulders hunched over the clay, one leg kicking, the other braced, grunting now, part of the grayness—so fundamental, and yet so complexly choreographed.

When she started to pull the clay upward, transforming the blob into a tall, gleaming wet thrust of clay, her face lifted, her arms and leg eased their work. And now her hands seduced the clay, fingering it, burrowing in it, scoring it, making of the pillar of clay a receptacle of clay, cupping hands along the pillar, inserting fingers into the receptacle, squeezing, shaping, kneading.

I wondered if she could read, or sense, my thoughts. She looked at me as she pulled the pillar up and plunged her thumbs into the shiny wet crown, spreading it into a round, endless lip. Then she looked down at the clay and began to talk over the soft whirling sound of the wheel.

"It starts with centering, centering the clay. It always helps me think, organize my thoughts. I wanted you to see this. I don't know why. There was something I wanted you to know. Maybe after you think about this, you will know. Please, don't ask me any questions. I've answered so many.

"I told you, I thought I found the house gone through. There were things Judy wanted you to see. I had hidden them. I don't know if you know about the chest."

She had created a bowl. She stopped the wheel and removed a plywood disc on which the bowl sat. She put the disc—a "bat," she called it—and the bowl on a shelf, pulled a lump from a pile of clay, hurled it on a table, and began strenuously pumping and kneading it. She did not talk while she did this, except to say, "Wedging. Getting the air bubbles out." When she was satisfied with the condition of the lump, she flung it on a new bat and started again.

She told me about the chest and how Judith had taken it to Mrs. Jordan's. O'Neill said that on the night of Judith's death she took the chest back to her apartment. I expected that the next thing I would be told was that the chest was missing.

"I just didn't want to leave it lying around, in Mrs. Jordan's or in my place. Judy felt that my place was vulnerable, and I had no reason to doubt it. I felt, though, that no one would bother down here." She looked up and smiled. I smiled back. This gray little room certainly was too messy for there to be anything serious going on in it. I was beginning to appreciate her and even understand her a bit. Reticent. At the edge. Never in the center.

"Did you go to a parochial school?" I asked.

"Does it show that much?" she said. She was still smiling.

"Only in the nicest of ways."

"My grandmother used to call that blarney, Mr. Phelan." She went back to seducing her clay.

"I haven't heard that word in years," I said. "And the name is Phelan. No mister."

"No first name?"

"I don't like it. Francis. They called me Franny when I was a kid. Anyway, back to the chest."

"If you insist. But I'd like to hear about your parochial school image theory some day, Phelan." She said this in a surprisingly coquettish way. She did not sound as if she was used to sparring with men, verbally or otherwise. I wondered why I felt that this was true. I was trying to answer my own question, and I missed what she had been saying.

"Excuse me, Miss O'Neill. I lost you for a minute."

"The name is Barbara. No miss. You looked far away. Where were you?" She was pressing down on a wet pillar of clay and spreading it into another round lip.

"I was trying to figure you out, Barbara."

"Good luck," she said. The way her body turned just then, her breasts were fully outlined against the blue sweater she wore under the smock. At the moment I remembered the photograph labeled *Judith Longden and Barbara O'Neill.* And I began to realize what she was doing. She probably got some of those photographs, too. She was trying to show me that they weren't true. She did not have to convince me that she was heterosexual, but that was what she was doing, here on her own turf, here where she could center herself.

"What have you figured out?" she asked. She sat back on the board, legs spread, feet up on the braces of the flywheel frame, hands on her hips.

"Not very much. But enough to convince me."

"You were given some photographs?"

"That's right."

"What do you think they were trying to do with those photographs, Phelan?" Barbara suddenly tensed. I realized that what I had been seeing as coquetry was a psychological primping to make herself able to mention the photographs. I assumed she had been told I had a set. I wondered who else had them.

"I think they were part of a half-a—, a half-baked plan that could have been concocted to prove Judy was a smuggler, or to discredit her."

"And me?"

"I think they dragged your name in for other reasons." I waited for her to ask the reasons; she didn't. So I continued. "This may be a little rough, but bear with me, Barbara. Kovacs told me that Caslon—and I guess the AEC guys, and now the FBI—suspected Judith of smuggling plutonium. Maybe in her . . . person. If so—and I don't know a discreet way of saying this—one way to get evidence would be to examine anyone who may have been . . . physically . . . in contact with her. With those photographs, I got a report on Judith's trip to Los Alamos. She was given a thorough g-y-n examination. The report also says you and Art went to Los Alamos. I think someone was trying to tell me that all three of you had . . . had something going. Maybe that all three of you were involved with plutonium. I asked Art about Los Alamos. He said he was not given a genital examination."

The color was rising in her face through my words, but she was ignoring her blushing as best she could. Her hands were now primly folded on the wheel, and her legs were drawn together. I wondered if I had gone too far. I feared that my clinical descriptions were more threatening to her than obscenity would have been; she could have pretended not to understand obscenity. But I plunged on.

"So the photograph that is supposed to be of Judith and you . . . it just doesn't make sense. To them—whoever the hell *they* are—that photograph was just something to . . . to blur her image. Unless"—Barbara looked up at me—"unless, at Los Alamos. You see, if you were given an examination and Art were not, it would indicate that they thought . . ."

"That we were lesbians? Yes, I can see your reasoning. I think the photograph was just one more obscenity—on their terms, obscenity—to smear Judy's character. That's what I think, Phelan." She was composed now. "I was not given a genital examination, by the way. But I have been aware of what has been said, what has been implied by them. One reason I'm aware is that Judy, in a frenzy, suggested that they—I don't know who *they* are, either—were . . . were interested in my sex life." She smiled for an instant. "Such as it is."

I felt on a spot. She was attractive enough, especially now, after going through this strange gray parley with me. But I did not want to try to play a scene out of *Tea and Sympathy*. Nor did I want to complicate my life in the wilds of Caslon Wells.

She must have seen the reflections of my thoughts in my attempt at blanking my face. She smiled again—with some relief, I think—and started trimming excess clay from the pots with a looped-wire tool. It was a much less sensual occupation than the shaping of wet clay had been.

"Back to the chest," she said. "I took it down from Mrs. Jordan's and put it back in my closet. I took out the things that Judy had put in, except for some things I didn't quite know about." I started to ask a question, but she held up the tool to silence me. "I'll get to that. Anyway, as I said, I was afraid that the apartment would be searched, and so forth. I hid the material I found and replaced it with some things I had around: a training manual, some Facility newsletters, with items randomly circled in red; a notice we had received about a tornado alert. When there's an alert, we have to put all the plutonium in a special vault. Management's sensitive about that.

"When I came back from Corpus Christi, as I said, the FBI was here. They had a search warrant, I must say. And they took the chest, with all the material *I* had put in it. I still think that somebody was in here *without* a search warrant, but that's beside the point." She looked up to await questions.

"Did the FBI take anything else? Anything of yours?"

"No. And they were very courteous. But they began questioning me. Nothing strenuous. Here, at work, and then in the backyard. They wanted to know whether anyone besides me had access to the kiln."

"Do you know why?"

"They didn't say, but I assume that it has to do with treating plutonium oxide. I *think*—I don't know, you understand—but I think that if you apply enough heat, and do some chemical things, you can produce pure plutonium."

"And why do you think anyone would do that?"

"To make a bomb, I suppose." She touched the bottom of an inverted bowl lightly and cut away the center of its round foot. She turned to me. "Well, wouldn't you suppose that, too?"

I said yes, but I could not think of the prospect calmly.

"You saw them questioning me about temperatures. And they took away some things for further tests, they said. There were also some Caslon men, who worked with them. Running alpha scanners over the kiln, my apartment—and down here. That's what really scared me."

"Why?" I asked. But I had hardly spoken the word before she pulled back the right sleeve of her smock and sweater and reached into a five-gallon drum that stood next to the table she had been working at. She had been dropping bits of wet clay into the drum, which was half-full of water. She extracted a tightly knotted plastic bag that once had been yellow and put it on the table.

"You'd better open it and take them out," she said. "My hands . . ."

I eagerly reached in and found a small green notebook, a thick file folder, five tape cassettes held together with thick rubber bands, and a vinyl blue loose-leaf notebook that seemed identical to the one that I had found in my motel room. I scanned the file; it was about Scinto. I thumbed through the notebook and saw the entries of a journal. I turned to the last page. I know now that Judith wrote this, her last entry, just before Orr confronted her. Within an hour or so after she wrote this, she began the flight that ended in her death:

> OCT. 19: In outer change room. I guess I've been taken off SNM work. Am going to quit anyway. Just killing time. They have to pay me, though. Will have quiet day till 4. Must get journal ready for H's friend. And other stuff.

I was lost in her journal for a long moment. And the tapes. What would be in the tapes? I looked up from the journal finally. Barbara was smiling again. She was obviously relieved.

"I know she wanted you to have this," Barbara said. "But there was more. Some more things. I don't know what happened to them. When I switched the material in the chest on the night she . . . on Monday night . . . I looked." She explained about the secret compartment. "I unlocked it. It was empty."

She was wiping her arm with a gray towel. There was a smudge on her right cheek. I pointed to it, then rubbed it off myself. Barbara blushed.

She began busying herself, cleaning up around the wheel. "I don't know what was in the compartment. But I do know that she was taking something with her to meet you on Monday. She was frightened. I know she thought they were closing in on her. I thought she was paranoid. But she was right.

"I didn't help her enough. I didn't know, Phelan. I really didn't know. Her life-style. Her . . . her *ability* to cope. I thought that was enough. That I could stay off a ways from it. I do that, you know. Stand off. Anyway, on Monday . . ."

She told me about her last hours with Judy. It was a matter-of-fact narrative. In recounting the maneuvers with the chest, Barbara said she did not actually see what it was that Judy was going to take to carry to me.

I told her that Art had seen an inter-office envelope and, through its holes, something shiny black and maybe something like a manila folder. I asked Barbara if she had ever seen anything that had been in the false-bottom of the chest.

"Yes. Once. Just for a second. Folders. Manila folders—the kind in business files. And x-rays. What looked like x-rays."

"From medical files?" I asked. "Something from her medical files?" She did not answer. "Well, do you have any idea what they might be?"

Barbara shook her head. The nuns teach you that. If you just shake your head and you do not actually say "Yes" or "No," then you are not exactly lying, not really sinning. Up to that moment, Barbara had answered my questions openly. I had not picked up a hint of evasion. Now, as clear as the blue eyes she turned away from me, she was holding out. She would not lie. I knew that. But she had been told, by somebody, more than she was telling me. I knew, too, that she had decided to stay on the side, to stand off from the center.

14.

I TOLD BARBARA I just could not stay any longer. I had to start reading the journal and listening to the tapes. She understood. I said I would be checking in with her later to get a guided tour of Caslon Wells. I didn't say how much later. I did not want to tell her I was getting out of Caslon Wells as quickly as I could. I did not want to spend a night here with material that some other people would like to have once they found out I had it. I did not think that would take very long.

I drove directly to the motel, checked out, drove to the Tulsa airport, and dropped off the car. Within an hour after plucking the material from the yellow bag I was in an airport bar, at a table in the corner, back to the wall, eyes on the door. Just like Wild Bill Hickok, I thought, and the idea was funny enough to make me relax.

I had a seat on the next plane to Corpus Christi. The plane would start boarding in about thirty minutes.

The journal, tapes, and other material were in the carry-on bag I had slung over my shoulder. I had no other luggage. I slipped the shoulder strap off and put the bag on the seat next to me. As I did, I thought I saw a slight movement at the table next to me. I tried to remember whether the man at that table had been there when I came in. He had not. I reached for the bag—and so did he.

I managed to slip my arm through the strap. I spun away from him, enwrapped the bag in my arms, and hugged it to my chest. I kicked out in his direction, knocking over a chair and causing enough commotion so that the man bolted toward the open door. He pushed a waitress against a table, sending it and her sprawling.

I almost took off after him. But I decided that he knew the place, might have a friend or two, and may have wanted me to chase him. All this went through my mind very rapidly, along with a notion that the man vaguely resembled the equally vague description Harry and Art had given me of the man named Geiser.

I sat down. The fallen waitress had risen. She walked to me calmly and asked me if everything was all right. I wondered what this place was like when something really happened. She picked up the dollar tip on the table next to me and asked me again. I said I'd take my check. I left her a dollar tip, too.

I waited until I knew the men's room was empty: Clutching the bag and my raincoat, I went in, locked myself in the only booth, and clicked open the loose-leaf notebooks. I stuffed the pages in the pockets of my trousers. I put Judith's journal in my back pocket. I creased the file folders so that they would fit in my jacket pocket. I distributed the five tape cassettes and my own cassettes through my pockets. I felt like Captain Kangaroo, but I knew that anyone who grabbed my bag now would not get much more than a tape recorder, a couple of empty looseleaf holders, and some dirty laundry.

I came out of the men's room intent on finding a security guard. I would rush up to him and say—what? I remembered what Phil had said—terra incognita. I certainly was not going to trust any private or public lawmen.

I finally decided to walk rapidly to the gate. Never before had it taken so long to get on an airplane—the passing through the metal detector with my bulging pockets, the waiting in the lounge, the straining to hear if that was *my* name some sinister voice was summoning. But the plane took off on time, and with me on it.

Judith's mother lives alone in a trim little house near the Gulf. Janice Longden is a small woman, slim and quick-moving, as I imagined, and now know, Judith was. I had expected to find Mrs. Longden bereaved. But she had a calm about her that was the calm of the detached. It soothes and sustains the possessor but unnerves and disorients the observer.

She talked about Judith in distant tones. "Judith spent most of her life where she could see and smell the ocean," she said. "It seems strange she died so far inland."

She explained, finally, that her "acceptance" of Judith's death had come from a recently acquired acceptance of Jesus Christ as her personal savior. I told her I had the impression that she and Judith had been Catholics.

Janice Longden turned her head away from me and toward a living room window that framed the gray sea and sky of the Gulf. The sky suddenly had darkened.

"The storms come quickly here," she said. And, hardly pausing, she went on. "I left the Church just before I got my divorce from Mr. Longden. I believed that the same . . . the same thing happened in Judith's life."

I asked her if she had heard anything directly from Caslon about the accident. She obviously believed that Judith's death was absolutely accidental. A company representative already had visited her and given her a check that covered the work pay and earned vacation pay due Judith, the uncashed $300 check for apartment restoration expenses, a settlement on the quarantined items taken from the apartment, and the full amount, calculated with double-indemnity for accidental death, of the company-paid life insurance policy. "Caslon was very nice about it," Mrs. Longden said. "A very nice man came here with the check." She said she deposited the check immediately, at the representative's suggestion. She also signed a paper which, for Judith's mother and employer, effectively ended the matter of Judith's death.

Once money was out of the way, Mrs. Longden began talking about Judith by refracting her through the prism of Janice Macauley Fogarty Longden. She poured me tea and told me how Judith had been conceived. She left the room to answer the phone, returned, and told me how upset she had been when Judith became pregnant by Michael York. She left again and returned with a photograph album, and skimming through it, showed me only the photographs of Judith with her mother. I could see other photographs of Judith alone, and with the man I took to be her father, and with men, women, and children who were strangers to me. But we never stopped to see those photographs.

I quickly cast out Mrs. Longden from the photographs I was seeing and saw only Judith. Judith in a plaid skirt and white blouse on her first day of first grade. Judith standing in front of a Quonset hut in a seven-year-old's nurse costume. Judith in the uniform of a Brownie, a Girl Scout (matched by her mother's), a ballerina. Judith in a two-piece bathing suit on a beach blanket, squinting into the camera. She looked to be about 15. She sat, cross-legged, next to her mother, who wore a dark, one-piece suit. The hand, wrist, and hairy forearm of someone leaned on the edge of the blanket. The photograph had been cut. I assume the arm had been part of Mr. Longden.

The photographs of Judith ended with a formal portrait of her in her high school graduation cap and gown. There were only a couple of more pages to the album, and I assumed that there were no photographs of Judith on those pages.

Mrs. Longden hardly spoke during the ritual of showing me the photographs. She silently closed the album, got up, left the room again, and this time came back with a cardboard box. On all four sides were printed RELIGIOUS BOOKS and I'VE FOUND IT! SALVATION! I was expecting a farewell armload of religious tracts.

"I was putting these things together when you called me," Mrs. Longden said. She placed the box next to my chair. The top was open, and I could see papers and books in it. "They are all of Judith's things that I still have. I was going to burn them. You can look them over. Keep them if you like."

I must have looked shocked, for she began to speak more quickly, in explanatory, self-justification tones: "She was my little girl, Mr. Phelan. She is dead. She was not part of my life for a long time. I have not seen her since she left her husband and her child." Her voice began to soften, and I thought that for the first time there would be a sign of grief. "Not since she left her husband and her child," she repeated. The phrase was worn by much use. Then, as if to keep some kind of psychic balance, she said, "I have not seen her—and she has not seen Michael Junior, either. Or Michael Senior. I see them all the time. Almost every week."

I took a closer look in the box. School papers. An autograph album. Several diaries, some with a clasp and keyhole. A dance program. I said these were relics of her life and I could not keep them.

"Then I will burn them, Mr. Phelan. I am not as heartless as I am sure you think I am. I have memories of Judith. But I have no use for these things, Mr. Phelan. They remind me of a daughter I had a long time ago. They do not remind me of the girl, the woman, who died. And I have Michael Junior to think of. She is not part of his life. She is not his mother now."

I took the box.

Paul Longden was at the shop, banging a dent out of the right front fender of a new green Ford pickup. I introduced myself and as obliquely as possible tried to tell him what I was doing.

He nodded, shifted the rubber mallet to his left hand, shook hands with me, and went back to work, rhythmically tapping. "Usually, they bring them to the place where they bought them, when they're new like this," he said, staring at the slowly disappearing dent. "But, if they know me, and have been coming in, hell, they just bring them in here, and I do a little job like this for nothing."

He talked on about his shop, about the problems of running a small business these days. And as he talked, I became aware of another man who had been operating a grinder on the far side of a car at the other end of the shop. The man, still holding the now silent grinder, came around the car. He looked at me for a moment, and we both looked away. I knew it was Michael York, Judith's former husband.

Paul Longden had finished now. He wiped his brow and looked at me directly for the first time. He wore metal-and-plastic framed glasses. His face was dark, leathery. I assumed he fished and hunted. His eyes were the eyes of Judith: direct, clear, the kind that never looked away from you. His jawline was firm, and he carried no excess flesh on his face or, as far as I could see, on his body. He asked me if I would like to have a cup of coffee in the office.

"I won't be able to spare you much time, mister. I'm a working man." He said it with the authority of a man who knew that only men who worked with their hands really could say they worked. As we entered the small, glass-paneled cubbyhole, he jerked his head in the direction of the other man I had seen.

"My ex-son-in-law. When I told him you were coming, he said he wanted to meet you. Not to talk, though. Not to talk.

He said that. You understand?"

I nodded. Longden had a way of making things clear.

"I never thought much of those goddamn Volkswagens," he said. "Too small. Engine in the back. Nothing to take the punch in the front. That's what makes them so goddamn dangerous. Goddamn rolling gas tank. I've heard them called that." He paused and looked at me. "Did it burn?"

"No. It didn't burn."

"You saw the wreck?"

"Yes."

He made us both coffee by pouring a quantity of instant powder into two white cups and then taking a kettle from a hot plate and pouring just about enough hot water to cover the powder. He did not offer any milk or sugar because there was none. He sat on the edge of the small desk. I sat in an old swivel chair. I wondered where Michael York would fit.

He came in carrying a can of Coke. He stood next to Longden. There was not enough room to close the door. York was about 30 and gone to fat. His belly hung over his belt. His jeans were tight. His denim shirt's middle buttons were missing. Under the shirt he wore a dark-blue T-shirt which said something in gold letters. His hair was dark brown and shingled in what had been a flaring style a month before. His moustache covered his upper lip and looped across his cheeks to join his sideburns. His complexion was paler than Longden's and his hands were cleaner. I did not imagine they hunted or fished together, and I assumed that on the job Paul Longden had to tell York what to do, specifically and frequently.

"She called me when she was going to buy that 'VW," Longden said. "She knew a helluva lot about cars, you know. She liked to learn. Cars. Chemistry. History. Anything. She was quite a girl. Quite a girl. I taught her to drive, with a stick shift on a '64 Chevy—and she learned just like that." He snapped his fingers and then looked at the calendar on the door for what seemed like a long time. The calendar had a large color photograph of a sailboat racing before the wind, her blue-and-yellow spinnaker billowing against a pale morning sky.

"I guess Mrs. Longden told you that she was the beneficiary. They was never close, her and Mrs. Longden. But when she took the job in that goddamn place, well, she called me. Every once in a while she'd call me. She said there was this life insurance. She had some kind of thing happen to her, right in training, she said, and she was thinking of quitting. And then she decided not to, and there was this insurance. She said she wanted to make Michael Junior the beneficiary. She had to put down somebody's name. He was kin. And it was a way of doing something for him."

Longden paused and I glanced at York. He had picked up a clipboard and was looking over a job order. He took a pencil from his shirt pocket and wrote something on the paper.

"I told her that it would be best for her to stay out of Michael Junior's life. As far as he's concerned, I mean, he's got a new mummy, I said, and it might be better to leave it that way. Well, she got sad—and mad, too—at the same time. The way she could. And she said I could go to hell. And I guess that's how Mrs. Longden got to be the beneficiary."

He talked a little more about Judith. He called her Judy. I could see York edging to leave, but I knew he would not leave until Longden was through talking about his daughter. Finally, there was a long pause. York turned toward the door.

On the desk was a picture of a child, a boy about six or seven: dark hair, parted on the side, those direct eyes, a pale face that narrowed to a sharp chin. The image of his mother, I could hear people say of him. I picked up the photograph. "Is this Michael Junior?" I asked.

York turned, leaned forward on the desk, and said, "That is *my* son, Mr. Phelan. Not hers, not anybody else's. She walked out on me and him." It had been bottled up, and now it poured out. "Walked out. She said she wanted to see him when he was twelve and he could travel. Goddamn. Imagine that? She could *wait* to see him?

"Christmas. Christmas times. That's when she'd call. I wouldn't answer. And I told Mary Ann: no calls. No way, do I talk to her. Mary Ann's my wife. Michael's *mother.* That's who Michael Junior's mother is, Mr. Phelan. It's Mary Ann York. Far's Michael knows—or ever will know—that's who his mother is.

"I don't know what you're going to do with this, Mr. Phelan. And I can't care less. I really can't. But, I'll tell you, Mr. Phelan, as far as I'm concerned, Judy, she was dead a long time ago. We told Michael Junior that, you know. We told him a long time ago she was dead."

15.

THERE WAS A point beyond which none of them would go. Not her mother, her father, or her ex-husband. Not Art, Harry, or Barbara. Not the people she worked for, the people who watched her, the people who suspected her. None of them. They would never go beyond describing—and toward understanding, toward explaining. To all of them, she died a mystery.

Until I got her journal and her tapes, there was a point beyond which I myself could not go. I had reports, files, hours of interviews on my tapes and in my notebooks. In Caslon Wells, in Washington, and in Los Alamos, the official kind of people would talk to me, give me reports—even surveillance reports and transcripts of bugs and taps. They wanted to convict Employee A (or Individual A), as the official reports referred to her. Everything about her was merely data. And disclosure did not matter. She was dead.

But she is Judith Longden. She is not Employee A. She has an identity. She lived a life. I needed truth about her, *from* her. And, with her tapes, her journal, and the box of memories that were almost burned, I have some of that kind of truth. I can see her, at least dimly, as she sometimes saw herself.

I never went back to Corpus Christi, but I did go back to Caslon Wells. I talked to the people at the Facility again, and to Art, and to Barbara, especially to Barbara. I got to know quite a bit about Judith through Barbara, and in a way hard to explain, I got to know at least a little about Barbara through her reflections about Judith. And I got to like Barbara enough to forgive her.

A fragment, from Judith's last day, told to me by Barbara:

Just before Barbara left on the four-to-midnight, Judith asked, "How old are you, Barbara?"

"Twenty-nine," Barbara replied, startled. "I'll . . . I'll be thirty in March."

"That's right. I forget. Pisces. I'm Cancer. That's too much, isn't it? Too much. Anyway, I'm twenty-six. And I could die. I'm working in a place that could kill me, make me one of those numbers on that sign at the Facility. I'm going to tell that reporter about that sign, when I tell him about that place and that stuff, that awful stuff."

Judith's journal gave me a truthful, vivid counterpoint to the official "chronology of employment of Employee A" that I had found with the photographs in my motel room. The journal entries were mostly telegraphic observations about the Facility: accidents and near-accidents, violations of AEC regulations.

> MAR. 12: Gasket in Glove Box No. 5 in SX Room 12 leaking again. Room on respirators 0215 to 1115 (fifth time I know of).
>
> AUG. 3: Asked Fenwick why no handles on emergency decon showers in air-lock corridor. He said people turned them on for hell of it, so Orr had them removed.
>
> AUG. 6: CAM monitor alarmed in SX 14—and all Fenwick did was press reset button! CAM's supposed to alarm at half MPC. [For the uniformed reader, she wrote in Continuous Air Monitor and Maximum Permissible Concentration.] Wonder what our dose *really* was.

The journal apparently was Scinto's idea. He asked her to keep a record of events in the Facility. But her journal also contains personal, undated, cryptic passages that seemed to focus on the two topics that most concerned her after she met Scinto: love and death.

> Gold cross hanging over me. Like the tattoos on PL. Then blood on him, all over his chest. Matted hair. Red fleece.

• • •

> AR—like being married. Easy, no big deal. Makes me hate MY—even hate his initials—more. Scinto. Scinto, Sin with Scinto. [This seems to have been written at least two months after Scinto was killed.]

I won't play psychiatrist about her using initials for her father, for Art, for Michael York, but using Scinto's full name. And the tattoo reference obviously compares him to her father. She was in love with Scinto, and it was his recruiting of her to help him in the union that led to her death. To say they both died for the union puts it too dramatically. They died because of where and when they happened to be living. I'm sure neither of them would want to make it more than that.

Unlike her journal, her tapes were always intimate, always about her thoughts, her loves, her fears. Judith had what she called listening tapes and talking tapes. A listening tape could be anything from a store-bought cartridge of a bluegrass group to a homemade tape of something her recorder pulled from a country radio station or from a noisy night at a local saloon called Carry's Place. A talking tape was a kind of erasable diary.

Driving in the car, lying on her bed, or pausing any place where she could be alone, she would record a thought or an idea. Usually, she would soon erase it by talking words over it. So there are often layers of words, some only partially covered by the words flung over them.

> "It's no good, that goddamn stuff. No good for me. Not with booze. Dizzy. Don't need. Getting. And black. Was a she. And he said, I remember Dad said, I was coming about. Coming about. Feeling up. And out. Real. A bitch. A goddamn son of a bitch. Didn't stop me for speeding. He just—"

And then, on the same tape, on one that spun with her through the Southwest in the summer before she went to work in Caslon Wells, there are voices and the faint, whisking sounds of dry winds. The voices become stronger.

• • •

House made of dawn.
House made of evening light.
House made of the dark cloud.
House made of male rain.
House made of dark mist.
House made of female rain . . .

There is a break, and then her voice takes up the chant. In the interval, during that break in the tape, I could imagine her driving and playing and replaying that tape. She apparently had attended a Navajo ceremony somewhere and had become captivated by the chant. She memorized it. So have I.

The five tapes she left in Barbara's chest were precious to her, I think, the way certain memories are precious. We don't know the reason. We just know the feeling.

A cowboy song, *Utah Carl,* is bawling out of a country station.

Long we had rode together,
We'd ridden side by side;
I loved him as a brother,
How I wept—

Then her voice appears. The radio clicks off.

"I've been learning about Indians. I've been reading about how they were screwed. They never told us that. In school, they never told us that."

There is the unmistakable thump of a VW engine behind her voice. Then the engine stops. I can picture her by the side of the road, opening a book, reading silently, and then switching on her recorder. (There is no engine sound behind her voice now.) And in some stretch of desert, where the air ripples with heat and the road narrows ahead like the thin blade of a knife, she speaks again:

"This is something I'm going to learn. I love the words, maybe because they are about death, and I don't know much about death. I wonder why I like this, why I read this. It's called the Formula to Destroy Life. It's Cherokee. I'll read part of it.

• • •

I have come to cover you over with the black rock.
I have come to cover you with the black slabs, never to
reappear . . . Now your soul has faded away.
It has become blue.
When darkness comes
Your spirit shall grow less
And dwindle away . . .

"I guess what I want is there to be some mention of death on this tape. I don't know why."

Only one of the tapes left with Barbara was not strictly about Judith. That tape contained what seemed to be almost a verbatim account of what Scinto had told Judith about an accident at the Facility. The accident, which involved plutonium, killed one man and nearly killed Scinto. Her concern about that accident, and its criminal implications, gave her information that was dangerous for her to possess. Perhaps that is why she left that tape behind.

She made a tape on Saturday, the day after the raid on her apartment and the day before she, Barbara, and Art went to Los Alamos. She made the tape at Barbara's while awaiting a federal official, Dr. Ann Garvey, who was going to question her. Parts of her conversation with Garvey, and later with Barbara and Garvey, are on this tape, apparently with their knowledge.

On the tape, while she is alone, Judith talks about her sexual life. She is obsessed by the idea that people at the Facility believe she has been violating her body with plutonium. In those last days, plutonium had become almost carnate, a thing trying to violate her, to kill her by penetration.

Her feelings become part of what happened to her, and my own feelings tell me that I do her memory no harm in writing about what she felt, what she feared, and how her mind and her body reacted to threats and cruelty.

I think I know her voice well enough to write about her, going beyond describing, going toward explaining, toward understanding.

To try to understand the girl-woman who preceded Employee A, I had to enter her diaries, which were among the articles in the box her mother gave to me instead of to an incinerator. I had to break the clasps on the diaries. The entering of that first diary was brutal, a kind of rape. I felt as if I were violating a young girl. And yet I did it. There was no other way. I had to do this to her, I told myself, in order to understand her, to know her. There was no way to enter her life except to force my way in.

What happened with Jeff today was this . . .

When Judith was twelve, her father's port was Norfolk, Virginia. The family had an apartment on base in what was called Navy Housing. One of the children in the rows of garden-type apartments was a boy named Jeff. He took the school bus with her but was a grade ahead of her. One hot day, just before school ended, he and she were alone in the backyard that was common to the apartments. They were climbing on the redwood frame that supported an empty plastic swimming pool. Jeff made believe that the pool was filled. He jumped in.

The blue, crinkled lining was warm to lie on. They talked while they lay there, with the sun beating down on them, and Jeff taught her how to rub her eyes and make colors inside her head. While she had her eyes closed, Jeff touched her between her legs and asked her if it made her feel good.

Then he asked her if she wanted to get cool. They crawled over to the shady part of the pool, and he took his shirt off. He said he would like to help her take her shirt off, but she said she did not need any help. She took off her sneakers and T-shirt and jeans, but she kept on her panties and her new training bra. Jeff grabbed her and kissed her on the mouth. Then he pushed her and tried to get on top of her. She yelled and started to cry. Jeff called her a dirty word she was never able to remember, and he climbed out of the empty pool. Suddenly, she was all alone.

. . . I was so scared!! Shaking all over. Prayed nobody saw . . .

Happiest news in my whole life!! Leaving nasty stinking, vomity Norfolk!! . . .

When the family moved from Norfolk to Corpus Christi the next year, she was told that they would never have to move again. Her father was retiring from the Navy and they would live in a house of their own in Corpus Christi, where her father was buying an auto-body shop.

The move to Corpus Christi meant that something she called a dream would come true. She would live in one place for a long time.

She entered junior high school in Corpus Christi with the enthusiasm of a convert to learning. Permanency became the motive for a striving that she had never experienced before. She felt propelled by herself for the first time, and she had proof of her success. The proof was still there, in that box. Report cards with straight A's. A recital program with Judith credited as second violinist in the orchestra. Girl Scout awards. A scrapbook of clippings, A+ English papers, first-honors certificates.

Then, in her third year of high school, in a diary that often has entries that merely say "Dull Dull DULL" or "Damn Damn DAMN," Michael York enters, filling one of the longest entries in the diary.

> . . . Dad told Mom and I [crossed out and replaced by "me."] about HIM today. Dad says he hired HIM because his hands look good. Dad says they're quick hands. Didn't dare say I already saw HIM and TALKED to HIM!! Downtown. He talked first. Saw my picture in Dad's shop. He said don't tell Dad. Didn't. He's older than I. Not too. I told him Dad says he took a liking to him. HE says maybe I'll take a liking to him too. May-BE!! . . .

"Take a liking to him." The phrase blossoms in the diary. Her father started bringing Michael home from the shop for supper, and he would stay, to watch her wash the dishes and do her homework, and to watch television with her father.

After a while, she and Michael began to be alone. He did not talk much, and his eyes did not speak much, either. Boys her own age had curious, shifting eyes that looked at her breasts and looked at her legs and tried to look up her dress. She could understand those eyes. Michael was five years older than the boys she knew, and his eyes swept over her in a different way. He seemed to know what he was looking at.

Before she could decide whether she liked him, whether she

took a liking to him, he was making love to her. The first time was at the drive-in, where they both knew it would be. The movie was *A Thousand Clowns*. Michael never said a word. He put one arm around her shoulder. His fingers rested there for just a few seconds, and then they tightened. With his other hand he began unbuttoning her blouse. At that moment she thought of Jeff in the empty swimming pool. But in the car there was less terror and a feeling of warmth, of awakening, of opening.

There were other times in that summer between her junior and her senior year. And then Michael had walked away, sauntered away. She never knew whether her father had figured out what was happening and had fired Michael.

Around Christmas, in the happiest time of her senior year, when she once more had found confidence in the endless spiraling rewards of scholastic achievement, when she could stare out a school window at the horizon and see it as a metaphor of a wide and beckoning future—when she no longer thought every day of Michael York, he returned to her life. She did graduate as fourth in a class of 236, she did win membership in the National Honor Society, and she did have three college scholarships to choose from. But she was pregnant.

Judith and Michael and Michael Junior lived with the Longdens for a few months and then moved into a new garden-type apartment complex on the outskirts of the city. Michael drove a customized, metallic-plum, 1957 two-door Bel Aire to the body shop every day. The trip took forty-five minutes. But after a year or so, the trip started taking a couple of hours—and longer—at least twice a week, and Judith got the feeling that Michael had a girlfriend. She never accused him because she really did not want to know. And after a while, it did not matter whether Michael had a girlfriend. Nothing much about her marriage mattered.

She did not keep a diary then. But she wrote letters to herself, folded them tightly, and stuck them, randomly in her high school and junior high diaries. She was still the earnest A+ English writer, correcting her mistakes, writing about herself carefully and, it appears, honestly. She always seemed to be honest.

She and three other wives remarkably like her in appearance, accent, and mood had coffee nearly every afternoon while their children, on the periphery of their mothers' vision, crawled or creeped or fell and cried. "Shall I have an affair?" one of the women asked the others one day. "If you have to ask, forget it," another said, and they all laughed. But, to Judith, it seemed like a sensible question. Not long afterward she met a divorced policeman who was living out his lease in the complex.

It seemed as if it all could have gone on indefinitely. Everybody knew what everybody was doing, but no one was talking about it. She wrote of having a sense of being in an unending, ever-expanding pageant—the kind they had in school, where you stood silently on stage representing somebody or something while someone in authority pretended that a real event was taking place and told this lie to the audience.

The day before the policeman's lease expired, when he told her he was going away and when she felt again the memory of that day in the empty pool, Judith decided that she would quit the pageant. She would make straight A's again, somewhere else.

She tried to tell Michael about it in a long, rambling letter that she never mailed.

> I want to stop faking it, Michael. I don't want to make believe any more that I am yours and you are mine. I know what I want to do about me, and I guess I know what I want to do about you. I just don't know what I want to do about Michael Junior. I have to think that out. I have to think it out a long time.
>
> What I want to do about me is go away. That takes care of you, too. I have to go away from you. It's just that I don't love you any more. I love Michael Junior—*Mike*, I mean. I want to call him *Mike.* I love him very, very much. But Mike shouldn't have to be some kind of toy that we push around between us. I want to make it something else for Mike. I don't know what that is yet. But tell him I love him and keep telling him I love him, no matter what . . .

She folded and unfolded the letter so many times that it became two pieces of stained paper.

She called her mother and tried to tell her what was happening, what she was planning to do. Her mother cried, but Judith didn't.

She finally just called Michael at work and said, "Mike, when you get home, I won't be here. Michael Junior is at Debbie's. I've told Mom, and she said you should call Hopkins—the lawyer she and Dad used? Tell him whatever you want. I'm going to Houston. I'll stay at Kathy's. Goodbye."

Michael called the lawyer as soon as she hung up, charged desertion, and was awarded custody of Michael Junior.

16.

KATHY, A HIGH SCHOOL FRIEND, treated Judith like a casualty: first aid but no long-term treatment. Kathy is married now to a NASA engineer. They live with their daughters, Denny and Amy, in a townhouse just beyond the Houston city limits. Kathy seemed to enjoy talking about the days when Judith lived in Houston. That time had strong memories for Kathy, but they were not all bitter.

"There were parties, lots of talk. Endless rounds of love affairs. Drugs. Not much—Quaaludes and booze to get a high. Lot of speed. Some guys back from Vietnam with heroin. I never took any. I don't think she did. There were long bad nights. A suicide. You wake up and you find somebody isn't there any more. A lot of groping. We were hearing about things for the first time. That the war was bad, that women could be themselves, that queers weren't queer. We didn't get big into anything. But we knew things, or maybe it was that we were *beginning* to know.

"I only took her in for a little while. Then I told her about a place where she could live with people. We lost track a little, and then, when she went back to school, I saw her a little now and then. She was conscientious, like in high school, typing her notes, doing extra things, recording her lectures. She said she was starting to think a lot. Maybe that was what we were doing. Not *knowing* exactly, but thinking."

Judith moved into a room in what had been a one-family

house in a Houston neighborhood that had been slowly running down and now seems to be making a comeback. It's almost fashionable today.

Four other people lived there: three men in their early twenties and a thirty-two-year-old woman who immediately told her age and that she had just stopped being a nun. She still lives there, and it takes a while now for her to tell you that she used to be a nun. She remembers Judith quite well.

Judith assumed that the place would be a commune; she had read about communal living, and she thought that this would be a way into it. But the philosophy of the place was that each person stayed out of everybody else's way.

At Kathy's suggestion, Judith registered at a temporary-employment agency which sent her out on secretarial jobs (typing, no shorthand). She was bright, attractively non-hippie, and dependable. The old attributes of the Girl Scout and the National Honor Society scholar were reappearing in the woman. She managed to earn enough money to enroll in Houston Community College. She registered for a full-time schedule, surprised to feel again the sense of striving, the need again for straight A's. In a little less than two years, she would get an associate degree in applied science.

She knew almost from the first day that the house was an unfriendly place, but it made sense. Life there was safe, cheap, and unchallenging. Sensible. Being sensible was important to her. If she had run away merely because she wanted to find an adventure, then her running away had been meaningless.

She had classes in the morning and afternoon. She had a steady job, four nights a week, from five to eleven, in the admitting office of a hospital. She was changing. And changing consumed so much time, so much energy.

After a few months in Houston, whatever it was that had made her run away had settled deep within her. She could not give a name to her feelings. She did not know what she was, but she knew what she was not. She was not a wife, not a mother, not even a daughter, and except for seeing Kathy now and then, she was not a friend.

She was not a lover, either—except for some groping, except for some weekends when she would go to Dave's or to Ed's and she would leave on Sunday night or Monday morning with what Dave had called her goodies bag because in it she carried her nightgown, the plastic case that held her diaphragm, and the tube of Preceptin.

She told Kathy that Michael had insisted she use the pill. The first kind she tried made her throw up and break out in a rash. She changed to another kind, and it still made her sick. They did not want any more children. Michael Junior was enough. "Even if it makes you sick," Michael said, "it's got to be better than having another goddamn baby."

She had switched to the diaphragm, but Michael had hated that. He would reach across the bed and touch her breast, and she would know that she had two choices. She could take the diaphragm case and the tube of Preceptin out of the night table. Then, sitting on the side of the bed, she could arch her body and smear the jelly on the diaphragm and insert it, and wipe her fingers on the sheet or somewhere on her leg, where, she hoped, Michael would not touch the stuff and then, in palpable disgust, wipe *his* fingers on another part of her leg. Or she could get up, go into the bathroom, close the door, and perform the ritual in private. Either way, Michael would lie there, sighing or snorting in impatience and anger, his erection threatening to recede. As soon as she lay down beside him, careful not to touch him, he would roll upon her, thrusting fast and desperately, his spasm a burst of anger—even, perhaps, mutual punishment: a quick lay, he called it.

Sometimes she would insert the diaphragm before he came home. But he did not like that, because it seemed to him that she was trying to take the lead, trying to tell him when she wanted him instead of waiting for him to begin.

"You can bet your ass I'm not going to lay here and wonder whether you've got that goddamn rubber thing in you and got hot pants. If you want it, that's just fine. But if you're laying there and you've got that thing in you, then it's not just that you want it, but that you want me to do it, and that's one helluva different fucking thing."

She kept using the pill and getting sick, and she supposed that was one reason she left.

For a long time in Houston, still uncertain, still poised to return, she had been looking for reasons to stay or to go back. She had the feeling of a memory. Up the ladder to the highest diving board at the dependents' pool at the base in Norfolk. Out to the end of the board. Looking down at the blue-green water. Turning around and going back down. In Houston there was a moment like that, a moment that would become a memory.

English 236, Appreciation of American Poetry. She had never heard of the poem, *Nancy Hanks*, by Rosemary Benét, but she read poetry well on sight, and when Mr. Cowles asked her to read, she began—

If Nancy Hanks
Came back as a ghost,
Seeking news
Of what she loved most,
She'd ask first
'Where's my son . . .'

She almost managed to get to the end of the fourth and final stanza . . .

'Did he grow tall?
Did he have fun? . . .'

But she broke down. She faked a coughing spell, trying to cover up the dry sobbing burning her insides.

That night she called her mother. She wanted her mother to summon her home. She wanted to be told that Michael Junior—Mike—was ill and calling for his mother. She wanted to rush home to love, to love of some kind.

She hoped that her mother would say something about Mike—"Michael Junior," she knew her mother would say. But her mother said nothing. And Judith did not ask about him. She told her mother that she was getting straight A's, and that was nearly all she said.

When Judith hung up, she went into the kitchen. Margaret, the former nun, was at the table, having her bedtime cup of tea. Judith filled a pan with water, put it on the stove, turned the dial to high, took from a cupboard a Maxim instant-coffee jar labeled JUDITH, and stood by the stove, watching the burner's outer black rings turn a dull red. She did not speak.

People rarely spoke to each other in the kitchen, the center of ill-feelings in the house. Food was individually purchased, individually prepared, and eaten in solitude. Since there was only one refrigerator, perishables were subject to depredation. People might speak to each other in the common living room, where disputes over television programs usually were settled by attempts at consensus. But the kitchen was a place for confrontation and silent accusation, not conversation, and so Margaret was startled to be told there, "Margaret, I have to talk to somebody."

Judith sat down opposite Margaret. While the water boiled away, Judith told Margaret about the marriage, the baby, the running away, and finally the reading of the poem. Margaret waited a moment before she said that she did not want to talk to Judith or to anyone else because talking was a waste, an externalizing.

"You are still a nun, Margaret," Judith said, and that was the last time Margaret spoke to her, even to say hello.

She had had enough of Houston by the time she got her degree, along with an offer of a scholarship to the University of Texas. The two years had given her a degree—and confidence. She told herself that she could go back to Corpus Christi. She would stay with her mother, see Michael and Mike, and after a couple of weeks she would leave. To where, she did not know. She quit the hospital job, cashed in the U.S. savings bonds her father had given her when she married ("Don't tell Michael"), bought the VW, and spent the summer driving in the Southwest, listening to the Southwest, talking to it. She did not drive toward Corpus Christi.

She reached Grand Canyon National Park just before sunset on a day near the end of August. The sight of that reddening, then darkening infinity held her at the rim. She decided to stay the night in the lodge. The next morning at breakfast she heard two waitresses talking about leaving. Impulsively, she asked the hostess for a job. She stayed for six weeks, mostly to see the sunsets. She had not seen many sunsets in her life.

At the last sunset, while she waited for the shadows to fill the last shimmering ridge below, she knew there was still a chance that she would go home. She began driving through the night, southward, with some vague plan to go back. She would not stay there in Corpus Christi, in the past, with her first life. She would just visit there. She would visit, and then she would leave to start a new life.

In a little town north of Phoenix, she stopped at an all-night cafe and pulled up alongside a Mustang. Its engine was racing. A slim young man was angrily snapping the handle of the door on the driver's side. As he stooped and picked up a rock, Judith shouted, "Don't. That's a classic."

He turned and glared at her. "Mind your own goddamn business, honey. It's my car."

She slid across the seat to get out on his side. He lowered his eyes to her shorts and tanned legs and smiled, still holding up the rock.

"You've locked yourself out," she said. "But I suppose that's obvious even to a dumb-ass like you." She stood next to him, glaring back, eye to eye. She was as short as he was, though slimmer. "Go in and ask them for a clothes hanger, a wire one." He did not move. "OK. We'll go in together. You order us coffee. I'll get the hanger, come outside, open your goddamn car, turn off the engine, and come back in to drink the coffee and give you your key. And nobody inside will know you're a dumb-ass."

"I'll go in," he said. "I want to see this."

He returned with a hanger, which she opened and straightened. She slipped the hooked end of the hanger between the rubber strips of the vent and the rolldown window and tugged the knob. The vent window opened, and she reached in, switched off the engine, took out the key, and handed it to him.

"My name is Art," he said. "Thanks."

"You're welcome, Art. My name's Judy."

"Where are you going, Judy?"

"Driving. Driving south. I just finished with a job."

"Looking for a job? Are you looking?"

"Sort of. Yes, I guess I am. I have to have a job."

"A real job? I mean, one that isn't just fooling around, like being a waitress or something like that. A real job?"

She laughed and said she had a degree in science, and that was real enough. So she thought she would get a real job, not a waitress job.

He told her he was on a week's vacation from his first real job. He said he was a laboratory technician in something he called a Facility. He said it would be easy for her to get a job there. The turnover was considerable. They were working three shifts. She asked him what they did at the Facility. He said they worked with plutonium.

Art was staying at a motel about a mile from the cafe.

"Where are you staying tonight, Judy?"

"You ask a lot of questions, Art. I'm not staying anywhere. I'm just driving. Driving south. I told you."

"There's not really any place to go, this time of night, Judy, except to a motel."

"You're funny, Art," she said. First sparring with Art, then talking to him in real words because he had become someone she wanted to be real with, she felt, for the first time in her life, an intimation of maturity. She was older than he, but not much older—three years? "You're really funny, Art. Suppose I do go to your motel. How do I know they're going to have room for me there?"

"You *know* you've got no worry about that, Judy."

They were sitting side by side in a booth. She was against the wall. He stood up. She told him later that if he had not done that, she would not have gone with him. If he had sat there, trapping her, she would have gone back to driving through the night. He had the sense to not try to trap her.

They spent two days together. After Art drove off, early in the morning, she spread a map on the bed and looked for Tulsa. She took a spool of white thread from her duffle bag and measured the straight-line distance from Phoenix to Corpus Christi. Then she swung the thread around to Tulsa. The distance was almost exactly the same. It was, she once said to Art, as if there was no difference which way she chose to turn.

17.

WHEN SHE ARRIVED in Caslon Wells, Art invited her to move into his apartment. She said she would stay there, but she did not want to move in.

"I don't see much difference," Art remembers saying. "Either way, we're sharing one bedroom."

"I've got more on my mind than this bedroom."

"You don't act that way."

"What way?"

"I mean, you seem to like being here—being in bed with me."

"Sure I do. You're good—very, very good. OK? But there's more to me."

"Oh Christ, Judy. I know that."

"Do you?" She waited for an answer, but Art got out of bed. She heard three sounds—the click of the TV, the slam of the refrigerator door, the pop of a beer can's opening—and in the silence that followed she managed to fall asleep. Sometime during that first night he returned to bed. When she woke up, Art had already gone to work. Alone, she had a vague feeling that they had made love again. She also had no sense of time. She told Art she did not have a keen awareness of time, and he suggested that the vagueness and the timelessness resulted from a combination of wine and grass the night before.

Art had the idea that she would wait a few days before she began her new life, which was to start with her applying for a job at the Caslon Nuclear Facility. But that morning's sense of timelessness apparently had the effect of making her want to use time. She told Art she felt an urgency. She decided to go to Caslon that morning instead of waiting for Art to pick up an application for her. He felt that she did not even want that much help from him.

Getting a job at the Facility was as easy as Art had predicted. Her two-year degree in applied science gave her the basic qualifications for being a laboratory technician (whatever *that* was), and she scored high on the aptitude tests. She always did well on tests, especially on ones that asked for a selection among answers that were already there. She felt as if she were passing the final examination to the real world.

Michael used to taunt her about that. He said he was in the real world, and she was in the place where the wives lived. But that had changed. In Houston, and on the road, driving aimlessly through the Southwest, talking, listening, becoming aware, she had changed. She was Judith Longden, a woman on her own. She proclaimed it on a stretch of tape otherwise full of country music and remarks about clouds and mirages on the road ahead: "I guess what I feel the most right now, right this second, is that I am alone, just Judith, and I am happy. I am in the real world, Michael, you son of a bitch."

She had not noticed the sign at the gate on her job-interview trip to the Facility. But on the Monday that was her first day of training, she stopped and read the sign: SAFETY FIRST: 724 DAYS WITHOUT LOST-TIME ACCIDENT. The digits 724 were in a slot; as she drove up, a guard was taking out the 4. She watched him put in a 5. "It's a scoreboard," she told Art later. "They keep score on us." For all her time at the Facility, that sign would trouble her. On that day, she wondered what had happened there 725 days before. And each new day would increase her wonder.

The training session started in the cafeteria with a showing of *Welcome to Caslon*, a film about the corporation—its gleaming headquarters building in downtown Tulsa, a couple of refineries, a few gushers, a pipeline or two, a smiling Caslon service manager. Spliced on to the film were crudely filmed scenes of Facility buildings and security measures; the only view inside the Facility was one in the cafeteria. There was no mention of what went on in the Facility.

After the film came a swift tour of the Facility: Main

Building, Uranium Processing Plant, finally Plutonium Processing Plant. The dozen or so new workers filed out of P Plant's first-floor cafeteria behind a tall, slim man in a long white lab coat. He was pale and his hair was so close-cropped it was colorless in the fluorescent light of the central hall. They clanged up the metal stairway and crowded around a landing at the top. Their guide, who introduced himself as, "Mr. Gildea of the Industrial Safety Team," pulled at the flanged metal door. She felt her hair ripple, not to the play of a wind but to the tug of some kind of pressure. The door hissed shut behind them. They were in a long, narrow corridor.

Gildea motioned them to line up along one side. He stood across from them and fidgeted with the nozzle of a fire extinguisher. It was one of five that Judith could count along the corridor. The trainees began fidgeting, too, and looking around, waiting for Gildea to speak.

The high ceiling seemed to be supported by strips of metal that made her think of a long venetian blind opening onto nothing. Pipes ran below the baffle, and from them were suspended fluorescent light fixtures. That kind of light would always disturb her in a subtle, unreasonable way; perhaps because in its fullness and totality it deprived her eyes of seeing shadows. The walls were stark and white. Doors with porthole windows broke the cinderblock pattern. Like the door they had just passed through, these seemed designed never to open, or to open with great mechanical reluctance.

"We are in an air-lock corridor," Gildea began. "For reasons that you will learn later it is necessary to maintain a negative-pressure atmosphere in the laboratories. There's no need to go into technicalities about the system.

"Let me tell you about a few of the features of this corridor—it is called an access corridor because it's the only way out. For that reason, it has many safety devices. You'll learn about them on your regular work shifts, but I'll quickly point them out to you now. I am trying to anticipate your questions, you see."

He pointed up. "The baffle, for technical reasons not worth going into, will retard the movement of fire and fumes. You'll notice that the fire extinguishers are not all the same. *Never touch one.* You may make matters worse. Each extinguisher is for a different kind of fire. Trained personnel are to handle them, *not* production employees. At intervals along the hall, at every other laboratory doorway, you will see signs that say EMERGENCY SHOWER. Your supervisor will tell you more about the shower procedure."

Judith was leaning against a cold pipe that emerged from the wall near the floor and arched out to a shower-head about seven feet up the wall. She noticed that the valve-stem on the pipe had no handle. The shower could not be turned on by hand. The two other shower pipes near enough for her to check also lacked valve handles.

"You'll notice a lot of gizmos hanging on the walls—electric panels and lights and such. All you need to know about them is that they are part of the alarm system. If the ordinary electricity goes out for some reason, an emergency battery-powered system comes on. It's designed to work no matter *what* happens. I hope you never have to see them come on, but those lights hanging at intervals along the corridor are access lights. They are made of thick glass and covered with a fine mesh so they can't be broken by flying objects. They are connected to the emergency power system. The lights are blue. If you ever have to evacuate and you can't see your way because of darkness or fumes or what-have-you, just follow the blue lights. OK? Let's be moving on."

A woman next to Judith had been raising her hand, and Gildea had been ignoring her. As he turned and began leading the group down the corridor, the woman yelled, "Wait a minute, mister." Her voice brought everyone to a stop, and Gildea had to turn. "Wait a minute," she repeated. "What the hell is it that we're supposed to do here that's going to be so dangerous? When are you going to tell us that?"

Everyone had been issued temporary identification, a cardboard label with an adhesive back. Gildea walked up to the woman, leaned down to read the label on her red sweater—"Mrs. Wilkinson, is it?"—and jotted it down on the yellow lined pad clamped to his clipboard. Stepping back, addressing all of them, he said, "You are not going to be doing anything dangerous. You are going to be following procedures that have been developed by highly competent, highly intelligent people—and approved by an agency of the Federal Government. We are a safe place. There is nothing dangerous here."

"I don't believe you, mister," Mrs. Wilkinson said. "I

promised my husband I wouldn't work in a dangerous place. So I quit." She walked to the door and pushed down on the metal bar across it. Nothing happened, and she pushed down again, harder. She pushed so hard her feet left the highly polished floor. She stood before the door and began pounding on it. Finally, Gildea walked over, raised the bar, paused, then pushed the bar down and put his right shoulder against the door. It opened, and Mrs. Wilkinson squeezed out. Gildea pulled the door shut, returned to his place at the head of the procession, and with a jerk of his head, resumed the march down the corridor.

The laboratory door, also flanged and heavy, bore a yellow sign with the black, three-triangle symbol of radiation. The door had a standard brass handle on a brass plate. Gildea needed two hands to pull the door open.

"Please do not touch anything," he told the trainees, who crowded around him in a half-circle. "You are in an RMA. Those are important initials around here, so I'll repeat them: RMA, radioactive materials area. People who work in here *must* follow RMA procedures. You will be told about these procedures by your work supervisor."

It was a white box of a room, its walls uncluttered, its ceiling bearing only partially recessed light fixtures. Along three walls were people, their backs to the visitors. Each person sat on a stool before a stainless-steel box on metal legs. Although the hunched-up shapes in the white coveralls were different—a thin-shouldered figure with hair to the collar next to a fat-backed figure with a thick pink neck, and so on down the line of humps—there was a strange sameness, as if these white shapes, all somehow connected, were the visible parts of an organism whose other parts were as yet unseen.

Judith could see that the people's arms were thrust through two gasketed holes in the boxes. Just above the holes a diamond-shaped window was inset in a riveted metal frame. Judith could not see through the thick window to what was inside the box.

Gildea was talking: ". . . special glove boxes for handling plutonium." It was the first time she had heard anyone in Caslon speak the word. Gildea acted as if he had let slip a dirty word. He was flustered. "That is to say, special glove boxes for the handling of radioactive materials. It does not really matter, really, *what* the stuff is inside the glove box.

What matters is that it is radioactive, and we are handling it here in a safe and sensible way.''

His voice slipped back to its normal frequency for talking to trainees. "There still is another negative-pressure level maintained in the glove boxes. The air inside is dry to minimize the effects of humidity. There is an outlet filter and an inlet filter. We have a four-air supply system so that the air in this building keeps flowing toward the next lower pressure area. That keeps the radioactive material inside the glove box. Simple."

Gildea's radiation talk came on the second day of the five-day training course.

"You can read a lot of nonsense about radiation, from people who don't know what they're talking about. Well, x-rays are radiation, and every year about 137 million people get x-rayed—that's more than half the population. Sure, x-rays can give you cancer—if the x-rays are turned on so high and given to you so much that you get an overdose. And even then you might not get any cancer at all. Radiation is highly overrated. There are a lot of other things to really worry about. Like cars.

"You all drove here today. There's no other way to get here than to drive on Route 85. Right: Well, let me tell you, the chances of getting killed or injured out there on Route 85 are much, much greater than getting injured in this place.

"You just follow the rules around here, and all that's going to happen to you is you'll live to a ripe old age and get your Social Security.

"Now, about that old bugaboo, radiation. The Atomic Energy Commission sometimes measures it in 'sunshine units,' because you can get a pretty good dose of radiation from the sun. You ladies who go out in your little bitty bikinis and get a sunburn, well, you're probably getting more radiation than you'll ever get in here—where, I'm sorry to say, you'll be wearing more clothes."

Gildea began to drone from a Federal Government pamphlet on the measurement of radiation. Judith wanted to ask a question. She raised her hand—it was such an old, quaint gesture; she had raised her hand so often in so many schools, usually out of confidence, not curiosity. But this time she had a real question, not a bright statement that would show she had done her homework. She wanted to know what kind of radiation could be expected. And she wanted to know about the substance she assumed she would be handling here: plutonium.

Gildea ignored her hand, which she began waving with the insistence of a National Honor Society veteran. "No questions," he finally said. "We have too much we are obliged to cover."

The training day was supposed to consist of four hours of classroom instruction and four hours of on-the-job training with a work supervisor. There was no classroom instruction. All Gildea did was read from an AEC manual and refuse to accept questions. He cut off the session after two hours because the cafeteria crew needed to set up for lunch.

She and three other trainees, two of them men, had as their work supervisor a slight, hollow-cheeked foreman named Haskins. He was about forty-five, and he spoke with a heavy Southern accent. He told them on the first afternoon that he was in charge of the first, or eight-to-four shift in the SX Laboratory, but he did not describe what work was done in the SX Laboratory, or even what SX meant. He introduced a younger man who had thick black hair and wore large, black-framed glasses whose lenses were faintly tinted green. "This is Doug Fenwick, and he's the laboratorian assigned to Room 14, the lab room you'll be working in." Haskins did not say what a laboratorian was.

On Friday, the last training day, Haskins gathered them in a storage room full of barrels bearing the yellow-and-black symbol for radioactivity. Fenwick passed out hooded white smocks. He told them that when they started work full-time, they would be issued coveralls—"initial cost and replacement costs deducted from your pay."

Fenwick also handed them white nylon shoe covers. They were told to tie the covers' drawstrings tightly around their ankles, put on the smocks, but ignore the hoods. They all signed papers that said they had been issued safety clothing. Then they clumped off, like big white rabbits, behind Fenwick and Haskins, both of whom wore coveralls but not shoe covers.

Haskins led them into Room 14. Fenwick followed and closed the door. Judith had become accustomed to the sounds of air rushing in and out of rooms. But she was still not used to people who did not look up when she entered a room. She counted nine figures, each hunched before his (or her?) glove box.

The twelve glove boxes in Room 14 were arranged in four bays. Two of the boxes in each bay were occupied; the middle stool was empty. Each of the trainees was assigned to a middle stool. Judith found herself flanked by two men. The one on her left moved his head slightly toward her and nodded when she sat down. His hood was so closely drawn that his face seemed to be floating, unattached to his body.

"Each one of you is at a box," Haskins was saying. "OK. Now don't turn around. Just listen. Doug is passing out gloves. Now just put them on and sit there. Don't put your hands in the boxes." Fenwick gave her a pair of translucent plastic gloves. Her hands were sweating and shaking; she had trouble pulling the gloves on. The fingers in the gloves were nearly an inch longer than the fingers on her small hands. She tugged at the cold, smooth fingers while Haskins talked.

"Now in a normal day here you'd be working on a pass-through. You'd be part of a bay team assigned to a specific SX job. Today, though, I'm going to give you a break. You won't have to work. Just try it out. It's pretty simple.

"OK. Everybody got their gloves on? Now take a look at what's in front of you. Three big holes, right in a row. Now there are three holes, but we know you only have two hands. *Ha. Ha.* The three holes are so you can work inside the box with either your hands close together or far apart. OK. There's a long sleeve hanging out of each hole. The sleeves end in fingers, like big gloves. OK. The sleeves are all tied together so that the negative pressure in the box won't suck them in. You might say this box sucks." He and Fenwick laughed. The shoulders of the men next to Judith wiggled to signal to her an appreciation of Haskins' joke.

"OK. Now untie the sleeves. All three hanging there in front of you? OK. Tie a knot, not too tight, in the middle one. Doug will check them." Haskins waited a moment. "OK. Now stick your arms into the sleeves. The way to do it is to sort of take turns, wiggling your arms and pulling up your sleeves as you get your arms further and further in. Now, when your hand reaches the hole it will feel like a heavy piece of rubber with slits in it. Just force your hand through that hole. Not too hard. You don't want your hand to punch into the box—it might break something." He paused again.

"OK. Now, everybody got their hands in?" Apparently at least one person had not been able to perform the maneuver because Haskins said, "Doug. Give that guy a *hand*. Ha. Ha." Haskins spoke the laugh, as if it consisted of two words.

"OK. Everybody set? Now hold your hands up, palms toward you, so you can see them through the window."

Her hands looked detached and far away. She turned them, very slowly, and they seemed to respond even more slowly than she had commanded. They acted like puppets of hands, with stiff, lifeless fingers. Beyond and below her hands was the brilliantly white and unshadowed box. Peering through the thick, diamond-shaped window, she lost for a moment the reality of the box's size; its starkness produced an illusion of infinity. Her puppet hands were performing on a boundless white stage. Haskins' voice broke the spell.

"You'll see a lot of valves and pipes inside, against the back wall. Forget them. *Don't touch anything yet.* Just move your hands around. Slowly. Touch your hands to each other. Get used to the view." Haskins waited perhaps thirty seconds. "OK. Now directly in front of you is a beaker and a shallow dish. To your right is a round tray mounted on a wheel, like a lazy susan. You can only see a part of the round tray because it is pushing through a slit in the gasket that connects your glove box with the glove box on your right. Glance to your left. Same thing. That lazy susan pass-through is connected to the bay on your left." Another pause.

"When I say 'go,' the operator to your right will turn the tray and you'll see some small bits of metal on that tray. *Go!*" At the word, the tray turned to bring into view several pieces of silvery-white metal. "*Don't touch,*" Haskins commanded in a loud, harsh voice. Judith's eyes never left the pieces of metal on the tray.

"That's plutonium you're looking at. It's nothing to be scared of. You just have to be careful, that's all. It's crumbly. And it's a little hot to the touch. Your gloves will protect you. OK. Now I'm going to ask you to do some things with it. I'm going to give instructions, then I'm going to say 'go.' Don't do anything until I say 'go.' OK. The first thing that I want you to do is pick up a piece—just *one* piece—and put it in the dish." A pause of about ten seconds. Then: "*Go!*"

Judith did as she was told. The metal felt warm. Her hand was shaking as she moved the gray little chunk to the dish. It was strange not to hear the sound of the metal striking the dish, which seemed to be made of glass. The air inside the box seemed dry, warm, and in circulation. She was sweating. Her hands—poised now, awaiting instructions as much from Haskins as from her—were sticky against the inside of the gloves.

"Next—but not till I say 'go'—pick up the beaker and pour a few drops of liquid on the metal. When you do that, there will be a little reaction. But don't worry. *Go!*"

At that moment, Judith heard a scream to her left. She turned sharply, forgetting that her arms were in a box. She leaned awkwardly past the hunched shoulders of the man at her left. He had turned, too. Hardly a second had passed since that first scream.

She could see someone at a glove box topple backward off a stool and land heavily on the floor. His feet were entangled in the stool legs.

She recognized him as a trainee named Jim, who was tall, had curly blond hair, and was about nineteen years old. She remembered he had told her he had never been good enough to play high school basketball because the coach said he was not well coordinated.

As he fell back, his gloved hands shot out of the sleeves of the glove box. There was blood on his left hand. She turned her gaze toward her own window to see what her own hands were doing. They were suspended, one over the dish, the other over the beaker.

"Don't move! Don't move!" Haskins shouted. Her mind jumbled the separate sounds she heard in the next moment: feet slapping on the tiled floor; the clicks of switches; a sharp, loud, pulsing buzzer. She could not see what was going on, and she could not move. She was blind and trapped in the midst of something she could not understand.

"*Keep your hands in place. Don't move!* Goddamn it! I said don't pull your hands out! Doug. Tie up those sleeves. I'll get him. Let's get the masks on them."

Something white flashed before her and then slapped against her nose and mouth. She felt an elastic band pressing her temples and hair. Her hood was yanked up, and she was in a cowl, her vision even more limited. By moving her head slightly, she discovered she could see herself in the glove box's window. She was shimmering, transparent. She was wearing a mask, the kind nurses and doctors wore around an operating table. Then beyond her own masked face she could see the door opening and two figures in bright yellow coveralls.

They seemed to be wearing masks that covered their heads. In the filmy reflection she saw them do something over, or to, the man on the floor and then pick him up. As soon as they passed through the door, a third figure in yellow appeared and did something at the door. Judith could feel a slight pressure, as if the air had become heavier.

The figure moved and lost its translucency, startling her as it entered her vision and became wholly real. The figure wore loose-fitting coveralls with white, thick-fingered gauntlets. Its black boots were partially covered by yellow covers. The head covering looked like a yellow football helmet combined with a rubbery mask. The upper half of the mask was windowed so that an image of flesh was visible; the lower half, which pulsated, consisted of two small canisters, just below where cheeks would be, and a thick black ridged hose that ended in a tank strapped to the back.

"I am a health physicist," said a woman's voice from inside the mask. "There has been a slight accident. Please follow my instructions. I am placing this room on respirators. Trainees first. Trainees, I want you to slowly withdraw your arms from the glove boxes. Just sit there. We will come to you."

She changed the tone of her voice; more sharply, she said, "Haskins, you handle number one. Fenwick, this one. I'll take number three."

Judith felt a hand on her right shoulder. The voice, gentle now, said, "Turn around, please," and in a moment the paper mask was replaced by a respirator. It covered the lower half of her face, a black, flexible mask with perforated metallic discs as cheeks. The health physicist tightened the respirator's head-girding strap, but the facepiece did not feel snug against Judith's cheeks, and she tried to say something about it. She was looking up at a pair of blue eyes that pierced the dull sheen of the windowed visor.

"Save your breath," said the voice, sharp again. "You may need it." The blue eyes strayed to the temporary ID tag, and the voice softened to say, "OK, Judith?"

Judith looked at the round face in the ID tag dangling

above her and managed to read the name just before the tag and the figure swung away. "OK, Barbara," Judith said to the back of the yellow figure.

The figure named Barbara returned to the door and leaned against it. "Relax, everybody," she said. "We're all going to be here for a while until the dust settles."

With a movement of her hands too fast to follow, she removed the hosed helmet-mask and replaced it with a respirator that looked the same as everyone else's. The change produced a kind of masked democracy, a sense of an unknown danger now shared.

18.

JUDITH NEVER SAW the young man named Jim again. "A lot of people drop out," Art told her when they met in the parking lot that day, the last day of training. Art had managed to get the same shift and had suggested a celebration; a graduation, he called it. "They drop out, but they get replaced." He ran a finger along a line on her cheek. "On respirators? Christ, what an introduction! But I guess it's good to know about right away."

"You mean it happens a lot?" she asked, rubbing the line he had just traced.

"Often enough. I've spent plenty of time on respirators. Once I spent three days in a row and so did just about everybody else in P Plant. A big spill."

"Is that the accident?" He knew what accident she meant: the one implied by the numbers on the SAFETY FIRST sign. He had not wanted to talk about it, and she saw the same stubborn look returning to his face. She quickly kissed him and said, "Let's go celebrate graduation."

They drove in Art's car down Route 85 to Carry's Place, reputedly the site of the first Oklahoma saloon that Carry Nation attacked with her hatchet. The country music in Carry's Place was usually honest and never amplified. The beer was served in frosted glass pitchers, and the frozen pizza was thawed and cooked in a few seconds in a microwave oven. There was a jukebox that kept indifferent music in the air between sets.

When Art and Judith walked in, *Save Your Kisses for Me*

was playing. A wobbly patron was kicking the jukebox and yelling, "I didn't push that goddamn number. That's a shitty song." Bud Jennings, the tall, beer-bellied young man who ran Carry's Place for the Tulsa lawyer who owned it, whipped off his shapeless Stetson and whacked the jukebox kicker across the back of his jeans, handed him a quarter, and told him to sit down.

Jennings picked up a pitcher from the bar and led Art and Judith to a table along a wall. At the next table Judith saw a woman she thought she had seen before. She mentioned this to Art, who turned—and waved. "Barbara O'Neill," he said. "She's an HP."

"She's *the* HP," Judith said, "the one I just told you about. I only saw her with the hood on. Let's ask her over."

Art shrugged to indicate some reluctance, but he waved his hand and moved his head enough so that Barbara did come to stand by them, sipping her small glass of beer. Within a minute, Bud had led a couple to Barbara's table, and now it was she who shrugged. She sat down and accepted a half-glass of beer from their pitcher.

They sat through one set, unable to talk much between songs. A red-bearded man was singing. His denim jacket and jeans were truly faded and truly patched, the clothes of a genuine hitchhiker. He picked a guitar that had been punched around as much as he had been. He was singing one by Billy Joe Shaver:

> We're all wayfaring wandering gypsies, alone.
> Looks like lookin' for is where we'll always be.
> Cursed to be born as serious souls
> No one will take seriously.

After the applause and cheers, in a moment of relative quiet, Barbara leaned toward Art and Judith and said, "I've got a great album by Shaver. And Willie Nelson singing. And I've got something better than frozen pizza. Would you like to come to my place?"

At Barbara's they ate a parsley-and-basil omelette and hot biscuits with jam made of strawberries Barbara had picked. Art, a fried-egg man, did not like the omelette, but he liked everything else, particularly the atmosphere. He remembers feeling comfortable there with Judith mostly because she seemed to relax. She had been tense all night, and he knew that tension early on a Friday evening would probably mean the rest of the weekend would be tense.

They were sitting listening to records and drinking Almaden chablis from ceramic goblets. Art began to roll a joint, but Barbara touched his arm and asked him not to, pointing to the ceiling and saying, "Landlady." Art said, "Oh, shit," filled his goblet, drained it, and filled it again. He was going to suggest that they leave, but he noticed, dimly, that Judith and Barbara were talking, and congratulating himself for having such good sense, he kept his mouth shut and listened.

Judith was sitting against the wall, her goblet in her left hand, her right arm on a low table, her hand cupping her chin. Behind her arm was a candle set in a latticed ceramic chimney. The light flickered on her cheek as she spoke. Art would always remember her face that way, a face that lived, vibrantly, in the lights and the shadows.

The music had stopped. Barbara had settled into a big brown chair with puffy round arms. Her cat, Grayfur, was in her lap and could be heard purring between Barbara's words.

"Trainees are always doing that, getting into accidents," Barbara was saying. "I always make sure I know if there are any trainees in P Plant when I'm on duty. He wasn't badly hurt—as far as we know."

"You mean you don't really know?" Judith asked. She turned her head, and Art could see that her jaw was a sharp, white line in the dark.

"I mean Caslon doesn't monitor people after they leave," Barbara said. "And a lot of them leave." She signaled Art for the bottle and held it out for Judith's goblet.

"You're left-handed?" Barbara asked.

"No. I do pretty well with either hand most of the time. But I'm right-handed. Why?"

"He was left-handed. I noticed that. I guess what happened is that as Haskins was telling them to pick up the plutonium in their right hand and the beaker in their left hand to pour the solvent over the plutonium, he tried to cross his hands. I think the heat of the plutonium surprised him, too. Maybe scared him. Anyway, he dropped the beaker. It broke, the tray cracked. He was cut, I guess, trying to get his hands out."

"But why would that be a big deal? I mean, the buzzer and the people in the yellow suits—and you—all charging in like that? It looked like an overreaction."

"If anything, it was an underreaction. He still had the plutonium in his hand when he pulled it out. There were plutonium particles all over the place. That's why I put the room on respirators."

"But it was only a scratch. I still say, what's the big deal?"

"Plutonium's the big deal. Didn't they tell you anything about it?"

"I know it's radioactive—alpha rays, mostly. I looked it up in the encyclopedia at the library." Judith rattled off what she knew. "Plutonium is man-made, created when uranium fissions. It's in atomic bombs and in nuclear reactors. It's dangerous, but since it's an alpha and beta emitter, it's not too dangerous outside the body. A piece of paper can stop an alpha ray and a piece of cardboard can stop a beta ray."

"I'll give you a C-minus," Barbara remembers saying. She sensed the good-pupil rhythm in Judith's recital. "But no cigar. You may know a couple of things about plutonium, but you don't know anything about what it can do to you. It's probably the most dangerous stuff on earth."

Judith did not immediately respond, and Art took the opportunity to say, "I guess maybe we should get going. It's late."

"No," Judith said. "Wait. I want to ask a couple of more questions." She was tense again. She had moved her head back into the shadow. But from her voice he could tell she was tense again.

"Maybe I could answer them—on the way home," he said. "Or at home. Let's go, Judy. I'm tired as hell."

"One question."

"OK."

"When I left the plant today, the sign still had the same numbers on it as when I went in. Seven hundred and twenty-nine days. Why didn't they change it back to zero?"

Neither Barbara nor Art immediately knew what sign she meant because both of them had long before stopped looking at SAFETY FIRST and its numbers. "Oh," Barbara said, "*that* sign!" She looked at Art, and they both laughed.

"Hell, Judy," Art said, "that sign *never* goes back to zero. It's sort of a joke."

Judith turned to Barbara. "But why—" Judith began, but Art reminded her that she already had asked her one question.

Judith did not speak during the short trip home. Art tried to convince himself that her silence meant that she was looking forward to being in bed with him. But he knew that this was not so. In the seat next to him she was stiff and cold; he could tell without touching her. She was staring straight ahead, her eyes not on him, her thoughts not on him.

The questions began to burst from her the moment she followed him through the doorway: *How long had he worked there?* Nearly a year. *With plutonium?* Most of the time in P Plant, with the plutonium. At first in U plant, with the uranium. *What did SX mean?* Solvent extraction. Part of the process. *Do you understand what you're doing, what you're working on?* Yes. More or less. *But you're not worried?* No. *And you don't care if I'm worried?*

"For Christ sake, Judy. You're the one who just took the goddamn training course." They sat on big black beanbag pillows on the floor in his living room. He wanted to smoke, but he knew she would take it as evasion. "Judy, honest to God. I don't think it's a big deal, the danger. And, please. I just don't want to go into all this shit when I'm here. *This* is where I am. Where *we* are. I don't want to be *there*."

"Maybe I'm leaning on you too much," Judith said. "Does it bother you that I'll be working where you work? Is that it? Am I threatening you somehow?"

"Cut that shit, Judy. I love the idea of you working there. It makes us closer. I thought you knew that."

"Sometimes I don't think I know anything—anything about you, anyway. And you don't know anything about me. It's important to me, Art. Really important to me that I have this job. It's part of a whole new life to me. And I'm confused, maybe scared. I wonder if I should be doing this."

"What's *this* supposed to mean? You just don't mean working at Caslon, do you? You mean me, too, don't you?"

"Yes. I guess I do. It's all so new, and it's all so . . . It gives me questions to answer, this starting everything. I wonder if I've really finished with my old life." She told him how lately she had been thinking about her son. And she told him about the time she had to read *Nancy Hanks* out loud in class.

"I can see how that poem gets to you. I can see that. That's what poems are supposed to do. But she was dead, Judy. You're alive. You're even sort of born again. No. I really mean that. You *are* sort of born again. It's the past that's dead, Judy."

"That's just it. I want to start and I want to start right. I want to know what I'm doing. They aren't telling me. That on-the-job training was a lot of bullshit. They don't tell me what the hell I'm supposed to be doing. I just stick my hands in a glove box and I do what they tell me in that box. Or try to."

"Well, I'll tell you one thing. You *better* be doing it right."

"What's that supposed to mean? If I'm in danger, tell me about it." She stood, started toward the kitchen, then turned and looked down at him. "You know what that accident was, don't you? Why won't you tell me about that accident? You and Barbara thought it was so funny, me—my—asking about that."

"Maybe it wasn't an accident? Is that what you're trying to say?" Now he stood up; he did not like her towering over him. "What the hell is your game, Judy? Why are you so goddamn curious?"

"There's no game, Art. Unless *you're* playing it. I'm going to work in a dangerous place, and I want to find out about it. You're my friend. You work there. And I asked you. No games—not from me."

"Are you going to join the union?" he asked. The question surprised her. She went into the kitchen, opened the refrigerator and took out a beer. With the door still open and her back to him, she asked, "You want one?"

"Yes, thanks," he said. Then, in the same tone, again: "Are you going to join the union?"

She opened the two beers and sat down. Art dropped down and squirmed to a spot closer to her than he had been before.

"I haven't given it much thought," she said. "I didn't think the union there amounted to much."

"It amounts to a helluva lot right now. There's going to be a strike."

"Is that why you were asking me why I was asking questions? Because you think I'm a scab? You're a goddamn fool, Art. I don't play games—never. No games, Art."

"OK. OK."

"How do you know there's going to be a strike?"

Art shrugged and did not answer.

"Look, Art, the way I find things out is I ask questions. If you don't like that, then you don't like something that's very big in me."

"Dick Scinto. He's the head of the local, Local 1010. He wants us to go out, and he's pretty damn sure he has the votes."

"Why? What's the issue? Money?"

"Sure. It's always money. But this time it's something else, too. Look, you know how much plutonium is worth? You're not supposed to know. Well, *I* know. I've heard guys right in this town say they could get $100 or $200 a gram. A goddamn *gram*. Christ." He drained the beer, stood up, got two more, handed her one, but did not sit down again. He began pacing around the room.

"Art, I don't see what this has to do with the strike. Or why I should join the union."

"You know why people'd pay so much for plutonium?"

"I guess because you could make bombs with it. But you need a whole factory, Art. Only a country, a big country, could do it. It's not like gold—or heroin."

"Lots of people could make bombs out of it."

"So what? What's that got to do with the strike? Art, I think you're not making much sense. Maybe we should just call it a night."

"Bullshit. You keep asking questions all night, I keep telling you answers. It's Scinto, see? It's strategy. He's getting the word around that if there's a strike and P Plant shuts down, it would be wide open for a heist. That's Scinto's word. A heist. There could be a heist."

He realized that he was repeating himself and that he was feeling drunk. And he did not want to give her the satisfaction of knowing it. So he deliberately tried to act sober. This had the effect of making his talk so deliberate and his movements so slow and careful that there could be no doubt he was just drunk enough to be trying to act as if he were not drunk.

"Art, did you get this stuff about the heist right from Scinto?"

"Not exactly."

"Well, who told you this?"

"A guy at the Facility. Friend of Scinto's."

"How do you *know*, Art? How do you know that this guy

is a friend? Maybe he was just giving you some line to get Scinto into trouble."

"Yeah. Maybe. Judy, let's go to bed."

He did not want to talk any more, and she realized that she did not want to talk, either. "Hey," he said, reaching down for her hands. "We're supposed to be celebrating . . . something." He pulled her to her feet and kissed her. She told him she could not remember what it was that they were celebrating. Art thought at the time that this was a strange lapse of memory. It seemed to him that her mind was trying to blot out the Facility. Then she must have remembered what they were supposed to be celebrating, for she stiffened for an instant in his arms.

And he told her again they were *here*, and *there* was not until Monday. She did not have to think about Caslon or plutonium or her new life until Monday. She did not have to go into the real world until Monday.

19.

IF JUDITH'S CAREER at Caslon started because she happened to meet Art, then her career continued because she next met Barbara O'Neill. Sensing Judith's apprehension about working with plutonium, Barbara telephoned her at Art's on Saturday morning. Barbara directed Judith to the Caslon Wells Public Library. There she would find a *Fortune* article on Caslon, one of the companies on the magazine's annual listing of America's 500 Leading Corporations. Barbara believed that if Judith knew what she was doing at the Facility, she would have less to fear.

Two years before Judith arrived in Caslon Wells, Caslon had won a contract from the AEC to manufacture fuel rods for an experimental nuclear reactor. The proposed reactor would be, *Fortune* said, "as much an evolutionary departure from conventional reactors as the jet turbine is from the Wright Brothers' twelve-horsepower engine." Conventional reactors were cooled by water. The water also acted as moderator to "slow down" neutrons, which, when striking the nuclei of the fuel's atoms, produce the power of fission. The fuel of these reactors was uranium.

The AEC was developing a Liquid-Metal Fast Breeder Reactor. Its coolant would not be water but liquid sodium, which, at 210°F, could still cool off fuel rods and keep them from melting. The "fast" referred to the fact that there would be nothing in the reactor system to slow down the neutrons. The reactor was called a "breeder" because it could produce fuel—virtually "breed" it—during the process of consuming fuel.

The principle had been known for years, but the "breeding" process had been confined to the top-secret federal production reactors that were the source of the key material for nuclear weapons. That material was plutonium. The fuel for the Liquid-Metal Fast Breeder Reactor would be plutonium.

The manufacture of plutonium begins with uranium-238. In a conventional reactor, some uranium-to-plutonium transmutation takes place. Thus, small amounts of plutonium would be among the fission products in the reactor's fuel rods. The rods are sealed metal tubes about one-half inch in diameter and twelve feet long. Inside are fuel pellets about an inch long. When the fuel rods are spent, they are cooled off in tanks of water for months, then chopped into small pieces.

This is where Caslon comes in. The bits of metal are delivered to Caslon for an industrial operation known as solvent extraction. The uranium and plutonium are separated and, each in its own plant, they are bathed in chemicals that extract them for other, less valuable fission products. Purified, they can be reprocessed as fuel.

In Caslon's P Plant, the process continued beyond extraction and reprocessing. The experimental fast-breeder needed a new kind of fuel rod, and Caslon had contracted to produce the rod. P Plant was producing plutonium and shaping it into fuel pellets. The ultimate product would be fuel rods with plutonium pellets sealed inside.

Plutonium fuel rods were vital to the AEC, which was virtually staking the future of nuclear power on the breeder reactor. Uranium was disappearing. "Without the breeder," said an AEC official in the *Fortune* article, "we can tap only one percent of the potential of uranium. This would make uranium equivalent to our oil reserves—and they, of course, are rapidly running out. With the breeder, we can increase the power potential of existing uranium by fifty to eighty times." The future of the nuclear-power industry rested on plutonium. Within the next decade, *Fortune* said, "this man-made element will play the role that gold has played for centuries. Already, in the corridors of the AEC and in the executive suites of energy firms, there is talk of 'the plutonium economy.' "

• • •

On her first day of work, Judith was to report to Personnel at 3 P.M., one hour early for the four-to-midnight shift. She sat in a cubicle, awaiting her assignment. She hoped that it would be P Plant. She liked the idea of being a pioneer in the plutonium economy, she had told Art. He had laughed. "It's just a job," he said. But she believed it was more than a job, it was an opportunity to begin something. Her concern about plutonium—not fear, she said, but apprehension—still bothered her. She had done some reading about the biological hazards of plutonium.

She looked up to see that the man approaching the cubicle was Gildea. She was surprised because she had expected a Personnel man, not a safety official. He took command of the table between them by placing a plastic-wrapped package in front of him and then opening a file folder and spreading its paper.

"Well," he said, "it didn't take you long to get an RD checkout." He looked down at one of the papers. "Let's see, we did cover the bioassay sampling program in training, didn't we?"

"Not that I remember," Judith said. It took her a moment to realize that she really did not understand what he was saying. "Mr. Gildea, I don't know what RD means. I have not the slightest idea what a bioassay sampling program is."

"Miss Longden, in that incident in the SX lab on Friday you may have received a slight uptake of plutonium. We wish to check you for RD—radioactive dosage. The way we will do this is put you on a bioassay sampling program, which simply means that for the next two days we would like you to containerize your urine and feces in the containers I will give you. You'll find further instructions with the containers. Each day you should bring them into work at the beginning of your shift and deposit them with the HP—health physics—personnel. Simple. Nothing to be concerned about."

"How can you say that?" She wanted to shout, but at the same time she did not want Gildea to see her as an hysterical, ignorant female. She had read enough to know that "a slight uptake" of plutonium could be highly damaging.

In school, sometimes before a test, she would see the phrases she had memorized appear as a hazy projection in her mind. Now it was happening, and she tried not to show Gildea any panic. In the instant that she was asking, "How can you say that? I know . . .," she was seeing and reading in her mind: *Radiation has many effects: on genes, causing mutations; on cells, preventing them from dividing or killing them. The most radioactive tissues in the body are those that divide most often: blood-forming organs, reproductive organs, skin, and intestines.*

"I know that there is nothing slight about an uptake of plutonium," she said. "How slight? Give me some numbers."

The cells lining the small intestine are extremely radiosensitive. A small amount of radiation in the abdomen can induce nausea and vomiting. The intestinal lining sloughs off, the bloodstream is invaded by bacteria that belong in the bowel . . .

"The numbers, as you call then, Miss Longden, are not particularly significant. I doubt very much if you would understand them. Now about the bioassay . . ."

"Give me the numbers, Gildea. What was the dpm per liter that the air-sampling filters picked up?" He had not noticed that she was reading one of his papers upside down. A dpm—disintegrations per minute—figure is a measurement of the decaying of plutonium, a radioactive substance; the dpm rate is also an index of the amount of radiation being put out in the room as a result of an accidental release of plutonium.

"I'm sorry, Miss Longden, but I am not empowered to give you that information."

"What is the maximum permitted lung burden?"

"I'm sorry . . ."

"I'm sorry, too, Gildea. I can write to the AEC and find that number out for myself."

"Sixteen nanocuries, I believe."

"And the volume of the room? I can get that too, you know. All I have to do, I guess, is write the AEC and . . ."

Gildea looked down at a paper. "The volume is 27,187 liters."

"And the concentration?"

"We estimate from the air-sample filters that the air concentration was 0.7165 dpm's per liter."

"And what do you figure is the number of liters I could

have breathed before I was given the respirator?"

"A woman engaged in light activity has a breathing rate of"—he glanced at the paper—"approximately nineteen liters per minute."

"If I was taking in nineteen liters of air a minute and the concentration of plutonium particles was 0.7165, then I don't see how I could have got much of a dose. They had a mask on me in, I'd say, less than thirty seconds and the respirator in maybe five or six minutes. On the outside let's say eight—even ten minutes—to make it easy. One hundred and ninety liters of air. Round out the dpm's to seven-tenths, and I figure I got maybe, what?, thirteen and something dpm's. I can't translate that to nanocuries, but it doesn't sound like much. Not with a respirator on."

"The room was on respirators for the remainder of the time you were in it," Gildea said. "Approximately one hour and forty-five minutes."

"That's about right. I figured they kept us there maybe to show us what it was like to wear a respirator for a long time. Or maybe to keep the room sealed until the particles had been pumped out. But of course they didn't tell us that. I'm beginning to think people don't like to tell you things around here."

"Quite the contrary, Miss Longden. I *am* here to tell you things. You were exposed to at least a marginal uptake of plutonium for approximately one hour and forty-five minutes. Since lung retention of insoluble particulates is twelve and one-half per cent of the intake, we believe that the ultimate lung burden could not be more than 0.07 nanocuries. However, as a precaution—"

"Wait a minute," Judith interrupted, aware that her voice was rising—*Ingested plutonium can severely damage tissue. A speck in a lung can induce fibrosis, a small quantity can cause lung cancer*—"Wait a minute. I had a respirator on nearly all the time."

"I am aware of that, Miss Longden. As a routine procedure, we examine the respirators. There seems to have been some difficulty with one respirator. It had defective filters. It need not have been the one you were wearing."

"The one I was wearing didn't fit too well, either."

"All the more reason. I hope you will be cooperative."

"Oh, I will. Don't worry. I'll give you all the piss and shit you want. One more question. What was the defect in the respirators?"

"It did not have filters in it."

"You mean whoever was wearing it was breathing that air straight?"

"Yes, but—"

"Somebody forgot to put the filters in? Somebody in HP"

"It is not an HP function. That is maintenance."

"You mean a goddamn janitor's in charge of respirators?"

Gildea scooped the papers into the folder and stood up. "I have been asked by Personnel to tell you that you are to report to the Metallography Laboratory in P Plant."

She sat in the cubicle for a few minutes. The blackboard of her mind was clear; no more textbook sentences. Textbooks did not help much in the real world. She could walk out now, the way that woman had on the first day of training. But walk out to what? She had just walked *in.* And she already had taken on so much: new town, new job, Art. To walk again, to seek out some other place, some other job—and, maybe, some other Art? She could not do that. Not yet. She would hang on.

She would ask questions. And not let them get away with anything. She could cope with work. She could learn to see danger, and if there seemed to be too much danger, she would quit. But coping with the rest of her life was different; there, she was in control. No one could assign her a place to live. She did her living on her own. She could not stay with Art. She had to be on her own.

And yet. It would be good to have someone to talk to, someone who would listen to what had happened today. She got to Art's a little past midnight, her first day's work a blur. Art was on the day shift, eight to four, and would be in bed.

"Is that the working lady?" Art's voice came from the dark bedroom. "Come on in and see what I've got for you."

She was carrying the bioassay containers. She had used one set of containers in work. The process had been humiliating; she later told Art it had brought back stinging memories of her first period, which had arrived in Miss Sanderson's American History class. She did not want Art to see the containers. She entered the bedroom and groped for a chair at the foot of the bed. She stumbled. Art was naked and sitting in the middle of the bed. She half fell and was half pulled onto him. She was still clutching the containers. He instantly knew what they were.

"Jesus," he said. "Jesus." He began stroking her hair. "What happened?"

She told him about the report from Gildea. She lay next to him, on top of the bedspread. He was slowly undressing her and softly kissing her on her lips, her eyes, her throat.

"Can we take a chance?" he whispered. She was naked now and feeling the chill of the room. Art slept with the window open. Her mind was full of him and his hands and his lips; full of numbers and fears; her mind was sensing cold and discomfort. Her mind, she told him, was now supposed to remember what day it was and then calculate the number of days since, and presumably until, her next menstruation. And her mind was also supposed to determine the odds against pregnancy (with an additional factor of her moral, psychological, and physiological attitudes toward a potential abortion). Her mind was to do all that and still feel the throb of passion and respond to the urgency of Art's swollen penis.

"I don't want to take any more chances today, Art," she said. Later, her diaphragm in place, her bioassay chores done for the night, she was ready for him. But he turned away, muttering something about spoiling a mood.

"Art, for Christ's sake. Don't make this a big thing. Just try to think it from my side. Bioassays. Chances. A new job, Jesus! My mind has been fucked up all day long. I'm in a fog. And the people I work with. Zombies in white hoods. I look at them and I try to see myself, and I wonder if I'm doing the right thing.

"I'm scared, Art. I'm scared of so many things. The job. Plutonium. You. Yes. *You.* I don't want to belong to anybody. Not now. Don't you see? I like being with you. I love making love with you. But I had problems tonight, Art. Big problems. I had more on my mind than fucking when I came home—when I came to this *place.* I can't really call it *home,* Art. I really can't."

He swung out of bed. He took a cigarette from the pack in the pocket of his shirt, which was hung on the chair. He lit the cigarette and sat in the chair, his back to the bed.

"I thought you were giving those up," she said. "See? That's part of what I mean. We don't really share a lot of ourselves. Do we?"

He did not answer.

Clutching the bedspread around her, she moved down the bed toward him. She draped the bedspread across his bare shoulder. She rubbed and kissed his neck.

"Come back to bed," she said. "Please. Let's talk a little bit more. And then let's make love. I think that's all we're good for, anyhow. And that's not so bad. That's not so bad."

He went into the bathroom and than came back to the room and got into bed. He did not speak for about two minutes.

"I *am* trying to give them up. A guy in work told me that if you carry them around like that it can make you even stronger. That was the first one I've had in about three days."

He turned toward her. They lay in each other's arms. He started to speak, but she kissed him.

In silence, they made love.

They were drinking coffee at the kitchen table. For the first time since she moved in he had packed his own lunch. Now the tempo of rushing off to work was speeding up their talk and movements.

"So you'll start looking today?" he said. "No rush, I guess? I mean. Well, you know. You can stay here forever. But I guess I know what you mean. Having your own place. But still seeing me, right?"

"Right," she said. "Seeing you, being with you, making love. But not living with you. That's all."

Within a week she was living in the west end of Caslon Wells, "the new end." Her apartment was in a complex of red-roofed, imitation-adobe buildings which welcoming roadside signs called "CW West, a Community Planned and Built by Caslon, the Energy Company."

CW West was extending the edge of Caslon Wells ever westward. To the east, in the old end, where Barbara lived and where the town had its heart, there were remnants of a past. Streets emerged from the countryside of ranches and small towns that flanked the town. The streets began as dirt roads and acquired blacktop status as they neared Route 85, the spine of Caslon Wells. The town had shaped itself by some natural process, by an uncultivated growth. To the west, however, the growth was prim and orderly. Moving westward toward the Facility, toward the plutonium economy, Caslon Wells was becoming a town that was leaving its heart behind.

Judith lived in—shuttled between—two worlds: between her need for Art and her need for herself; between the plastic plants in the lobby of CW West and the planters flowing with living green in Barbara's windows; between the stark glove boxes of P Plant and the life and the music in Carry's Place. Judith was learning to shuttle in the real, the doubled real world. She talked about her world on her tapes, which became extensions of herself. Some were so secret that she instantly erased them.

Barbara once stopped in when Judith was in the midst of what she called a wipe-out session. "Why do you do it?" Barbara asked.

"Do what? You mean, make my own gaps, like Nixon?" Judith laughed and shrugged. "I guess because there are things I only want to say to myself once, things I only want to hear once. I talk. I listen. And then I throw it away. It's like being able to throw time away." She paused. "It's on, you know. Right now, it's on."

"I didn't realize that," Barbara says on the tape.

"Yes. It's on. And, you know what, Barbara? I think I'll keep this. I don't think I have ever got your voice—your real voice—before."

By the time Judith had been on the job a month, the strike Art had predicted was imminent. She was confronted by a choice that was sharply edged: choose sides between those on the company's side and the handful of workers who were for the union.

She kept watching the safety sign, seeing the numbers rise, wondering what had happened 732 days ago . . . 750 . . . 759 days ago. She told Art she wanted to meet Dick Scinto. She would join the union only if Scinto told her what had happened on that day when the numbers had turned to zero and the counting had begun again.

20.

THE CENTER OF Caslon Wells is a stretch of Route 85 about nine blocks long, with pickup trucks and cars parked diagonally along both sides. The streets that come into town randomly from north and south end at the highway in a pattern that seems strange to the observant visitor. And then comes the realization: there are no crossroads. As a result, the two sides of the highway have become distinctly different, each with its own character.

On the south side was a grocery store and a cafe that had no bar and sold no wine, beer, or liquor. There also was a small department store, whose owner asked—and probably still does ask—where a stranger is from when a stranger buys something there. Next to the Best Buy Department Store was a drug store and a beauty shop.

On the north side was a barber shop, a pool hall whose broad window and glass door were always covered by faded green shades. Next to a Caslon gas station (named for the brand, not the town) was the sagging Highway Garage. A gleaming red wrecker was poised for accident duty; a side yard was heaped with hubcaps, tires, and rusting piles of parts.

And on one of the north-side corners was a storefront whose plateglass window had been replaced by a sheet of plywood that bore a name daubed in dripping white paint that apparently had been laid on by a three-inch paintbrush: JACKS. A professionally observant visitor to Caslon Wells would not have to be told that Jack's is on what is locally called the men's side of the highway.

The door to Jack's once had been a screendoor. Springs of wire fringed the frame, to which plywood panels had been nailed. The frame was scabbed with peeling layers of paint pasteled by time. The door handle was the metal silhouette of a Coke bottle, which innumerable hands had burnished to the color and the feel of pewter.

This was the handle that Judith Longden grasped. She pulled the door open with a knowledgeable slight hoist and stepped into a room as consistently cool and dark as a cave. To her left was a bar that Jack had built with his favorite material. The bar looked like a packing case that had lain for years in a damp warehouse. Though it had the chest-high, arm's length dimensions of an authentic bar, it trembled to the touch and few patrons dared lean on it. So as not to offend Jack, however, patrons would stand at the bar for a few moments while Jack chatted and served them. Then they would carry their cans or bottles of beer or tumblers of red wine to one of the tables.

Judith stood in the middle of the room for a moment, looking around. It was too early for the night crowd.

Late afternoon at Jack's is for the regulars: old men silently gazing at rows of Pabst Blue Ribbon bottles before them. And Jack's squaw, Mary. Jack never calls her wife, only his squaw. She is one-quarter Choctaw. No one knows for sure whether they are married. They live in a three-room bungalow a block behind the bar.

Mary can be found in Jack's almost any afternoon. She likes to talk to people. But most of the people who come into Jack's talk to Jack, not to her. Mary makes flowers out of Coors beer cans. With a small pair of shears, she slices the top out of a can and then cuts narrow strips to within a quarter-inch of the bottom. She coils the strips on a pencil, sometimes inwardly so that the tight little blossoms show the silver of the interior, sometimes outwardly so that the blooms are blotched or striped by the tan, pink, black, and white of the exterior.

Mary was gathering several blossoms into a bouquet and binding it with fine copper wire when she saw Judith. Mary smiled and nodded her head sideways, toward an inner room. As Judith passed by the table, Mary held up a bouquet. Judith took it into her hands and admired it.

The bouquet glittered in the light of an unshaded bulb that

hung on a long extension cord wrapped around an exposed beam. For a moment the bouquet glistened, and in that instant there was a pathetic beauty about Mary and what she had created. "They look so real that I can almost smell them," Judith said. She carefully placed the bouquet back into Mary's upstretched hands.

They did not talk for long, but they always did talk. Mary still likes to talk about Judith. Mary has never forgotten Judith.

Judith crossed a piece of sidewalk and passed through an open doorway to the inner room. Next to the doorway, at a window opening, Jack was passing four bottles of Pabst to two men who sat at a table.

The doorway and the window opening mark the former location of the exterior of the building. Caslon Wells is in a part of Oklahoma known as Tornado Alley, which has been hit by more tornadoes than any other area of comparable size on earth. A tornado had passed through the town fifteen years before and had leveled most of the business center. In the rebuilding, the sidewalk line had been shifted, and some of the exterior standing walls had been incorporated into the restored structures.

On one side of the far wall is a toilet, its battered door usually ajar. On the other side are two booths, their seats parallel to the far wall.

From where Judith stood near the inner doorway, the booths looked empty. Then a head suddenly jutted out from the farthest booth. She recognized Dick Scinto.

He was thirty-six, though his hair was gray and lightly flecked with black. His face was long, his brown eyes heavy-lidded and puffy. They widened for a moment as she approached, and she took the glance as a wink, an inverse wink, that momentarily annoyed her. But the flaring of his eyes was involuntary, a kind of tic. Even when she later realized this, she found herself fascinated by the effect. On a tape she made of this meeting, she says that when his eyes suddenly move, you realize that the eyes are real and they are flashing behind a mask.

She sat across from him and told him she was interested in joining the union because she wanted to get involved in making the Facility safer. She said she already had been contaminated, had thought of quitting, but also had thought that maybe there was a chance the union could make a difference.

"Art says you're quite a gal," Scinto said, not quite interrupting her, but obviously not interested in letting her have a monologue. He opened a can of beer and handed it to her. She reached across to the other can, opened it, and took a long drink.

"Quite a gal," Scinto repeated. He would later learn that Judith did not like to be called gal, girl, or lady. But even now, seeing her merely stare and not speak, he had sense enough to know he had not made a good first impression.

"All right," he said, "Art didn't really say you're quite a gal. *I* said that. OK? What Art said was that you ask a helluva lot of questions."

"Does that bother you, Mr. Scinto?"

"*Dick* Scinto. You don't call many people Mister, I'll bet. I'll bet most guys you know, you know pretty well. Right?"

"Look, I'll call you what you want—and you can call me what you want. No big deal. But let's get something straight. No bullshit about my being the good old big union president's friend. OK? I'm not here because I was dying to meet you. I'm here to decide whether I should join your goddamn union."

"I like getting things straight, Judy. I've been in unions before this one, in other places. A big town, a big shop, say, and you're big in the union, lots of time the gals just flock all around you. It sort of comes with the job in a place where there are gals on the work force, and they have special grievances. Yeah. And if they want to hop in bed with you, that's all right, too. But"—his eyes widened, and she began to understand then about the tic—"not here. I don't fuck around here, if you'll pardon my French. I got a wife and two kids. And besides that, this whole goddamn town is bugged, and all they need is to get something like that on me. So you and me can just relax. OK?"

He seemed actually, visibly, to relax. She sensed he was not used to making speeches about himself and his attitudes toward people. But he obviously enjoyed talking about the union and what went on at Caslon.

"We don't have many members, you know—the production work force, as of today, is one hundred and thirty-seven people, that's the number in the bargaining unit. And we've got a membership, as of today, of forty-four. You'd make forty-five, Judy, and we'd love to have you. I brought along an intention-to-join card. It's a good union, Judy. We protect our members, and in this business you've got to give them maybe more protection than you have to give them in a lot of other businesses, like the union I used to be in—the State, County, and Municipal Workers Union, where bad working conditions lots of time might mean short coffee breaks and not enough light to work by.

"But Art said you wouldn't join until you found out about the accident. OK. Well, when I finish telling you about the accident, I think maybe you'll understand why Art was slow in wanting to talk about it. I mean, first of all, it didn't happen to him. He wasn't there.

"I had just really got here. I was in the plant—P Plant. It was going only a couple of months. Well, I guess you can figure exactly *how* long ago, from that safety sign that you've been watching. About two years ago. P Plant had just gone into real production.

"I was going to try to organize, but I had to start out by working here. I've got an A.A. degree in industrial physics and I had a year and a half on a nuclear sub in the Navy. So I didn't have much trouble getting a job. Anyhow, they were hiring practically anybody then because they had just got that juicy contract. How the hell they got that I don't know. Or I guess I do. When Caslon wants something, it usually gets it.

"Anyhow, they had set up the line at first by getting some plutonium from the AEC, a sort of pump-priming. The idea was that they would start working with the plutonium, experimenting to see what would be the best kind of fuel-rod pellets. You know, what kind of form. Plutonium is allotropic, you know. Like carbon? You know how carbon can be like coal or like a diamond? Anyhow, they got some plutonium in, and they put it in a vault, they called it. The stuff was in little cans—like aerosol shaving-cream cans but screw-on tops—and it was racked on a thing like a kid's jungle gym, only with clamps on it. The rig made it so that the cans could be arranged in certain angles from each other.

"Now, you've got to understand that at that time things were even worse here than they are now—I heard about that missing respirator filter, Judy. It's not the first time, let me tell you. But at first things were even worse.

"They thought that since plutonium didn't put out big old

gamma rays the way uranium does, they figured that they could sort of fool around with it a little. Cut corners. The AEC guys were here when the stuff was delivered and first stored away, but they left pretty soon. And Caslon was on its own.

"I knew about plutonium, from being on a Polaris sub. I knew about safety measures. I mean, the Navy doesn't fool around with nuclear warheads. And I knew about criticality. You know about criticality?" Judy started to answer. But he had signaled to Jack for two more beers, and Jack was on his way. Scinto motioned for her not to talk until Jack shuffled off.

"Now, I trust old Jack, but not a helluva lot. Well, criticality—I'm sure you've heard of it. Critical mass. Bring two masses of uranium or plutonium together in just the right way—and *bam!* Critical mass.

"Well, there's also something called geometric configuration, and lots of people don't know about that. Plutonium has to be stored just right. You can put a little bit in a container in one end of a vault and a little bit in another container, and if they happen to be a little too close or even if the containers happen to be angled wrong to each other—angled, you know, so that the neutron flows can intercept, well, you can get criticality. And that can be the ballgame. The AEC boys, they call a situation like that a 'superprompt critical condition,' and I'll tell you, if that condition gets too superprompt, and if the geometric configuration is just right, well, there's another name for what can happen. A nuclear explosion. Small, maybe. But a lot of people would cash in.

"Now most of the Caslon types involved with plutonium are oil men to begin with, and then they got into uranium—mining it, refining it, getting chummy with the AEC, getting in on the weapons programs. And then came this chance to get into the plutonium economy—that's what they call it, you know—and they jumped. Maybe a little too fast.

"Anyhow, the accident. I hadn't been here a month before I started passing out certification-election cards. Now under the law the way you organize a place is to find out whether the workers want a union. There is a certification election, if enough workers sign up for it. And there's not a damn thing—legally, anyway—not a damn thing that management can do to the people who sign up.

"I wasn't keeping any secret about it. I was working for Caslon and I was working for the union. It was legitimate. But with the name I've got, all of a sudden, around these parts, anyway, all of a sudden, I'm the Godfather. Eye-talian. The Mafia is trying to take over the plant. There's a lot of excitement and they try to fire me. But they can't. So they take me out of the plutonium operation, for what they say is security reasons.

"But their problem is that they can't just do it right away. They had to train someone to take my place. And they send in a young guy named Walker. Paul Walker. Nice, quiet kid. Oklahoma born and bred, graduate of Oklahoma Christian. Nice, but kind of dumb. He was the nephew of a guy on the Caslon board. Learning the business.

"Well, Walker was assigned to P Plant and criticality control. He was supposed to learn my job, which was logging the plutonium in and out and watching over the vault. We were supposed to have a boss, but he spent most of the time on the first floor, hanging around with his girlfriend in the Big Room. So Walker and I were mostly on our own. It was just one shift then, you know, and when you finished for the day, you could lock up and go home and come back the next day and be pretty sure that things would be how you left them. Lot different now, with three shifts.

"On the day of the accident—it was in the last week for me to be in criticality control—I started to lock up the vault when Walker said that he wanted to stay a while and read some manuals that weren't supposed to be taken out of the criticality control area. I said OK and left.

"I was about half-way down the hall when something—I don't know what, maybe a reflection of the light, maybe a noise, I don't know. They say rats can smell radioactivity, you know. Maybe I was around the stuff so long that I smelled it. Anyway, I turned back toward the vault, and just then I heard the howler horn. There's no other sound like it. Howling. Like it would split your ears. The howler was sounding criticality.

"No one did what they were supposed to do. First of all, everybody was supposed to get out. But what happened was all hell started to break loose. People were pouring down the airlock corridor, and it wasn't air-locked any more. They were pushing me against the wall. But I managed to get to the vault and get the door open. And there was Walker, lying on the floor. He was in the middle of a blue haze. I took one look—I caught maybe 50 rads in that second—and I knew he was gone.

"He had an open container in his right hand, and it was arcing to a container low down on a rack. I was holding my breath. I didn't have time to put on a respirator. There was a foam extinguisher near the door. I aimed it at the open container, hoping to poison the neutrons, stop the flow. I laid down the extinguisher so it was squirting foam at the haze, and I grabbed Walker by the ankle and dragged him into the hall. It was empty. I turned on a shower and pushed his head under it. He lay on the floor, the water pouring down on his head, and it moved, and I knew he was alive.

"I ran down to another shower and got my hands and my head under it. Then I turned it on full blast and stood there for a couple of minutes, keeping my eye on Walker. I still figured he was all through, but I wanted to get him out of there. I knew now he wasn't as hot—that he couldn't do me much damage.

"Well, I got him to the HP room. It was empty, too. His face and neck and hands were bright red. He was dying so fast I knew he wouldn't have time to blister.

"I was beginning to feel sick. I started throwing up. I knew I had caught enough so I'd be sick for a while. I knew I wasn't going to die. Buy he was dying. He started convulsing—quick jerks, like somebody was pulling a wire inside him, and then he stopped jerking, and he was dead.

"By that time, the howling stopped and people were drifting back. I found out later that management spread the word that it was a drill.

"Well, there were two people who knew goddamn well it was no drill, and one of them was dead.

"The first guy into the HP emergency room was Bailey Orr, the Facility superintendent, and the second one was Deckman, head of security. Orr figured it out right away. He locked the door, and he started giving Deckman orders. I started going under at that point, and the next little while is hazy. I had to put together some of what happened from what I picked up later."

He finally paused. Judith had questions, but she held back, not wanting to interrupt a stream of words welling up from somewhere deep inside him and emerging almost tonelessly. The touch of cold metal to her lips made her think of the plutonium container, and she put the beer can down.

"I still don't see," she said, "why Art didn't want to tell me about this."

"I'm getting to that, or getting to what I think was making Art keep his mouth shut." Scinto leaned toward her. "He's scared, and he's afraid you might get hurt if you find out some things."

"What Art doesn't understand about me is I get scared when I *don't* know something. I've already found out about their goddamn respirators. But I don't like to find things out the hard way. Listening to you is an easy way." She wished she had not said that; it had sounded coquettish. She wanted to turn off that notion immediately, and so she blurted out: "And I know some things already."

"Like what?"

"Like there's going to be a strike."

"What else?" he snapped.

"Somebody wants to buy plutonium."

"You?"

"No. Not me."

"What's your angle?"

"I don't have an angle. I just . . ."

"Yeah. I know. You just want information. Yeah." Scinto suddenly reached across the table and wrapped each of her wrists with a circle of his thumb and index finger. He did not apply pressure; her wrists lay on his thumbs. She moved her wrists, and he coiled his other fingers so that she was lightly, painlessly pinned to the table.

"Who are you, sweetie?" He tightened his grip, but not enough to inflict pain.

"You know goddamn well who I am, Scinto. Is this how you recruit members?"

"We know they've got Pinkertons on the payroll," he said. "In production. Informers. Goddamn informers."

"You think I'm a Pinkerton? How come I drew a lousy respirator? Or was that a phony stunt?" He did not answer, so she pressed on, talking more quickly. "Is Barbara O'Neill a Pinkerton? Or Art? You sound paranoid, Scinto."

He let go of her wrists. She turned her hands palms upward, and for a moment his hands lay on hers. "Maybe I am. Maybe I think that place is going to kill me."

He pulled his hands away and rubbed them along his temples. His fingers were long, the backs of his hands were tufted with black hair. He cradled his hands in back of his head and rhythmically rubbed his arms against the dark wood of the booth. He seemed to be trying to unflex something deep inside, from where the story came. He looked at her intently, his eyes widening as he spoke. "It's bad here, Judy. Bad. Maybe you should quit."

"Why? Why should I quit?" He had more to say; she knew it.

"I think some people are lucky. Some aren't. You're not one of the lucky ones, Judy. You got a dose too fast. And you're on a piss collection again? In, what, a month?"

"This second one, they said, was just to take another look. No incident this time."

"Bullshit. You smoke grass? Take any fancy drugs? Don't answer. But don't forget they can check out those things in the bioassays. And they do. It's a shitty place to work." He looked at her evenly, boldly. "You're young, pretty. You can get another kind of job."

"You don't like women working there, do you?"

"No. But not for reasons you might think."

"Never mind what reasons I might think. What are your reasons?"

"Little bits of plutonium can stay in the body for a long time; they get breathed in or taken up with food. In a man that means he's got a pretty good chance he'll get cancer. In a woman, it means that, too. But if she gets pregnant, I don't think anybody knows what that means to the kid inside her."

"I'm not planning on having any kids. OK?"

"It could happen. Lots of things could happen."

"It won't," she said. She drained her beer. "Don't worry. It won't." She set down the can. "I've got another question. Do you ever tell your members stuff like that? About the dangers?"

"Sure. Safety programs, that sort of thing. How about another beer?"

"OK. But I've got to go to the john." She started to slide out of the booth.

"Got your piss bottle?"

"No. Damn it. In the car. Oh, the hell with it."

"Don't worry. Jack stocks them. Look on a shelf next to the mirror. Compliments of Caslon HP."

"You mean that many workers are on bioassays?"

"Well, that—and also a lot of bioassay types come into Jack's."

She was standing now, looking down at him, trying to gauge whether he was kidding. She decided he was not. "What is a bioassay type?" she asked.

"Lots of time, I mean *most* of the time, it's somebody in the union," he said. "So maybe you qualify."

"I don't sign until I hear the rest of your story."

"Fair enough. Hurry on back—and don't spill."

He told her he suspected that Orr and Deckman had talked Walker into stealing plutonium but that something went wrong. "He may have just been practicing that day. I think he was trying to find out if you could get away with it—just a little now, maybe more later. The goddamn fool—and Orr and Deckman, too, I'm sure they were in it—they all thought it was like stealing gold or jewels.

"I'm sure that the reason I was put in charge of criticality control in the first place was so they would pin any detected theft on me. As it turned out, they did hang the accident on me. They had FBI and AEC guys swarming all over me.

"I told them exactly what had happened. But I didn't tell them my suspicions. I can't even tell you how I know that there were plans to steal some of the stuff. It's not important that you know *how* I know. I figure what's important is that a lot of people—people I pick—know that I think there were people in management who were out to steal plutonium. And still are."

"But you won't tell any of this to the FBI or AEC?"

"No. Judy, paranoid is a good word for how I feel. I don't trust the feds. They've just got to know what's going on. And they don't do a damn thing. It's like—it's like they *want* people to walk off with the stuff."

"What about the strike? Is Art right? He said you thought there would be a heist during the strike."

"I never said that." His eyes flared. "Where the hell did Art get that?"

"He said it was some friend of yours."

"Bullshit. They're trying to set us up. Jesus. It just spins and spins in that place. The bastards never give up. They're always setting somebody up. I've got to talk to Art. Jesus. He should know better."

"What about you?"

"What?"

"What about you? Shouldn't you know better? You let them hang the accident on you."

"I figured it was better than cashing in the way Walker did. I told you I was out like a light for a while. I think I got hit on the back of the head. I think they were going to dump me back in the vault. I think there was plutonium already missing then, and they were going to say I stole it. And I would be dead. But a kid in HP—a guy named Miller, Chip Miller—came in then, as far as I can figure. He was coming up the road to the plant when he heard the horn. And he roared in, right through the gate without stopping. A brave guy. He ran into the room just when Orr and Deckman had me under the arms and legs, starting to carry me. He told me this later. They told him they had carried Walker and me out.

"Miller gave a quick check to Walker's body and then ran an alpha scan over me; he knew they were lying. I was in too good shape for their story to be true. But Miller's a smart guy. He didn't let on that he saw there was something phony. But they got smart, too, and I'm sure they know now that Chip knows almost as much as I do. Or suspects as much. He wanted to join the union, and I told him, 'Forget it. Things are bad enough for you already.' "

"Why don't they just fire you—and him? And everybody else who's a pain in the ass?"

"I figure it's better for them to keep us on. They can pass the word that I let an unauthorized guy alone in the vault and that there was a slight accident. They can say that Walker died of a heart attack brought on by stress. They can say he had a latent heart condition. They know that nobody will buy that. But they can say it. They may admit that there was an industrial accident—caused by *me*. Big deal, they change the number on the sign. That's my number. *I'm* the accident. They can say whatever the hell they want. They run the place. If they don't fire me, then they are big-hearted Joes who don't punish people for mistakes. If I walk out and start moaning to whoever will listen—and who's going to listen?—if I walk out, then I'm just some pissed-off type with a grudge. If I stay on, and maybe some of us have to because jobs aren't that easy to find, if I stay on, they can keep an eye on me. They can even look at our piss and shit if they want to, so they can find out what we're drinking or smoking or sniffing."

"This is coming pretty fast for me, Dick. You're beginning to sound like you're raving."

"Maybe I am. All I know is if there's a strike—and I think there will be—I'm probably a dead man. That's why I'm raving. This is one helluva place to work, Judith. Maybe you should quit it."

"I'm hung up on it now, Dick. I want to sign the card."

21.

ABOUT TWO WEEKS after Judith met Scinto, she and Art went to a Local 1010 meeting at the Cherokee Motel. The negotiating committee reported that it had not been able to get any of its demands. The committee recommended a strike vote. Dick Scinto said that in all honesty he could not urge the members to vote for a strike.

"We can't shut them down," he said. "There aren't enough of us."

Somebody asked him how he was going to vote.

"I'm going to vote to strike," he said. "I'm just talking about me, Dick Scinto, not about the president of Local 1010. I don't feel like him at all tonight. I feel like me." He began rambling about his life.

"I'm going to vote to strike," Scinto said again. "I'm going to do that because I started down a road and that's where it leads." His eyes looked around until they found Judith. "It doesn't lead anywhere, but I'm on it."

Scinto walked out of the room without speaking to anyone.

When Judith and Art left the meeting, she asked Art if he knew what had been depressing Scinto.

"Depressed?" Art said. "I thought he was just drunk."

"Have you ever seen him drunk?" she asked. "This is my first union meeting. I mean, does he usually act this way?"

"No. I guess it's the pressure. Yeah, I guess that's it." Art turned and looked at her. He remembers doing that; he rarely takes his eyes off the road. He looked at her to see her reaction as he added, "You ought to know. You ought to know what's going on with him."

Art and Judith had been regularly seeing each other, talking, smoking, making love, sometimes at her place, sometimes at his. They made no demands upon each other, but they had what Art thought was an understanding that neither of them would get involved with anyone else. They had not slept together since Judith met Scinto. One night Art had driven to her apartment on impulse and had seen Scinto's car in the parking lot.

Now, in the car, driving from the meeting, he had made his first oblique accusation. She was silent for a moment, then she said, "I've seen him a couple of times. He's been having problems. He thought I could help him."

"Yeah. I'm sure you can."

"Why don't you just stop this goddamn car, Art? I don't have to take this shit from you. I don't have to tell you this. I am not sleeping with—not fucking—Dick Scinto. The problems he has are about trusting people. In the union. He wants me to keep an eye on some things for him. I have an idea that he had asked you to do that and you turned him down. Just an idea, Art. But am I right?"

"You bet your ass you're right. I don't do spying for anybody. And let me tell you something else. He may tell you he doesn't fuck around. But he does. You're not the first girl he's asked to help him. He's got a rep for that. Only the help is that you jump in bed with him."

"So what? What if I do? It's none of your goddamn business."

"Right. None of my goddamn business. OK. It goes both ways, then. Both ways."

They drove a couple of miles without speaking.

"Listen, Art. We've got a couple of things going on here. I like you, like being with you. Let's not change that. But I've also got to talk to you about Scinto. He is a *friend,* Art. I can have a friend. So can you. OK?"

"Not exactly OK. But let's just cool it right now. What about Scinto?"

"I thought you might know something about why he's depressed, Art. Do you? Honest to God. I saw him last night. At Jack's, if you have to know. He was full of strategy. He was mad at some people. But he was up. He wasn't like this. I think it has something to do with what you mentioned to me when you first were talking about him."

"What do you mean?"

"I think maybe he's mixed up in selling plutonium."

"If he is—and I say *if*—then it's not like you think. What I hear is that he's trying to find out what's going on. That's all. He's not stealing anything. I'd swear he's not doing anything like that. And for Christ sake don't ever say anything like that to anybody. That's dangerous stuff, Judy. Goddamn dangerous stuff."

That night, not only because Scinto had asked her to help him but also because she was falling in love with him, Judith added to a tape that would be almost entirely devoted to Scinto—perhaps, in a way, dedicated to Scinto. She went over her recording of her first meeting with him, adding comments of her own. ("There are so many sides to him . . . I wonder how much he tells his wife . . .") She reported on the union meeting, her talk with Art. She seemed determined to keep a record of Scinto's involvement with the Facility. That record would become a prelude of one she would keep on herself.

The day after the union meeting, at the end of the eight-to-four, she went to her car in the Facility parking lot and opened the door. On the driver's seat was a matchbook that had not been there before. It was yellow, with a border that was supposed to look like the coils of a lariat. In black letters was JACK'S BAR, and under that, in smaller letters, was J. E. Cushing, Prop. Crowded in even smaller letters on the other side were several messages: 7 Words to Live By Are Live, Love, Learn, Think, Give, Laugh & Try . . . Please Read Psalms 19 & 1 John, Chapter 2 . . . Ladies Welcome. No Gambling.

Scinto used the matchbook-drop technique to pass the word of certain meetings to certain people because he had begun to distrust phones and some union members. He had told her about the drop, but he had never before summoned her with it.

Scinto was sitting in the back booth, facing the doorway. She sat down opposite him. He passed her a can of beer, which she opened.

"Thanks for coming. I'll make it fast. I wanted to tell you—tell someone, and it's you—what was going on with me last night. Listen. If anything happens to me, anything bad—getting killed, getting arrested, anything bad—you tell people that it was because I found out there was plutonium being stolen in this place. You can tell anybody you want, Judy. Anybody."

"When? When, Dick? When should I tell them? Dick. This is all so sudden, so screwed up. I don't know what to do. Why me, Dick? Why me?"

"Because I trust you. Because you don't have anything at stake in me, in Caslon. Nowhere. There aren't any strings on you."

"But what the hell is this, Dick? Who is doing the stealing? What kind of proof do you have?"

"I can't go into that, Judy. Not here. This goddamn place. Jack. I don't know about Jack. But I've got to talk. Listen. I got a telephone call. Just before the meeting last night. The guy said that my kids . . . my kids . . . The guy on the phone said that they'd get my kids. I said, 'Me. OK. Get me. Not them.' And the guy on the phone said, 'Fair enough, Scinto. Fair enough. You stop the shit you're into. Or we get you.' That's what he said."

"Did you call the police?"

"That's why I like you, Judy. You've got a great sense of humor. No. I didn't tell them. Just you. If anything happens, I want you to know I didn't steal anything. I want you to know, Judy." He took her hands in his. "Especially you." He squeezed her hands and suddenly stood up. "Got to go. The strike starts at midnight."

She recorded every word, spinning it out of her memory and onto the tape. Then there is a pause. And the tape begins again. This time she records not only every word but also, it seems, every thought, every feeling.

• • •

It was on the eleventh day of the strike. Scinto called her about nine o'clock at night. He told her that he wanted to pick her up in fifteen minutes at her apartment. They drove in his car to a vacant lot next to Jack's bungalow. In the lot was a van, a black van with bulging, beetle-eye plastic windows and orange, pink, and blue sunsets lacquered on the sides. The door of the van was unlocked.

Scinto had not spoken on the way to the van. Now, as he lighted a Coleman lantern and put it on a fold-down table, he said, "I sent my wife and kids to her mother's. I think for good. It's all coming together, Judy." He took a pint bottle of bourbon out of his jacket pocket, found paper cups, and poured two drinks. "I've been kind of lousy to her, I guess. Anyhow, I got the phone call. I know about these things. They won't try it when I'm with somebody."

She was sitting on the narrow bunk. He was still standing by the table. He reached the paper cup down to her. She took it and moved slightly. He sat next to her. They did not speak. They looked directly at each other, and they saw each other clearly in the lantern light.

She lay back on the bunk. There was a melting away, as soft as the light. And then an urgency. So much had been unspoken until this moment, and nothing was said as the moment appeared. They lay together afterward, talking softly, their words like the light: flickering, illuminating little, but precious. He had marked her tonight, he said. He had shown the ones who watched him that she was on his side. It was, he said, probably the most selfish thing he had ever done. But he had wanted to mark her.

"He said *mark*. That was his word," she says, her voice on the tape at once tense and steady. "I felt it like a brand, like a tattoo. I understood what he meant. The way I understood how he wanted me to tell the world he had not done anything wrong. I knew there would come a time when I was supposed to tell. But when it happened, the next day, when it happened, I couldn't tell anybody. He was right. I was marked."

She was also watched. The company report on Scinto notes:

> . . . Subject and JL entered a van registered in the name of Charles P. Miller, a Health Physics technician (Employee Number 578) which was parked in a lot in Caslon Wells next to the

> home of John E. ("Jack") Cushing, owner of Jack's Bar. CPM and JEC remained in the bar while Subject and JL were in the van, a period of approximately two hours. . .

The next day, on the twelfth day of the strike, Judith and a few other picketers were gathered around a fifty-five gallon drum set up at the intersection of Route 85 and the road to the Facility. Someone, a veteran of other strikes in other cold places, had banged a few holes around the bottom of the drum, thrown in a couple of handfuls of leaflets, and started a fire. Someone else had dumped a pile of scrap lumber next to the drum. The fire was kept going night and day. Picketing went on through three shifts, though the Facility was on only one shift.

Caslon hired extra guards and erected saw-horse barriers across the road near the intersection. Cars entering the plant were stopped there, and the people inside were asked to identify themselves. Most of the people in the cars were regular workers. The strangers were imported strikebreakers. They lived in well-guarded rooms leased by Caslon at the Cherokee Motel. The out-of-town strikebreakers ate there together and went to and from the Facility in a convoy escorted by sheriff's deputies.

Each day, at the beginning and end of the single shift, the picketers assembled near the drum and, as the strikebreakers' convoy stopped at the checkpoint, the pickets yelled "Scabs!" or "Pricks!" or "Cocksuckers!" But if Dick Scinto could get them to shut up for a moment, they would chant in ragged unison:

Union Yes!
Caslon No!

Union Yes!
Caslon No!

And, shouting louder and faster, they would move on the saw-horses.

. . . Union Yes!
Caslon No! . . .

• • •

Judith is chanting as she pushes against one of the saw-horses set up parallel to the road, creating a passage for the strikebreakers' cars. Dick is directly across from her, mouth to a white loudspeaker that is connected by a black, tightly coiled cable to a battery pack slung over his shoulder. Their eyes meet, and he takes the bullhorn away from his lips so that she can see he is smiling at her. One of the cars speeds through. Another is pulling up, blocking her view of Dick. The car stops for a moment. Then it roars through so fast that a guard steps back and almost falls. The second car passes the first, which swerves to the right, then swings in hard behind it. All this happens at the leftside edge of her vision. In front of her, where she now focuses her entire vision, Dick's arm drops. His eyes flare. His mouth gapes, but in the sudden quiet there is no sound from him. He begins to fold, knees bending, head and body bending, all of him lying there on the black pavement of the road. The saw-horse seems to dissolve as she and the other pickets rush across the road to him. He rolls toward the culvert. Someone grabs a lapel of his sheep-skin coat. He lies face up at the edge of the culvert. There is a round red hole in the front of the coat, and the grimy white shearling that edges the coat is turning red. She bends over him and opens the coat. She looks away from the pulsing red spreading across the denim. A gold cross glints in the mat of black hair at the V of his shirt, where the flesh is brown and sweaty and unstained by red. That cross had swung over her last night. That had happened just as suddenly as this. She looks at his face. His eyes are still flared.

She testified at the coroner's inquest. She told what she had seen from the opposite side of the road. She was asked if she could name all of the union members who were present at the picketing site. She said she could not but that she could name many, if that was necessary. She was told to just answer the questions. She was asked if it was not possible that Mr. Scinto had been shot from her side of the road, perhaps by someone who was standing nearby. She said that was impossible. She was asked how she could say it was impossible when she had just testified that she could not name all of the people there. She replied that she *knew* that the shot had been fired from a car. She was asked how she *knew*, and she retold what she had seen from the opposite side of the road. She was asked if she could name . . .

The coroner's verdict was that Richard Anthony Scinto had been shot by person or persons unknown. Death was attributed to a gunshot wound caused by the entrance into the body of a flat-nosed or hollow-point bullet which severely damaged vital organs. The bullet was apparently fired from a handgun, and expert testimony indicated the probability that the handgun was a Smith & Wesson .44 Magnum revolver. The sheriff's deputies who were present at the scene testified that no weapon of that type or any other unauthorized handgun was found in a thorough search of the cars that passed the deceased just prior to the shooting. Nor did the deputies' search disclose any unauthorized weapons on the persons of the occupants of the cars nor in the immediate area. It was the conclusion of the coroner that, while the occupants of the cars could be ruled out as suspects in the homicide, further investigation of certain persons along the roadside would be in order.

She had wanted to say that he had done nothing wrong, that he had believed he would be killed because he had suspicions about . . . About what? No one at the inquest had raised the issue of motive. No one seemed to want to know why he died. And she did not want to start suggesting what it was that he had *not* done. She knew that whatever she said would be twisted. She had been marked. She had been marked as being on his side. And now she was, without quite knowing why.

22.

THE LEADERSHIP OF the national union, which had not taken much notice of the small Local 1010 before, reacted immediately after news reports about Scinto's murder reached the headquarters of the union in Washington. The president of the union, who had never heard of Dick Scinto, announced that the Nuclear Workers Union would pay a $25,000 reward for the arrest and conviction of Scinto's murderer. "He was assassinated because he was a union leader," a union press release said. "We will avenge his death. And we know that the rank and file of Local 1010, despite their anger and grief, will not falter. The strike will go on. Our just demands will not be changed. Dick Scinto will not have died in vain."

The union president then conferred with his vice president for public relations and with two representatives from the outside public relations firm on retainer to the union. The consensus was to refrain from any more public moves until the union received confirmation that Scinto had indeed been killed because he was a union leader. There was always the possibility, as the cautious public relations vice president put it that "he was up to something else, like screwing somebody's wife." Harry Skirvin, as a vice president who watched over locals in the Southwest, was sent to Caslon Wells and told to find out what was happening out there. He was also expected to keep the strike going as long as he could, at least for public relations purposes.

When he walked into his room at the Cherokee Motel, he found a file folder containing a report on Dick Scinto. The report would become smudged and wrinkled from being passed around so much, and it no longer resembles the pristine report Skirvin found that day. The report was so neat and so well typed (on an IBM Executive) that he had no doubt it was not only a Caslon product but also undoubtedly from the front office. There was no attribution for the collection of rumors and quoted statements about Scinto's rabble-rousing and occasional flings. Skirvin had no reason to know whether any of this was true, and he had no reason to care. He noticed that a Judith Longden appeared in the report shortly before the strike started. Harry vaguely wondered if she might be the source of some of the "confidential information." Much of the twenty-six-page report had the feel of an informer; someone in the union, Skirvin thought.

Though nothing in the report itself initially interested Skirvin, he was intrigued by pages of a transcript stapled to the back of the folder as if they were an afterthought. The transcript consisted of a series of Q's and A's, with the source of the Q's not identified; the first A had been crossed with a line and *Scinto* had been written in. Skirvin could think of a dozen reasons why the transcript was probably a fake, but he began reading.

Q. You were in Mexico City on July 12, 13, and 14.

A. So what?

Q. You talked to a man named José Arteaga-Castillo.

A. I didn't talk to anybody but waiters, bartenders, people in shops. My wife and I were on vacation there.

Q. Do you know this man by his alias, Cesario Cortina—or as Cesar?

A. I don't know him by any name. What the hell is this?

Q. Did Cesar suggest that you meet him again in Ciudad Acuna, Mexico?

A. I don't know anybody named Cesar.

Q. And did Cesar suggest that you bring some of the stuff?

A. What do you mean, stuff? You trying to hang a drug thing on me?

Q. The stuff Cesar was referring to was plutonium.

A. Oh, Jesus. You're on that again.

There was a break in the transcript. The Q. and A. resumed, but the typing was different.

• • •

Q. State your full name.
A. José Arteaga-Castillo
Q. Are you also known as Cesario Cortina, and as Cesar?
A. Yes. Yes. Those are my other names.
Q. And why do you have other names? Is it part of your job?
A. Yes. Part of my job.
Q. And what is your job, Señor Arteaga-Castillo?
A. I am an undercover agent for the Mexican Government, for the *Federales*.
Q. Is that all you do? I mean, do you have another job?
A. Yes. I am the manager of a night club in Mexico City.
Q. I am showing you a photograph. Do you remember seeing this man in your club?
A. Yes, yes I do.
Q. And when was that?
A. In July, I think. Yes, in July.
Q. And how did this man identify himself? Did he have a name?
A. He called himself Jonesy, just Jonesy. But I know it was not his name.
Q. Now, in your own words, what did Jonesy tell you?
A. He told me that he had heard around that I was a good person to see about . . . about handling things. I ask him what kind of things. He said hot stuff, very hot stuff. I told him I still didn't know what he meant. And he said that the hot stuff was very valuable stuff from a nuclear re—a nuclear machine. I tell him again I didn't know what he meant. And he said it was stuff that you could make big bombs, atomic bombs, out of.

There was no more to the transcript.

At their first meeting, Harry Skirvin gave the report and transcript to Judith. Harry immediately dropped his theory that she was an informer. (He never did identify an informer in the union.) He knew that she was beginning to trust him, too. He felt that she was seeing in him an extension of Dick Scinto. He had seen in the report mention of the visit to the van by Scinto and JL, and he began wondering how far she would go in identifying him with Scinto.

After reading the transcript, Judith told Harry she agreed with him that the transcript was probably a fake. But she told him that Scinto had expected to be accused of stealing plutonium, probably because he had uncovered evidence of plutonium thefts by management.

She told Harry that, at Scinto's suggestion, she was keeping a journal about what was going on inside the Facility. She said that Scinto had asked her to proclaim his innocence if he were ever accused of a crime. Harry, stunned by the emergence of plutonium theft as an issue in what he had thought was simply a strike, told her not to proclaim anything. She would be doing more for the memory of Dick Scinto, he said, if she would help keep the strike going.

Harry had underestimated her.

"Bullshit," she said. "The strike is over, and you know it. All you have to do is accept what they offered in the first place. Which sure wasn't much. The big thing here is not the strike but what this goddamn company is getting away with."

She waved her journal at him, and he knew he was going to be spending more time than he had planned in Caslon Wells. Like Scinto, she had chosen a collision course with the company. For the union's sake, Harry would have to keep his eye on Judith Longden. But he had been a union professional long enough to know that whatever the company had been doing, it would have to slow down after a murder on its premises. He bet himself that it would be about three months before there was a collision.

this once to you, Miss Longden"—his gaze swept the table—"and to everyone else. The amount of plutonium missing from the Caslon Facility is sufficient for the manufacture of several nuclear weapons of substantial power."

Judith felt that the others had not shown a sufficient reaction; she assumed that Rosen already had made this statement to Orr and probably to the others. Her heart was pounding, her hands trembling. She wanted to hide her hands; she pressed them against her thighs.

"Remember. I said that plutonium is the dominant problem. There are others. We are involved here with a constellation of problems, Miss Longden." He picked up the notebook in his right hand and slapped it against his left hand again and again, as if he was applauding an event he was seeing in his mind. "Not the least of these problems, Miss Longden, is your physical condition. There are certain . . . classic . . . methods in which small, valuable objects—diamonds, for example, or narcotics—can be smuggled."

"Oh my God," Judith said. "Are you saying that I put . . . plutonium in my body?"

"I am *not* saying that, Miss Longden. What I am saying, however, is that you are going to be placed on a full bioassay program, beginning immediately, and that you are going to be given a full-body count at Los Alamos on Sunday. You are to make no mention to anyone about the MUF. You are familiar with the term?"

She nodded. *Nuclear Material Unaccounted For after processing*. It was a terrifying phrase that could not be uttered, and so MUF had been devised as a way to say the unutterable.

Rosen signaled to Orr and his secretary, ostensibly to put the room on record again. He waited a moment and then resumed. "Yes, the dominant problem is plutonium contamination. Dr. Garvey here is particularly concerned, from an occupational hazard standpoint, and of course, the AEC is concerned because of the plant-safety questions involved. And so, Miss Longden, we have prepared this report, a kind of outline of the events leading up to your possible contamination.

"I have found that in making an inquiry into the causes of something, it is best to start with a chronology. We would like you to read this chronology and help us trace the possible contamination. You will recognize that the situation is urgent, I am sure, and will understand why it is necessary to begin as soon as possible."

Judith nodded.

"For the record, please," Rosen said.

"What?"

"For the record, Miss Longden. Do you agree to go over this chronology with Dr. Garvey or myself?"

"Yes. Yes, I do. And now can I go to work? And I need my ID. Feeney has my ID. And a dosimeter. I need a dosimeter. For the lab. I really have to get going. Really."

She heard herself speaking with an exaggerated air of politeness; she saw herself standing in front of Miss Purcell in the tenth grade and asking permission to leave English Comp early so that she could try out for *A Midsummer Night's Dream.* She won a part, Helena. A page of the script appeared in her mind, with words underlined, just as she had learned them:

> *Hel.* I will *not* trust you, I,
> Nor longer stay in your *curst* company.
> Your *hands* than mine are quicker for a fray,
> My *legs* are longer though, to run *away.* [EXIT.]

She discovered that she was mumbling, that some of the words had slipped out of her mind and across her lips. She leaned to steady herself, but somehow her fingertips could not quite reach the table. She saw a blurred movement at the side of her vision. Ann Garvey had leaped up, grabbed Judith's right shoulder with just enough force to keep her from falling forward, and eased her back into the chair. The move was so swift and graceful the others did not realize that Judith had lost consciousness for about three seconds. Still on her feet, Garvey pulled off her black-rimmed glasses. Dangling on a finely wrought chain, they heaved to the tempo of her breathing and her finger-tapping as she glared across the table at Rosen. "This woman has had enough of a day, Dr. Rosen," she said. "This was supposed to have been an inquiry into a personal contamination, not an interrogation. I'm sure you have further discussions here. But I am concerned with Miss Longden, not the Facility. I want to take her home."

"I have no home," Judith said, the words flat and impersonal.

"Well, where are you staying?" Garvey asked.

"At Barbara's. My friend Barbara's."

"Then we'll go there, all right?"

"Yes. Thank you."

Doors opened and closed, and she was standing next to Ann Garvey, who turned to Judith and smiled. It seemed like a long time since anyone had smiled at her.

She began telling Garvey about Miss Purcell and *A Midsummer Night's Dream . . .*

Judith, accompanied by Garvey, stopped in at Health Physics, down the hall from the Big Room.

"Bioassay kits for four days, please," she said, arbitrarily picking a number of days. The technician on duty, Chip Miller, stood behind what employees called the check-in counter. To the left and right of the counter were doors that led to the check-out counters—the examining rooms and the bioassay samples depository.

"Again, Judy?" Miller asked. He was a friend, and she knew he worried about her just as she worried about him. She had stayed up with him all one night, listening to his story—premed, medical school, Vietnam, heroin, detoxification—and, that night, another bummer on mescaline. He looked Garvey over swiftly; the glint in his eye said to Judith, *Narc.*

Judith thought she could ease his suspicion about Garvey by introducing her as a doctor, but "from Washington" would have been enough to make Chip vault over the counter. So Judith merely smiled and said, "I hope it won't be anything this time, Chip. Anyhow, I'm taking my business to the bigtime HP—Los Alamos."

Garvey walked over to a wall rack and was looking through a pile of government leaflets, one of which she had written. Miller whispered to Judith, "Watch it out there, Judy. That's Secrets City." He reached under a counter and handed her the kits.

Judith insisted that she was recovered and able to drive. In the parking lot she gave a last assurance that she would indeed drive carefully—and slowly, so that Garvey could follow in her rented car.

When Judith opened the door of her car, she saw one of Jack's matchbooks on the seat.

She drove to Barbara's and waited in the car, engine running, until Garvey parked behind her, got out, and walked up to the VW. Judith reached across to open the passenger window and yelled, "Barbara's home, I see her bike. See you in a while." She gunned the engine and sped away.

Harry Skirvin was standing by the frail plywood bar at Jack's when she walked in. He picked up two cans of Coors, nodded his head toward the inner doorway, and led her to the farthest booth. He handed a can to her, unopened.

He told her that a contact in the AEC had told him about the raid. He said he had someone in the union drop the matchbook in the VW. He did not give the man's name, and she did not ask for it. In fact, she spoke little, and he remembers wondering at that moment whether she trusted him.

He softly tapped his can of beer on the dark, stained wood. "Judy," he said, "I think you may be in a jam." He waited for a response. There was none. "Maybe I should say *we* are in a jam. A lot of things are coming together."

"I can see why *I* might be in a jam," she said. "I'm the one going to Los Alamos—I guess you know about that, too. I guess you know that they think I might be poisoned. And Art and Barbara."

She was not good at concealing bitterness, or many other emotions, Harry thought.

"Let's get out of here," he said. Taking her left hand in his right hand, he started to rise. He felt her resistance, and he sat down again, still holding her hand.

"Where are we supposed to go?" she asked.

"I'm at the Cherokee."

"How's your wife?"

"That's not fair, Judy. What's past is past. I don't think you really want to know. But the fact is we're separated. Not divorced. Trying to work it out."

"What about your son . . . Frank?"

"Fred. He just entered Cornell. My daughter's still at

home—she's sixteen—and she's taking it pretty well."

"Sorry," she said. "That was a cheap shot. I guess I was trying to tell you that I . . . I don't want to get involved with you again. Not now, Harry." She took a sip, put down the beer, smiled, and said, "Nothing personal."

They both laughed.

"Believe me, Judy, when I said let's go, I had no intention of . . ."

"Let's not push it too far, Harry. Don't tell me you're *not* interested. That's almost as bad, you know."

"Christ, Judy. You can twist things into more goddamn shapes. I'm here—I flew all the way here—to help you. I wanted to be here before you went to Los Alamos, and I want to be here when you get back. That's when this will all come together."

"When *what* will come together, Harry? For God's sake, can't you see? I'm in the middle of something I don't understand."

"Remember the last time we were here?" She looked up at him sharply. He acted as if he had not noticed. "We were winding up the strike. Trying to make something out of nothing. The union was falling apart. You needed help then. You need help now. I came here—"

"You didn't come here just to help me, Harry. You came here to help your goddamn union. Christ, if you knew how much bullshit help I've been getting. Christ. The cops wouldn't help. Art wouldn't help. Barbara doesn't know from anything. The goon squad. Feeley. B.O. Deckman. Every son of a bitch you can name—and two new ones from Washington. And now you. All of you bastards who are going to help me." She had drained her beer, and she stood up and waved to Jack for another. "Oh, Harry, if you only knew how phony you seem. How phony you all seem."

"I'm sorry you're feeling persecuted, Judy. And probably paranoid. I can't blame you. I know you must be half-nuts. I can't blame you for being pissed at me, either. Just about every time I show up in this town, it's meant trouble. But hang in there, please. This isn't going to last forever."

"OK. Judy's calm now." Two more beers appeared. "Thanks, Jack." She waited until Jack was behind the bar again. "I'm sure you can help, Harry. But, please, no more bullshit. You work for the union."

"Judy, you practically *are* the union in this town right now, don't you realize that?"

"No, Harry. Let me get something straight with you. Right now I am thinking only about me. Not you. Not Local 1010. Just me. Now if you want to help *me,* fine. But I need to know that it's me that's being helped. Get it?"

"Got it. How can I help?"

"Well, without getting old Jack too interested," she said, "I am going to snuggle up to you and put something in your pocket." She shoved the douche bottle into his pants pocket and told him about it.

"I'd like the stuff analyzed, Harry."

"Done," he said. "Have you told anybody else about this?"

"Just Barbara. Why?"

"I'm wondering if you should tell the AEC: the people from the AEC—I assume that's who you were talking about—the two from Washington."

"One's from the AEC—Rosen? Sam Rosen? A tough guy who doesn't look it. The other one's a woman, Ann Garvey. But she's not from the AEC. She's from O-Sha-Hay? Occupational . . ."

"Occupational Safety and Health Administration. Yeah. They have a fairly big shop, but I thought I knew just about everybody in it . . . But Garvey? Don't know her. I'll check her out. What else?"

"Do you know about a thick report—a federal report, I think—called *Nuclear Crimes*?"

Harry turned, frowned, and waved his hand at shoulder height to get her to lower her voice. "Sure. I've heard of it. It was done by a think tank for the AEC. It was supposed to be classified, but it was leaked by a senator. Turner, I think. What about it?"

She told him what she had seen and her suspicion that she may have been deliberately shown it.

"I'll look it up. And the bottle. And Garvey. But not by phone. I don't trust the phones—or much of anything else—in this town. What about that book in your lap? What's that?"

She told him what it was and what she was told to do. He nodded, as if little or nothing of what she had told him was a surprise.

"Play along. Do what they say. It may help when they start asking questions at Los Alamos. Get the whole story straight in your head. And don't forget, you've got some things of your own. They didn't grab that, did they?"

"No. They're hidden. I put . . ." She hesitated.

Harry held up a hand. "Don't tell me. Just have it ready when we need it."

"And when is that going to be? And is it going to help me—or the union?"

"Judy, it's going to help everybody. Just about everybody. You're not just going to be talking to me when you get back from Los Alamos."

"I don't get it. Who will I be talking to?" Suspicion and resentment sharpened her voice.

"The *Washington Post,* Judy. The *Washington Post.* They're sending a reporter. I'm meeting him here Monday night. That's when we'll get our—*your*—story out. So tomorrow, do your homework, just like they told you to. Only you'll be doing it for yourself, not them."

She nodded. Harry looked at her and saw her drifting from him, toward some point where he was not invited. He knew there would be no more talk. He said he thought it would be a good idea to call it a night.

Harry insisted on walking her to the car, and she insisted that he not follow her to Barbara's in his rental car. She didn't need him tonight. She just wanted this day to be over. She adroitly managed Harry's goodnight so that it became a quick but friendly hug and a placid kiss. Then she got into the car, jiggered the wires, and at the first sound of the engine, hit the accelerator for a fast takeoff.

She slowed at the highway and turned east. Hers was the only car in sight. Through her rearview mirror she could see the lights of a car as it swung out of a parking space that looked to be about in front of the drug store, nearly across the highway from Jack's. Harry. Damn him. He was going to follow her. She decided not to speed up and give him an excuse to make a game out of chasing her. But the lights were growing large and closing on her fast. It was a pickup, not a car. She thought she saw the silhouette of two men. The pickup's headlights drilled into her mirror.

She wrenched the steering wheel to the right. The VW's left wheels lost the road for a split-second. She felt the car begin to tilt. She touched the brake to increase the friction of the right wheels on the road. Now, four wheels on the ground, she swung the steering wheel sharply right. The VW skimmed across a short stretch of grass between the road and the culvert. The VW nosed into the culvert and swept along like a toboggan down a chute.

The instant her lights picked up a slab bridging the culvert ahead, she touched the brakes again, nudged the steering wheel to the left, and spun out of the culvert. Her right rear wheel thumped down on the slab as she cleared it. She skidded across the grass, tapped the brakes, eased the wheel through a sinuous left-and-right, and was on the highway. Ahead, the pickup's tail lights were tiny red eyes vanishing into darkness.

She thought of pulling off the road. But her hands held the wheel like claws; her arms, shoulders, legs, feet—so fluid and quick before—now were sore and leaden; the thud of her heart echoed in her throat and stomach and back of her skull so that her body seemed thin-walled and hollow. She could not stop because if she did she would fall apart and not be able to start again.

She turned off at the next side road and traveled parallel to Route 85 until she was opposite Barbara's street. She shot across the highway, circled Barbara's block to look for strange cars or the pickup, and pulled into the driveway along the side of Barbara's house.

Her head was pounding, just as it had been this morning. She felt as if she was going to vomit. She had to hold herself against the door with one hand while her finger stabbed in the darkness for the doorbell. The porch light came on and she saw Barbara standing like a dark shadow in the hall. Barbara yanked open the door and started to tell Judith that Garvey had gone and was angry and that they both had worried about her and where did—. Then Barbara stopped talking.

She led Judith through the living room to the bedroom. Judith sat on the edge of the bed and struggled to untie the alien blue sneakers, trying to remember how they had come to be on her feet. She peeled off the pink strangeness of the pants suit, whose origin she also could not quite remember as she fell into a sleep, her body diagonally across the bed.

Somehow, the angle of her body became a vector of a dream, and her body was a car veering off a road, off a bed.

Her body twitched and her head filled with light, two lights burning into the head of the body, into the head of the car—going off the road, off the bed. There was a click. The light was gone, and in the sudden darkness, she perceived dull flecks of colors behind her eyes, and she was finally asleep.

28.

Saturday, October 17:

She awoke not knowing where she was, but she felt no anxiety. She lay still for a few moments, waiting for her mind to come about. That was what her father called it, coming about. He had taken her sailing a few times in Corpus Christi, and he would shout, "Coming about!" She would duck as the boom swept over her and the *Snipe,* no longer one with the wind, would be still. Then the boat would come into the wind and the mainsail would tremble, and the boat would heel, sailing again full and fast. Judith first had learned then that a boat was a *she.* She wondered why, and her father had said that when she woke up she sometimes was like a sailboat coming about: her eyes were open but her mind was blank—and then, from nowhere, came the wind, and she was under way.

In the half-wakeness, she remembered the *Snipe,* remembered her father, and, coming about, she swung out of bed. The *Snipe* and her father and the coming about would be part of what she would remember and record today.

She took the recorder from the closet and started talking to it. She had sorted out what day it was and where she was. And the journal. The journal would be important today. She put the recorder on Barbara's bureau. Then she took the small green notebook from the pocket of the pants on the floor, found a pencil on the bureau, and wrote, "Oct. 17. A day to put it together."

She remembered that she had to use the bioassay kits that were in the car. She put on the pink pants, found a blue sweater in Barbara's closet, and padded, barefoot, to the kitchen. Barbara was there, starting breakfast.

Judith made a rapid roundtrip to the car and back, and holding up the bioassay kits as silent explanation to Barbara, hurried into the bathroom. She emerged carrying a bottle of urine and a bag of feces. Barbara pointed to a large, white, translucent-plastic box on the drainboard of the sink. She had been through bioassay programs herself.

Judith put the bottle and bag into the box, placed an air-tight cover on it, put the box on the bottom shelf of the refrigerator, and sat down at the table before a mug of black coffee and a tall glass filled with a frothy liquid the color of old ivory.

"I forget its name," Judith said. "And what's in it."

"Lassi. It's Indian—*Indian* Indian, not—"

"Right. And what's in it?"

"Buttermilk, some ice, a banana, dash of vanilla, brown sugar—"

"And nuts. I can taste nuts. It's not bad. Aren't you having any?" Judith put down the half-filled glass.

"Had mine already. I'm trying to get organized."

"For what?"

"Going over the chronology. Ann . . . Ann Garvey told me about it. She was really peeved with you, you know."

"Pissed, Barbara. Why can't you say pissed?" She took another long gulp; the lassi felt cool and, although she would not use the word, pleasant. "Peeved! What the hell do I care if she was peeved?"

"She expected to have a chance to talk a little with you last night. And then you zoomed off, leaving her standing there."

"You're beginning to sound like my mother, Barbara." She drained the glass. "Now, my mother wasn't bad. I loved—love—my mother. But she sure did yell at me a lot, especially at breakfast. She would . . ." Something, probably Barbara's mention of zooming off, summoned up the pickup truck on the highway. For a moment she could feel the thud of her heart, as if she were feeling a memory.

"What's wrong?" Barbara asked, startled at Judith's sudden paleness.

"Something that happened last night. I . . . I wasn't remembering it. Remembering other things, but not that."

She told Barbara about the pickup and the lights burning into the mirror. Barbara listened without asking any questions.

When Judith finished, Barbara said, "Drunk. It could be a drunk. Or some nut who was not drunk but wanted a good time scaring a woman. A woman looks all alone out there. Once a guy pulled up alongside me on the motorcycle and his buddy leaned out and grabbed my arm. I hit the brake, and the pull of the truck broke his grip. I almost wiped out. But I managed to keep her up, and I just took off and passed that pickup."

Barbara poured the dregs of the lassi into Judith's glass. "So," Barbara said, "I wonder if something like that wasn't what happened to you last night. I mean, no connection with what's going on at the Facility. Not everything has to be connected, you know."

"OK. You might be right. All I really know then is that I was scared as hell. It's making a wreck out of me, Barbara."

"You look all right to me. Pale. Maybe a little too thin. But I'll bet you didn't take any of those pills last night."

"Tranquilizers? No. I don't have anything."

"And you look it. Your eyes. You look clear-eyed."

"Now I'm beginning to think you *are* my mother."

Barbara shrugged. She started cleaning up and motioned Judith to stay seated. It was always difficult to help Barbara, especially in her kitchen.

"We better set up," she said, when she had finished at the sink. "Ann Garvey will be here around noon."

"Do you think she is who she says she is?" Judith asked.

"What makes you say that? She seemed OK to me. Smart. Concerned. Asking questions about women in the shop."

"Harry said he hasn't heard of her and he knows a lot of people in that outfit of hers."

"Well, he might not know her because she's a specialist in women workers, and his union isn't famous for having a lot of women in it. She's legitimate. I'm sure."

"Did you find out what she's a doctor of?"

"She's a psychologist."

"A goddamn shrink."

"No. A psychologist. She tests people, finds out how people feel about their jobs, working conditions, that sort of thing. I think she's more interested in what Caslon may be doing to you, and the rest of us, than what you may be doing to Caslon."

"Why do you say that—'doing to Caslon'?"

"I don't know. I guess because you've been, well, sort of keeping track of things there for the union. Haven't you?"

"Yes. But I'm not doing anything illegal. You know that, don't you? I'm not committing any crimes."

"Well, who said that you were?"

"Nobody—not exactly. But I know there is something big going on. That guy Rosen said there's a lot of plutonium missing. I'm not supposed to tell you that."

Barbara looked as if she were about to speak. She turned away and went into the living room. Judith followed her. Barbara set up a card table and then went into the kitchen for two chairs. She picked up two, but Judith managed to get one away from her. They put the chairs on opposite sides of the table. Judith went off to get her copy of the chronology, and when she came back to the table, Barbara was sitting at it. Judith sat in the other chair and opened the chronology.

"Are you going to be asking me questions, too?" Judith asked.

"No. I'm sort of sitting in for Dr. Garvey. I thought . . . I thought you might want to sort of practice."

"OK. Ask me a question, doctor."

"Judy. The stuff in the chest upstairs." She broke off, as if to wait for Judith to say something.

"There's nothing dangerous in the chest, Barbara, I swear it. But when we get back from Los Alamos, I'll take the stuff off your hands. I'll have a place—a person—to give it to." She told Barbara about the meeting set up with the reporter. Barbara nodded solemnly, glad to hear the news. Barbara did not like anything she did not understand.

They talked a little about the trip to Los Alamos. Barbara did not seem to be worried; to her, health was basically a psychological phenomenon. At Caslon, her rationale was that she would expose herself to a hostile environment almost no matter where she worked, but she could offset some of the probable damage with a sensible, nourishing diet.

"I suppose what we'll be eating there is that government cafeteria junk. I think I'll bring a survival kit. Speaking of which—" When Barbara said that, it meant she was about to make a suggestion. So, at *which,* Judith, whose attention had been drifting, came about. "Speaking of which, it looks as if you're not going to be able to get to Tulsa for clothes. Would you trust me to pick out something? You can't keep wearing that pants suit."

"OK. I guess just duplicates. A pair of jeans. Prewashed, if you can. Slightly flared. Twenty-four, twenty-five waist, or small. I don't know how they come. I guess a couple of shirts—the plainer, the better, size seven, I guess. None of that polyester crap—well, you know that. Maybe a turtleneck. Yellow, solid—like golden?—yellow. And how about a navy blue one, too?"

"You want that, you may have to get some polyester, maybe cotton-polyester."

"You judge. OK? But can you spend this much? I haven't cashed the check, and—"

"I can handle it. Don't worry. No gifts. What about shoes?"

"I just need something temporary. But I do need something. Maybe moccasins, the kind that have laces like shoes have. Size five or five and a half. And some cotton bikinis. Size small, and cheap. No bra."

"You think you want a dress, or a skirt and blouse or something?"

"A dress? Hell, we're only going out in the middle of the desert. You're not figuring any big times out there, are you, Barbara? I mean, you're not bringing a dress, are you?"

"Just checking." Barbara smiled, trying to remember the last time she had seen Judith in a dress. "OK. I better get started. No need for me to be here when Ann Garvey gets here, and I can do some chores. Saturday is when I go to the farmers market. I guess your car would be best. OK? The key! Maybe I'll be able to get one. At the garage I use. It's on my way. But for now you'll have to show me how to start it."

Judith went into the living room and sat down at the card table. She opened the blue notebook to the first page, which read:

LONGDEN, JUDITH A. EMPLOYEE NUMBER 807.

" . . . I've looked at that page as long as I can," this part of the Saturday tape begins. "And I think, 'That's not who I am.

Not who I am. And what I am is not what they think I am. I'm not Employee Number 807, and I'm not putting plutonium in myself, and putting it in my . . . my deepest self . . ."

She talks about herself, about her feeling that where she works has become where she is. But her monologue gets back to Rosen's implied accusation.

"They all want to put something there. Harry, Art, Michael, Dick, Jeff, they all did. Harry again. They all want to put it there. And now they're saying I put that stuff, that awful stuff there. 'Step on a crack. Break your mother's back.' Put it in your crack. Break your company's back . . . 'Nuttin' hot there,' Feeley says. He could put the tube up. Squirt. Squirt. Put it up . . ."

She goes back to her first days at the Facility. She skips through her journal, reading excerpts. She speculates about Bailey Orr's sex life. She talks about her father a great deal, her mother a little. She is reeling through experiences near and far, untethered to the reality of anything more than perception, when the phone rings. The tape keeps spinning. The phone rings again. She answers.

"Who? Who are you? Oh, Harry. Yeah. Yeah. No. I'm all right. It's hard to explain. Like I was asleep. And you woke me up. No. Not really. *Like—as if*—I was—*were*—asleep."

Harry said he might not be able to see her before she went to Los Alamos. He reminded her he would be meeting her on Monday, at eight o'clock on Monday. "With my friend. Remember my friend? He'll be here with me."

"Your friend?"

She sounded vague to Harry, as if she did not quite know where she was. Trying to talk in some kind of code, he gave her another reminder: "And you'll bring your records? The records? He'll enjoy hearing them."

And that is when she said, "I'll bring them. I'm sure he'll like *Way Out in Idaho.*"

29.

THE TAPE FLICKS on and off as she awaits Garvey. She keeps talking about her life and her body, sometimes in terms that are so personal as to be incomprehensible. At other times, her words are sharply focused on plutonium and how it must be poisoning her.

" . . . Never. Always. Never. Always. In and out. Out and in. Boxes suck. Finger in. Finger out. Art think's it's there. He thinks it. Cancer of the cock . . ." The words can be spun through a listening mind again and again until the listening mind shares her perception.

Interspersed, usually in a distant, melancholy voice, is her description of her day. The tape remains on through much of the conversation with Garvey and later with Barbara. The microphone apparently is voice-actuated. There is enough on tape to reconstruct that day of searching.

She went to Barbara's closet and pulled out the square black wooden chest. She jiggled one of the brass hasps, listening for a click. The false bottom of the chest snapped open enough for her to get her fingers under the edge and lift it up on hidden hinges. She examined the material, took out the Scinto report, closed the false bottom and the chest, and pushed it back into the closet.

She returned to the living room and began reading the chronology Orr had presented to her. The doorbell rang. She welcomed Ann Garvey with an apology for running out on her the night before. Judith took Garvey into the living room. They sat at the card table.

"I've been reading the chronology and I got as far as the strike," Judith said. "At that point, I think, you need more than the company's chronology to know what was going on. I want to tell you some things." She said she would be selective about what she told, but that she would not lie and she would withhold little. She also said that she had been taping her thoughts about what had been going on, and she wanted to continue, taping her discussion with Garvey.

"Fair enough," Garvey said. "Let's start with the chronology. It doesn't say all that can be said, I'm sure. It looked to me as if someone was trying to build a case against someone who was building a case. Do you see what I mean?"

"You're saying that I was building a case and the company saw it—sees it—and has put together this book to show what I was up to. Or what the company thought I was up to."

"Right," Garvey said. She fished her copy of the notebook out of her bag. "There's also something else suggested here, between the lines." Garvey paused, as if to wait for Judith to ask a question.

"I think it's called nuclear diversion," Judith said. "Stealing plutonium. That's why I wanted you to see this report on Scinto. I guess you know who he is and what happened to him."

Garvey nodded.

"OK," Judith continued. "I think that this report on Scinto is probably a lot like some report somewhere on me. I think that this blue book they've allowed us to read is *part* of the report on me. They either haven't finished making up the report on me yet or they haven't shown it to me or, I assume, to you."

"They know I'm supposed to be here from Washington for reasons of safety, occupational safety," Garvey said. "Sure, they've talked to me about you. They've given me the impression that you're a troublemaker, a crybaby about contamination—running to HP with complaints, the sort of stuff I hear all the time."

Garvey leaned back, tipping the chair on its rear legs. She saw Judith flinch—the instinctive gesture of a small person who sees a large person tip a chair—and shifted forward. The chair firmly on the floor, her arms firmly on the table, and her head and bosom thrusting forward, she began speaking as if she were testifying at a Congressional hearing: "Most people we deal with don't like the Occupational Safety and Health Administration. We remind the unions that their members are risking their health and maybe their lives, and the members don't want to hear it. We warn management that it is making money at the expense of their workers' health, and management doesn't want to hear it. Ralph Nader says we don't try hard enough, and George Meany says we try too hard.

"There are some industries where you wonder how anybody can work at all, how anybody who calls himself human can hire a worker. I've seen asbestos workers going upstairs backwards. You know why? Because they can hardly breathe; they've all but lost their lungs. They can take only one stair at a time. Then they have to sit down. They've learned that they use less energy, need to breathe less, if they sit their way upstairs instead of stepping on a stair, then turning around and sitting on each stair. So you see that in an asbestos plant—men going upstairs by sitting on them."

She finished her coffee and turned down an offer of another mug. "The nuclear industry is worrying some of us. Lots of attention to reactors, little attention to a place like this. I was sent out here to find out about safety here. Especially as it involves women. O-Sha is trying to build up its interest in women; you know, the way everybody else is. But I think I'm here for something more."

"What do you mean?"

"I mean I think I'm supposed to be some kind of *witness,* a potential witness. Part of the Federal Government presence. That's the word Rosen used. Presence."

"What else did he tell you?"

"He talks in a convoluted way," she said, and for the first time in the conversation, she started sounding guarded. "He was trying to get something across to me. That's the only way I can think of putting it. 'Get across.' I've met the type so many times in government. He wants to say something, but he wants to say it in a way that is impossible to quote, impossible to repeat. Nothing anecdotal or rememberable, like my asbestos workers on the stairs. You'd never catch Rosen giving you an image. He's a dealer in abstracts."

Garvey pushed her chair back and began walking around the room. She seemed unsure of what to say next. She went to the window. Only later, when Judith told Barbara about Garvey, did it seem strange that Garvey had gone to the window just then. When it happened, it seemed natural, a coincidence.

Garvey suddenly motioned Judith to the window and pointed to a green Impala sedan that seemed translucent as they looked at it through the yellow organdy curtain. A man wearing faded blue coveralls and a red cap with CAT on the front got out of the car and walked rapidly across the street. He opened the door to Garvey's rented Pinto, which was parked in front of the house.

"He put something on the seat," Judith whispered. "It looks like an envelope."

Garvey turned and looked down at Judith. "Something about you, I'll bet."

The man hurried back to his car and drove off. Judith leaned forward far enough to see the car pull to the curb near the highway intersection.

"Special delivery," Garvey said. She went out to the car and returned with a thick envelope. Inside was a report on Judith Longden. In general appearance, it resembled the report on Dick Scinto, which Judith now showed Garvey.

Both apparently had been typed on the same typewriter. Attached to the back of the report was a transcript, shorter than the one in the Scinto report.

At Judith's suggestion, they scanned the transcript in the Scinto report first. Then they looked at the transcript in the report on Judith.

The beginning of the Q. and A. litany was almost identical to the second half of the Scinto transcript: *Q. State your full name. A. José Arteaga-Castillo* . . . and so on down to *Q. I am showing you a photograph. Have you ever seen this woman?*

" 'Answer,' " Garvey read aloud, " 'Yes. I seen her in Phoenix. At Phoenix airport. In the parking lot there.' "

" 'Question. And when did you see her there? What was the date?' "

" 'Answer. On August nineteenth. Yeah, on August nineteenth. This year.' "

"What?" Judith asked. "What was that date?"

"August nineteenth," Garvey said. "Does it mean anything to you?"

"Harry. Harry Skirvin and I. I guess that was the date. He had to go there, had to go to Phoenix for a union meeting. I met him. To talk about the Facility. I had been contaminated. Two days. We were there two days."

"But you never saw this José or Cesar or whatever his name was?"

"No. Never. I swear."

"But you could be placed in Phoenix on August nineteenth? Airline ticket? Something like that."

"Yes. Oh, yes. Sure. The bastards. And pictures. Pictures of us. Harry told me later they took pictures of us. They sent some to his . . ."

"That's OK," Garvey interrupted. "The pictures are something else. I'm not interested in them. But in the transcript this José says he met you, and you and he talked about getting plutonium out of the Facility. Now is that true?"

"No. No. No. I never saw that man. I never, never stole anything. Nothing. I never stole. But they put it in me. Somehow they put it in me. Don't you understand?"

"But that's the *name,* Judy," Garvey said. "That's the *name.*"

"What name?" Judith asked.

"Arteaga-Castillo. You swear that name doesn't mean anything to you?"

"No. For God's sake. What the hell is this, Garvey? Are you some kind of cop or what?"

"Rosen told me to find out if you knew anybody by that name," Garvey said, a sigh in her voice. "It was the one definite thing he said. I was supposed to talk to you and make an estimate—his word, an estimate—of your reliability. Your reliability factor."

"So you're not here for safety!" Judith exclaimed. "Jesus Christ! Nobody! There's nobody who's playing it straight with me."

"I *am* here to look around, Judy. That's the truth. Mostly for safety. And for you. To find out about you. I told you that, Judy."

"No. You didn't really tell me that. *I* tell people things. People don't tell *me* things. Pretty simple. But I never get it."

Her voice started to rise; she was nearly shouting. Then, abruptly, her voice softened.

"I have not stolen anything," she said quietly, slowly. "I have tried to make the place I work a safer place, a better place. And I think I may have been contaminated. Contaminated, Dr. Garvey. I think that somehow they put plutonium in me."

It was at that moment, Garvey remembers, when tears appeared in Judith's staring eyes. The tears created two dimly gleaming lines on her narrow, waxen face. Garvey touched Judith's hands, first the right, then the left, as if to detect a sign of life. The hands were cold.

"I do want to know about the contamination, Judy. Look." Garvey held up the report she had got from the car. "There's a part in the report about that."

"There is? They have it down there?"

"Yes. You feel up to reading it?"

"You bet I do," Judith says, her voice suddenly strong. "I'd like to see what the lying bastards have to say."

They began to read the section of the report entitled *Investigation of Employee A and Residence in Regard to Possible Contamination with Plutonium.*

30.

SOURCES OF INFORMATION

Information in this report was obtained by way of official records, interviews of cognizant individuals, observations by employees and management personnel, and other sources.

" 'Other sources,' " Judith said. "Informers. Lying bastards."

"Let's just read a while, Judy, and keep the comments for later."

"What the hell. Why not?"

On Wednesday, 14 October, Employee A—

"That's me? I'm Employee A?"

"Yes. I assume so. Something happened only four days ago?"

"Yeah. That's when it was. In Metallography."

"Right. Well, let's go on."

On Wednesday, 14 October, Employee A was performing various kinds of paperwork in the Main Metallography Room (Met Room 12) of P Plant. At approximately 5:15 P.M. Employee A took a break. Prior to leaving the work area she monitored herself and found no trace of contamination. At approximately 5:30 P.M. she returned to Met Room 12 and proceeded to her next task. She put on coveralls and 15-mil neoprene gloves, taping them to her wrists, per standard procedure. She began grinding plutonium samples in Glove Box

No. 4 and later shifted to Glove Box No. 6, where she polished the samples and ultrasonically cleaned them.

At approximately 7 P.M., Employee A monitored herself at a hand-and-foot counter console with audible alarm and visual readout, the standard procedure prior to leaving RMA—

"What's that mean?"

"Radioactive Material Area."

. . . and no contamination was recorded. She removed her coveralls and went to the cafeteria for a 30-minute lunch break.

When she returned from the cafeteria, she again put on her coveralls and, returning to Glove Box No. 6, resumed polishing and cleaning plutonium samples. At approximately 9 P.M., Employee A began to secure Glove Box No. 6. She withdrew her hands from the glove box and, per standard procedure, monitored her hands. The console visually and audibly alarmed in an indication of contamination, and a Health Physics technician was automatically summoned, arriving at 9:12 P.M.

The HP technician made a preliminary direct reading on Employee A's hands and arms, using an Emerline PRM-6 portable alpha survey instrument. The survey indicated contamination up to 20,000 disintegrations per minute (d/m), a substantial level above the Maximum Permissible Contamination level of 500 d/m. With the aid of a female HP clerk, Employee A was taken to the Medical Decontamination Facility and—

"Like hell I was. You try to find that. They just took me into a regular lab that had a shower and they gave it that name in this report. The lying bastards."

"OK, Judy. Let's read on."

. . . and decontamination procedures began. She removed her coveralls and submitted to a survey which showed contaminations of both hands, upper arms, the neck, face, and hair. Nose smears showed a contamination level of 200 d/m. Nasal irrigation minified this level to 10 d/m. Showering and a scrubbing further reduced contamination about the arms, neck, face, and hair to a level less than 500 d/m.

Employee A was given a urine kit and a fecal kit and asked to provide samples *in situ.* She was then released to return to work at approximately 10:35 P.M.

• • •

"My God!" Garvey said. "You mean after all that you went back to work?"

"This isn't one of those soft-ass asbestos plants, Garvey. Sure I went back to work. So far, this is how it really was."

> Within the hour of Employee A's exposure to possible contamination, the filter papers in the air sample units in Met Room 12 were removed for examination and the room was placed on respirator status for the remainder of the work shift. At the conclusion of the shift, but prior to the entrance of the incoming shift, an HP technician surveyed the room in a search for a possible source of contamination. Readings of 5,000 to 3,000 d/m were found on the gloves in Glove Box No. 6. Subsequent examination of the air sample filter papers showed airborne plutonium concentrations of twice to three times the average concentrations permissible in occupied areas.
>
> On Thursday, 15 October, Employee A returned to Met Room 12 on the mid (four-to-twelve) shift and did routine work that did not involve any authorized use of any glove box. At approximately 7 P.M., preparatory to leaving the RMA for the cafeteria, Employee A monitored her hands. The console visually and audibly alarmed in an indication of contamination. An HP technician immediately responded.
>
> Preliminary findings were that her hands, neck, and face were contaminated beyond permissible levels—

"No figures this time, I notice."

"Funny. I think they were about the same, up to 20,000 d/m. Wonder why they didn't put them in."

> . . . and Employee A was given an emergency decontamination.

"A goddamn shower out in the hall, that's what that was."

> She was then taken to an HP facility, and a more thorough scrubdown was commenced. Fecal and urine samples were also taken. She requested that a nasal smear be taken. The smear from one nostril showed 22,000 d/m and 15,000 d/m from the other nostril. Employee A appeared to be agitated at this point and further decontamination procedures were hampered.

"I'll say I was agitated. Sweet Jesus! I figured the first one could be an accident. But the second one? I was alone in the room just before it happened. It was like somebody *poured* plutonium into the room. I was half-crazy. I thought—*think, still* think, right now—they were trying to kill me. I was calling that queer HP every goddamn name in the book.

"I kept calling for Chip Miller, and I guess that was a mistake. It must have sounded like he was an accomplice or something."

"What do you mean, 'accomplice?' "

"You know. They were after me, suspicious of me. For *something.* This was not just an incident that came out of nowhere. There's got to be more in that report—before this week—before these two incidents. It's happened to me before. Last August, it happened. It should be in there."

"OK," Garvey said. "Let's look for it. But this week's incidents, the Thursday one, there's more about it." She started reading again.

> A preliminary survey of the fecal and urine samples showed extraordinarily high levels. Employee A and the urine and fecal containers were taken to E Building for a more detailed survey. Decontamination procedures began immediately. Large portions of P Plant were placed on respirators.

"You're going to have to translate all this for me, Judith."

"E Building is the emergency building," Judith began, sounding as if she were giving instructions to a classroom. "It's a first-aid area. There's a special entrance. Anybody brought in through that door is supposed to set off an alarm. You walk into an air-lock. Supposedly, everything in that part of the building is air-tight so that any airborne plutonium that gets into the room stays there.

"They brought me in and they told me to strip—there was a female HP there, a little dykey, I think—and she put a paper kind of smock on me. I could hear alarms going off, and I was never more scared in my life. I felt as if I was going to puke, but I wouldn't give the bastards the satisfaction.

"They told me to lie down on the decontamination table. They—well, not they; now it was just the female HP, her name is Helen Reynolds, I think—she told me to take off the smock and to lie down on the decontamination table. She had complete radiation gear on—bright yellow coveralls, heavy gloves, and a hood like a motorcycle helmet with a mask built into it—that's the high-exposure respirator. Anyway, she hooked up a hose with a shower head on it and she squirted water over me.

"The water drains from the table into holding tanks. Art says that the table sounds like the kind he saw in a mortuary in Vietnam, where they got guys' bodies ready for shipment home. Anyway, there are drains built into the table. After she gave me the water treatment, she started scrubbing me with a detergent. I started yelling, and she stopped. But she made me scrub down. And I had to shampoo my hair in some kind of caustic they have for decon."

Judith suddenly stopped speaking. She drummed her fingers on her knees for a moment. Garvey could not tell whether Judith was angry or exhausted. Judith was breathing hard, and Garvey thought that it was almost as if Judith was living through the experience. "I guess you want to hear the rest," Judith said, as if she were talking to herself.

"They have a wound monitor there. It's a special kind of detector. It looks like one of those water picks? An HP can make a very precise measurement to look for a tiny bit of plutonium. If you get a wound, it can get into the wound or at the edge of the wound and show whether there is any plutonium inside. That's the worst thing that can happen to you. Getting it inside you.

"Well, when I saw that wound counter, I thought, 'Oh my God! They think it got into me.' I thought of the nasal smears, and I thought, 'She's going to shove that thing up my nose.' I started to sit up, but she pushed me back. I don't usually faint. I think I'm tough. But I felt myself beginning to go under."

Judith paused again. She had not noticed that Barbara had come into the house. Garvey saw Barbara standing in the kitchen doorway. They nodded to one another, but Barbara did not speak.

"I knew all along, I guess, what she was going to do. She pushed my legs open and she put that wound detector all around my vagina, and I could feel it just poke me, just right at the edge of myself. And I started yelling.

" 'I'm getting out of here, you queer bitch,' I said, or something like that. I just remember it all in pieces. I jumped off the table, and I thought I was going to hit her, but she was bigger than me. I kept yelling. I don't know what I yelled. I tried to find my clothes. All I had was that paper smock, and I was tearing it. And then I remember she came around the back of me and she put an arm under my chin and I felt her sticking a needle in my ass—on the rump, not up my ass. It was a shot. She was knocking me out."

Garvey looked again at Barbara, who still had not moved or spoken.

"When I came to, I was on a couch in a little room off the decon room in E Building. At least I figure that's where I was—oh, hello, Barbara. I didn't see you come in. Well, you've heard all this."

"I didn't hear that," Barbara said. "You didn't tell me about that examination with the wound monitor. I never ever heard of anything like that, with you or anybody else. Never."

"Well, it happened. I don't know why I didn't tell you. Anyway, it was probably just Reynolds being queer."

"I don't think so," Barbara said. "You told me that Rosen was trying to say he suspected you were smuggling plutonium in your vagina."

Barbara sat down on the red leather couch, facing the card table. Grayfur appeared from nowhere and settled into Barbara's lap.

"Grayfur," Judith said. "I haven't seen her all day. Where's she been?"

"I don't know," Barbara replied. "She just turns up. She seems better."

"Lovely cat," Garvey said. "She's been sick?"

Barbara nodded. "I've been wondering about resuspension. But she seems OK right now."

"Resuspension?" Garvey asked.

"Plutonium particles can travel in a lot of ways. You rub your nose and wipe it on your sleeve. At the end of the shift, you change clothes, but maybe some stuff still sticks. How much of the stuff will you be taking home for resuspension? I thought maybe Grayfur got some, but on second thought I decided her sickness had nothing to do with . . . with whatever else is happening."

"This resuspension," Garvey said, "that's why they can get into an apartment and survey it? That's what they call it, don't they? Survey?"

"That's what they call it," Judith said. "I'd like to see what the report says about that. And what it says about Feeley."

Garvey handed the report to Judith. She skimmed it for mention of Feeney, but members of the survey party were not identified by name. The report concentrated on numbers, and the numbers seemed believable, given the premise that plutonium had been in the apartment.

"If they're building a case against me," Judy said, "the numbers in here would stand up. They just can't be making this up. Jesus! The place was really hot. They can't be making this up."

Each room had been "surveyed." In most of the apartment "only minor levels of contamination" had been found. The radiation measurements of contamination were in disintegrations per minute. Apparently for the convenience of readers who would be unfamiliar with the measurement system, the anonymous compiler and distributor of the report [Kovacs] had attached a brief explanation of disintegrations per minute and a table indicating dpm danger levels. The table showed that anything below 500 dpm was not considered dangerous.

Counts ranging in the tens of thousands were recorded on the kitchen floor, in cabinets, and on counter tops. Similar readings were made in the bathroom, where the toilet seat showed an incredibly high reading of 110,000 dpm.

Foods in the refrigerator also showed high counts, ranging from 2,000 or 3,000 on such items as butter and cheese to 375,000 on a salami. This astronomical figure meant, according to the report, that a "significant" number of particles of plutonium—not just traces of it—had to be on or in the salami.

The report had a surrealistic quality. Plutonium in a salami. On a toilet seat. "Jesus. Jesus," Judith kept muttering as she read through it.

The report carried the survey even further—into the Caslon Wells sewer system. Yellow-suited, hooded men extracting water from the toilet bowl in Judith's apartment, then tramping to a raw-sewage treatment plant and dipping out samples of fetid water.

"Why?" Judith asked Garvey. "Why in God's sake did they do all this?"

"I don't know, Judy. I honestly don't know."

"Honestly. My ass, honestly. If there is anything to this goddamn report—into the sewers for God's sake, into the *sewers*—if there's anything to it, then you know what it means? I'll tell you what it means. It means I'm full of that shit. That shit is in my lungs and it's going to kill me. Jesus. That shit is in me. In *me!*"

Judith stood up so abruptly that her chair fell back. She flung the report across the room. The report hit a drape and landed on the window seat. Grayfur jumped down from Barbara's lap and dashed to inspect the new object that had appeared in one of her favorite sunning spots.

Judith hovered at the table for a moment as if she was not sure where she was going to turn. She stood rigidly, her body trembling, her arms at her sides, shoulders raised so that the lower half of her face seemed to be jutting from a suddenly deformed body. Garvey would remember looking at Judith and mentally flicking through lists of shock symptoms and drug symptoms, trying to give a name to what could be causing the agony in Judith's mind. The moment passed, and Judith seemed to relax as swiftly as she had knotted. Garvey wanted to ask her what had gone on in her mind during that long, frozen moment, but Garvey knew that whatever Judith could have expressed about that moment had been expressed with her body and face.

Judith replaced the chair and sat down. "I'm sorry," she said. "I got worked up." Her calm voice was nearly inaudible. "I've been reading a lot. I've been trying to figure out my chances. If there really are a lot of plutonium particulates in my lungs, I don't have a chance."

Barbara and Garvey began to speak at once: "Not true" . . . "Don't know" . . . "Need tests" . . . "Los Alamos" . . .

"Never mind," Judith said. "We'll find out how we are tomorrow. Right, Barbara? Maybe we should celebrate, a last—oh, hell, not *last.* Christ. I don't want to be talking like that . . . Let's call Art and Harry. Let's go to Carry's . . . You, too, Dr. Garvey."

"No thanks. And call me Ann . . . I should be going. Read the report. Digest the material. Study up . . ."

"Yes. Ann. Very busy, Ann. We'll see you tomorrow? On the Los Alamos special? With our pal Rosen?"

"Yes. Yes. I'll see you then."

Garvey made her goodbyes and rapidly left. Judith sat at the card table, her eyes on the tape recorder. It seemed to Barbara that Judith was talking more to the recorder than to her.

"I've been reading about the lousy business we're in, Barbara. I just read about one of the ones who started this. It happened in 1946. He was a physicist. He was working on what the AEC calls nuclear devices. Bombs. His job was to test for critical assembly. He called it tickling the dragon's tail. He would push two subcritical assemblies close to each other until the distance was just right to set off a chain reaction. He would nudge them, nudge the two assemblies until they were just a hair from going critical.

"He was doing this for the fortieth time when his hand slipped or something. He took 800 rads. Right in the face. Somebody figured out this was like being less than a mile from ground zero at Hiroshima.

"I already knew that you could die in a criticality accident. Dick told me about that guy Walker. Walker was lucky. He died quick. And what Dick told me were just words from a nice guy talking about seeing another guy die. It could have been an automobile accident. They always tell us that, don't they? It's more dangerous on the highway than in P Plant?

"But I read about this other guy, the physicist tickling the dragon's tail, in a medical book, and it was in those medical words that make people like a piece of meat.

"It took him nine days to die. The AEC brought in ten doctors to try to save him. But they all knew it was no use. He died. Nine days. That's what the goddamn stuff does to you, one way or the other. It kills you, mostly slow. Jesus.

"Know where that guy died?" She looked up at Barbara. "He died in Los Alamos."

31.

EITHER WILLIE NELSON himself or someone who looked very much like him—scraggly hair and ginger beard, dark, wide-set eyes—was singing at Carry's Place when they walked in. Barbara entered first, then Judith, Art, and a couple of steps behind, Harry Skirvin.

The man sitting on the bar was not Willie Nelson. Judith could see that now, pushing through the tiny box of an entrance, the windows of its inner and outer doors dimmed with the frost of the night and the breath of the Saturday-night crowd. She could see that this was the same man who had been there long ago, or it seemed long ago, when Art and she had come here to celebrate the end of her training.

Barbara decided that Judith was happy at that moment, and perhaps she was. She thought Judith looked good in the jeans and the yellow turtleneck. Judith had liked everything Barbara had bought. They had had a few minutes to talk, while they were getting ready to leave. Judith had seemed unusually grateful, because, Barbara had realized, Judith rarely let anyone do anything for her with an exchange of favors.

They all got to the back edge of the jostling, loud-talking, joint-passing crescent of people around the center of the bar.

Bud Jennings strode up to Harry Skirvin and began pumping his arm and slapping his shoulder. It had been Harry who had picked up the tabs when the Local 1010 strategists had met here in the waning days of the strike, and saloonkeepers do not forget people who pick up tabs.

Bud found them a table by plowing through the broadest part of the crescent to a table where Bud's girlfriend sat with two other young women. Without a word, Bud's three model patrons vacated the table and plunged into the crowd. They left behind a half-filled pitcher, which Bud emptied into four glasses he had managed to scoop up from the bar. The singer, who called himself Red, had a clear, vibrant natural voice and now was into Willie Nelson's labyrinthine *Time of the Preacher*, a ballad that could go on forever.

> Now the preachin' is over and the lesson's begun . . .

"Garvey sends her regrets," Harry half-shouted over the song and the ebbing din. "She asked me to say goodbye to you."

"What?" Judith asked.

"Garvey. She says she had to go back to Washington right away."

"Why?"

"She didn't say," Harry said. "She's a funny lady."

"I think she's a fink, Harry."

"Maybe so."

"You said you had business. That you couldn't see me," Judith said. She sounded to Harry as if she were accusing him of something.

"You called me. You asked me to come here. And I'm here," Harry said. "I was going to call back anyhow. I had to see you. On business."

"You always used to say that," she said, smiling at him.

"Say what?"

"That you'd call me."

"I meant it tonight, Judy. It's business. Serious business."

Harry was on Judith's left, Art on her right. He glared at Harry, trying to figure out why he was there, what he was saying, why they seemed to be so intense.

> It was a time of the Preacher in the year of '01.
> Now the lesson is over and the killin's begun . . .

Suddenly, none of them was speaking. The song became loud and insistent. The words of the ballad, only occasionally understandable, drifted across their silence. They were not speaking because none of them quite knew what it was that any of the other three might wish to hear. The silence lasted for less than a minute, but it seemed longer, and the one who broke the silence—Barbara—broke it with the deliberation of someone swinging a hammer at a plate of glass.

"Harry, since you're the only one *not* going on the plane tomorrow, maybe you should tell us why you're here." She lifted her glass. "You want to propose a toast?"

Harry lifted his glass, but only to take a long draught. Then he spoke.

"OK. I wanted to say this to Judith alone, but she probably would be telling you and Art, anyway." He leaned in closer to the table, to make what he said more confidential, but he had to speak louder in order to be heard. He was practically shouting over the music—

> And just when you think it's all over
> It's only begun . . .

—and the loud, liquid sounds of talk from the tables jammed around them. "LISTEN. TODAY. I JUST FOUND OUT . . ." The words of the song faded as Red picked out the theme on his battered guitar. And Harry found himself shouting against a sudden new wall of quiet. His words seemed to echo. " . . . THAT THE FBI. . . ." He heard the startled hush and lowered his voice. "The FBI is in town. That was the business I told you about, Judy."

He turned to her, and though his words could easily be heard by the others, they knew that he was speaking only to her. "They asked me why I was in town. They said they were doing a routine background investigation of a Caslon employee. They didn't say who, but I was obviously supposed to know who. There were two of them. I've talked to the FBI before, Judy. It's usually just one. One agent. When there are two, it means that the case is big enough for them to put heavier manpower on it, and it means that it's hot enough so that the FBI wants one agent to be hearing what the other agent is hearing and saying. Insurance."

"This is no place to be talking about this," Art said, his voice hissing in a loud whisper.

"Maybe it's just the place," Harry said. "You want to bet on any place in this town not being bugged?"

"What were they questioning you about?" Judith asked.

"Nothing you could put a finger on. They're good at just making you *feel* that something criminal is going on. They asked me if I were here in an official capacity, or whether it was a private visit." Art was glaring at Harry again. "I knew what they were getting at. The bastards.

"I said I was here on confidential union business. They asked me how long I was planning to stay at the motel. I said until Tuesday. They asked me if I planned to be speaking to any people who were not actually members of Local 1010. I figure that means they knew I was meeting Phelan, the guy from the *Post.* I told them that I did not want to discuss union business with them any further. I said that I would cooperate in anything formal that the FBI did—I felt I had to say something like that; I didn't think it was a good idea to tell them to go to hell. But I said I wasn't going to just talk to them like that, informally, they called it, in a motel lobby. They said . . ." The ballad finally ended in a ragged chorus of performer and audience—

> But he could not forgive her, though he
> tried and he tried
> And the halls of his memory still echoed
> her lies . . .

—and Harry had to raise his voice again: "THEY SAID THAT THEY WOULD BE BACK IN TOUCH WITH ME IN WASHINGTON IF IT PROVED NECESSARY. THAT WAS THEIR PHRASE, 'IF IT PROVED NECESSARY.' "

"WHAT DO YOU . . ." The music stopped. " . . . make of it?" Art asked. He noticed that Judith had looked away when Harry had begun talking. Art tried to see what Judith was looking at.

"It seems to me," Harry said, "that they are nosing around but don't have anything solid. I guess it's just as well that you all three heard about it from me. But I'm sure whatever it is, it's focused on Judy. Judy?"

Now he also saw that she was looking away. When he turned and followed her gaze, he knew what she saw: Geiser, the man from Personnel, the man Harry had pointed out to her in Jack's months ago as a smalltime hood. But she was not looking at Geiser, for she had got used to seeing him in the plant; she was looking at the man across the table from

Geiser. He still wore a red cap with CAT on the front. The man who had put the report in Ann Garvey's rented car.

She identified the other man for Harry and Art. "It's just that they're together," she said. "I guess that's what bothers me. That they're together and they're where I am."

"Do you want to go?" Art asked.

"I want *them* to go. Let's have another round. And I'm going to have a good time."

They stayed for another hour, but Judith's eyes continually strayed toward the table with the two men. They seemed never to speak, never to move. The glasses on the table between them never seemed to be lifted.

Harry thought about going to the men's table and asking them to leave, but it would have been a crazy thing to do. Harry was feeling a bit uncomfortable, anyway. This was not his kind of place.

He said that, during the between-sets quiet, just before they left. He asked Judith, "What is it that you see—or hear, I mean, in this music? It's western, I know that much. But some of the lyrics—'You told me once you were mine forever' and 'Can I sleep in your arms tonight, lady?'—I didn't think anybody still wrote that kind of stuff. Old songs?"

"New," she said. "This is outlaw stuff. They call themselves outlaws. No Nashville shit. If you listen close, you'll notice—well, *you* might not notice, but other people can—you'll hear something real, something that's not plastic. It's hard to get it across. I guess the words aren't all that's to it. There's more, to the music, I mean. It's mostly the music, but it wouldn't go anywhere if the words weren't that way."

"What do you mean, 'that way'?"

"Corny. Honest. Nobody trying to play tricks with you. Saying things as if there really was a way to say things."

"You're getting deep."

Art had been watching them. "You want one more round, Judy?" Art said in a tone that expected a "No."

"No. I guess we should be leaving." She stood and turned her head once more toward the table with the two men. "I wonder if they'll leave, too."

Red started singing again, just as she stood up.

At a time when the world seems to be spinnin'
Hopelessly out of control . . .

• • •

She sat down.

There's deceivers and believers and old in-betweeners
  That seem to have no place to go.

"I guess we should go," she said, half to herself. But she stayed sitting until Red got to the end:

I looked to the stars, tried all of the bars
  And I've nearly gone up in smoke.
Now my hand's on the wheel of something that's real
  And I feel like I'm goin' home.

As soon as the break started after the song, they filed out and left the parking lot in three cars: Art alone in his Mustang Stallion hardtop with racing mirrors, forged aluminum wheels, and two-tone paint; Barbara and Judith in the faded-red Volkswagen that now could be started with a key; Harry in his Ford Granada from Hertz. He turned east, toward the Cherokee. The Mustang and the VW headed west on 85. And about a quarter of a mile behind them was a green Impala.

Judith was humming and sometimes singing the words—

Now my hand's on the wheel of something that's real

—and feeling good. She wondered if Art would turn when she turned off 85 to Barbara's street. He did, and so did another car.

She parked in front of Barbara's and told her that she was going to stay with Art for a few minutes. He pulled his car up to within inches of hers, and he hit the brakes so hard they squealed.

Barbara, who had not talked much on the way home, said, "OK. I'm going to bed. They'll be here to take us to the airport at seven thirty."

Barbara entered the house without acknowledging Art's presence. Judith walked to his car and snuggled in close to him. He draped his arm across the back of the seat but did not quite touch her.

"I thought you might stay with me tonight," he said.

She did not answer, but reached up and turned the rearview

mirror so that she could see out the back window. A car was parking about two blocks up. Its lights flicked out. She kept looking in the mirror, a blackness framing a faintly glinting hood and windshield.

"What's the matter?" Art asked.

"They—I guess it's the guys from Carry's—I think they're parked behind us. They followed us. But why?"

"I don't know." Art's voice had softened. "It's scary, isn't it? All this? That's why I thought . . . that it might be better, you might feel better, with me."

"I'd like you to take care of me, Art." She raised her head for him to kiss her, and he did. His arms closed about her. She broke away from his lips, slowly and gently. "I'd like that, Art. But I've got to get all this worked out. I'm scared; just this minute I got scared. I want to go in, Art. I don't want them looking at me.

"I want to talk to you, Art. So much. I was thinking, when we get back tomorrow night. We could be together then. I want to talk."

"OK." He swung his right arm off the back of the seat and grabbed the steering wheel with both hands. He was looking directly ahead. He adjusted the rearview mirror so he could see in it again. "I'll drive around the block and pull up behind them. I won't get out. They won't get out. I just feel it. I feel like there won't be any trouble. They'll just go away, and I will, too. You get out now. I won't start up until you get inside."

In the darkness of the living room, again through the organdy, she looked at the green car. Then Art's Mustang was jackrabbiting off, wheeling around the corner, and reappearing, its lights swelling as they silhouetted the Impala. She could see the black profiles of two heads, one with a cap. In a few moments the Impala started up and drove slowly down the street. When it passed in front of the house, the man without the cap—Geiser—rolled down the window on the passenger's side and waved. His face was turned up to the window she stood at, and he seemed to be smiling.

32.

Sunday, October 18:

The driver was a white-haired man who wore a Stetson low over mirrored sunglasses. His words were not sentences but only orders spiked with the impatience of a man who has done more and better than this. By his third command—"you up front, ladies in back"—Judith was convinced he was a retired cop. Later, she decided Pinkerton; she whispered the single word to Barbara, who nodded. They traveled in almost complete silence. There was little traffic on the highway, and when Art remarked upon that, the driver merely grunted.

At the Tulsa International Airport terminal, the driver parked in a No Parking zone and ushered them through silently opening doors. He barged past them in the lobby and led them away from the Continental ticket counter and directly to the walkway for Gate 8. The driver stood at the side of the electronic surveillance arch as first Judith, then Barbara, then Art passed through without reaction by the machine or its operator, a stocky, part-Indian woman trying to look tough by looking bored. The driver stepped through the arch, and the metal-detector produced a sizzling sound on the operator's console. He glared at her, and she waved him through.

The driver led them to a small lounge at Gate 8, where the 8:45 A.M. Continental flight to Albuquerque was posted. The driver walked over to Rosen, who was standing near a large window, his back to the lounge. A Braniff airliner was taking off, and Rosen swiveled his head, following the plane, a streak of Calder colors, as it angled against the cloudless blue of morning. They could see their reflections in the window; they knew he could see them. The driver stood for a moment at Rosen's side. The driver said something, and Rosen nodded. With a rubbery motion of his right arm, Rosen waved the driver away. Rosen spun around and with another swivel of his head took them in. "They should be calling the flight in about ten minutes," he said. "We'll change planes at Denver. We will arrive in Albuquerque at eleven forty local time. We'll catch a Los Alamos shuttle flight there and get to the lab a little after noon. It will be a long morning, but I must ask you not to urinate or defecate until you get to the lab." He looked at each of them, stopping his swing at Judith's upturned face. He resumed lecturing.

"The tests you will be given are extremely important. Details will be explained to you at the lab. The people there . . ."

"Why are we going there?" Judith asked. Rosen seemed to intensify his gaze on her.

"Because, Miss Longden, you made a contamination complaint. There was some positive response. And, as you well know, there were some positive responses on the part of Mr. Reeves and Miss O'Neill."

"No, I did not know much about that," Judith said. She was seated between Arthur and Barbara. Looking at him, then at her, she said, "And he didn't tell me . . . And she didn't tell me. People don't tell me things."

"Friday," Art said, a defensive tremor in his voice. "Friday, when you saw me with Deckman? He told us. He told Barbara, then he told me."

Judith stared at him for an instant. "Not HP? It was Deckman? I thought . . . I don't know what I thought." She looked up at Rosen. "How much of this is security, and how much is health? Where is Ann Garvey? What is the real reason we're being taken away?"

A Continental attendant appeared and handed Rosen five boarding passes in exchange for the tickets Rosen held. "There will only be the four of us," Rosen told the attendant. "Dr. Garvey will not be coming." They exchanged the ticket and boarding pass.

While this was going on, Judith had stood up. The attendant walked away. "Answer my questions!" Judith exclaimed. She grabbed Rosen's arm. "Answer my questions!"

He glanced at his watch and then half-turned to look out the window.

Judith let go of his arm. She whirled and took one step as she said, "I'm not going."

In a surprisingly swift motion, Rosen reached out his right hand and grabbed her wrist. Several people who were waiting for the flight had put down their newspapers and magazines and were watching Judith and Rosen. He simultaneously responded to their attention and to Judith by pulling her toward him, holding her head against his chest with his right hand, encircling her waist with his left. He was acting as if he was consoling her; but she felt a harsh, menacing strength. He spoke loud enough for Art and Barbara to hear: "I am authorized to sedate you if necessary. There is a federal air marshal aboard the aircraft. Don't do anything silly."

As he was saying this, the flight was called. The other passengers filed ahead of him and were given boarding passes. He kept his right arm around Judith's waist, propelling her toward the covered ramp connecting the lounge and the plane.

The stewardess collecting the boarding passes looked at Judith curiously. Rosen took the boarding pass out of Judith's hand and gave it, with his, to the stewardess. "My patient may need a little extra care," he said. The stewardess looked at the telex message on her clipboard. "You and your patient are assigned to A-9 and B-9, doctor. Have a good flight."

Rosen took A-9, the window seat, and Judith B-9. They had to squeeze past the occupant of C-9, the aisle seat. He was a beefy man in a brown suit, white shirt, and black string tie. Rosen wriggled out of his overcoat and motioned to Judith to remove her parka, but she slumped deeper into the seat, staring at the back of the seat in front of her. Rosen handed his coat across her to the man in the brown suit. He nodded to Rosen and put the coat in the overhead compartment.

Barbara glanced at Judith, gave her a sad smile, and disappeared into seat A-8. Art, impassive, looked at Judith with a quick jerk of his head, took off his suede jacket and sank into B-8. The man in the brown suit alternated between C-8 and C-9 during the flight to Denver, but he spent most of the time in C-9.

"Do you want something to help you rest?" Rosen asked Judith, his voice surprisingly gentle.

She shook her head and closed her eyes. "I think I can go to sleep on my own," she said.

"I have some Thorazine with me," Rosen said.

She had been taking Thorazine occasionally for the past few months. The last time she saw the barbiturate was in her medicine cabinet in her bathroom. They all seemed to know so much about her, but she was no longer surprised. She shook her head again. "No thanks."

In Denver, Rosen and the man in the brown suit escorted them to the VIP lounge on the upper deck of the terminal. Now the security tightened enough for them to feel it. The man in the brown suit seemed to report formally to an older man in a blue suit. Two other men in dark suits were standing around, one by the door. He looked uncomfortable in a white Stetson that seemed to be an attempt at local-costume disguise. They all had a way of looking at each other but not at three of the arrivals. "I just thought of a name for us," Judith stage-whispered to Art as they sat at a low table. "The Caslon Three. Has a ring, doesn't it?"

Art shrugged and reached for a *Denver Post* on the table. The man nearest him took a notebook from his inside pocket and wrote something down. Art put the *Post* back.

"Jesus, Art," Judith urgently said in a slightly louder voice. "We're in some kind of *custody.*"

"Maybe they're passengers," Art said, shrugging.

"That's Manzano Mountain," Rosen said as the plane began its approach to Albuquerque. He leaned back and beckoned to Judith so she could look out the window. He had become talkative in the last few minutes, and there was an aura of excitement about his speech and mannerisms. In a way, he was going home. "Manzano Mountain," he repeated. "Our largest nuclear-weapons storage site. The Pentagon's Nuclear Weapons School is here, too. It's quite a city, really."

At the Albuquerque terminal they lost the man in the brown suit but picked up two uniformed guards. Everyone quick-stepped to the private-plane terminal, where they boarded an

AEC plane that immediately took off.

"I thought it would be a desert," Judith said as the plane began its long approach to the controlled air space around Los Alamos. The windows filled with mountains mantled by spruce and sprinkled with the soft gold of aspen. Then amid the mountains a tableland of mesas appeared, and upon a mesa more than a mile high glinted the intrusion of a city. Or probably a city; it looked more like an installation, for it was spread thin; its parts were scattered; and its dominant color was white, a metallic white. A city from the air usually has a continuity, a form, and a pastel prettiness. Not Los Alamos. It sprawled on a mesa not because its founders had been inspired by the beauty of the wilderness, but because they had been enchanted by the desolation of the site.

The plane landed on an air strip. Two cars pulled up to the plane. The guards entered the first car; Rosen and The Caslon Three piled into the limousine.

"When I first came here in 1950," Rosen was saying, "it was a closed city, the only one, I think, in American history." His listeners were not listening well, for their minds were on a collective desire to urinate.

A roadside sign said:

> Los Alamos—The Atomic City—Birthplace of the Atomic Age and A-Bomb. Site of the Los Alamos Scientific Laboratory and Museum. Good Lodging. 18-Hole Championship Golf Course. Picnic Areas.

"It still had a touch of mystery then. I was in weapons design. Of course, I couldn't say that then. They had only started to let people even use the word physicist here. Some of the restrictions had been lifted when we got here: you could use a Los Alamos mailing address. But you couldn't get in or out of town without a pass. Nobody. There's where the guard house was." He pointed to a squat building that blurred by. "It's a restaurant now." He sounded disappointed, an old grad returning to a changed campus.

Technical Area 14, or TA-14, was enclosed by a high, barbed-wire-topped, chain-link fence that extended as far as the eye could see. The guard at the gate politely asked them to get out of the car, which was straddling a metal plate sunk flush into the road. Rosen stood next to the car; the others stretched, moved about, and fidgeted. The guard made a swift, professional search of the interior of the car, ran a hand-held detector around each hub cap, and motioned the driver to stand by the car for an expert frisking. The driver got back in and drove through the gate.

The car carrying the escort guards had already parked; they were inside the TA-14 entrance complex preparing for the visitors. TA-14 was a Protected Area whose access points were maintained under strict AEC security regulations. Within the Protected Area itself were Material Access Areas, where plutonium and other Special Nuclear Material were handled. These inner areas were guarded even more elaborately than the access points.

Rosen, Judith, Barbara, and Art entered a square, windowless concrete building that jutted from the perimeter fence, next to the vehicular gate. They were met in the reception room of the building by the escort guards, who photographed them and passed out plastic cards that looked like credit cards. They were literally the keys to a computerized security system that guarded each of the TA's in Los Alamos. The system monitored all copy machines, which could be operated only by use of the cards, and maintained a real-time and stored-memory record of the movement of all people, packages, and vehicles in and out of each Technical Area.

The Technical Areas were the vestiges of the closed-city era. Until 1957 no casual visitors had been allowed in Los Alamos. The Federal Government then owned everything in the city. No building could even be painted without permission. Housing was allocated on the basis of salary and tenure. There was no private enterprise; all stores were run by Government contractors. Municipal services were performed by a contractor hired by the Government. Senator Caslon held the controlling interest in a company that performed such services. That was how Caslon got started in the nuclear-energy business.

Los Alamos was only the name of a desolate canyon until the 1920's, when it became the site of a spartan military academy for boys, the Los Alamos Ranch School. One of the relatively few people who had ever heard of the place was J. Robert Oppenheimer, a young physics professor at the University of California. He often backpacked into the mesa country and had stopped by the school. Soon after Pearl Harbor, when he was asked to pick an isolated site for the building of the first atomic bomb, he suggested Los Alamos Canyon.

The Army took over the school and assumed control. The Army called it Los Alamos Site Y and operated it like a military base. Laboratories were shut down by MP's at 5 o'clock, and physicists had to learn to pick locks to work in the labs at night. Personal identities were top secret. Food and gas ration books, automobile registrations, insurance policies, income-tax forms—all were processed by code number to avoid revelations about who was at Site Y.

All mail was censored and went through Post Office Box 1163, Sante Fe, New Mexico. By December, 1944, the population was 5,000 and included children whose birth certificates bore only the Santa Fe postal address. The citizens of Site Y could not get divorced, vote, adopt children, or have their wills probated. The man who ran Site Y, Brigadier General Leslie R. Groves, called his realm's only product the atomic bomb.

"It was the wrong name," Rosen was saying to his charges. Another story from the old grad. "Every time I see that sign Atomic City, it disturbs me. *Nuclear* is the word. Every damn bomb is atomic—so is everything. A stupid, imprecise term."

Around the time of the arrival of the young and newly doctored Samuel Rosen, his alma mater, the University of California, was a major contractor in Los Alamos. The project then was the making of the hydrogen bomb. The basic fuel for this bomb would be plutonium, manufactured in AEC production reactors and processed at Los Alamos.

Plutonium's use as a fuel would not come until the 1960's with the development of nuclear reactors for the production of electric power. By then Los Alamos was an open city, but it remained the Atomic City and its obsession with security never diminished. Now, with the basic secrets of the bomb in encyclopedias, what was guarded here was the stuff with which bombs could be made—not by nations but by people.

The escort guards lined them up before a revolving door that connected the reception room with the access passageway to TA-14. On the otherwise bare white wall to the right of the door was a sign that said:

> CONTRABAND
> Cameras, film, bombs, incendiaries, fieldglasses, binoculars, electronic sending & receiving devices, dangerous weapons, alcoholic beverages, firearms, explosives, codes & ciphers. WARNING: Persons having such unauthorized items in their possession are subject to such penalties as may be provided by law, dismissal, or other administrative action. (U.S. Atomic Energy Commission)

Within the louvered frame of each wedge of the revolving door was an explosives detector. The segments of the door kept to a minimum the amount of air in which the vapors of chemical explosives could circulate. The detector was capable of sniffing as little as 200 grams of dynamite, TNT, or other explosive nitrogen compounds. If explosives were detected, the door jammed. A guard in an adjacent bunker could push a button and incapacitating gas would fill the door segment. The glass in the door was bulletproof.

In the windowless passageway was the arch of a metal detector which, by AEC standards, was "capable of detecting a minimum of 200 grams of nonferrous metal placed anywhere on the body." At the inner door a closed-circuit TV camera swung and focused on the individual approaching. The image would be retained for as long as the security-system computer instructed the videotape to retain it.

At the direction of the escort guard, each visitor inserted the plastic card into a slot in a key-reader box next to the door. The electronic key-card system recorded the identity of the card (including by whom it was issued), the time of entry, and the estimated time of the visitor's exit from the Technical Area. If the visitor did not exit within fifteen minutes of that time, Central Security would be notified, and the stored image of the card-carrier would appear on access-point security consoles with orders to detain.

One by one, they passed through the access passageway's inner door. They were now in a maze of buildings, the AEC Medical Center and Scientific Laboratory. They had arrived in Atomic City No. One, where the hazards of radioactivity were not considered hazards, where the dangers of nuclear energy were called challenges.

And here were the strangers, come to be examined because they might have been exposed to too much plutonium. Barbara, seeking a metaphor in her Catholic heritage, said later that the command trip to Los Alamos was comparable to the summoning of a medieval heretic for examination in Rome.

33.

AFTER THEY ENTERED the Occupational Health building their uniformed escorts disappeared and were replaced by Gary Hobson, tall, black, in his mid-thirties, and Susan Poole, short, round-faced, and in her late twenties. Their names were printed in white on black rectangles they wore on lab coats. Each had a dosimeter clipped on the coat collar.

"We are to see Dr. Montgomery," Rosen said.

"I want to see a bathroom," Judith said. "I'm in pain."

"That's first on the agenda," Poole told her. "We're all set up for you. Three total *in vivo's.*"

"And hold the mayo," Judith said.

"What?" Poole asked.

"Never mind," Hobson said. "Let's get these people into Montgomery."

Dr. Joan Montgomery was sitting on a high stool at a laboratory table covered with the graceful folds of a long computer readout. On a shelf behind the table was a computer terminal and several monitoring devices with digital displays. At the end of the table was a small glove box.

She nodded to Rosen. "Long time since Vienna," she said. Smiling at each of the other visitors as she was introduced, she looked at them over red-framed half-glasses whose sidepieces disappeared into shingled gray hair. She pulled off the glasses and let them hang down on her buttoned-up lab coat. She had a dosimeter clipped on her pencil pocket. She did not have a name plate.

Hobson had slipped out of the room. He returned and handed bioassay containers to Montgomery.

Their fidgeting had become frenzy. Art was all but hopping as he shifted his stance from one foot to the other. Barbara's system was to rub her hands against her hips while softly humming and bouncing on the balls of her feet. Judith paced, and, at the same time, bent her body from side to side, hands on hips.

"You will be designated A, B, and C," Montgomery said. "And we will begin with bioassay. Miss Longden, you will be A. Will you please take these . . ." Judith, looked upon with envy by B and C, grabbed a plastic bottle and a plastic box from Montgomery's hands. " . . . and go into the lavoratory through that door . . ." Judith was already out of the room.

"Mr. Reeves, you will be B." Art now was hopping in front of her. He swept two bottles and a box from Montgomery's table. "Down the corridor two . . ."

Art trotted, saying over his shoulder, "I know where it is."

Barbara groaned. She was biting her lower lip. She imagined she would simultaneously bite off her lip, urinate, defecate, and faint in a pool of her own waste. She estimated that she could hold out for two minutes. She began counting, her chin quivering with each number. She sidled toward the door Judy had entered. At the count of one hundred and two the door opened, and Judith flattened against it as Barbara charged past her.

The containers of the urine and the feces went into an assembly of anonymous hands, along with blood samples, locks of hair, fingernail parings, spittle, and puffs of breath in plastic bags. The laboratory processing was swift, efficient, and unhindered by any human warmth.

"We're theoretical here," Montgomery told them when they reassembled in her laboratory. "By which I mean we turn out a lot of studies, set a lot of standards, and send a lot of reports to the AEC. But . . ." She paused and smiled. "But we don't see people very much.

"All right. Now what is going to happen. You will be given total *in vivo* counts. All that means is 'in life,' as opposed to *in vitro*, 'in glass,' or in a test tube. We want to know what is going on inside your bodies. We have special ways of doing that. You'll be gone over for radioactivity in a research facility that is underground. The reason for this, as I'm sure you know, is that we have to block out as much confusing background radiation as possible. We're a mile above sea level. A change from sea level to a mile up can be as much as 150 millirems.

"Just to remind you, even if you didn't work in the nuclear industry you'd still be getting radiation from natural sources, and from x-rays, luminous watches, TV. We've been using x-rays for more than 70 years. In an average year about half the population . . ."

"We've heard all that, Dr. Montgomery," Judith said. "I know that sounds rude, but we've come here to find out whether we have plutonium in us, especially in our lungs. We've heard all the positive statements about radioactivity. My big question is how much of that stuff do I have in me? We're involved with an aerosol, not x-rays."

Montgomery looked at Rosen, who was frowning and shaking his head. He impatiently waved his hands, obviously signaling the lecturer to cut short her talk.

"Yes," she said, casting an abbreviated smile at Judith. "Aerosol. In the lungs. Particles." She was having trouble getting back to what it was she wanted to say. "We will be doing counts on your lungs, of course. And on your entire body." Her pause was just long enough for Judith to speak without quite making another impolite interruption.

"When will we find out?" Judith asked. "Will we get rem-count printouts?"

"We will give you a verbal report. Detailed reports will be forwarded to your employer. And the counts will be in nanocuries, not rems."

"It figures," Judith said.

When they stepped from the elevator, Art tugged Judith's right arm, and they fell back from the group. "What the hell was that all about?" he asked. "Rems, printouts. You're such a smart-ass sometimes. It's only going to get us in more trouble."

"I'm not in any trouble with anybody. I want to know about my health. Period."

"Bullshit. You were trying to put her on."

"She was the one with the bullshit." The others were standing by a door up ahead, waiting for them. She began talking faster. "This is screwy, Art. *Biological* measurements are in rems. Rems means roentgen equivalent, man—it's a way of assessing biological damage. Nanocuries are for measuring *amounts* of radioactivity." The others were so close now that Art thought Rosen could overhear her—if she cared. "Rems would be for *us*; nanocuries are for *them*."

Montgomery was still smiling. She pointed to the half-windowed door. "I'm afraid I must be leaving you here. We all have a busy schedule today. Oh, yes. You'll need to use your cards at this door. Gary and Miss Poole will be seeing you through this long day. A pleasure to have met you."

They also left Rosen behind. As they passed through the door marked RESTRICTED RESEARCH AREA, Barbara heard Montgomery say to Rosen, "No cafeteria today, Sam. They've finally got a good Chinese restaurant here . . ."

"Are you HP technicians?" Judith asked their escorts.

"No," Susan Poole said. "I'm an animal attendant and Dr. Hobson is a veterinarian."

"Jesus!"

"Surprised?" Poole asked. "Well, so were we. We don't have many people, like Dr. Montgomery said." She looked down at her clipboard. "Room 212. You're Individual A?"

"Right. Good old A." Judith looked up at Hobson. "And Montgomery's a vet, too?"

"Her doctorate is in radiology. I believe that her thesis was on the environmental behavior of radionuclides released by nuclear reactors. She's smarter than she talks."

"What about you?"

"I just do my job. My specialty is mammals. Any mammal."

"Room 212," Poole said cheerily. "Here we are."

She flung open the door, revealing a small room which had in its center a stainless-steel box about the size of a three-drawer filing cabinet. The box was sheathed by Plexiglas. There were four ports in the sheath, and out of each one protruded a length of flexible black tubing which led into a Plexiglas box just big enough for a beagle to sit in. The boxes were low in back, high in front, so that the beagle inside could only sit. Each dog's head was strapped into a gray muzzle connected to the end of the black tubing. One dog was rolling its eyes, straining to look sideways at them. It had seen the door open. The beagle managed to raise its hindquarters enough to wag its tail, which thumped twice against the box.

Poole reached to close the door, but Judith stepped into the room. Hobson grabbed her arm, not hard, but with enough force to stop her from going farther.

"I don't want them disturbed," he said.

They stood there a moment, Hobson's hand still on her arm. "I'm not ashamed of this," he said. "They're better cared for here than in most homes. Fed, groomed. And they won't be sacrificed. It's not that kind of experiment. They keep on living. We keep on watching them. Been going on for years. These are the twentieth group."

"What are you trying to find out?"

"Plutonium aerosol," he said. "Your thing. Only they're getting a lot more than you could get. They get an aerosol, a mist of air with a few thousandths of a gram of plutonium oxide in varying particulate size. We measure how much they excrete and otherwise metabolize. And we just wait."

"For them to die?"

He nodded.

"How long?"

"It's still going on, you know. We don't have all the data."

Barbara and Art were in the doorway, looking from the dogs to Hobson and back again, listening, waiting for an answer.

"How long?" Judith repeated.

"We think about nine years."

"Lung cancer?" Barbara asked.

Hobson looked relieved to be able to turn away from Judith's unrelenting gaze. "Yes. But we're still working . . . We still don't know. Anyway, I'm not the one who's writing this . . . I don't know all the elements."

"You've got to know one thing about this," Judith said. "You know how long a beagle usually lives."

"About 18 years," he said. "It seems that most of the time this stuff cuts their lives just about in half."

"This is the wrong room," Susan Poole said.

"Maybe it isn't," Judith said.

34.

HOBSON AND POOLE led Individuals A, B, and C farther down the hall and directed them to separate rooms. Each assumed that the three rooms were identical and that what went on in one room would be the same as what went on in the other rooms. The rooms assigned to B for Arthur Reeves and C for Barbara O'Neill were basically the same; high-ceilinged, white, brightly lit boxes.

In Art's, the attendant was male; in Barbara's, female. Both attendants wore white, disposable paper coveralls, shoe coverings, Mother Hubbard-type hats, and surgical face masks; their thin plastic gloves were single-use. They revealed their gender by their voices; their gestures and their orders were almost identical:

"Remove your clothing behind that screen" (pointing) "and seal them in the carton you will find on the stool."

Then (eyes averted from the genitals): "Please step into the vault and lay on your back on the examination table."

The vault was well named. It looked like a bank vault, a metallic cube about eight feet to the side. The door stood open, revealing the six-inch thickness of the walls. To the right of the door was a long window set low enough so that an operator could sit at a console and observe the vault's interior.

The heavy door swung closed and clanged shut with a spin of a spoke-handled wheel. The inside of the vault was bathed in light from recessed ceiling fixtures. The walls, smooth and shiny, were made of a special shielding alloy. There was a flutter of air in the vault; the controlled atmosphere entered through a filter near the floor and expired through another filter system near the ceiling. Affixed to the ceiling was a continuous-air monitor.

Suspended from the ceiling was a white metal plate which hung directly over the examination table.

"Just relax," came the muffled voice through the intercom. "I'll be lowering the analyzer panel above you in ten seconds. It will not touch your body."

The room which Individual A entered was about the same as the others. The female attendant was an HP technician, as were the attendants in the other rooms. The preliminary procedure was similar: Judith stripped behind a screen and entered the vault. But it was not empty.

Two people were standing in the vault, one on either side of the examination table. They were masked, and they wore a higher-grade version of the technicians' protective apparel.

"Please get on the examination table and lay on your back," said a voice.

Judith stood at the foot of the table, her back to the door. She turned to look at the window. The technician's masked face looked back at her. There was a rumpling movement under the mask, and the voice repeated the command. Now Judith noticed an intercom speaker alongside the window. She could hear a click on the speaker; a tape recording began.

The man to the right of the examination table took a step forward. "My name is Dr. Goddard. I am a gynecologist. I am going to conduct the internal examination." He seemed to bow slightly. "Please get up on the examination table."

"Who are you?" Judith asked, glaring at the other man.

He did not speak.

"My associate," Dr. Goddard said. He motioned toward the table with his right hand. He wore yellowish plastic gloves.

"Where does he practice?"

"Here," the other man said. "At the Medical Center. My name will be part of the official report. Now please get up on the table."

She sat on the right side, to keep her back to the unnamed man. Then she lay back.

"Please spread your legs," Goddard said softly. "I am

beginning an inspection of the external genitals." His voice raised slightly; she was sure now the room was bugged. "Hair distribution regular. No swellings or discoloration. No skin lesions. No vaginal discharge. Clitoris normal."

He inserted his middle finger. "No indication of cystocele or rectocele."

"What's that mean?" she asked. She wanted to sound angry, but she knew her voice was feeble.

"No sign of hernia of the bladder or bulging of the rectum into the vagina." His voice resumed its cadence of mechanical recital. "Gland of Bartholin normal; cysts negative; Skene's glands normal." He removed his finger.

"Who the hell are you talking to?" she asked angrily. "This is the damndest vaginal examination I ever had. I thought this was supposed to . . . "

"Please be quiet," the other man said. "We are trying to make this as pleasant as possible."

"*You* be quiet," Judith said. "I don't even know who the hell you are. *Pleasant?* Jesus!"

Goddard resumed his recital. "I have inserted a speculum and have begun a visual examination for lesions or inflammation of the vaginal walls." He paused for a couple of seconds. "Normal." He paused again. "I am obtaining a scraping of tissue from the cervix." She could hear what seemed to be the opening and clicking shut of a container.

He inserted the index and middle fingers of his right hand into her vagina and moved his left hand along her abdomen. "No indication of inconsistency in the size or position of the uterus, tubes, or ovaries. No indication of abnormalities. Vagina appears normal."

Goddard deftly shifted Judith's body and legs so that she lay on her side, her legs drawn up in a fetal position. He inserted a lubricated finger into her vagina and a finger into her rectum. "I am examining the adnexal region. Pelvic organs well aligned. No indication of lesions at anal margin. Hemorrhoid normal. Adnexal region normal."

Goddard shifted her again. "Now my colleague will do an *in vivo* radiological." Goddard moved to the head of the table and firmly but gently pressed her shoulders. "Just relax," he said.

She did not try to resist. She stared at the white metal plate above her, at the recessed lights. She shifted her gaze and looked into Goddard's green eyes, framed by thick, grayflecked eyebrows and the white mask. He looked away, down toward where his eyes and his hands had been. She saw no alternative but to lie there and wait for this all to end.

"Conducting an *in vivo* radiation count on Individual A with an Eberline Plutonium Wound Counter," the harsh new voice said. "Instrument adjusted to . . ."

"Jesus!" Judith exclaimed. She pushed away Goddard's hands and tried to sit up. "That wound counter bullshit again. You're looking for it *in* me like *I* put it there. Jesus! My lungs. Look at my lungs!"

" . . . adjusted to detect at seventeen keV." He passed the wound counter over Judith's lower abdomen. The wound counter was a pencil-like metallic rod. It was connected by a thin white cable to the radiation dosimeter, a stainless-steel case about the size and shape of a toaster. The dosimeter, a portable alpha survey instrument, stood at the edge of the table, near his left hand. He continually shifted his eyes from a dial on the upper side of the dosimeter to the site of the rod.

The rod's rounded tip followed the white, puckered scar of an appendectomy incision and then slowly moved along the abdomen to the navel. The rod traced a faint line of down to the border of skin and hair. The rod stroked from thigh to thigh, rippling the hair, sometimes touching the hair-hidden flesh. "No detectable activity in pubic hair," said the voice.

"I'll need your help, doctor," the voice said.

"Please relax," Goddard said. "I am going to . . . resume my examination." He released his gentle pressure on her shoulders. "This will take only a moment." For the first time there seemed to be a trace of embarrassment in his voice.

"Dr. Goddard is dilating the vagina." The rod entered the vagina and touched the walls.

Again Goddard rearranged her body. The rod entered the rectum. The sphincter reacted, but there was no discharge. "No detectable activity in rectum," the voice said. "End of pubic area radiological *in vivo.*"

Staring at the white panel above her, she heard the door to the vault open and close. Then she saw Goddard's unmasked face above hers.

"Now that wasn't so bad, was it?" he said. He was smiling. His teeth were remarkably white and even.

"Jesus," she said softly. "Jesus. Why are you doing this to

me?" Her voice began to break, but she did not cry.

"I told you, miss. A routine g-y-n for radiation. No one is *doing* anything to you. If anything, you are the one who's doing things."

"What the hell do you mean?" Anger cleared the tremor from her voice.

"You know what I mean. You know why you're here." He paused for an instant, drew his face closer to hers, and whispered, barely parting his white teeth. "You know why we had to do this. Don't play it so innocent." Then he straightened up, and as if to talk to someone else, he spoke louder and dispassionately. "The general *in vivo* count will now commence. The HP technician will give you further instructions."

The door again opened and closed. She heard the hiss of the air in the vault.

The examinations of A, B, and C were otherwise nearly the same, and in all three vaults the procedure was similar. Each was asked to lie on the examination table, hands at side, facing upward, while the metal plate descended to within about two inches above the torso. After a few minutes the plate was raised, the individual was asked to turn over, and the plate descended again, this time hovering over the back.

The plate was a large-surface-area detector for an elaborate, extremely sensitive dosimeter located outside the vault. The technician read and recorded the counts on the console. The system was designed to find incredibly minute concentrations of plutonium in the body by detecting alpha rays.

After the plate had sought for any indication of alpha rays emanating from the whole body, the search was narrowed down. The HP technician entered the vault carrying a portable dosimeter similar to the one that had been connected to the wound counter. The attachment on this dosimeter, however, resembled a flat bar with a handle like that of a garden trowel. The portable dosimeter had two cables; one ran from the bar, the other plugged into a wall receptacle.

Holding the instrument in one hand and the bar in the other, the technician passed the bar over the chest, abdomen, hands, feet, head, and finally the pelvic area of each individual. The alpha-ray counts showed on a meter on the instrument and were also transmitted, through the wall connection, to the console. The counts were recorded and passed on to a computer. A printout would show the results of the *in vivo* counts.

The appearance of the reports on the three *in vivo* counts would be the same and would be made part of the official record of the examinations of Individuals A, B, and C. Results of the gynecological examination of Judith Longden would be sent directly to Washington for analysis by the AEC and the FBI.

"We don't get printouts?" Judith asked Rosen.

The four of them were in the snack bar off the closed cafeteria of the Occupational Health building. Their table was so tiny that she had to keep her elbows close to her side to avoid touching Rosen.

"No. At least not yet. They are being prepared. As I told you. However, as I told all of you," he scanned the table, "the counts seem to give you all a clean bill of health. The indications are that there was no detectable activity." He looked at his watch. "The car will be at the gate at six o'clock. We should be on our way."

The return trip was nearly a duplicate of the morning's journey, except for new escorts. As far as Denver, there had been a letting down, a lessening of tension. The Caslon Three were feeling relieved, for an unknown event had become a known experience. Soon after takeoff from Denver, however, the relaxation began giving way to sullenness, a snapping of a few words—"Well, excuse *me*!"—then silence. They were A, B, and C again, each isolated from the other.

When the stewardess came down the aisle taking orders for drinks, Art and Barbara ignored her, but Judith said, "A bourbon, please."

"No," Rosen said, not to Judith but to the stewardess.

"*What?* Who the hell do you think you are?" Judith twisted in her seat. She never unbuckled her seat belt, in an attempt to ease a fear of flying. She looked up at the stewardess, whose smiling face was turned to Rosen. "I said, 'a bourbon, please.' "

"I'm sorry, miss." Now the stewardess aimed her dazzling eyes and smile toward Judith. "Doctor's orders."

"What the hell is that all about, Rosen?"

"I want a nice quiet trip home, Miss Longden. I don't have any data on how alcohol affects your behavior. I don't want any drugs in you, including alcohol."

"Why can't I go into the toilet and gulp down something?"

"Because you are not carrying anything."

"How the hell do you know?"

Rosen pointed to the green notebook in her lap. "Just write it down in your journal. Another suspicion. Make it another 'Personal Theory.' That's what you call them, no? So write it: Quote. I think they went through my clothes while I was in the vault. Unquote."

She had been writing since they had been reunited in the cafeteria. She had exchanged few words with Art or Barbara. She wanted to think—and to write. She was working out what had led up to today. She had suspected that they—Rosen, and whoever worked with him—had gone through their clothing. She told him this now. And she told him she was not surprised that her clothing had been searched, her journal read and probably copied.

"Well, if nothing can surprise you any more, then I suppose you have something all figured out." Rosen spoke to her in an infuriatingly condescending tone, and he knew it.

"Yes."

"And is this ultimate 'Personal Theory' of yours a secret?"

"No."

"Well, why not tell me?"

"OK. What I have figured out and what I've written down here is that you are part of some group, some Government operation, that is trying to get me—and maybe Art and Barbara, too—but trying to get me, basically, to *admit* something. You—your group, probably in cahoots with Caslon—think we did something and want a confession. Or you know somebody else did this something and you want to pin it on us. You're trying to break us down. Break me down, especially. To get me to confess."

"Confess to what?"

"I don't know."

"Come now, Miss Longden."

"I don't know. I honestly don't know. You read the journal. My theories. Guesses. Honest to God, Rosen, I do not know . . . Let me start again. I *know*, but I don't understand, what I think is going on."

"Your rhetoric is quite charming, Miss Longden. But I cannot follow you."

"OK. I think you or the AEC or Caslon or the whole damn bunch figured I'm a disgruntled employee who causes too much trouble. Well, for that I should just be fired. But you're . . . you've made it a federal case. That's what I don't understand. It's out of proportion."

"Miss Longden, you—and your journal—are quite convincing in making it appear that you are blissfully ignorant. But there are certain *physical* facts involved here." His voice hardened. "And you *know* there are. You *know* what was in your apartment."

"I do not know. But I guess what you're getting at is that you think I stole plutonium from the plant. That's it, isn't it?"

"Do you know what it would mean if you were formally charged with that, Miss Longden?"

"No, I don't." She almost succeeded in keeping her voice from wavering.

"The law provides for a $20,000 fine or life imprisonment or both."

The safety belt light had flashed on, and the plane began to approach to Tulsa. Rosen looked at the checkerboard of Tulsa's lights. Judith's face appeared on the dark glass, startling him. The faintly mirrored face was pale and hauntingly innocent. He hesitated about saying the rest of what he had begun to say. But he had decided on his strategy, and he would go through with it. He turned his head away from the image of Judith to Judith herself.

"You know, I had never really thought about that," she was saying, almost inaudibly. "I mean, I had never seen in my own mind being arrested, being in a courtroom, being in jail. Jesus!"

He leaned closer to her, trying to hear and also wanting to be close to her. He was rarely confused about his emotions. He was now. He wanted to believe her. But it was too late. He would say what he had planned to say.

"There's a reward, you know. You could be worth a half-million dollars to somebody. All somebody has to do is turn you in. Think about it. Do you know anybody who would choose you over half a million dollars?''

She said it without hesitation: ''No. I don't.''

''Well, instead of meeting that reporter tomorrow, why not go somewhere with me?''

''Where?''

''To the U.S. Attorney's office here in Tulsa. We could go right from the airport. Tonight.''

The plane rolled along the runway, then braked. The relief of feeling herself on the ground again was so strong, it eclipsed her new fears. ''We've landed,'' she said. ''We made it.''

''Well?''

''What? Oh, no. No. I won't go there now. Maybe later. Maybe after I talk to the reporter. I have to do that. I said I would, and I will.''

''We'd rather you didn't talk to the reporter,'' Rosen said.

Art, Barbara, and the federal air marshal were filing out, along with the other passengers. They stood up, and Rosen placed his left hand on her right shoulder. It was a gentle gesture. ''We'd rather you didn't,'' he repeated.

''Hell, I know that,'' Judith said, suddenly laughing. ''Come on, let's get out of this damn plane. People'll start to talk.'' She laughed again. Rosen insisted on helping her with the parka.

35.

STILL IN MIRRORED SUNGLASSES, the white-haired driver of the morning was at the airport when they arrived. Rosen saw them to the car. "Take the Caslon Three home, Mike," he said.

There was little talk during the drive, and when Barbara and Judith arrived at Barbara's, they maintained silence until Art appeared. They had all agreed, hastily whispering in the terminal, after he was dropped off Art would drive to Barbara's and that the two women would not talk until he got there. He and Barbara had promised they would listen to what Judith had to say.

"The Caslon Three. I'm sorry I ever thought it. But that's what I thought we were. I saw us all together." She looked at Barbara on the window seat, Grayfur in her lap; then at Art, sprawled sideways on the red leather couch. Again, Judith was at the card table, facing them, they thought, like a judge. The tape recorder was still on the table. If Barbara and Art noticed, they did not mention it.

"I seem . . . It looks like I've got you in some trouble. It looks that way. OK. You wouldn't have been there today if it wasn't for me. OK. But there's something else. It's tough to say, but I wonder where I would be if it wasn't for you or maybe one of you. I think we should do some straight talking before I go to see that reporter tomorrow."

"Maybe this isn't a good idea," Barbara said. "It's been a long day."

Judith ignored her. "I've got a question for you, Art. Did you get a rectal examination today?"

"What?"

"And you, Barbara, did you have someone jam a wound counter up you?"

"No. But . . . I'll make some tea."

"You have anything stronger?" Art asked.

"Wine. Judy?"

"Thanks. Is that all there is to it? Jesus! Don't you two see? This whole thing was staged to examine *me.* There was nothing wrong with you two, or with me. They just wanted to see if I had any traces of plutonium in my vagina or rectum. That's all. Did you know that, Art?"

"Know what, Judy?"

"Jesus! Did you know this whole thing was a goddamn charade?"

"No. No, I didn't Judy. I don't understand all this. I don't understand."

Barbara came in with a half-filled bottle of Almaden chablis and three ceramic goblets. She poured Art's wine and went to the table. She sat next to Judith and patted her hands, which were spread before her. Barbara lifted Judith's right hand, wrapped it around a goblet, and filled it. Judith smiled and lifted the goblet.

"Wait a minute," Barbara said. She filled her goblet and raised it. "To the Caslon Three. All for one and one for all."

"I'll drink to that," Art said. He sipped his wine, walked to the table, and put his arms around Judith. He kissed her hair. He pulled up a chair and sat next to her. He and Barbara glanced at each other.

"Are you quite sure about that examination, Judy?" Barbara asked. She had tried to keep the touch of kindly indulgence out of her voice, but in a split-second she knew she had failed.

"Jesus H. Christ!" Judith pounded the table, which shuddered on its spindly legs. *"They* think I'm a crook. And *you* think I'm a goddamn loony. Yes. You can bet your sweet little ass I'm sure, Barbara. Are you sure they didn't poke you? I mean, you might just not notice."

"This isn't getting us anywhere, Judy," Barbara said. "You're on the eight-to-four tomorrow."

"Don't be in such a hurry, Barbara. There are a couple of

other things. You talked to Deckman on Friday. So did Art. Did he tell you anything about a reward, a half-million-dollar reward?"

"Captain Deckman told me that if I ever heard anything about any SNM missing that I should tell him," Barbara said. "And, yes, he did say that there was a U.S. reward and that it could be as much as half a million dollars."

"Art?"

"Yeah. Deckman told me. I didn't believe him, he showed it to me in a book."

"What was the name of the book, Art?"

"I don't remember."

"Could it have been *Nuclear Crimes?*"

"Yeah. That sounds right."

"Did either one of you think this had anything to do with me?"

They nodded.

"Goddamn it, Judy," Art said. "I didn't really believe it. I mean, I don't think you really knew that you stole any stuff."

"What the hell does that mean?"

"Well, there's been talk. You know that."

"That I'm a pain in the ass to management?"

"Yeah. And that you're some kind of crusader. And you ask a helluva lot of questions."

"And you don't give me a helluva lot of answers. Lover. What else did Deckman tell you?"

"Deckman told me about what they found in the apartment. You know. . . ."

"No, Art, I do not know."

"Plutonium. There had been plutonium there. He said they found awfully high counts, and that's why they took all your stuff away."

Judith glared at Barbara. "And that's what he told you, too?"

"Yes. There's the water boiling. I'll fix the tea."

"Yeah. You do that. I've got another question, Art. Just for you." She leaned closer to him. "Did Deckman tell you he thought I was smuggling the stuff out in my . . . well, I guess Deckman would say my cunt. Did he say that, Art? Did he say I was stuffing plutonium in my cunt?"

"Yes. Something like that."

"And did he tell you to watch out, Art?"

"For God's sake, Judy. Turn that goddamn thing off. This is private stuff."

"You bet it is, Art. Private *me.* I'll erase this tape when I've got it all down, when I've got it all figured. Now, tell me, Art. What were *you* figuring to do last night? What were you figuring when you said you wanted me to sleep with you last night? What were you figuring, Art?"

"Jesus, Judy. What makes you this way?"

"I'm the one asking questions, Art. You want me to guess?"

"No. I was figuring . . ."

"You were figuring that you'd get me to blow you and then you wouldn't have to worry about getting cancer of the cock. Right? But Art, suppose I was smuggling plutonium in my mouth? You think of that?"

"I . . . I thought of using a rubber, Judy. That's what I thought. And the other. OK. I did think of the other."

"Art. I'll go home with you tonight, and we can fuck all night, Art. But no rubber. OK?"

"OK."

"Not very convincing, Art. For God's sake, Art, don't you see? I've got to prove this to you—and you've got to prove it to me. You have to show you trust me, Art. Art, for God's sake, Art. This is crazy. They're trying to make me crazy."

Her hands went to her face, palms cupping her eyes. He reached toward her, but somehow she knew his hand was there, and she turned her face away before he could touch her. At that moment, Grayfur leaped into her lap. Judith screamed and bolted out of her chair, knocking over the table.

She kept her palms pressed against her eyes, shutting out Art and Barbara, who had rushed, clucking, into the room; shutting out them, all the *them*'s. She stumbled onto the couch. The leather was cold against her cheek. She withdrew her hands from her eyes and pressed her face into the cold pungent smell of animal. Grayfur was purring, near her right ear. She reached out to pet the cat and slowly turned her face just enough so that with one eye she could see a blur of rippling silver gray.

"And Grayfur, Barbara," she said, so slowly, so softly that they could hardly understand her. "You really felt that I might be killing her? Did he tell you that?"

"Captain Deckman said there may have been contamination—resuspension. I thought of Grayfur, he didn't."

"Anything else, Barbara? Did Deckman think of anything else?"

"No."

"He didn't have your psych profile there in front of him, Barbara? And he didn't ask you if you ever were married or whether you had any boyfriends?" She was speaking more rapidly now, but the force and the tempo of her words were out of phase with the slow motion of her body. She was slowly, seeming with pain, rising from the couch, turning around, looking at them, her face streaked with tears and creased by the seam of the pillow she had pressed against. The red crease cut diagonally across her face, from above her left eye to her narrow chin.

Barbara looked away from Judith's wretched face and from what Judith was saying.

"Did he come right out with it, Barbara? The old square son of a bitch. I'll bet he didn't. He could say cunt to Art, but I bet he couldn't say lesbian or pussy licking to you."

"Jesus!" Art said.

"You don't know what you're saying, Judith." Barbara's eyes were glassy, but the tears never moved from them. Her voice was tight, but it did not crack. She was holding on, her hands gripping the seat of her chair. "For the record, Art. For the record. I am not a lesbian. I have not . . . I have not been a lover . . . a lover of any woman. I told Captain Deckman that. It was very, very difficult for me to say that. I thought it might help you, Judy. I thought it might help you."

"Thank you, Barbara. I'm sure you did your best. Deckman's a bastard. They all are. Let's clean this place up. I'm sorry I . . . I'm sorry I got out of hand."

There often was a tension when they got into bed on a night like this, a preordained night. They sometimes made the tension part of the game, a game of who would make the first move. They rarely talked about it. Tonight, lying on his back, body stiff, Art spoke. "Sometimes, Judy, you don't understand—or don't want to understand, maybe that's it. I didn't tell you about Deckman because, in some stupid way, telling you would make it look like I believed him and not telling you would make it not seem that way." He turned his head toward her.

He remembers their last night, and, if he cannot quite find all the words to tell of it, he can convey the impression. And he can let it be known that there were no regrets that last night. It was a fine night for them.

She was propped on her right hand, her face close to his. He could feel the rhythm of her breathing and the warmth of her. He turned his body toward hers. She reached down for him, to his softness. Nothing happened. He rolled over, on his back, staring upward. Now her head was on his chest, but her hand was on him, lightly cupped, slowly moving.

"I'm having trouble, Judy. I don't know why. I can't get it up."

Then without reason, her hand trembled, and her fear was strangely stimulating. He began to harden, but her hand was gone. Her body stiffened.

"Judy, Judy. Relax." He turned toward her again. He stroked her shoulders and traced her spine to the roundness of her hips and then around her taut belly. "Relax." He was kissing her now, her eyes, her mouth, her throat, her breasts. She would stir now, her hips would move, her back would arch. His hand would find a moistness, there would be an opening of her.

But it was not happening.

Only rarely, in a spastic, triggered moment of alliance, had he tasted that moistness. Never had he so sensed himself deliberately planning, patterning his mouth as he planned and patterned his hands. Now, tonight, if there were some special need, some reason, he would *do it.* (His thoughts, if they could be set down, would have been like these. If he were to speak of what it was he was planning, patterning, the words would be *do it,* you know, *go down.)* He began to move his head along her, past the firmness of boned flesh, toward the soft hollow. But her hands were on his head, tugging him toward her face. "No," she said. "Put it in. Put it in."

And she was suddenly alive to him. All she would have done, she was doing. They made love in the gathering frenzy they both had learned and taught each other, and they achieved what they both had sought.

Now they laughed at the moments of groping, the fears.

"For a guy who couldn't get it up, you did OK."

"Judy. It was so good. And so strange, so strange tonight. So damn strange."

"Something's happening to me, Art. Something that I think is bad when it's coming over me, but I think it's good afterward. Like this. I guess what happened in bed was like what's been happening outside."

"Would you like to smoke?"

"Yes. Yes, Art. I guess I want that, too. Art, the good part tonight? Let's keep up the good part. It's like that with me lately, Art. You know, coming back? Tonight, coming back? In the plane? Rosen started getting very, very heavy." She took a deep drag. "He was laying on the reward shit . . . and telling me to stay away from the reporter . . . and making me feel down, down. And then all of a sudden I was smiling, laughing like hell . . ."

She began laughing, and Art began laughing.

"I had to do that scene at Barbara's. I knew I was getting in hard at you and her. But I had to, and I had to go nuts . . . The chair, the wine. Jesus! And the goddamn cat. Petting the cat. Wanting to get fucked. Wanting to know what the hell Deckman said . . . Art, Jesus, Art. They think I was putting that shit *in* me. And you thought it, Art. You thought it."

Her voice cracked, and she sounded as if she might begin to cry. Art could not tell what it was that was happening to her. Later he thought that what was happening was that she was going away, somehow going away . . .

Then she was back again, back from somewhere. " . . . I wanted to find out and I didn't want to find out. You know? It was like I had syphilis or clap or something. Or you thought I did. I don't know. A test. I guess it was a test. To see if you'd do it. If you loved me. It's all a test. Quiz. Examination. All a test. I guess I'll quit that goddamn place, Art. Like you. Love you. Quit. No more of that shit in me." She began to cry now. "It's not in me. It's not really. That shit's not in me. Not in my lungs. Nowhere in me. It's not in me."

36.

THE NEXT DAY she was dead. The next day I saw Caslon Wells for the first time. The next day is when I started writing this.

I have been able to write about her because she left a legacy of information that she had gathered and recorded. I did not have to imagine her. Writing about her to this point was a kind of collaboration.

But to write further, to write beyond the point of description, toward understanding, toward explanation, I have to write about why she died. And for this she left a legacy, too. Her death has produced innumerable reports. There are tapes and transcripts of tapes. There is a full record of her visit to Los Alamos. And there are officials eager to give me information about Employee A, who in death became Suspect A.

My friend Phil, who had given me the CIA-endorsed, FBI-suppressed warning while I was in Caslon Wells, had been right about where to look. The web of events and people may have been centered in Oklahoma. But the threads—the answers and explanations—were in Washington. The people there, though, were as reluctant to let the truth be found. No one, for instance, would tell me what 43719 might mean, let alone what it did mean. That number became for me the essence of Judith's legacy.

I had asked about that number several times in the few days I had been back in Washington. I think that is why I got the call from the Iceman. I gave him that name because his voice was cold and sharp.

"Phelan, you ask too many questions," the Iceman said on the first call. "What you're writing won't be printed. You want the real stuff about her, you be nice and just wait. It'll come."

I called Phil at his Langley number. He did not say that he knew about the call from the Iceman, but he did not sound surprised. I said something about the Government's involvement in Judith's death.

"Negative," he said in his most crisp CIA voice. "You have a lot to learn. Do you realize how complicated it is to arrange a Government killing?" I could never quite tell when Phil was kidding. "You need a thug for an asset, and he's almost always undependable. You need permission from a fairly high level for what they used to call 'executive action' and which I'm sure is called something else now. And, believe me, Phelan, it's not done to keep a young woman from complaining about working conditions or to keep a fairly well connected reporter from writing a half-assed story that won't have many facts in it, anyway."

I told Phil I would like to see him.

"OK. Give me a couple of days to sort through what this is all about. I'll call you." He hung up.

I was still on leave, but I spent a fair amount of time in the newsroom, mostly making phone calls. About seven o'clock or so on the day I called Phil, I left the paper, had a drink with a friend in a nearby bar, and began walking to my apartment, which is on Massachusetts Avenue, about a half a mile from work.

I thought I was being followed, but I thought it in a self-doubting way that I did not take seriously.

I walked up to my apartment, which is on the second floor of what once had been an elegant townhouse, and unlocked the door. I pushed against it, but it would only open part way. Something or someone was braced against it. I thought I heard sounds behind the door. The apartment was dark. I could somehow tell by the resistance against the door, though, that I was pushing against a person, not a chair or a bureau.

I pushed for perhaps ten more seconds. Then I bolted down the stairs and across the street to a drug store. I dialed 911 and reported to the policeman who answered that my apartment was in the process of being burglarized. I then called the press room at Police Headquarters and told MacBride, our man there, what was happening. I checked my watch.

In five minutes a patrol car pulled up and two police officers leaped out. One ran up the front stairs. Her partner leaped a low fence on the side of the house and headed for the fire escape in back. I was impressed at how well they knew the house. In another five minutes, they were back. And the night lieutenant from the precinct rolled up in his car, responding not to the burglary but to the power of the press. We recognized each other.

The two police officers followed the lieutenant and me upstairs and into the apartment.

"We figure," Officer Gladys Franklin said, "that they—there were two, I think—that they had the place cased well enough so they took the fire escape *up* and then to the house next door and down the inside stairwell that opens up on that roof. Pretty slick."

"We'll need a list of what's missing," the lieutenant said. He cast a professional look around. "Stereo. Sony. Typewriter. Camera. A Nikon. You know, Phelan, you should put that away. Funny. It's a mess. But they didn't take the good stuff. You'll be able to watch the Late Show tonight. You're lucky."

Some luck. Every drawer was dumped. Every shelf was empty. Even the cabinets in the kitchenette. Cans and smashed bottles on the floor. And things *were* missing. My tape recorder, which had been on the table in the living room, was gone. So was the bag I had carried on my trips to Caslon Wells, Corpus Christi, and Los Alamos. It had been full of tapes and notes. A couple of hundred pages of manuscript were gone, too. They had been piled next to the typewriter on the same table.

I had been paranoid enough to make duplicates of the tapes and photocopies of the notes and most of the manuscript. But I decided to go along with the apparent loss. I reported what was missing to the lieutenant. I called MacBride back and told him what had been taken. I figured that if anyone happened to be listening in, it would sound as if I had been badly set back by the theft. "I don't know how long it'll take to rewrite this stuff, or if it's worth it," I told MacBride. He decided to handle it as a straight short police story for the Metro section. He interviewed me; I declined to discuss what the subject of the story was, and he wrote four paragraphs about a "mystery theft."

The next morning I found outside my door, set on top of my morning paper, a cardboard box. It was full of shredded paper and chopped-up tapes. There was a handwritten, block-lettered note on yellow lined paper. "This could be you," it said.

I decided that from then on I would write this in the safety of the newsroom. My extracurricular work was approved by the assistant national editor who had been so skeptical on the first night I called from Caslon Wells. He even said that perhaps the paper would publish some of this some day.

Within the next few weeks I developed what Judith had called in her journal a Personal Theory. I began developing it by asking myself a question: Why had Ann Garvey suddenly left Caslon Wells?

I did not find Ann Garvey at the U.S. Department of Labor's Occupational Safety and Health Administration. When I finally managed to get through to what I had been told was her Osha supervisor, he said, "Dr. Garvey is no longer with Osha. I have no further information."

I put the question to Phil when we met a couple of days after the burglary. He chose the elegant oak-paneled barroom of the Hay-Adams Hotel on Lafayette Park, opposite the White House. He sipped a German beer, a taste acquired in Berlin in the 1950s.

"First of all, Phelan, this is not our show. Domestic stuff. You know that. You should be talking to the Bureau."

"The Bureau doesn't have smooth operators like you," I said. "But if you really mean that, I could probably get something more than what the FBI is putting out. We could press the Bureau. All they say now, though, is that they are investigating the death, Judith Longden's death. I'm interested in things *around* the death. Like Garvey. What was she doing there and what happened to her?"

"We have been developing her as an asset. She *is* a psychologist, and she was on Osha's payroll. She even wrote some pamphlets, I understand. We were hoping to develop her to get her on the staff of an international agency. Routine thing."

"International Atomic Energy Agency in Vienna?" I asked.

Phil shrugged. The game had started. I would ask questions and get answers only if a specific answer fulfilled some agency need. I might be given an answer to lead me astray, but I also might be kept more or less informed correctly. Shrugs and silences usually meant I was on track.

"Well, let us say a sister agency—domestic—made some inquiries about getting a safe person to look into a matter the sister agency was interested in. No big deal. Just a computer personnel and resources search."

"So the Atomic Energy Commission—maybe somebody named Rosen?—asked the CIA to find them somebody who might look into a possible nuclear materials diversion case? Christ, that's some computer! A woman involved, so the computer finds a woman to put on the case."

"You make it sound simple, Phelan. Much, much more complex. But, to carry on. There was a slight flap. She was told to get her ass back to Washington."

"Who called her back—your guys or the AEC?"

"That's not important," he said, just sharply enough for me to sense that the question was important. I let it pass.

"OK," I said. "She did not go back to Osha. Where is she? I want to talk to her—strictly about Judith."

"Talk to her all you want, Phelan. She's no longer a potential asset." He gave me the address of an apartment house in Arlington.

"You mean you dropped her? She's out of a job?"

"Not exactly, in response to your first question. And she's going to work for a small think tank in answer to your second. And may I give you some advice?"

"Always welcome, Phil."

"Don't push too hard on this. Nuclear stuff is a hard, hard ballgame. I brought you a clipping." He handed me a Xerox of what looked like a story from a French newspaper. He knew I spoke a little French.

The story was short. It was from a 1968 edition of a Paris paper. It said that thirteen nuclear weapons specialists had been killed in a plane crash. Somebody had typed, in English, along the bottom of the clipping, "Happened a week after announcement France planned to develop H-bombs. Needed plutonium, anyway."

I started to ask him a question, but he grabbed the clipping back, handed me the bar check, and stood up to leave.

"Take my advice, Phelan. Keep this thing in Oklahoma."

Ann Garvey told me that on that Saturday night in Caslon Wells she had been summoned back to Washington for an urgent meeting of her department. I let that pass. She also said that she had quit Osha to take a position in private industry, and I let that pass, too.

Garvey was sitting on a straight-backed chair near the stark white wall of her apartment. I sat across from her in a chair that had some padding on its seat but no arms. There was a sterility about this apartment that fascinated me. I felt I was dealing with someone who had trouble being self-indulgent and cared little for appearances. She wore a black and white tiny-checked double-knit pants suit that was too tight for her. He hair was drab. She technically did not chain-smoke because she snuffed out a cigarette in a large glass ashtray before she lit the next. They were Dorals, which to me represent an attempt to stop smoking.

"I never was completely frank with Judy," she said. "Now I wish I had been, and I'm not going to make the same mistake twice."

I wondered how frank she was going to be.

"She was in trouble. She had found out a dirty little secret. She had found out—lived through—the fact that a plutonium economy is going to eat up people like her."

My first surprise had come when she said it would be all right to record what she said. My next surprise was that she really seemed to be talking.

"We've known about the connection between cancer and radiation for more than a century. We know now that for centuries before that miners in Germany came down with something they called *Bergkrankheit*—'mountain sickness.' It was radiation sickness from the uranium in the ore they mined. Now we have miners digging up uranium in mines that are sometimes more than two hundred times over safe levels.

"The AEC's Division of Occupational Safety concentrates

on things like safety shoes and safety glasses. And neither the AEC or Osha has bothered to learn much about plutonium."

She actually picked up the recorder and began talking into it. I had the feeling that a frustrated bureaucrat was becoming a crusader before my very eyes. I wondered why.

"It's insidious. It gets in the body, and there's nothing—almost nothing you can do. There aren't many people working with plutonium. Maybe a few thousand. Now. But we know that among some groups of plutonium workers the death rate from cancer is about twice what statistics would predict. And, theoretically at least, they had been exposed to safe levels of plutonium. You know what the level is? Less than six hundred *billionths* of a gram!"

I guess she realized she sounded as if she were preaching. She put the recorder on the white plastic cube table between us. But she did not switch it off.

"Judy had breathed in—perhaps ingested—more, of course. Much more. We will know eventually. Or should know. There's a federal register of plutonium workers, you know, and when a worker dies, he or she gets an autopsy. It's called the U.S. Transuranium Registry. It's for people who have got transuranium materials—mostly it's plutonium—into their bodies. Judy went on the registry the first time there was a contamination report on her."

I asked her if she suspected that something Judy had learned had somehow led to her death. It was the broadest way I could put it; I didn't want to scare off Garvey at this point.

"Whatever she found out—whatever you're finding out—I'm telling you, there's worse. That Facility is dangerous and life-threatening. Work there is humiliating—the bioassays, the surveillance.

"You know what that Orr told me? He told me he really liked those bioassays because they could pick up a lot of other information on employees. He was laughing when he said it. I had hardly met him. But there he was, telling me intimate details about his workers. He said what he liked was seeing the reports on a minister's daughter who probably had syphilis and how some Mormon was on drugs. Incredible."

"That's not enough to get killed over," I said.

"I suppose you're right, Mr. Phelan. I suppose I'm just getting carried away. But don't forget this. If she had ingested or inhaled enought plutonium to contract fibrous carcinoma of the lungs, she would be dead in a few weeks, and there could be no doubt as to how she died. She would be the first casualty of the plutonium economy. A martyr."

"And you think somebody didn't want that to happen? Is that what you're saying, Dr. Garvey?"

"I'm saying what I said, Mr. Phelan."

I felt I had all I was going to get out of her without digging so hard that she would stop talking. But I had nothing to lose at this point. I told her that I had information she had been planted in Osha and then, in effect, planted in Judy's life. I wondered why.

Garvey paled. It doesn't happen often. But when you see the color suddenly leave somebody's face, it is startling.

"I'm just not going to talk about that, Mr. Phelan."

"You've already talked about a lot of things, Dr. Garvey. Controversial things."

"Nothing I have said to you is a violation of national security, Mr. Phelan."

"And talking about why you were there, that would be a violation?"

"I think you had better go, Mr. Phelan. I don't want to be rude, but you said you wanted to talk about Judith, about safety considerations. And that is what I did. If I think of any more things to say on those subjects, I will call you."

She never called. I found out later that the think tank she went to work for was in Aiken, South Carolina, near the Government's Savannah River nuclear-fuel reprocessing plant. I wonder sometimes what she is doing there.

I kept Harry Skirvin filled in on what I was learning. I thought that the more I told him the more I would get from him.

Harry's first revelation was about the so-called douche bottle that Judith had strapped to her thigh the day of the raid on her apartment. Harry had had the fluid analyzed. He said there was a trace of plutonium in it, enough to register on a sensitive alpha-scanner if she had douched herself, as instructed, with that liquid.

"OK," Harry was saying. "So now we know there *was* some kind of setup. She wasn't just paranoid."

We were in the Department of Commerce cafeteria. Harry is a connoisseur of cafeterias; he does not believe a union official should be seen in an expense-account restaurant, at least in Washington, at lunch.

"We really went into this, Phelan. We hired experts: radiologists, gynecologist, psychologist, you name it. If she had taken that douche on Friday morning, the way they wanted her to, there would have been enough of a trace of plutonium there for the g-y-n radiation exam to pick it up at Los Alamos on Sunday."

"What about her period? Suppose—oh Christ, Harry." I put down my notebook. I felt disgusted, with the story, with myself, with whatever they had been doing to her. "This is horrible stuff, Harry. Are you sure of this?"

"I'm sure about the trace of plutonium. The rest? Why not? They held all the cards. They could have set up the raid, the Los Alamos exam, everything. The gynecologist we talked to said that when she did have her period, say in a week, the plutonium would have passed out of her. The gynecologist is like you. He can hardly believe what we're telling him. But he says, that given the idea that people wanted to *frame* her but not *harm* her, it's even possible that no great harm would come to her from this."

"What's he, a goddamn Government doctor?" I asked. "He must be full of shit, Harry. Plutonium's got to harm you."

"Not quite, Phelan. We've gone over this. On a scale of harm, the worst thing would be to breathe it or to eat it. There was an experiment, at Los Alamos, right after World War II. The Government injected it—I'm not kidding, *injected*—plutonium into terminal patients. Nobody died of plutonium. They all died of what they were supposed to. Except two, last anybody checked. So it is possible to claim, if you're backed up against the wall by, say, a newspaper reporter, that plutonium in the bloodstream is not lethal and may not be highly injurious. If I sound like a goddamn bureaucrat, Phelan, it's because I just had to explain all this in a confidential memo to my boss."

"If what you say is true, what happened when she fooled them? She didn't have any plutonium in her because she didn't take that fake douche they handed her. Then what could they find in her at Los Alamos?"

"I think they found it, Phelan. I think they found it, maybe not in her sna—maybe not where they thought, but in her. If she had been clean, the whole deal would have been off."

"She—and Barbara and Art—they were all told they were OK."

"So?" Harry shrugged and finished his soup. "So somebody lies. The whole Los Alamos thing was a psychologist's setup anyhow. That's what I heard."

"Heard where? What psychologist? Garvey?"

I didn't tell him about Garvey's double role, but I told him about Garvey's condemnation of plutonium in general and Caslon in particular.

"Bullshit. I heard from someone in Osha that she's some kind of plant. The AEC sicced her on the case. She was trying to psych them. The way I figure it, Garvey set up everything: the raid on the apartment, the douche, the trip to Los Alamos. Everything. To break them down."

"What for?" I thought I knew, but I wanted other people to say it; I wanted to not be the only one talking about stealing plutonium.

"You know damn well what for. They were trying to frame her for something *they* were doing." He held up his hand, like a traffic cop. "And don't ask me again that bullshit question about who's *they*. You know who they is . . ."

"Yeah. Everybody who's not us." I laughed. Harry didn't.

"They were trying to frame her. And you know why?" He didn't wait for an echo. "I'll tell you why. Because of that day when the criticality happened and Judith and Barbara and Art saw Orr, Deckman, and Kovacs in that room trying to cover up something. Right off, Kovacs—he's the biggie, you know—Kovacs knew the only one he had to worry about was Judy. The only one with guts."

"So you're saying that Kovacs—one of the big *they* crowd—tried to frame her, and when he couldn't, he had her killed."

"*I'm* not saying that, Phelan. You're saying it."

And I almost said something about guts, but I didn't. What I said was, "Where do you put Scinto in this?"

Harry leaned toward me. "Don't ask, Phelan. Just don't ask. It's a real queer one."

I thought I knew Harry well enough to realize that he had not said this to induce me to pursue the Scinto angle, but of course that was the effect on me of what Harry said.

Harry and I met frequently for several weeks after that, but no conversation was as intense as the one in the Department of Commerce cafeteria. Not even when I asked him about her, about her and him. I knew it had nothing to do with her death—and that was the subject I was supposed to be pursuing. But I had to ask.

"I almost left my wife for her, Phelan," he said. "Almost. I kept finding excuses for going out there. It was a little local—and getting littler, mighty damn fast. They kidded me at first in headquarters, and then it had an edge on it. 'How's that nice little local doing, Harry?' That sort of stuff.

"It only lasted maybe two or three months. It ended in a Phoenix motel. I had to go there for legitimate business, a regional meeting. I got her to fly there.

"It wasn't all . . . all being in bed, Phelan. There was that. It was beautiful with her. Beautiful. She had a marvelous body. And there was an evenness to her. I don't know how to explain it. She was *there* and nowhere else. She was always with you."

He looked around, which he frequently did when we were talking. We were in a cafeteria on K Street. The place was patronized mostly by senior high classes from Iowa. "I guess I marked her in Phoenix, Phelan. Like Scinto marked her. It was a setup. Not by me, Phelan. Honest to God.

"But I was stupid. They set us up. They sent me a set of those photographs. They sent her a set. And they sent my wife a set. They made sure she got them, my wife, in the mail, addressed to her, when I wasn't home. It just about ruined me, Phelan. Just about did it. But it was over then. I told my wife it was over. And it was. It was Judith's idea. She didn't like me making a commitment to her and her not making one back. She said she couldn't do that."

From that point on, Harry seemed more guarded toward me. Eventually, he broke off. My phone calls to him were not returned, a note to him unanswered.

37.

I FINALLY MET Rosen at a party. I don't go to many parties. But the invitation to this one came from Phil, and he suggested that I come alone, which for me is easy.

The party was at somebody's house in Virginia. I was introduced to a dozen or so people, including my host and hostess, one or both of whom apparently worked with Phil. I spotted Rosen near the self-service bar. I had not been able to reach him at the AEC, though in Caslon Wells he had agreed to an interview when we both were in Washington. I was not so naive that I thought it was a coincidence that Rosen was at the party. But I assumed that it was Phil who wanted to talk to me and that Rosen was there to give Phil technological backup.

Rosen had poured himself a dry vermouth over ice cubes; it had the advantage, I suppose, of looking like a martini. I had a bourbon, which I made pale because I knew I would be working.

Rosen said he was slipping off to a study on the second floor where we would not be disturbed. He suggested that I join him in about ten minutes.

Phil was also in the room when I arrived. I assumed it was a safe room, at least from their viewpoint; any bugs would be theirs. I began by aiming a question at Phil, but he shook his head and pointed toward Rosen. "Dr. Rosen has agreed to talk to you about safeguards, Phelan. I'm just here to listen—and maybe learn something."

So Phil was a kind of public-relations presence for the agency. The principal was Rosen. He said he was willing to talk about safeguards but that he would have to be discreet in any remarks about what he called the Longden case.

"Why discreet?" I asked.

"There are aspects of the case which are still pending."

"Such as?"

Rosen looked at Phil, who showed no reaction. "Such as," Rosen said, "a very delicate investigation."

"Of stolen plutonium?"

Rosen looked to Phil again.

I elaborately closed my notebook, put it in the inside pocket of my jacket, along with my pen, and stood up.

"What's wrong, Phelan?" Phil asked. He seemed genuinely surprised.

"Come on, Phil. I'm not going to spend the whole damn night being played with like this. If you guys are trying to feed me something, leak me something, then why not do it? This is bush."

"Dr. Rosen is not used to talking to journalists, Phelan."

"Then why is Dr. Rosen here in this room pretending to talk to me, Phil? We're playing a game here."

"I'm sorry, Mr. Phelan," Rosen said. "Perhaps you could suggest a better way to do this."

He sounded as if he was not being sarcastic, but merely practical.

"I suggest, Dr. Rosen, that you tell me in your own words what happened to Judith Longden. You were there. You saw all the records. And you saw what was in the envelope she was bringing to me. Let's start with that." I turned to look at Phil and said, half to him, "And let's just stay in Oklahoma."

"The envelope was taken from . . . the body at the request of Mr. Orr," Rosen began. "This was perfectly legal, since it certainly was the property of Caslon. However . . . as the senior federal official on the scene, I asked to see the contents. I had reason to believe that they included material of federal interest. I was right.

"At the final fuel-rod assembly station in P Plant there is an x-ray unit, which looks for flaws in the fuel rods. By the time the rods have reached this station, the plutonium fuel pellets, encased in ceramic, are inside the rods. The rods are sent to the AEC for use in the experimental fast-breeder reactor the Government is building at a demonstration site in Tennessee.

"The contents of the envelope included x-rays of fuel rods. The x-rays had been crudely doctored. Flaws in the rods had been covered up by inking over them."

I tried to get Rosen to explain what the effect of defective fuel rods would have been on the fast-breeder reactor. He said he did not want to speculate because it would not be fair to Caslon. The matter was being studied by AEC quality-assurance engineers, he said. And he added, rather sharply, that since I had suggested that he tell me what happened in his own words . . .

"Miss Longden was a seriously ill young woman, physically and mentally," he resumed. "She did not realize how irresponsible it would be to show you those x-rays. Or to make unreasonable charges of hazards at the plant.

"But that was not our principal concern about Miss Longden. We had reason to believe she was diverting plutonium from the Facility.

"I believe you have acquired certain documents that mention a Mexican connection, that show the presence of plutonium in her apartment, that show her life-style was erratic, that she was susceptible to suggestions from others. We also have a psychological profile that may be of interest to you. It shows that she could be induced to commit a criminal act.

"She was not the only one engaged in the diversion. But we had a case against her, we were building a good one, and it was getting better. She knew this. I warned her on the plane returning from Los Alamos. I told her about the federal statutes: if a person engages in the diversion of special nuclear materials, and if the intent of that person is to injure the United States or aid a foreign nation, then life imprisonment is the ultimate penalty. It used to be death. If you recall, the Rosenbergs were executed for selling atomic secrets. I'm not convinced it should not still be death.

"I also told Miss Longden that the Atomic Energy Rewards Act provides for up to $500,000 in rewards for anyone giving information that leads to the recovery of the diverted SNM.

"She refused to cooperate with the Government, Mr. Phelan. She said she was going to meet you. From what she had in her possession, I would say that she was planning to *use* you. She was going to portray herself as a victim of plutonium contamination, a victim who was being pursued by a malevolent, criminally irresponsible company. She was going to use this to cover up her real self, and what was really about to happen to her. Within twenty-four hours of her meeting with you, Mr. Phelan, she was going to be arrested for the diversion of special nuclear material.

"No matter how sorry you may feel about her tragic death, Mr. Phelan, you should feel some professional relief at not being used as a cat's-paw."

There was a ring of rehearsal to what Rosen told me. I could understand why. Obviously, he had been briefing people at the AEC and elsewhere in the Government for weeks. But I knew I was being given a small piece of the pie. I did not know who baked it or what the ingredients were. Washington doesn't have an information labeling law.

I used Rosen's dramatic pause to compose a question which, I hoped, would deflect him from his rehearsed narrative and give me something more spontaneous.

"There was something else in the envelope, I understand, Dr. Rosen. Something with the number 43719 on it. Could you enlighten me about that?"

"The other documents in the envelope were comparable to the x-rays, Mr. Phelan. Allegations, shall we say. And comparable, in some cases, to the drivel in her journal. I assume you have her journal. Certainly there were numbers, file numbers . . ." He stopped for a moment and looked at Phil. "There were many numbers on the papers, which had been taken from Caslon, and were Caslon property. I do not remember any specific number."

"Could you give me a general idea about the contents of the documents, Dr. Rosen. As you did about the x-rays?"

"There was nothing significant."

"Well, not to be argumentative, doctor, but she must have attached great significance to them. She was bringing them to me. Isn't it possible for *you* to show them to me—with an interpretation?"

"No. That is not possible, Mr. Phelan. As a matter of fact, that envelope and its contents were accidentally destroyed."

"By whom, doctor? I mean, who committed the accident?"

"It was a mistake by those two Caslon employees who made the contamination check of the car and the body. They mistakenly thought that they were to destroy any material thought to be contaminated. They got their instructions wrong. Unfortunate."

I did not say anything, which, I suppose, was the most impolite thing I could do. I could see that Phil was almost wincing; he looked away when I turned my professionally pursed smile on him.

I asked Rosen about the visit to Los Alamos. He told me that the examinations were routine and that I would be sent a report on them. The reference to Los Alamos got him reminiscing.

"Quite a place. Quite a place. There's a woman there now, a biologist, I've known her a long time. She came there as a young girl, with her father, who worked on the bomb, the first bomb. She told me that she remembers playing hopscotch there, and the Los Alamos variation had a certain square, and you had to avoid that square. It was called contaminated. The contaminated square.

"The point is that people know how to live with nuclear energy there. It could be any city. People learn to live with what they need to live with. We could learn a lot from Los Alamos."

I nodded politely. I had stopped writing anything down. I looked to Phil, who smiled, relieved. The interview was over. To Phil, I assumed, the interview had been a success. But Rosen was still back in Los Alamos . . .

"It was a strange, fascinating place in 1950, when I arrived there. Out of Berkeley, young, bright—though if you were a physicist then, the word was always brilliant. But it was a tragic year. It was the year that shaped me, Mr. Phelan.

"The Rosenbergs were arrested that year, and, as one of my colleagues overheard somebody saying, I was only a syllable away from them."

I began paying attention. Rosen's voice was rising, not only with the fervor of reminiscence but also with a remembered anger.

"It all started, you know, with David Greenglass, Ethel Rosenberg's brother. He was involved with the theft of uranium. The wartime theft of uranium!"

I felt obliged to remind him that it had not been exactly wartime.

"Cold war!" he exclaimed. "And then Korea. Russia was

the enemy then. Still is. I never became sophisticated about Russia, Mr. Phelan. Never!"

Phil looked stoic, but I knew he wanted to break in; Rosen was spoiling the story. He was not just a sober scientist helping to track down modern plutonium thieves. He was Dr. Rosen of Los Alamos, Class of '50, redeeming himself and his two syllables.

"They're still at it, Mr. Phelan. We're putting men with semiautomatic rifles on the plants soon, you know. And armored personnel carriers. We have to defend our plants now. The so-called terrorists—Marxists, all of them. Do you know there already have been acts of sabotage—actual sabotage? Some thefts? Some losses? Arson at Nuclear Fuel Services. Arson at the Indian Point reactor . . ." I started scribbling down the names. "Dynamite found at Point Beach Reactor in Wisconsin . . . And don't try to shush me," he said, glaring at Phil.

"They are trying to get plutonium, Mr. Phelan. The MUF—that means 'material unaccounted for'—is rising. They've got it somewhere. She must have known where it was. She must have known."

Phil had got out of his chair and was standing between Rosen and me. "That will be all, Dr. Rosen," Phil said, in a stern voice I had never heard before. "That will be all." Phil turned to me and said, in that harsh, curt voice: "The interview is terminated."

Rosen looked like my last chance at finding out what had happened to Judith. Phil had given me all that the agency had felt safe to give and had even produced Rosen to perform for me. But the performance had got out of hand. Now, of course, Phil had closed up on me, and Rosen had become totally unavailable. I had nowhere else to go—except to Capitol Hill.

Two committees were cautiously circling the potential issue of Judith Longden's death. Just enough had been published about the incident to give some people the idea that an issue could be constructed. It was possible that she could be made into a martyr . . . for organized labor . . . for women's liberation . . . for opponents of nuclear power. The idea was being discussed in talks among activists searching for a new cause, in a few counter-culture newsletters, in phone calls to Congressmen's issue people on the Hill.

And so scouts for two committees had hit the trail to Oklahoma, looking deep enough into Judith's death to determine whether it was a safe issue and one worth anything to their principals. The scouts had access to FBI field reports and other federal information that could be made available to a friendly Congressman's aide but which a reporter could not expect to obtain.

The scouts were back now, reporting to their Congressmen. In that atmosphere, I could pick up—and drop—crumbs of information. I began a round of trade with one of the scouts. He had found out enough for me to develop my Personal Theory beyond what Rosen had told me. The scout, in exchange for my account of Bim's description of the accident scene, gave me something: a lead on my number, 43719. He had an information retrieval specialist on his staff. He asked her to work over the number.

"She thinks it's somehow related to the Caslon docket number," the scout told me. "She has seen the first four numbers in AEC files on Caslon. You want us to look into it more?"

I put him off by telling him it was not worth it. I remembered that moment's hesitation when Rosen used the word *file* in reference to the number. I went directly from Capitol Hill to the AEC reading room at 1717 H Street Northwest.

The Freedom of Information Act compels federal agencies to make available an amazing amount of papers. So much, in fact, that dispensing this information has become a secondary occupation of many agencies. The AEC does its dispensing through its reading room, a quiet, wide-windowed place on the ground floor of a downtown office building.

Beyond the reading room is the document room: rows of tall metal racks stuffed with thick file folders. I could see them over the shoulder of the clerk who leaned on the shelf of a dutch door. I had told her I wanted to look up something on Caslon but had only five digits of one of the files in the Caslon docket.

"Another clue?" she asked, with feigned weariness. I nodded. If she thought I was another FBI agent, it was her error. I saw no reason to tell her she was wrong.

She opened the lower half of the dutch door and led me to

the metal shelves that held the tens of thousands of files on possessors of AEC licenses: nuclear power plants, fuel-reprocessing plants, laboratories, waste-storage sites. The clerk knew exactly where the five or six feet of Caslon files were. She checked the 43719 on the call slip I had made out, but failed to sign. She pulled down the slim file.

"Caslon's got a lot of docket numbers," she said. "The 43 is the latest series. We use 71 as an SNM designation. Well, I guess you know that. This is the 71*9* sub-section material."

"There doesn't seem to be much," I said, trying to sound casual.

"We don't see this very often," she said. "The 9 designates special licensing."

"What kind of special licensing?" I asked. I had the folder in my hand now. She was examining the call slip more carefully.

"To export SNM," she said. I must have looked startled, because she explained it to me. "You know, permission to send weapons-grade stuff out of the country." She paused, looked at the slip again, and spoke quickly. "Hey. Wait a minute. This is restricted. Who are you, mister? If you're not FBI, you give me that."

I already opened the file. I only needed a moment. The file showed that Caslon had received permission to export to a commercial laboratory in Mexico small quantities of plutonium "for the calibration of alpha-scanner equipment and other scientific purposes." The latest entry in the file, dated a week after Judy's death, was a document from the AEC's International Safeguards Division. As the clerk angrily snatched the file out of my hands, I saw that the document ordered a withholding of Caslon's export license pending an "urgent, high-level review."

The order was signed by Dr. Samuel Rosen.

38.

It is nearly a year after Judith's death. No one has been arrested for her murder because it has been officially determined that she was not murdered. She was killed in an automobile accident that she somehow caused herself. She was a victim of fate.

There is some truth to this. There was a conspiracy of fate. But there was also enough reality so that there is no need to turn to Joan of Arc or Antigone of Thebes to explain the death of a slender young woman who confronted a powerful enemy.

The investigators of Judith's life and death never agreed on the reasons for, or the circumstances of, her death. But a consensus did develop, and that consensus is the basis for my Personal Theory (which I capitalize in memory of her usage in her journal). She could not go beyond theory. The investigators of her death could not go beyond theory. I cannot go beyond theory.

The conspiracy—of fate and of people—began when Dick Scinto discovered that men in management were plotting to steal plutonium. Scinto may have been approached to join in the conspiracy. This is not known. But it does appear that he saw the theft as an off-the-record issue, a way to get the company to deal with him on a contract. It was blackmail, yet not the kind that asked for personal payoffs. Scinto wanted nothing more than a good contract. The tactic got him nowhere; there was a strike. Angered, he told some people about the criticality incident, about his suspicions. The person he talked the most to was Judith, and he did his talking in places wired for eavesdropping, such as Jack's bar and Chip Miller's van.

The strike gave management an opportunity to get rid of Scinto; strikes often cover up personal grievances, and violence in strikes does not usually produce much police reaction. Scinto was marked for physical assault, not murder. But killing a man in Oklahoma is relatively easy. You shoot him. If you don't rob him, then the murder is strictly a personal matter. The frontier lives on in Oklahoma.

One of the imported strike-breakers was Geiser, a man with a gun. He was told that management did not want to deal further with Scinto. Geiser killed Scinto not so much to kill him as to take out insurance. Geiser wanted to settle down, to be on a payroll. He believed that blackmail worked best when it was not called that and when the payments could be made impersonally, as on a company payroll, and at no one's out-of-pocket loss. Kovacs understood this, and in a frank moment said as much to a federal investigator.

After Scinto's death, management began to intensify the watch on the few people who had been told about the plutonium theft. The watch soon focused on Judith, not because she was dangerous but because she was unpredictable. When surveillance was increased, the result was paranoia; believing she was being watched, she became more suspicious of Caslon. This helped to inspire her journal-keeping, her questioning.

Caslon Wells was a company town, and so it was easy for Caslon's security specialists to install wire taps and bugs. The line between plant security and national security was hazy. So was the line between the indisputable need for health surveillance and the manipulation of that surveillance to keep a watch on employees.

The motel room Bible-stuffer, incidentally, was Deckman. He's a born-again Christian, a lay reader in his church (Disciples of Christ), and a self-righteous moralist with the tolerance of a Savonarola. He learned to be a cop on the border, and what he learned on the border was there are good guys and bad guys. You do anything necessary to keep the bad guys from winning. He is personally against pornography, but he could understand why Kovacs needed those photographs, and so Deckman arranged for them with a hooker he knew intimately.

Fred and Bill, the so-called Health Physics technicians who checked Judith's car, are members of Caslon's corporate-level Security Services, whose headquarters is in Tulsa. Federal officials doubt if Fred and Bill tampered with the safety belt on Judith's VW. But investigators were unable to view the car. The VW was turned over to Caslon under the authority of State Police Captain French two days after the accident.

The car was declared contaminated—in what was later described as an administrative error—and was taken to the AEC burial site in Idaho Falls, Idaho. A compactor crushed the car to a featureless mass, and it was buried. French retired from the State Police and is now a manager in Caslon Security Services.

As a Health Physics technician, Barbara O'Neill was aware of the use of HP facilities as a cover for Security operations. Although she did not perform any specific services for Security, she saw enough to convince her that bioassays, for example, were being studied for more than plutonium—and on occasion were switched or adulterated. She told this to federal investigators, but not to Judith.

Barbara had to know that the unannounced entry of Judith's apartment on the Friday before her death was not a site survey by HP radiation technicians but a raid by Security personnel. Yet Barbara did not warn Judith. Barbara, on the edge, saw Judith as someone who was in the center, taking care of herself in a situation of her own making. Barbara is now a supervisor in the Caslon Nuclear Research Laboratory in Pasadena, California.

Neither Barbara nor Art told Judith the substance or the import of their interviews with Deckman. Nor did they reveal that they had been questioned separately by Kovacs in his hideaway office next to Deckman's. Barbara and Art were told that they could be charged with conspiracy to divert plutonium if they discussed the case with Judith. Both knew on Friday that her arrest was imminent and that they most likely would have to testify against her when she was brought to trial.

Soon after Judith's death, Art disappeared from Caslon

Wells. Concerned, federal officials searched for him. He was found in a town in New England, where he is working in a garage. Like Barbara, he is on the U.S. Transuranium Registry. Thus, there is a legal basis for federal surveillance of both of them for the rest of their lives.

The events leading directly to Judy's death trace to the launching of an AEC inquiry into "irregularities" in Caslon's plutonium bookkeeping. The AEC had been aware for some time that substantial amounts of plutonium were being diverted from the Facility. The arrival of investigators panicked Caslon's management. A coverup began. It resembled the Watergate coverup in one particular way; it was more improvision than plot.

Plutonium was being diverted not as a criminal plot for private profits but for corporate investment, blessed by high-level Caslon management. Uranium, which once seemed plentiful, had turned out to be scarce. The price had risen so sharply that nuclear power plants faced shortages. The uranium shortage had inspired a speeding up of development of the fast-breeder reactor. When it did become a reality, plutonium would be bred in the reactor and would become plentiful. Until then, however, plutonium would be more precious than ever. And Caslon, putting corporate profits ahead of AEC regulations, decided to stockpile plutonium by juggling SNM accountability records.

Kovacs, reporting directly to the chairman of the board, was in charge of the stockpiling. Through Deckman's border connections, Kovacs set up a drop in Mexico. What Caslon was doing was not only in violation of federal law but also jeopardized the United States, which, like Mexico, was a signatory of the Treaty on the Non-Proliferation of Nuclear Weapons. The treaty is monitored by the International Atomic Energy Agency. CIA agents in the IAEA—and CIA wire taps in Mexico—soon picked up the existence of Caslon's Mexican connection.

The problem was delicate. The United States wanted to shut off the plutonium leakage, but not openly. Caslon was too powerful to move against through direct legal action. There also was a certain attraction to the CIA in the existence of free-market plutonium, which might some day be used as a lure to friendly nations, much as heroin had been used by the CIA in Southeast Asia during the Vietnam War.

While the AEC and other federal agencies pondered the situation, Kovacs became increasingly aware of the investigation. He began developing the scenario that led to Judith's contamination and death. With the aid of Deckman, Orr, and Geiser, Kovacs transformed Judith from a dissident to a plutonium thief. The Mexican connection was modified and daringly used to implicate her and, posthumously, Scinto in trafficking in plutonium. Meanwhile, in hopes of providing at least paperwork justification for corporate dealings in Mexico, Caslon applied for an export license. The effect was to alert the AEC's most fanatic safeguards official, Dr. Samuel Rosen.

Judith Longden had become, unwittingly, the central figure in an immense and growing conspiracy.

The Wednesday and Thursday contaminations were real. Geiser injected plutonium into the room where she was working. The idea was to associate her with an unexplained diffusion of plutonium. It was also Geiser who planted plutonium in Judith's apartment. The raiders did discover traces of plutonium in the apartment—but not in the hall, not in her car. It was this fact which led Rosen and other AEC officials to believe that Judith had deliberately taken plutonium into her apartment. Had she accidentally tracked it in, there would have been a detectable trail.

When he was shown the preliminary report on the apartment raid, Rosen believed more than ever that Judith was an important figure in the group stealing plutonium. But Kovacs went too far. To convince Rosen that Judith had been smuggling plutonium in her vagina, Kovacs gave Rosen a confidential report that made an incredible charge. The report said that analysis of the salami had shown plutonium was on the outside because Judith had masturbated with it. Kovacs was unaware that in the report by Feeney, the leader of the raid, the salami was described as sliced. Kovacs had overplayed his hand. Rosen began seeing him as a desperate, top-level conspirator who was trying to frame an underling.

Rosen and Garvey became convinced that Judith was only a minor figure, a courier, in the conspiracy. They also believed that Judith could be frightened into revealing the conspiracy. The Los Alamos examinations were the climax of a campaign to break her.

Judith was not involved in any theft of plutonium. She correctly saw the accusation as a false issue created to frame her and silence her. She wanted only to expose the hazards to which she and other workers had been exposed. She had a deep commitment to the union and to the improvement of working conditions. She even said once to Harry that if what she was doing would close the place down, she could die happy.

Through a union contact in the plant, Harry helped her get the incriminating x-rays that she was to bring to me. Harry told me—and nuclear engineers confirmed—that if the rods were seriously defective, the reactor for which they were intended could be ruined. It was also possible that the reactor would go super-critical, out of control. And the worst-case analysis of that event was what the engineers called a "super-prompt critical condition" or an "extreme power excursion" or a "disruptive energy release." In other words, a nuclear explosion.

Revelations about the defective rods would have been a good story. The theft of plutonium would have been a sensation. The Government, the company, the union—all had reasons to want the diversion of plutonium unpublicized. Yet, somehow, Judith had heard the number 43719. I suspect that it was Rosen who somehow saw to it that a copy of the nuclear export license was in the envelope. We will never know for sure.

Soon after Judith's death the Atomic Energy Commission was abolished; two new agencies replaced it: the Energy Research and Development Administration and the Nuclear Regulatory Commission. ERDA promotes nuclear energy; NRC is concerned about safety and safeguards. Rosen became part of NRC. He is now stationed in Vienna, on loan to the International Atomic Energy Agency.

If what Judith had been confronting had been something less than the plutonium economy, perhaps there would have been a solution to her death. But her death raised questions and issues that could not be discussed openly and officially. The Government does not even want to use the word *theft* in association with plutonium; the preferred word is *diversion.*

All plutonium used in the nuclear industry today is weapons-grade. More and more of it will enter our lives if the fast-breeder technology becomes part of the nuclear-power grid. Until recently, plutonium was measured in grams. Now it is talked of in kilograms. We have started to become careless with it. The General Accounting Office, in a classified study conducted for Congress, estimated that two *tons* of weapons-grade plutonium and enriched uranium is unaccounted for.

Terrorists in possession of a small amount of plutonium can manufacture a bomb.

This was what was riding with Judith down Route 85 that night: the plutonium terror, the plutonium economy.

I imagine Kovacs throwing up his hands and saying some modern version of King Henry II's appeal to his knights for some relief from the burdensome Thomas à Becket. Neither Henry nor Kovacs actually ordered a murder.

She is driving down Route 85 that night. Behind her appears a dirty-white pickup, Geiser at the wheel, the man in the red cap—who has never been identified—at his side. Geiser says he will tap her car. Once before, they had come close. Tonight they'll tap her VW, just enough to scare the bitch. Red cap nods. She will be scared, maybe hurt. Not murdered. Hell, they're just foolin' around.

Judy tries to pull to the right. The pickup truck hits the VW on the right. The VW starts to fishtail. Judy turns into the skid, twisting the wheel to the left, trying to come out of the skid. But the pickup is still on her. It suddenly accelerates, then stops, firing her across the road—the pickup like a gun, the VW a bullet. The pickup drives on—and is never seen in Caslon Wells again.

Geiser was arrested three months after Judy's death. Because he had failed to report to his federal parole officer in Tulsa for three months, he was returned to federal prison to complete a twelve-year term for armed robbery of a bank. He will serve a prison term about equal in length to what probably would have been meted out for manslaughter by motor vehicle, the most serious charge that could have been lodged against him.

P Plant is no more.

A wrecking crew and a team of NRC inspectors arrived and dismantled the building. A hole was dug and the pieces of the building were buried. The most contaminated materials—the glove boxes, the pipes, the waste tanks, the solvent-extraction pumps, the wound counters—were packed into a trailer truck by men wearing respirators and hooded coveralls.

Preceded and followed by NRC security vehicles, the trailer truck left the mound of dirt and passed through the fences and the gates. The safety sign still stood, but it had no numbers. The truck turned onto Route 85 and headed for the Interstate. The driver and his armed companion were changed every four hours to protect them for overexposure to radiation.

Next morning, just after first light, the trailer truck was waved through the double gates of the National Reactor Testing Station at Idaho Falls, Idaho. A tail of cinders and desert dust flared behind the truck as it rolled nearly four miles across sagebrush-dotted flatlands to the ground burial facility.

The driver and the guard got out of the truck and went into a small building. A man in hooded, full-protection clothing emerged and climbed up into the cab. He followed a Jeep, which coursed through the burial ground to a ramped hole fifty-five feet long, twelve feet wide, and sixteen feet deep. The driver drove the truck down the ramp, got out, and was helped from the hole by the Jeep driver. The truck driver threw his protective clothing into the hole, lit a cigarette, and hopped into the Jeep. As it turned around, a yellow bulldozer hove up, a man in hooded coveralls at the controls. He lowered the blade and began pushing dry brown earth onto the trailer truck.

About a quarter of a mile away are the drums that contain Judith Longden's possessions. And the car she was driving down Route 85.

Everything is buried now, way out in Idaho.